"DEAR GOD, ANNA, DO YOU KNOW HOW YOU MAKE ME FEEL INSIDE . . . ?"

Chance spread his fingers across her waist and held her so close against him that their hearts seemed to pound as one. He lowered his lips to hers without thought, without logic.

The softness of her lips sent a jolt through him and for a moment his pulse seemed to stop. There was no wind, no river, no night. There was only the wonder of Anna in his arms. . . .

Suddenly her hand flew through the air and slapped the side of his face. The angry blaze in her eyes was hot enough to set the horizon afire.

"You said I could trust you. You said you wouldn't force yourself on me."

"All I did was kiss you. . . . I'm a man, Anna."

"You're an animal."

THE TENDER TEXAN

JODI THOMAS

DIAMOND BOOKS, NEW YORK

THE TENDER TEXAN

A Diamond Book / published by arrangement with
the author

PRINTING HISTORY
Diamond edition / August 1991

ISBN: 1-55773-546-8

Diamond Books are published by The Berkley Publishing Group,
200 Madison Avenue, New York, New York 10016.
The name "DIAMOND" and its logo are trademarks
belonging to Charter Communications, Inc.

PRINTED IN THE UNITED STATES OF AMERICA

10 9 8 7 6 5 4 3 2 1

To the love of my life:
my best friend, my husband,
Tom

1

Texas, 1846

As she walked away from the German camp, Anna pulled her wool hood lower and faced the bitter wind blowing in toward the Galveston coastline. In front of her, the raging waves slammed into the shore as though angry at having lost the small band of immigrants to the land.

"You've claimed your share of us," Anna whispered to the crashing water as she fought back tears. There was no time to cry—no time even to consider what she was about to do. The child she carried inside her made all other choices impossible.

Glancing inland at the setting sun, Anna focused on her goal: the campfire of the cattlemen. She was Anna Marie Meyer, of Biebrich on the Rhine, Germany, widow of William Meyer, and tonight for the first time she would be the master of her own fate.

The rain-soaked ground sucked at Anna's boots, fighting her progress. She had no idea whether the cattlemen were driving a herd to or from the port of Galveston, but she was thankful they'd camped within sight. Their fire was her final ray of hope in a foreign and hostile world as she moved toward them on her pilgrimage . . . fighting the wind . . . fighting the dark, twisting path . . . fighting her fear.

As she neared them, the drovers stood up. They were a dirty, drab lot with few social graces, but they recalled enough from their upbringing to know when they were in the presence of a lady. The pungent odor of cattle and dust clung to them, and their thin, wiry frames made them appear more like shadows of men than the rugged frontiersmen they were. Anna knew little of Americans and even less of these few who called themselves Texans. She knew only that her husband had been promised land in Texas, and she aimed to see that her child inherited that birthright.

Anna walked as close to the fire as her long skirts would allow. Then she pulled her hood back so the men could see her face. Her auburn hair was pulled into a tight widow's bun at the base of her neck, but a few strands had pulled free to brush across her pale, high cheekbones. Her husband had told her once that she was a fine-looking woman, and she hoped he hadn't lied about that, as he had about so many other things. From the reactions on the men's faces, she knew William had spoken the truth.

"I am Anna Marie Meyer." She squeezed her hands into fists inside her coat. The blisters along her palms throbbed, but the pain made her voice steadier. She'd practiced English for years and knew she spoke with little accent. "I've come to see if there is one among you who will marry me this night."

A rumble went through the crowd of men. She could hear a few crude whispered comments, but no one answered her. Anna forced herself to turn in a circle. In the twenty years of her life she had never felt so frightened, so alone. She held her head high. She would not beg, not even for the sake of her unborn child.

An old man, with whiskers covering his grizzled chin, stood. Several men pushed him forward as the unlucky spokesman for the group. He raked his slouch hat off his bald head and nodded at Anna. "Miss, beggin' your pardon, but are you tetched in the head?"

Anna suppressed a nervous laugh, for she was as close to letting her mind slip from reality as she'd ever been in her life. Insanity might have been her mother's way of coping, but it wasn't Anna's. "I must have a husband before the sun rises. I will pay one hundred American dollars if he will stay with me for a year and help me homestead a farm north of the Guadalupe River."

A laugh went up from the men, and Anna felt her face redden.

"Sorry, miss." The old man chuckled. "There ain't a man here who's cut out to be a farmer or he'd already be workin' his own homestead. Besides, we can make twice that much doin' what we're doin' without havin' to fight Comanches." He gestured at the sorry examples of manhood behind him. "These men ain't the settlin'-down kind."

Laughter sparked in small groups around the campsite. Several commented about already being married and how that was the reason they chose to roam. A few made offers to fill the job of husband for the night.

Anna pulled her hood back around her face to hide her shame. She'd humbled herself more than her breeding and standards ever should have allowed. Now their laughter was more than she could endure. Holding her head high, she walked from the campfire without showing a single hint of despair or a breath of weakness.

The cold evening wind assaulted Anna's face, and tears stung her eyes as she moved down the darkened ruts of the road back to the German encampment. As she approached, she noticed the tiny flickers of firelight that indicated each family's space. She saw no movement from this circle of temporary shelters and knew that the immigrants would be crowded beneath the central meeting tent for worship.

This was a savage land, this Texas, full of cruel, barbarian men. Anna would have given everything she owned to be a child again in her parents' home during those years before her father left. She thought of the sunny, endless days of listening to her mother play the piano and the long walks with her father after dinner. But now she had no home. Her father had been gone for more years than Anna could remember, and her mother's death was fresh and raw in Anna's mind. Anna blinked back her tears. She had nowhere to go.

Thoughts of her plight so consumed her that Anna didn't realize someone was coming up behind her until a hand grabbed her shoulder. She whirled around in the darkness, pulling away in terror. Was she to lose her life this night? After surviving a voyage ridden with storms and shortages of supplies, would she die on land without a soul to mourn her passing? She shoved hard against the shadowy attacker and bolted from his reach, but her feet became tangled in her thick skirts and Anna tumbled toward the ground.

Powerful arms encircled her, catching her before she slammed against the hard earth. Strong, muscled hands pulled her against a broad chest and set her on her feet. "Wait, miss." His words came fast, a blending of shyness and worry in his tone. The smell of cattle and sweat assailed her nose.

The moment her feet were firm upon the ground, he dropped his arms. "I've come to take you up on your offer of marriage."

Anna tried to see his features, but brooding clouds hid even the quarter moon's faint light. He was several inches taller than she, although at five feet eight inches she towered above most men. She longed to see his face before she spoke, yet she knew it didn't matter. If she didn't have a husband tonight, all would be lost. "You agree?" The words slipped past her lips in a whisper.

"One year, one hundred dollars. I'll help you start a farm along the Guadalupe River." His voice was lightly flavored with a southern drawl. He rubbed his gloved hands together nervously, and she could sense the hard power of his body, which seemed caged by restraint, like a wild animal forced into civilization. As he continued to speak, his warm breath fanned her face. "I have to have the hundred dollars now."

Anna didn't want to ask why. Be it gambling debts or his own guarantee of her half of the bargain, she didn't care. "If I agree, you must know the rules of this marriage."

"What?" His tone was matter-of-fact rather than questioning.

"I am three months pregnant. At the end of the year you will lay no claim to the farm. It is to be mine and my child's. You will leave without a word one year from today, January third, eighteen forty-seven."

"Agreed." He moved impatiently, kicking at the muddy road as though he disliked talking.

"And," Anna made her voice steady, "during the marriage you will lay no claim to me."

There was a long silence and she wondered if he might yet back out. Should she pray he did . . . or didn't? Suddenly the idea of talking of marriage to a man whom she'd never seen seemed insane.

The shadowy figure shoved his hat lower on his head. "Agreed," he said lightly, as though her last statement mattered little to him. "I'll meet you at the mission in an hour."

"No." Anna touched his arm, then pulled her fingers away, surprised at her forwardness. "Come to the tent in the center of the first German campsite. We will be married by my minister. He speaks English."

"The money first."

She pulled the money from her pocket. It was the last she had, her inheritance. "One hundred dollars."

"One hour." He took the money from her hand.

Her quick tongue lashed out before she thought. "And clean up."

A mumbled word she didn't understand reached her in the darkness as she listened to his footsteps fade away with only the jingle of his spurs for an answer. Had she offended him with her penchant for cleanliness? She stood in the darkness and whispered, "Dear Lord, help me. I'm about to marry a man whose face I've never seen, and I forgot to ask his name."

2

"You can't be serious, Anna!" The Reverend Mr. Muller roared so none of his followers would miss a word he said. "How could you have found someone willing to marry you? You know no one in this land. We've only been in Texas for two days. All the men from the ship have returned to it, and the men in our group are either married or they've joined up to go to Mexico and fight."

From the other side of the tent, Anna felt Walter Schmitz's lecherous yellow-brown eyes watching her. He was puffed up like a toad who'd swallowed the bug of benevolence. "She's only stalling, Reverend. My offer still stands. Anna may come live with me and mine and I'll treat her as one of the family." One eyelid winked slightly, betraying the lust in his heart.

His plump wife nodded her head in agreement. "She's welcome as long as she keeps that sassy tongue of hers in place and does her full share of the work. That is, if she doesn't think she's too highborn to dirty her pretty hands. We all know them that are well born sometimes forgets their place when they fall to the status of us common folks."

Anna knew the Schmitzes wanted a servant, and if she ended up with them she'd be doing all the work until Walter Schmitz forced himself on her. Then she'd be kicked out and blamed for trying to destroy their marriage. She lifted her chin and looked down at him and his wife. "I plan to marry this night. Tomorrow when we load the wagons to go establish our settlement, I will have a husband who can sign for my late husband's land. You did offer me that option, Reverend."

The minister nodded. "But who . . ."

The man of the cloth seemed at a loss for words, but Walter Schmitz's wife had no such ailment. She pushed her way through the others to stand beside the minister. "We've all had to endure your unsettled stomach for several weeks, Anna Meyer, so there's no need to tell us about you being in a family way. So tell me now, what kind of man would want a wife who carries another man's child?"

Walter stepped next to his wife as if they were bookends of decency. "My dear friend William has not been dead a month and you disgrace his memory by throwing off your mourning gown for a bridal gown. I had to watch him grow weaker each day at sea and finally die from the bad water and rancid food, but I'll not stand by and let you dishonor his name."

The minister held up his hand. "Now, Walter, she's not dishonoring William just because she wishes to marry another. A woman in her place can do little else but marry again."

"What decent man would take on a wife he knew not?" Walter snorted and his wife nodded her head in agreement.

Anna froze, unable to answer. She didn't know the stranger's name.

Then, from the back of the tent she heard a mumbling. Feet shuffled as the crowd parted, but she didn't turn around. The muffled jingle of spurs reached her ears, and a strong voice with a southern accent said, "I plan to marry her."

Everyone, including Anna, turned to watch as the stranger moved closer. A cream-colored broadcloth shirt and dark pants covered his tall, lean form. His slouch hat shadowed his face, but Anna's eyes were fixed upon the gun strapped low on his thigh. She'd heard stories of this wild land, but seeing the weapon riding on his muscled leg like an essential part of his being made her wonder again what she'd agreed to in the darkness halfway between the German campsite and the wranglers' fire.

He was standing beside her before she looked up. "I'm Chance Wyatt," he informed them in a cold, factual voice. He removed his hat, revealing a mass of black hair that fell over his collar. "Will you marry us, Reverend, or do I go down to the mission and fetch a priest?"

Whispers filled the tent, but speechless, Anna could only look into the clean-shaven face of the man beside her. Man? Her mind screamed at the lie. He was tall and self-assured, but his face told the truth. He was little more than a boy. In fact, she would bet her life that he hadn't seen his twentieth birthday. And yet she had staked her future on him, a boy who wore a gun like an extension of his body.

The minister startled her into responding. "Anna, you wish to marry this man?"

Anna managed a nod.

"And Chance Wyatt, you wish to marry Anna?"

"Yes, if she'll have me."

The obliqueness of his statement sent stifled giggles through the crowd. His words were quickly translated to German so all could understand and share in the humor. Anna looked up into Chance's dark indigo eyes and, seeing only sincerity, raised her chin higher.

Claudia Schmitz mumbled louder than the others. "I think he does not know of her sharp tongue and that she already carries a child in her stomach."

"Or of her mother," another buzzed.

Walter Schmitz added to the heckling. "Perhaps he is too young to know of such things."

Chance's swift turn startled Anna. Like an animal alert to the first sound of danger, he faced Walter Schmitz. "I know all I need to know of Anna." He slid his fingers along his gun belt to the handle of his weapon without taking his eyes off Schmitz. "And I know that from this night forward I'll tolerate no man speaking ill of my wife. I suggest, sir, you mark my warning well. I assure you I'm man enough to stand behind my word."

The tension in the tent was so thick a tidal wave couldn't have stirred it. Walter Schmitz pressed his lips together in anger but didn't speak. He could be quite brave when he knew he had the upper hand, but never when he was unsure.

"I'll go get my Bible," the minister blurted, suddenly in a hurry. "Everyone else move out by the campfire. It's only fitting we perform our first marriage under the stars for heaven to witness."

As the others shuffled out, a tiny woman appeared at Anna's side. She had the face of a child, but her ample bosom proved otherwise. "Are you sure, Anna?" Her words were thick with her heavy accent.

Anna smiled at Selma, her only friend among the group. "Yes. I have no other path."

Selma pulled her ivory lace scarf from her head. "Then you must wear this. It was my bridal veil."

Anna accepted the finely woven lace with tears in her eyes. "Thank you," she whispered. At least now her head would not be hooded in mourning color when she said the words with Chance.

The tiny woman/child was swept away on the arm of her husband, Carl, who nodded at Anna, too shy, as always, to speak to her.

As the young couple left, Carl's broad workman's frame and Selma's tiny body seemed an odd contrast in spite of their closeness. Anna wondered how she would appear to others on the arm of her new husband.

Looking into the eyes of the stranger at her side, Anna spoke bluntly. "You're so young. A boy."

Chance didn't seem bothered by her frankness. The hard lines were gone from his face now, and he looked younger than when he'd spoken to Schmitz. "There's nothing I can do about that, ma'am. I figure I'm not more than a year younger than you."

Although she nodded in agreement, Anna realized she thought of herself as older because she'd been married since she was fifteen to a man twenty years her senior. Somehow she had passed from a child to a married woman without ever being young. Last month when she'd torn the lace from her black dress to make her widow's weeds, all thoughts of herself as being young were ripped away.

Chance took her hand gently and placed it in the crook of his arm. "I heard what was being said. You have to marry or lose your homestead, don't you?"

Anna looked up, aware that his fingers still rested on her hand. How could he now appear gentle, even shy, when only moments before she'd seen a fire in his eyes that left no doubt he'd kill any man who questioned his word?

"I think I understand, ma'am. I'd like to say something from the first. You had a lot of guts doing what you did back there at the campsite. Some of those men would have killed you if they'd known you had a hundred dollars in your pocket."

His warm blue eyes darkened and the southern drawl was barely a whisper. "I've been on my own for some time, and I can take care of you for the year. You don't need to worry about being safe. No man, including your yellow-eyed friend, is going to touch you."

Anna's eyes widened. "You don't know Mr. Schmitz."

"No, but I've met his kind. I could see his lust as plain as a spot on a diamondback rattler's head."

"But he's a respected member of our society. Everyone looks up to him."

"Do you?"

Anna had never lied, and she wasn't about to start now. His dark eyes would see right through her anyway. "No. He was my husband's best friend, but I've always hated the way he looked at me."

Chance stepped toward the door, pulling her to his side. "Well, ma'am, I'm going to be your husband now."

Anna smiled for the first time in days. "I think you'd best stop calling me ma'am then."

His fingers slid over hers where they rested on his arm, and he lifted her hand to shake on the agreement. He turned her palm over in his hand, and a frown pulled his dark eyebrows together, wrinkling his tan forehead. "Those blisters need doctoring."

"I've had no time. We had to drag our trunks from the shoreline yesterday. The wagons won't be here until tomorrow morning, and I was afraid the sea would wash my one trunk away. The ground was so muddy we had to cut poles and drag our belongings along them."

"There are men—"

Anna pulled her hand from his. "I had to do my share. You must realize that there are many in the group who don't think I should be allowed to claim my husband's land." Anna couldn't bring herself to tell him why. How could she explain the hatred she'd always felt for the man she'd married, or that the others had resented her coldness toward him? How could she tell this stranger that her child had been conceived when her husband raped her on board the ship, and that she'd been afraid to cry out for fear the others might hear and hate her more. She'd feared, too, that he'd beat her as he had when he'd raped her once before. William had been a member of the society and she had always been the outsider. And now she was about to marry another outsider, a man she knew nothing about.

Anna's fingers tightened around his strong arm. "No one is to learn of our arrangement. As far as anyone is to know, we are husband and wife in every way."

Chance nodded. She felt his dark eyes studying her closely. "Anna." Her name sounded foreign in his warm, southern drawl. "You don't have to be afraid of me."

Her green eyes searched his blue ones. Had he read her mind so easily, or was he only guessing? "You're asking me to trust you?"

"Yes. Trust me or don't marry me. I don't want to see

fear in your eyes when you look at me every day for a year."

Anna knew he was right. If she lived in fear of him, she might as well be living with Schmitz. "I will trust you. Is there anything else?"

A slight smile lifted the corner of his mouth. "Yes. Don't ever call me a boy. I'm man enough to hold up my half of this bargain. One year from tonight I'll leave silently, with no words of regret and no looking back, but until then I'll protect you as though the Almighty had truly granted you to me as a mate."

"Agreed, Mr. Wyatt." Anna pulled Selma's scarf over her hair, remembering the lace veil she'd worn at her first wedding five years before. This time she knew the ways of men and she was determined to protect herself.

This time it was her decision.

An hour later they were husband and wife. They walked away from the campfire without a word between them other than those the minister had asked them to repeat. Chance tied his horse behind her tent while she undressed and crawled under her blankets. Anna tried to lay perfectly still as he entered the tent and spread his bedroll not a foot away from her own. He was only a shadowy outline again, as he'd been when they'd met, but now he was her husband.

The sound of him rummaging through his saddlebag broke the quiet. In the blackness, she felt him kneel beside her. "Anna, are you asleep?"

Anna considered staying silent. Whatever he wanted could surely wait until morning. "No," she answered, determined not to lie to this man. There had been enough lies in her first marriage to last a lifetime.

"Good." He moved closer. "Give me your hands. I need to put some salve on them."

"It can wait until morning." Anna wasn't sure she wanted him to touch her. She knew firsthand that men were not always the same in the darkness as they were in the light.

"No." His answer was as firm as hers. "By morning you might have blood poisoning."

There was no arguing with the truth; her skin was already red and sensitive around the broken blisters. Slowly she pulled her hands from under the blanket and held them out to him. After finding her fingers in the blackness, he gently held them in his hands and rubbed warm sticky salve over the blisters. Her flesh was tender, but she did not move or cry out as he continued to lightly apply the medicine to her palm. Laying one of her hands on his leg, he began to wrap the other. When she tried to slide her freed hand away, he grasped it firmly and placed it back on his leg.

"Hold still," he ordered. "I can't see much of what I'm doing. I don't need you moving around."

The warm feel of his leg beneath her hand made her nervous. She didn't need light to be aware of his nearness. The clean smell of soap and leather seemed to fill the small tent and she heard his every breath. The way his thumb slowly traced the palm of her hand blocked her awareness of everyone in the world except the man at her side.

"Thank you," Anna whispered, and she closed her eyes as Chance wrapped her other palm in cloth.

He moved away without a word, and she heard his breathing slow slightly, telling her he'd been aware of her nearness also. The outline of his body shadowed the wall of the tent. When he spoke, his voice was low. "I have to leave for a few hours, but I'll be back before daybreak."

Questions jumped into her mind, but she didn't ask where he was going. She wasn't sure she wanted to know. As he silently left the tent, she wondered why his absence didn't bring her the relief William's leaving always had. For hours afterward she lay awake, waiting, wondering if he would ever return. What if she was to be swindled now after he'd won a small portion of her confidence? Yet she thought over the few words he'd said and how he'd made her feel proud in front of the others. She thought of how gentle his touch had been when he'd doctored her hands. She thought of how little she knew of him.

An hour before dawn, Chance slid back into the tent and sank onto his bedroll with a sigh of exhaustion. After unbuckling his belt, he laid his gun in the space between their bedrolls. Within minutes his breathing grew regular and slow. He'd made no effort to touch her. Perhaps he truly was a man of his word.

Anna turned her back to him, and just before she crossed the bridge into dreams, she heard him mumble in his sleep.

"Maggie," he whispered. "Maggie, don't cry."

3

Leaning on one elbow, Chance studied Anna's sleeping form in the early dawn light. She was so close that if he had moved his arm six inches, he could have touched her cheek. But she might as well have been a hundred miles away.

She looked so beautiful with her auburn hair fanning around her face; its rich red-brown color reminded him of newly turned earth in the spring when the soil was still damp with winter. Some might not think of that as much of a compliment, but Chance loved the earth as only a boy born on river-bottom farmland could.

The gentleness of her face hypnotized Chance, and the way her long, dark lashes rested against her pale cheek fascinated him. He could not remember ever seeing a woman so perfect. Memories of the pockmarked and snaggletoothed young saloon girls he'd talked with flashed through his mind. And the respectable women he'd seen in Texas had sun-worn, wrinkled skin or tough, square features that reminded him of oxen. Most wore bored expressions as if they were permanently imprinted on their faces; it seemed like they'd seen all there was to see in this world. They always stared at him with vacant, hollow eyes, never with the flash of the fire he'd seen in Anna's forest-green depths.

How many times had he dreamed of meeting a woman like Anna? She walked with grace and her voice had a softness that made him wonder if she'd ever raised it at anyone in her life. And her cream-colored skin reminded him of a pearl. A man didn't have to know much about fine china to realize when he was looking at a rare piece. And Chance didn't have to see all the women in the world to know that Anna was a true lady. He could probably count on one hand the number of women he'd been this close to since his mother died. There'd been so many hard winters and lonely months spent in the saddle, that finally his memories of family and how they'd died had faded. Now Anna, with her proud stance and gentle movements, had touched him and rekindled a need he had thought long dead. She didn't know this land and how cruel it could be for women.

Locking his hands behind his head, Chance lay back, forcing himself not to stare at her. He must have been crazy to have taken her up on her offer. The last thing he needed was a wife and a farm to worry about. There were other ways to get the money for Maggie. He'd supported his sister for the past eight years by paying cousins to keep her, and he could have continued to without tying himself to Anna. But, dear God, how grand she had seemed marching right into camp like a queen. After just one look at her he would have given much more than a year of his life for the heaven of touching such a woman.

Laughter rumbled from his chest. A year of his life was the price, only he'd spend it in hell because he'd agreed not to lay a hand on her.

"Chance?" Anna's voice was a whisper in the shadowy light. "Are you awake?"

"I'm awake." He wanted to say good morning or whatever people who sleep only inches apart say to one another, but he simply waited.

There was a hint of apprehension in her voice. "Have you seen the part of the country where my land is? I keep dreaming about it, but a picture won't form in my mind. There's a small settlement along the Guadalupe River called

New Braunfels. A group of our people went there last year, but their letters have been few."

Focusing on the dark creases of the tent, Chance tried to remember. "I was near there about three months ago, riding with a group of rangers. Don't know much about the settlement, but I heard a fellow say that the town was like a little German village. He said they even had a hospital shed and were starting a town church. The land around is rich earth, best as I remember, but hilly and rocky in spots." He suddenly wished he could tell her more, but they'd been riding hard and fast and he hadn't taken the time to see much.

Holding fast to her dream, Anna sighed. "I have waited so long. In a few months I'll have my own land."

A frown wrinkled his forehead. He remembered hearing his mother say the same words when his family first settled in Texas. You'd have thought their farm was one step outside heaven's door the way she talked about it. Her memory and the nightmare scene of her death had been the thing that had kept him going all these years. Every time he'd been about to give up, his mother's memory had driven him to make it one more mile. Her life had given him values, but her death gave him one driving purpose.

He clenched his fist beneath the blanket. One of these days he'd find Storm's Edge and he would leave that savage in a pool of his own blood the way the Indian had left Chance's mother. That was another reason Anna's offer had looked so good. Her people were heading right into the area where he'd heard Storm's Edge and his band camped in the winter.

Anna's soft breathing pulled him from his thoughts, reminding him of how other people live, of how others care about more than revenge. Somehow just thinking about Anna made him feel like he was betraying his family. His next words sounded sharper than he meant them to. "You people would be better off to wait a few months. Every teamster within a hundred miles has been conscripted to haul weapons and munitions for the army, and there aren't enough wagons left to haul supplies, much less people, that far inland. The trouble with Mexico won't last long; then you could go into the hill country better prepared."

He heard Anna rummaging in the small carpetbag that had served as her pillow. "We have waited. We have a few carts and drivers. The society has talked it over and decided we can walk to our land. If we stay on the coast any longer, this place will become a mass German grave. Many of my people are already sick and more come down with fever every day."

"The trip could kill more."

Anna's angry reply surprised him. "We will start today." She was as stubborn as she was beautiful.

Turning toward her, he tried to think of a way to talk an ounce of sense into her.

The sight before him in the early gray light made Chance forget his words. She was sitting on top of her blankets. Her white nightgown was buttoned to her throat with lace and ribbons crossing back and forth in a latticework pattern. She'd pulled her hair over one shoulder and was combing out the night's tangles with her fingers.

"I . . ." The vision before him was interfering with his brain. He'd lived his whole life without ever seeing a woman dressed like this. His parents had been poor farmers, and what little lace his mother made was saved for Sunday clothes. Anna's gown had lace all the way down to the swell of her breasts. He tried to make his eyes move away, but they were caught in the lace along her bustline as surely as if they'd been tangled in wire. "I . . ." Chance couldn't remember what he'd been talking about. He knew he'd been angry, but his anger was replaced now with a wave of another emotion.

Anna pulled the blanket around her. "Would you mind going outside while I dress?" Her voice was sharp and a hint of hatred colored her words. It was as though she'd looked at him and seen something evil, something poisonous.

Fire as hot as the Galveston sun in July inched up Chance's neck. He couldn't have met her eyes if his life had depended on his returning her stare. Grabbing his gun, he hurried out of the tent, trying to pull his boots on as he went.

Once outside, he wondered how to get through the day without making a bigger fool of himself. Around men he could hold his own, but he felt like a greenhorn around Anna. They might be almost the same age, but she'd been a married woman. Married folks knew about those quiet times between a man and a woman. To her, married five years and pregnant, he must have looked like the village idiot staring into a schoolhouse window. Hell, there was no telling what she'd think of him if she knew he'd never been with a woman. Yet, there he stood, acting like a kid and knowing that wrestling a longhorn was easier than talking with her, even if she was going to be his wife for a year.

Chance jerked the reins of his horse, Cyoty, and led the huge bay down to the creek. The half-wild animal was frisky and ready as always to prance, but Chance held tight. He'd named the horse after the Indian word meaning wild and alone. Sometimes he felt a kinship with Cyoty that was closer than he'd ever felt with a human. But this morning a herd of buffalo could have trampled him and he wouldn't have noticed, for he was lost in his own stampede of unfamiliar emotions. As he brushed the bay's shaggy mane, Chance fought the urge to confide in the horse as he had when he was younger. There was no question he understood horses a lot better than he understood women.

By the time Cyoty had taken his fill of water, Chance had made two decisions. First, he was going to treat Anna like she was his sister when he was around her. And second, he was going to stay around her as little as possible. He hobbled Cyoty so the horse could graze along the creek's grassy bank, then Chance walked back to the camp still deep in thought.

As he neared the tent, he saw Anna standing facing the

morning sun with her eyes closed, her auburn hair tied in a neat bun, and every emotion carefully hidden from view. She waited until he was standing beside her before speaking. "There is coffee in the main tent."

The anger that had dripped from her words as thick as cold grease only minutes before was gone. Her voice was soft and kind and sounded as though she'd had a great deal of experience hiding her feelings. She took his arm and as they walked to the main tent where people seemed drunk on the contagious excitement that sparked the air. Some folks were ill and many looked weak, but this morning everyone managed a smile. For today they would begin the last part of their journey to paradise.

Anna stood close beside him, introducing him to the few people she knew and translating when needed. Some of the older folks were determined to bring their native language with them, but many of the younger ones had decided to speak only English in this new land. Chance found their broken English almost as impossible to understand as their German.

"Good morn'," said a tiny young woman, smiling at Anna and Chance.

The sight of such a slight woman on the arm of her huge husband made Chance smile. "Good morning."

"Good morn—*ing*," she repeated, practicing her English.

"These are my friends." Anna leaned close to Chance as she introduced Carl Jordan and his wife, Selma. "They are from my village, but I didn't know them until the journey."

"They speak English?" Chance winked at Anna as Selma assured him that she did in words he barely understood.

The smile that touched Anna's green eyes made his heart miss a beat. "Carl is very quiet. I'm not sure he speaks at all." The laughter in her eyes and Selma's long-winded denial left Chance with the feeling that Carl's silence was probably more from lack of opportunity than from shyness.

"My husband," Selma rattled in broken English, "is a

carpenter and so he was allowed to bring two trunks." She touched his arm with pride. "He can lift our trunk alone, but the one with his tools is very heavy."

"I'd be glad to lend him a hand." Chance nodded toward Carl and the huge round-shouldered man smiled.

As they heaved the trunk filled with tools onto a wagon, Chance decided he liked this strong, silent man and his wife, who was like a noisy bundle of cheer. He was glad Anna had chosen them for friends.

That was more than Chance could say for Walter Schmitz. The fat, middle-aged man had been watching them all morning out of the corner of his eye. Finally, he meandered forward.

"Morning." Walter didn't smile as he greeted them.

Chance nodded once, but he noticed Anna didn't answer.

Walter moved closer. "How are the newly married this day?"

As he waited a moment for Anna to answer, Chance felt her hand tighten along his arm. He said simply, "Fine." He didn't like the way the older man looked down his nose at them as if he were lowering himself even to be seen talking with them.

Walter looked directly at Anna. "It is a sad day when the memory of an honorable man like my friend William Meyer is tarnished by his wife's marrying beneath her within days after his death."

Anna held her head high, and her fingers dug into Chance's arm as he took a step forward. Walter quickly moved away into the crowd, a touch of fear in his eyes when he glanced back at Chance.

"Anna . . . ?" Chance said uncertainly.

"Forget his words," Anna snapped, making Chance wonder how anyone could be so cold and so beautiful at the same time. Being around her was confusing him more every minute.

Within an hour Chance was given the solution to his problem. The Reverend Mr. Muller asked him to ride a few days ahead of the wagons as a scout. There were three other scouts, but a party of this size could use another man who knew the country and had a horse, and Chance knew the hills better than he'd ever known people. He welcomed the opportunity to be alone and agreed to leave as soon as all the carts were loaded.

As he talked among the others Anna never left his side, her anger now completely vanished. Now that he had been given a role, he found the people friendly and accepting. They were hungry for any news of Texas, and having a Texan among them made their dream seem more real. However, Anna's nearness and the light pressure of her fingers on his arm consumed his thoughts even as he talked about Texas. Once, as he drew a map in the dirt showing several men where they were headed, he was rewarded with a brief smile. For a moment, Chance was so lost watching the gentle curve of her mouth, he couldn't have answered to his own name. Another time, with several people watching, she brushed the suede of his vest with her fingers. Chance thought he might explode with the sudden pleasure her small gesture had given him.

By the time the last trunks were loaded onto the wagons, the sun was high, marking the hour of noon. Chance touched her fingers resting on his arm. "I need to saddle up and leave."

He wished she'd look up at him, but her eyes were shaded from his view as she spoke. "I will walk with you to your horse."

Chance glanced over to the trees where he'd hobbled Cyoty. There was no one by the creek and he knew they would be alone for a few moments before he left. His stomach was in a knot so tight the oxen hitched to the wagons couldn't have pulled it apart. He wanted to be alone with her, but a part of him was screaming to run away before he tumbled into the bottomless depths of her green eyes.

As they made their way toward the horse, Anna asked, "Do you have enough food, coffee?"

Brushing the branches of a live oak to one side, Chance waited for her to pass. "I'll be fine. How about you?"

They were in the shadow of the trees now, where light shone in thin sheets between the barren branches. "I can take care of myself." Her voice blended with the sounds of the stream, shallow now in winter, and the faraway cry of a bird.

"Take care then." He wanted to hold her close, to let her know that he cared about her safety, but when his arm encircled her shoulder he felt her stiffen. He pulled her closer, longing to hold her in his arms, but gone was the warmth she'd shown earlier; she jerked her shoulder backward as suddenly as though his touch bore the kick of a shotgun.

Her green eyes flashed angrily. "No!" Her hand shook as she pressed his chest, shoving him away.

"What?" Chance watched her in utter confusion. "What's the matter?" Could she be that afraid of him? "I wasn't planning on hurting you, Anna."

Wrapping her arms around her waist, Anna backed away. "I thought you understood. There will be no touching between us." Her voice was shaking as though he'd tried to molest her right there, not thirty feet from the others. "If you touch me again," she whispered, "I swear I'll kill you." She hugged herself tightly.

Chance was more confused than he'd ever been in his life. "But all morning you've been touching me, standing next to me."

"That was for the others' benefit. We are alone now." Her eyes were emeralds of fury, her knuckles white with fear. She studied him for a moment and seemed to relax slightly. "I'm sorry if I gave you the wrong impression, but there is never to be anything between us other than our original agreement."

Chance slapped his hat against his leg and swore under his breath. "So that's the way it's going to be. We're a couple when others are around, but when we're alone I'm not even supposed to look at you." He felt his face redden at the memory of the way he'd stared at her in the tent.

"That's the way it's going to be." She held her head high in challenge.

Dear God, why did she have to seem more beautiful every time he looked at her? The angrier he got, the more he wanted to touch her and the more she seemed to hate him.

Chance fought between the urge to grab her and kiss her, and the desire to turn around and leave her forever. Her softness had been so real earlier, and now her rage was just as genuine. He swung the saddle across Cyoty's back. "I'll be back in a few days," he said without looking back.

He didn't see the tear that stood in the corner of Anna's eye as she watched him ride away. He was her only hope for the future, her only road to independence. Yet how could Anna tell him of her fears, not just of him, but of all men?

The two days of scouting turned into a week as Chance crisscrossed the land searching for the best trails. Although he slept in his saddle, ever alert to the possibility of danger, ever vigilant, deep in the corners of his mind throughout all his waking and sleeping hours was the thought of Anna.

Why had the way she'd held her chin so high at the wranglers' camp made him willing to forfeit a year of his life to protect her? Especially when he should be looking for the renegades who'd killed his family eight years ago. He needed to think of his little sister, Maggie, and most of all, he needed to have nothing binding in his life.

The rain started the third day he was out, but the steady drizzle couldn't erase the memory of her lace gown from his dreams. By the end of the week the need to see her was like a pain deep in his gut that grew worse by the hour. After meeting up with one of the other scouts, he agreed to take the far point for another few days. Maybe he could starve this craving to see Anna out of his mind if he stayed away long enough.

* * *

Rain had pounded him for a solid week by the time Chance was finally reunited with the wagons late one afternoon. The sky was as low and brooding as his mood, with rain so thick it seemed to be hanging in the air instead of falling. He had a ten day's growth of beard and hadn't seen a hot meal for days. But all thoughts of a shave and a meal and even of seeing Anna were washed away by the sorry sight before him.

The wagons, which were little better than carts, plowed through the mud single file. The thick-legged oxen heaved as they pulled each hoof from the sludgy earth and planted another step into the soft ground.

People, like gray mourners, walked behind each wagon, trudging in the muddy ruts. Every few yards the exhausted men and women would lend a shoulder to push the wagon over a bump or out of a hole.

As Chance walked his horse slowly down the line of wagons, no one looked up at him; they were too tired to care who passed beside them. They'd walked for days in the rain and some of the travelers were so caked with mud that they seemed part of the liquid road they slowly plowed through.

Chance found the minister walking beside the third wagon, a sleeping child on his back. "Why don't you stop?" Chance shouted above the rain. "There're cliffs up ahead. You could build fires, dry out, wait for the rain to let up."

The minister shook his head. "If we stop, the Mexicans who drive our wagons will leave. We've come all this way. We will keep going until we reach the German settlement."

"But these people look half dead." Chance's anger was mounting. These families weren't tough frontiersmen. Hell, he thought, half of them didn't even have clothes that looked sturdy enough to last one good Texas winter.

"You've got to order the people to stop," Chance yelled above the rain as equal parts of anger and pity blended in his words.

The minister shook his head as he said in a deep voice, "Better they die striving for their dream than in a tent without hope. Tomorrow is Sunday. We will rest then."

For a few moments Chance walked beside the minister, trying to understand the logic of these strong, stubborn people. They had a dream of freedom and wide open space. Their dream had been his to hold all his life and he'd never placed much value in it. Chance wondered if they knew the price of such determination. Half of them looked like they might die before ever reaching their land, and those who survived this journey would find only hardship. This life they all longed for would rip the hearts out of those who were weak and crippled—out of all but the strongest. This land called Texas was wild and beautiful, but it could turn deadly in the time it took an Indian to string his bow.

Only when the afternoon sky turned from a yellowy gray to the color of smoke did the reverend call a halt to the march. The carts were abandoned for the night and each family spread out tents under the protection of nearby trees and huddled together inside their shelters. A few fires sputtered to life but most families were too tired to bother with an evening meal.

Chance walked through the encampment, wishing he could help, but the help of a hundred men probably wouldn't make a difference. He'd seen cattlemen who'd worked without sleep for weeks who didn't look as exhausted as these people. The sudden need to reach Anna and make sure she was all right became a pounding in his chest.

He found her sitting on the wet grass, her tent still rolled and bound in a bundle beside her. In her arms she cradled her carpetbag like a child holding onto a favorite pillow.

"Anna?"

Red, fever-ridden eyes looked up at him.

Chance knelt close. Her face was ghostly pale and her lips were colorless in the cold air. "Anna, why didn't you put up your tent?"

"It doesn't help the cold," she whispered. "I didn't put it up last night, or the night before."

Chance looked around and realized that the others seemed to ignore Anna. They all had their own families, their own problems. He grabbed her by the shoulders and pulled her close. Even through her wet clothes he could feel the fever in her body. "How long have you been sick?"

She closed her eyes and rested her head against his shoulder.

"How long?" Chance demanded as he bit his glove off his hand and rubbed her cheek with his warm fingers.

Anna shook her head. "From the day after the rain started. I'll be all right. I just want to sit here and rest." She looked up at him as if she'd never seen him before. "If I die, promise you'll bury me. We had a woman die yesterday and I heard someone say that we weren't taking the time to stop and bury any more."

Pulling her into his arms, Chance tried to warm her with his own body. He was used to living out in the weather. He'd been without a roof over his head most nights since he was twelve. But not Anna. "You're not going to die, Anna."

Her watery green eyes met his as she slowly shook her head. "I don't want to be left by the road in the mud. Promise me you'll bury me and say a prayer."

Her words ripped a hole in his heart as big as his fist. "You're going to be fine. I'm not going to let you die."

Anna leaned against his arm and closed her eyes. The rain dripped from her hood and tapped against her face, but she didn't seem to feel it.

"Stay here." He pressed his cheek against hers. "I'll be back in an hour."

She nodded as he stood. Without looking up at him she lowered her head to her knees.

Bolting onto his horse, Chance kicked the animal hard. Within minutes he was out of sight of the camp and riding north toward the break in the cliffs.

4

Anna no longer felt the rain tapping against her hood and the icy drops running down her face. She closed her eyes and thanked God she didn't have to walk any farther in the mud. Sleep's thick fog was clouding her mind when she felt someone lifting her like a child being carried to bed. She put her arms around his neck and held on tightly.

The stranger carried her to a horse and sat her gently atop the saddle. For a moment she was cold and alone, then his warm body was behind her, holding her in the saddle— holding her in his arms.

They rode in a slow, rocking motion for what seemed like hours. His arms were comforting and warm around her, his heartbeat a steady rhythm in her ear, soothing away the cold, blocking out the loneliness.

As the evening sky turned from soupy gray to deepest black, the horse stopped and the stranger carried her into a warm, dry place filled with shadows and echoes. She wanted to hold onto him, but he pushed her gently away as he whispered words in her ear she didn't understand. Anna closed her eyes and smelled the woody smoke of a long-burning campfire. She felt her wet clothes being lifted off her body and then a heated blanket was wrapped around her. When she lay down on a soft bed the stranger's warm lean body molded her into his own, holding her in his arms until she fell asleep.

* * *

Anna awoke slowly. The heat of a fire warmed her face and she smelled the soft scent of pine. Slowly, like a swimmer coming up from deep water, she took in her surroundings. She was lying on a bed of pine needles and straw, with her carpetbag as her pillow. The dark walls around her were made of rock, and the fire before her blocked most of the entrance of a small cave.

A hand drifted a few inches down her shoulder and a body moved behind her. Sudden, uncontrollable fear crawled just beneath her flesh. Anna twisted and saw Chance's sleeping face only inches from hers. His arm lay protectively over her. Except for his gun, which rested on a rock just above his head, he was fully dressed.

Where was she? Anna searched the shadowy cavity. The place was about ten feet wide and maybe twice that distance long. Chance's horse was tied up at the highest part of the entrance so that he was out of the way of the campfire's smoke as well as the rain. Where they lay, the cave was just high enough to stand up in and wide enough for one bed, and judging from the thick black soot on the ceiling many travelers had used this cave as a lodging. Her clothes had been spread along the jagged edges of the cave's walls to dry. Anger started to replace her panic.

Her fingers trembled as they traveled down to feel her cotton camisole and petticoats. Someone had undressed her. She glared at Chance. What else had he done while she was out of her mind with fever?

Anna slowly raised her hand and gripped the gun's handle. As she slid the weapon from its holster, she rolled away from Chance. Her sudden movement startled him and with instinct born on the frontier, he reached for his gun. Its absence brought him fully awake, but the alarm passed from his body as he turned and saw her.

"What have you done?" Anna's words echoed through the cave.

Wiping the sleep from his eyes, Chance sat up and ran his

long fingers through his damp, black hair. "You're better. Thank God."

Anna pointed the gun directly at his chest. "Where am I? What have you done to me?" She felt her anger slipping into confusion, so Anna gripped the gun more tightly. If this stranger had harmed her, would she have the strength to see him dead, or would she be a coward as she had been before?

Chance focused on the gun in her hand. In one fluid movement he stood up, bumping his head on the roof of the cave. He cursed colorfully at both the ceiling and at his forgetfulness. For a moment her anger and the gun seemed forgotten.

Rubbing his scalp, he took a step toward her. Anna jumped back, putting the fire between them. "Tell me where I am! Now! Where are the others?"

Chance leaned back against the cave wall, looking bone tired. He folded his hands behind his head and closed his eyes, relaxing, but the twitch of a tiny muscle along his jawline signaled his anger. When his blue eyes opened again, they were as cold as the metal of the gun in her hands.

"Either shoot me, woman, or put down the gun. I'm not planning on spending the rest of my life looking down a barrel."

Anna didn't understand his reaction. Why wasn't he afraid of being shot? Was the man she'd married completely out of his mind? Had the bump he'd suffered damaged his reasoning?

"You'll spend the rest of your life in the next minute if you don't tell me what you've done to me."

"I didn't do anything to you." His voice was still cold, as his eyes bored into her.

Fighting tears, Anna tried to steady the gun. "I told you I'd kill you if you ever touched me." She gripped the weapon with both hands.

"Then kill me now," he shouted, "and stop torturing me!"

It took a moment for Anna to follow his stare and look down. Her breasts were rising and falling with each breath and the ties of her camisole had become loosened, leaving the material curving softly to her body. She was revealing more of her flesh to this stranger than any man had ever seen. A blush warmed her cheeks as she looked up to see Chance move his eyes from her to the fire, and for a moment she thought the fire in his gaze equaled that of the flames.

With forced slowness he knelt down and threw another log on the blaze as calmly as though they were talking about nothing more important than the weather. Anna watched him in confusion. Was he totally without remorse for what he'd done? Or were his crimes only in her mind?

Outside a bolt of lightning flashed, lighting the entrance for a moment with a blinding white flash. The horse jerked against his ropes, fraying Anna's nerves as she glanced toward the animal.

In the second her eyes were turned, Chance skirted the fire and stepped up beside her. His fingers closed over the gun and twisted it from her grip with one mighty jerk. Then his arm pulled her against him so violently that Anna felt the air leave her lungs.

As he held her against him, he hissed into her hair, "Don't ever point a gun at a man again unless you're planning to shoot him."

Anna felt the hot tears welling in her eyes. "I'll kill you for what you've done to me."

His hands gripped her shoulders with bruising force, and he pushed her away from him and against the cave wall, preventing any attack she might plan. "I've done nothing to you. Nothing!" Anger twisted his features and his eyes turned the blue of an icy ocean bottom. "And if I ever do, it will not be when you're ill, but when you're out of your head with a fever I've stoked."

Twisting violently, Anna felt his body press harder against her, flattening her breasts against a wall of muscle.

The pounding of his heart raged against her own chest. With a sudden jolt she realized it was the same pounding warmth she remembered clinging to when she was so cold.

His warm breath came in gasps against her cheek. "If I ever touch you, it will be because you've come willingly to me."

"Never!" Anna turned her head away. Never would she go willingly to a man. She closed her eyes, fighting back the memory of that night on the ship when William had come to her bed. He'd whispered how sorry he was to have to rape her a second time, then he'd stuffed a handkerchief in her mouth to muffle her cries. The first time he'd been drunk, but on board the ship he'd known what he was doing and he hadn't cared that he was breaking an oath he'd made to her. The first time, Anna hadn't wanted to believe any man could be so truly evil, but the second time William had taken her, she'd let shatter any such childish thoughts. Never would a man touch her like that again.

Chance ran his fingers through her hair and pulled her face within an inch of his own. "Never is a long time. Almost as long as a year."

Her emerald green eyes met his smoky gaze. "If you live that long."

Chance's sudden laughter startled her. He eased his body away. "Tell me, did you make death threats to your first husband, or did you just shoot him outright?"

Watching him turn away, Anna debated attacking him, but decided against it; she'd felt his strength when he'd held her pressed against the wall. She forced her breathing to slow and made her fists relax against her sides. "I do not wish to discuss William with you or with anyone else."

Anna didn't move as Chance holstered the gun and left it lying between them on the rock. Despite his accusation, he did not seem threatened by her. He moved with ease about the campfire. Slowly, he lifted the blanket she'd been sleeping under and held it out for her.

Anna hesitated, then turned her back. She felt the warm

wool surround her from head to toe. Chance's arms were around her only long enough to secure the blanket in front.

"I'm sorry," he said from behind her, his words shocking her more than his light touch. "I shouldn't have said anything about your husband."

The blanket warmed her flesh, but his words touched her heart. She wanted to scream that she had hated William and that she'd thought of killing him many times, but all she could whisper was, "I don't want to talk about him."

Near the fire a cup of water boiled over, drawing Chance's attention. "Sit down and have some tea while I tell you what's been happening." He didn't look at her as he slipped a knife from a sheath inside his boot and began shaving parts of a twig into the hot water. "When I got back to the wagons, you were running a high fever. Everyone else in the camp had someone to take care of them, but you were just left out in the rain like some orphaned dogie. I don't think anyone noticed how sick you were, and I'd be willing to bet you didn't tell anyone."

Snuggled inside the warm blanket, her knees drawn up to her chest, Anna savored the hot, spicy aroma of the tea.

"I knew you'd be dead within a day or two at the most if I didn't get you dry, so I found this place, built a fire, and left my blankets to dry while I went back for you. Once I got you here, I started giving you as much of this tea as you'd take. Folks back East call this bush a spicebush, but the Indians call it feverbush and use the bark for tea. It's not half bad but getting you to drink it sure wasn't easy, especially that first night. You're about the stubbornest human I've ever met."

Anna looked up. "How long have we been here?"

"Three days. The wagons moved on yesterday, but they won't get far ahead of us in this rain. When you seemed to be resting easy, I rounded up as much of this bark as I could find and took it to the others. I don't know how much good it does, but the Indians swear it gets rid of the demons that cause the blood to heat."

The water in the cup boiled a second time and Chance shoved it from the fire. "I cooked a rabbit this morning. Do you feel like eating?"

Anna accepted the cup and nodded. "We've been alone here for three days?"

Chance looked up and smiled. "Yeah." A dimple, slightly hidden from view by his whiskers, creased his left cheek. "Don't look so frightened. I told you that you didn't have to be afraid of me."

All he'd told her slowly sank into her still groggy mind. He'd taken care of her for three days. He'd been alone with her in a cave and he hadn't had his way with her. Pieces of her fever-inspired dream blended with reality. Chance had quite possibly saved her life by carrying her to this warm place. To think that only moments before she had considered shooting him!

"Thank you," Anna whispered over her cup. It had been so long since anyone had been kind to her that she didn't know what else to say.

"Wait'll you taste it," Chance answered.

"No." Anna lowered her cup to her lap. "Thank you for helping me. I don't know of anyone else who would have done what you did for me."

"Anyone would have helped if they'd seen you in that shape. Did you tell Carl and Selma you were sick?"

Anna shook her head. "They were far back in the group. I hadn't seen them for days. Most people of our society are kind, but there are those who hate me." She bit her full bottom lip in an effort to control its quiver. "I should tell you . . ."

"You don't have to."

Anna chewed the corner of her lip. "No. I want to. My first husband was twenty years older than me and the wealthiest man in our village. Everyone thought I married him for his money." She couldn't bring herself to tell him the real reason she'd married William.

She sipped the steaming, bitter liquid without flinching.

"When he died, some blamed me for that as well." A tear ran down her face.

Leaning forward, Chance stopped its progress with the side of his finger. "You must have loved him deeply," he whispered, more to himself than to her.

Anna's head shot up, shocked by the amount of caring in Chance's deep voice. She wanted to shout that she had hated William and that if wishing him dead could have killed him, she would have done so without regret. But Chance was a stranger, someone who'd married her for a hundred dollars and would leave her in a year without a word of farewell. He was not someone with whom she should share her past. Nor was he someone she should grow to depend on. Anna looked away. "I'd like something to eat."

A few minutes later Chance pulled freshly cooked rabbit meat from the embers. Anna watched him moving about the fire, his lean, hard muscles giving him the grace of an animal of prey. She must be careful or she would reveal too much of herself to this man whose way of life told her he would never put down roots.

They ate in silence, then Chance cleaned the tin plates and mugs by holding them out in a stream of rainwater pouring off the cliff above them. He leaned against the opening and watched the rain for so long that Anna thought he'd forgotten her presence. Certain that he wasn't paying attention, she pulled her comb from her bag and set to work on her mass of tangles.

Moments later his voice startled her. "Your hair picks up the colors in the fire."

No answer came to her mind, for his words were more of a statement than a compliment.

After a long silence he tore his gaze from her and stared again at the opening. "It's hard to tell what time of day it is with this rain." He pulled a small gold watch without a chain from his pocket. "It'll be dark in an hour or so."

He walked back and sat on a log beside her. "Anna, I've

been thinking. We're going to be together for a year, so maybe we ought to get a few things out in the open between us."

Drawing the comb through her hair, Anna looked at him, waiting.

"When I woke up, I didn't much like having a gun pointed at my gut."

A smile touched Anna's lips. "I'm glad I didn't shoot you."

"Thanks."

"It might have brought this cave down on me." Anna couldn't suppress a smile. The strange tea made her feel light-headed.

One dark eyebrow rose and Chance looked unsure for a moment, then realized she was joking. His laughter was rich and low, reminding her of the way her father had laughed when she was a child.

"I've told you not to be afraid of me, but I guess that trust will have to come in time. Until then we've got to live together and try not to scare each other to death."

Anna laid her comb aside and began twisting her hair into one long braid as he continued.

"My mother died eight years ago and since then I haven't lived around many women. I meant you no disrespect when I looked at you the other morning in the tent. It will just take some getting used to, seeing a woman in all those things you wear."

She didn't know whether to believe him or not, but the thought of the way he'd looked at her that first morning sent fire to her cheeks.

"Maybe if I could start treating you like a sister, you could stop looking at me like I was fixing to murder you in your sleep every time I get within ten feet."

The depth in his honest eyes made Anna want to trust him, and she liked his laughter and the way he moved with such self-assurance. "Some men say one thing and do another." Her words sounded bitter even to her.

For several breaths neither spoke. Finally, Chance snapped a stick he'd been using to poke at the fire. The twigs flashed as he tossed them into the flames, making the cave brighter for a moment as Anna watched him turn to face her. Without taking his eyes from her face, he knelt beside her and touched her shoulders gently. "I give you my word. In this country all you really have to count on is a man's word."

"Brother and sister?"

A long sigh escaped his lips. The feel of his warm breath against her cheek frightened and excited her, and she fought the urge to pull away. This cave had been their home for three days and he hadn't tried anything. Perhaps he was worth trusting?

"I'll try," she whispered, and was relieved when he patted her shoulder and backed away.

"I'll get some more wood before dark. The rain looks like it's slacking up." As he pulled on his coat, he seemed in a hurry to be out of the little space.

The night swallowed him as though the blue-gray rain was a curtain across the front of the cave. Curling deeper into the blankets, she watched the fire dance along the walls. An hour, maybe more, passed. When Chance returned, his arms were full of wood. After he spread the twigs and branches over the rocks to dry, he banked the fire for the night. He fed Cyoty a handful of grass, and Anna thought she could hear him softly talking to the animal.

Closing her eyes as he neared, Anna listened as he pulled off his coat and boots, hearing the jingle of his spurs as he set them aside. One eye crept open just wide enough to watch him pull off his vest and damp shirt. His back was ribboned with smooth muscles that glistened in the firelight, and his wide shoulders tapered to a slim waist. A deep four-inch scar between his shoulder blades marred the perfection of his body, and Anna felt a strange anger at whatever had caused such an ugly brand on his back. As he turned toward her, she quickly closed her eyes again. A moment later, he lay down behind her, not touching her, but she could hear his breathing only inches away and feel the warmth of him so near.

As his breathing slowed he twisted and pulled the blanket over her shoulder, then brushed her hair lightly with his cheek. "Good night, Anna," he whispered, then relaxed beside her when she didn't answer.

The tight muscles along Anna's spine slowly relaxed. He'd held to his word and she felt safe for the time being, but she'd seen a promise in his indigo eyes when they'd fought over the gun. It was a promise that he might not always keep his distance—a promise that frightened her and warned her she must never let down her guard. But for now this Texan was the only person she'd been able to count on in this strange land. Perhaps he would prove to be the one man she could trust.

Long after Anna's breathing grew regular, Chance lay wide awake beside her. When he was certain she was asleep, he turned and gently pulled her against him. He loved holding her in his arms. He liked the way her body molded so perfectly to his. He loved the smell of her hair and the silky way it brushed his cheek.

He'd held her only three nights, yet it would be a lifetime before he forgot the feel of her at his side. The loneliness of all the future nights without her weighed heavily on his mind as he cradled her, trying to memorize every detail, dreading his own sleep, for it would rob him of this time with Anna in his arms.

Everything felt so right except for one thing: Chance had lied. He could say that it was true a million times, but it would still be a lie, and no matter how he tried, he could never think of Anna as a sister. The memory of the tear he'd seen on her cheek when she'd talked about her husband made it clear that she didn't want a lover. Probably just the thought of replacing someone she'd loved so much upset her greatly.

Well, if he couldn't be her lover he'd do his best at trying to act like her brother. It would have been much easier if the cave had been larger, if she hadn't gotten sick, and if he'd never held her to keep her warm.

It would've been better if he hadn't had this one last night of heaven to lie here beside her and smell the scent that was soft and feminine and definitely her own; or hear the slow steady whisper of her breath as she slept, reminding him of the gentle lilt of her voice with its old-world accent and musical quality. He couldn't erase the way her eyes had sparkled with green fire, threatening him with far greater harm than anything he'd have suffered by the gun. Chance knew he was going to have one hell of a time not thinking of her as his woman.

5

A sudden jerk on her arm startled Anna and she woke instantly. Twisting violently, she slammed into a hard wall of muscle as Chance pulled her to her feet beside him and clamped her mouth with his hand. "Get dressed!" he ordered, then shoved her toward her clothes.

Without taking her eyes off him Anna pulled on her garments. A hundred questions were in her mind, but his movements painted danger in the air. The pain left by his fingers pressing against her mouth was a silent warning not to take his order lightly.

Without another word Chance buckled on his gun belt and slid the weapon up and down in the holster, testing the ease of drawing it. Then he rolled up their blankets in a tight bundle and threw the tin cups in her bag. Moving soundlessly, he strapped the two bundles on Cyoty and checked the bay's saddle.

"Ready?" he whispered in his warm southern accent, but his blue-gray eyes were smoky with caution.

Tiny shivers of terror were climbing up her spine, but Anna managed to nod.

"Stay close and don't make a sound."

A suppressed scream blocked her throat as she tried to swallow, and the worry in Chance's stormy blue eyes only added to her fear. Something was wrong. His hand was almost crushing the bones in her fingers and she knew he wasn't even aware of her pain.

They moved out of the cave and into the bright morning sunlight, but the sense of danger in the air overshadowed the rain's end. Straining her eyes and ears, she tried to find a clue to the reason for Chance's wariness, but there was nothing, only the gurgling of a stream and the crackle of wet branches in the breeze.

Slowly, as if walking a tightrope, they moved down the cliff's edge and through the trees bordering the hills. Chance walked like an animal stalking it's prey, alert to every sound and movement around them. Anna's heart pounded so furiously she was sure he could hear it. Through the stillness, death seemed to laugh in the bright flickering of silver raindrops and dance in the brilliant rays of sun that blocked their vision as surely as darkness.

When they reached the edge of the trees, Chance pulled her against him and slowly raised his hand to point toward the sun.

For a moment Anna blinked in the light without seeing anything; then she saw them. Indians! A dozen, maybe more, were moving about the clearing, setting up a campsite on the edge of the creek. One white man dressed in buckskin moved among them like a brother. Anna's blood raced like rapids in a spring stream. The dark-skinned Indians looked frighteningly savage in their leather wrappings.

"Stay with Cyoty." Chance's words were quick, allowing no argument or answer. Pulling the knife from his boot, he placed its handle firmly in her palm.

"But . . ." Anna froze. He was gone. Crouching among the trees, Anna watched as he moved toward the Indians, his hands raised away from his gun and his lips pressed together to make a low whistling sound.

The Indians abandoned their work as he neared. As though his whistle had drawn them, they moved in a single herd toward him, all except for the buckskin-clad white man, who sauntered away from the others. The Indians circled curiously around Chance as if they were observing some animal that had just strayed from the woods. Anna saw no smiles on their faces, nor weapons in their hands. The strange people only stood before Chance talking in a broken language she'd never heard.

· One young brave, dressed in buckskin pants and a leather jacket much like Chance's, stormed up to him. He pounded Chance's chest as though testing his strength. To Anna's horror the Indian's angry voice rose and blended with the laughter of the others.

In the suddenness of a twitch, Chance threw his body full force into the tall Indian and they both went tumbling to the ground. Chance made no effort to restrain the man, and the Indian pulled away without fighting. Both men were seemingly unaware of anyone else in the clearing, and the Indian circled Chance, stalking him. Anna couldn't see the man's face, but he was yelling as if his pride had been trampled.

Turning his back to the angry man, Chance came toward her, his face frozen in concentration. Without a word he took her fingers in one hand and the horse's reins in the other, and then he pulled her toward the Indians. When he was within a few feet of the campsite, he stopped and slowly stripped off his shirt and vest. Only the tight jerk of the muscle along his jaw indicated the tension packed into his body.

As he unbuckled his gun belt and laid it over the saddle, he spoke. "Show no fear, Anna. Trust me."

Anna wanted to scream, *Trust you? You're the one taking off your gun in front of these wild people!* But she managed to nod. The group who had watched Chance so closely now gathered around her like she was the newest exhibit. One lifted her braid and laughed. An old woman with stubs instead of bottom teeth pointed at Anna's boots and chuckled with a noise that was somewhere between a donkey's bray and a goose's honk.

Moving closer to Chance, Anna place her hand lightly on

his back for support. His bare skin felt smooth and warm beneath her fingers, and his powerful muscles tightened at her touch. For a moment Anna forgot the Indians. Her father and husband had both been country gentlemen with muscles gone soft from inactivity. Touching Chance was like feeling marble wrapped in warm flesh.

Her touch drew his immediate attention, and when he pivoted to face her a smile suddenly lifted the corner of his mouth, revealing the dimple on his left cheek. "Don't tell me that my brave wife, who can take care of herself, is afraid."

She knew he was trying to make light of their trouble. And at this moment she hated him for it. Didn't he know he could be killed? *She* could be killed!

In horror, Anna watched as Chance first bent and pulled off his boots, then pried the knife from her hand and cut a leather strip that hung from his saddle. With a swift movement that Anna felt rather than saw, he slipped the knife into her pocket. To her shock, he winked at her as though he'd just whispered a secret and she was supposed to understand the meaning of his action.

Chance tied the leather strip around his wrist and pulled the knot tight with his teeth as he spoke. "Don't worry. Any woman who can threaten to kill her husband at night can surely fight off a few Indians come morning."

Anna didn't see the humor in his words, and she flashed her eyes angrily at him, thinking that she might consider helping these Indians pull the black hair from his scalp. His answering smile made her even angrier.

"I saw a white man earlier." Anna tried to keep her words steady.

Chance shrugged slightly. "He's around. If he's smart, he'll stay out of this. This is between the one called Walks Tall and me."

There was no time for questions as the tall Indian who'd hit Chance earlier stepped from behind the others. He too had stripped to the waist and removed all his weapons. His wrist was also bound with leather, but unlike Chance, his eyes were dark pools of concentrated hatred. Pointing at Anna, he said, "Your woman?"

Sweeping his arm between the Indian's hand and Anna, Chance pulled Anna against his bare chest. "My woman." Somehow the words seemed a challenge.

Anna would have clung to him, but Chance pushed her a few inches away. "Show no fear!" His fingers bruised her shoulders, emphasizing his whispered words. "No matter what happens don't cry out."

With effort, Anna managed a nod and looked back at the Indian. The tall man pointed to a tent at the back of the campsite.

Chance translated the silent command, his eyes never leaving the Indian. "Walks Tall wants you to wait in his tent."

"No." Something was about to happen between the two men and the last thing she wanted to do was wait inside. Her destiny might ride on this fight and she wanted to see what was to come.

Chance turned his powerful blue gaze on her, but instead of the anger she'd expected, she saw a hint of admiration. His words were kind as he put his arm around her shoulder and pulled her toward the tent. "Anna, you will be safer in there. Don't worry. No matter what happens, I'll come for you soon. The fight will not take long."

There was no room in his manner for questions or argument. Any trace of the boy she'd seen when they were alone was gone. The man before her was self-assured, confident. In the morning sunlight his tanned body shone like copper, and he looked as uncivilized as the savages around them. There was a wildness about him she'd never fully seen, a wildness no amount of clothing could tame.

Reaching up, she brushed an ebony curl from his forehead. She wanted to tell him to be careful, to come back, but there was no time for words.

He closed his eyes for a moment, then drew away before she could speak.

Several pairs of onlookers' hands shoved Anna backward into a large tent and laced the waist-high entrance closed. Anna fought the lacings, but all the ties were outside, out of her reach. Pacing the area, she found frustration and fear battling for control of her mind.

The air inside the walls of animal skin was thick and humid, pungent with the aroma of a hundred campfire meals. The floor was bare and still damp from the rain, telling Anna the tent had not stood on this ground long. An icy fear crept up from her legs and twisted around her chest, cutting off her breath, restricting the flow of her blood.

Outside she heard shouts. Screams, cries, and laughter blended into one unruly voice that rang harshly in her ears. She'd been told the Indians in south Texas were peaceful, but stories of Indian torture and savagery had crossed the ocean. They were bloody tales designed to frighten children and test men's visions of bravery. Were the people outside really cannibals, as some sailors had said? Would they kill Chance and leave her to die? One of the sailors had told of the Indians cutting off hair and scalp even while men and women were still alive.

The sound of flesh hitting flesh filtered through the air. Anna pressed against the hide wall and strained to hear. The slap of blow after blow continued until finally she knelt and covered her ears to block out the sound. If she couldn't see what was happening, why did she have to listen to the fight? She felt terror covering her, blanketing her from air, from life. The tent and the present slipped away in her mind and she was a child again . . . a child crying for a mother who never came . . . a child covered with blankets, smothering in the damp air.

"Mother!" Anna cried. "Mother!"

She jerked violently, trying to pull the phantom cover off her head, trying to climb back to the world of sunshine.

Rolling on the damp earth, Anna slammed into a pole.

The wood crashed into her forehead, shattering her nightmare and bringing her back to reality and pain. Blood dripped across her face from a cut at her hairline.

As she reached for her handkerchief in her pocket, Anna touched Chance's knife. Jerking the blade free of her skirt she stared at it, her bleeding forehead completely forgotten. The knife was her answer, her way out. Twice he'd handed it to her and twice he'd made a point of getting her to focus on it. But why? How could a knife help now? She could kill herself and avoid the worse-than-death future they might have planned for her after they'd had their fun with Chance, or she could wait and use the weapon on the first man who came through the door. She might kill only one, but she would defend herself.

Looking around the tent, Anna made her decision. She raced to the side opposite from where the flap was laced. Kneeling, she grabbed the knife in both hands above her head and slashed at the wall of hides with all her strength.

Fresh air and freedom flooded in, and without hesitation Anna shoved the knife into her pocket and crawled through the hole. She ran as fast as she could to the trees, afraid to look around to see if she was being followed until she was completely covered by brush.

From a hundred feet away, and well hidden in the undergrowth, Anna knelt and studied the campsite, praying for a way to help Chance. As she fought for breath, a few drops of blood from the cut on her forehead blurred her vision. Wiping the blood away with her fingers, she watched the circle of Indians in the clearing.

Chance and the one called Walks Tall were fighting. The leather straps they'd tied around their wrists were now tied together so that neither could move far enough away from the other to avoid a blow. Both were covered with mud.

Wiping more dripping blood from her eye with her sleeve, Anna tried to think. If she could get the knife to Chance, he could cut the strap that bound him to the wild Indian. But Chanced was surrounded. Even if he were freed, he'd have no chance to run. As she watched, the Indian swung one mighty arm and hit Chance on the side of the head. Bone cracked. Anna fought back a scream as Chance fell, the Indian tumbling down on top of him. Chance's skull must have been shattered with the blow!

There was no time to watch more. She could do nothing for Chance. He must have wanted her to run. That's why he'd offered her the knife. He couldn't say it, so he'd insisted on the only way available to him.

Gathering her skirts, Anna darted through the trees. She ran without direction, without any purpose except escape. Her heart began to pound in her ears and her lungs burned for air, but she didn't stop. She had to be as far away as possible before the Indians discovered she was gone. If they had killed Chance so heartlessly, what would they do to her?

6

Rolling away from Walks Tall as soon as the crunch of broken bone registered, Chance lifted their bound arms with his palm open, telling the crowd that the fight was over. Walks Tall was in too much pain to care. As the white man in buckskin stepped forward to cut the leather binding the fighters, all eyes were on the brave's broken arm.

Chance stepped back, allowing the others to surround the Indian. He would not dishonor his opponent by offering sympathy. The man in buckskin sheathed his knife and stood beside Chance, his tanned face emotionless. "Appears your head broke his arm, son."

As he pulled the remaining rawhide from his wrist, Chance sized up the man at his side. He was of medium height and rock hard like men get after they've lived off the land for years. A scar stretched across his neck from ear to Adam's apple, telling of a violent past, and dirt clung to him like a second skin. His hair and eyes were the same faded brown, as if God hadn't wanted to waste much time in designing him. His age was hidden in weathered wrinkles, but his movements told of a man not yet out of his forties.

"Thanks, mister, but I'm not your son."

"True." The stranger looked straight at Chance with an honest smile. "Name's Tobin Taylor."

There was an unwritten law that one man didn't ask another too many questions. Most people in Texas weren't

51

too free with personal information, but Chance wanted to
know more of this man who walked among the Indians as
their friend. He offered his hand. "Chance Wyatt. I've
known Walks Tall for years. We spent some time at a
mission home in San Antonio as boys. His folks were killed
by white men, mine my Indians."

Watching his words register on the stranger's face,
Chance continued, "There was a time when I thought we
could be friends, but the hatred over his folks' deaths
festered in him. Within a year we were fighting about
everything. Guess the only thing we ever agreed on was
running away from that home."

Taylor showed no interest in Chance's story. His face
bore the look of a man who'd lost interest in everything
except staying alive. He turned and checked the girth on his
horse. After a moment he glanced over his shoulder; his
eyes looked past Chance to Walks Tall. "I'll ride over to the
other camp." His words were spoken in the Indian dialect.
"I'll bring Medicine Man's widow back. She's the only one
around who Walks Tall is goin' to let set that arm."

Mounting his horse, the man looked back at Chance. His
eyes were hard with a lifetime of seeing and not living.
"Oh, by the way, son, I saw your woman running toward
the woods."

Every muscle in Chance tightened to the breaking point,
but he tried to keep his face calm and his walk unhurried as
he headed toward the creek. The cold water stung his face
and chest as he dipped waist-deep into the stream. He
whistled sharply and Cyoty trotted over. Chance wiped his
face with the shirt that had been tied to the saddle, shoved
his arms into his vest, and strapped his gun on before he
turned back to see if the stranger was watching.

With relief he noticed the man called Tobin Taylor was
gone. Chance's body exploded into action, swinging onto
Cyoty's back and heading for the woods. Why had she run?
What if she were in trouble? His mind spun in fear. Why
didn't she stay in the tent like he'd told her to?

* * *

Anna ran along the stream, following its crooked path, hoping it would lead her to civilization—if there was such a thing in this wild and hostile land. Her heart pounded noisily in her chest and she didn't take the time to notice if the moisture running down her face was sweat or blood. If she didn't get away fast, there would be more than a few drops of blood to worry about.

From behind her Anna heard a horse thundering closer at a steady, terrifying clip. "Run," the pounding seemed to urge her on. "*Run!*"

As the noise grew, Anna threw herself blindly into the brush. She crouched in the thick tangle of branches, afraid to breathe. Dried weeds and leaves blended with the tall brown grass to shield her from view, and she clenched her waist as a dull pain spread through her abdomen. She had no energy to run, no breath to calm her, no strength to fight the rumbling hell that moved closer to her even in the damp shadows of the brush.

The horse's snorts were very close now. Someone was moving the brush aside. The stomps of the animal and the jingle of spurs blended with the snap of leather as the rider twisted off his saddle and moved closer.

Anna closed her eyes as tightly as she could, as though not seeing what was coming would prevent her pursuer from seeing her. The memory of Chance falling as the Indian's arm slapped against his skull filled her mind, blocking her pain.

A branch near her head moved. Pushing hard against the twigs at her back, Anna waited. In her mindless terror, she barely felt the stabs of the brush against her.

"Anna?" a voice called. Another twig moved. "Anna."

Her eyes flew open as her own name registered, just as Chance spoke again. He was only a few feet from her, the sun shining off his damp, black hair, worry filling his dark blue eyes. His strong arms were carefully pulling the branches away from her.

Her terror transformed into joy as Anna jumped toward Chance. He was alive! Somehow he was alive! She threw her arms around him and hugged him as if he'd just rescued her from hell itself.

"Chance!" Anna couldn't let go. "Chance, I thought he'd killed you!"

Slowly, Chance pulled away from her enough to see her face. His smile dimpled his left cheek and mirth twinkled in his eyes. "So that's why you ran. I thought you were just tired of married life." His laughter was low and a little nervous. He seemed to have trouble knowing just where to touch her shoulders.

Hugging him again, Anna realized that only a day ago she wouldn't have cared if Chance lived or died, but suddenly she was very thankful he was standing beside her trying to make light of her fears. He was little more than a stranger, but as much as she hated being dependent, she knew without him she'd never live long in this savage land.

All her fears of the past days tumbled forth. The docking, the walk, the rain, the fever, the Indians. Her pride seemed to crumble like a house of cards. Anna moved into the warmth of Chance's arms and cried. For the first time since the night William had raped her, Anna cried.

Chance stood without moving as she pressed against him. Slowly, he embraced her, and he felt her sobs shake him to his very core. Although he wasn't sure what to do, he rubbed his cheek against the top of her silky hair and held her tightly, allowing the pain of her private hell to pass from her onto his strong shoulder. How could he tell her not to cry or that he'd protect her from whatever she feared? Chance wasn't even sure Anna wanted his sympathy, though she clung to him now.

Finally, Anna moved away from his shoulder, though his arms still held her waist against him. "I'm sorry." She lifted her chin and swallowed back her last sob. "I've never cried like that in front of anyone."

Slowly, Chance lowered his hands to his sides, suddenly

feeling as though they'd grown three sizes. He didn't know what to do with them. Here she was apologizing for clinging to him and saying she'd never done anything like this. Did she think he had? Touching her was as new to him as legs to an hour-old calf. How many times did she think he'd held a woman? It had been so many years since his mother last hugged him, Chance couldn't even remember the feeling of a woman's arms. The few saloon girls who'd rubbed against him with their large, loose breasts and whiskey perfume were worlds away from Anna. He wanted to tell her that he'd do anything to see that she never cried again, but his arms ached even now to feel her pressed closely to him once more. There she stood, looking at him with those wonderful eyes, expecting him to say something. His tongue felt like it was nailed down flat to the bottom of his mouth.

Anna wiped her face on her sleeve like a child and Chance smiled. Her action reminded him that she was very young and very new to this land. He pulled a handkerchief from his back pocket.

"You're a mess." He dabbed at the blood already drying over the small cut on her forehead. "Are you hurt anywhere except here?"

Anna smiled back and Chance felt his heart roll in his chest. Here she was, standing before him with her hair tumbling around her and full of twigs. Dried blood had made a small stream along the side of her face, and the dirt mixed with tears on her cheek was as thick as war paint, but still she was the most beautiful creature he'd ever seen. No matter what, she was a lady, a grand lady, and a little dirt could never hide that fact, just as a bath would never make him worthy of standing beside her as her husband.

Clearing his throat, he tried to speak as his finger brushed the dirt from her cheek. "Why did you run? You have nothing to be afraid of among these people as long as you are careful and show no fear."

With a sudden jerk, Anna pulled away. "I thought you

were dead. Why did you give me the knife if you didn't want me to use it to escape?"

Chance's eyebrows rose as he began to put the puzzle together. "That knife means a lot to me. It was given to my father by James Bonham only a few days before Bonham rode through Santa Anna's lines to die with his best friend, Travis, at the Alamo. I gave you the knife because Walks Tall and I fought over it the last time we saw each other. I didn't want him seeing it again."

"The last time?" Her voice was barely a whisper.

Continuing like a fool in his first poker game, Chance was oblivious to the warning in her words. "Sure, Walks Tall and I have been fighting since we were kids. A fight, for him, is an honorable way of taking what's mine. He's always wanted that knife but he's never been able to take it away from me. It may not seem like much, but it means a lot to me. I pulled it from my father's boot right before we buried him."

Stepping a few feet closer to Cyoty, Anna gave no sign she was even listening for a moment. When she did speak, her words were icy. "You've known Walks Tall for years?"

Chance awkwardly shoved his hands into his pockets. "Since we were boys. He was the only one of a group of Delawares who survived when white men raided their camp. His people had been peaceful, but there are whites who think the only good Indian is a dead one. Walks Tall must have some warrior blood in him somewhere, because he takes great pleasure in trying to kill me every time we meet."

Anna looked over her shoulder, her voice as low as faraway thunder. "And you let me think we were in danger for our lives."

Chance raised an eyebrow as he finally recognized the quicksand in her words. "I didn't have time," Chance quickly replied, hearing the anger in her voice. "He challenged me. I could hardly waste time talking with my squaw while he waited to fight."

"Your *squaw*?" The rage made her green eyes sparkle like diamonds. "Tell me, oh brave savage, what were you fighting over this time?"

Before Chance could answer, Anna had moved a step closer. Her hands were doubled into fists, ready to attack, leaving no doubt in Chance's mind that Viking warriors were charted in her bloodline. Her voice became louder with each word. "The two of you were fighting over me, weren't you? You risked my life over a childish test of strength. If you'd lost the fight, would I have spent the rest of my life in a tent made of hides?"

Chance's smile made the blood rush to Anna's cheeks. "How could you?" she yelled. "I'm not some possession like that knife. I was almost frightened out of my mind and you were only playing a game. I'm not something to be fought over and won like a bet at a gaming table."

His full laughter startled her into a moment of silence, then her fist swung in anger. Chance caught it effortlessly. "Stop. You're not only stubborn, you've got as quick a temper as a badger in winter." Lowering her fist to her side, he continued. "I hate to hurt your pride, but we weren't fighting over you; we were fighting over Cyoty."

"What?" Relief and embarrassment flooded through Anna's frame, making her want to crawl back into the brush and hide.

Laughter dripped from his words as he explained. "Walks Tall already has a woman to warm his tent, though I'm sure she's not as fiery as you. The Delawares are very civilized as Indians go. He would never dream of taking a woman against her will, anymore than I would."

"Oh, he only wanted to crack your skull, not damage your wife."

Brushing her auburn hair away from the wound on her head, his words grew serious. "My wife does a pretty good job of that without the help of Indians."

Anna jerked her head away. "I can take—"

"—care of yourself," Chance finished for her.

True, unrestrained laughter bubbled within Anna. She could no more control it than she could the tears that had fallen earlier. Something about this man and his country had eroded all the restraints on her emotions.

They laughed until tears ran down her cheeks, then Chance took her hand in the familiar manner of longtime friends and led her to the horse. "Come on, my fiery wife, we have to go back." He encircled her waist with his hands and lifted her onto the saddle.

As he swung up behind her, Anna leaned easily into his chest. "I feel like I've lived a month this morning. I haven't cried like that since . . ." She couldn't finish. She'd never tell anyone what William had done. He was dead. It was over. She forced herself to look straight ahead. "I don't remember ever laughing so hard."

Chance brushed his whiskered chin against the top of her head. She waited for him to speak, but he only nudged Cyoty into action. His silence didn't worry her, for the gentle way his arm braced her in the saddle told her he cared more than words ever would have. She rested her head against his chest and closed her eyes, remembering the way he'd held her when she'd cried. Anna silently added another brick to the bridge of trust she was building between them—a bridge she'd never even started with another man since her father left her. A tremor of anticipation of what lay beyond the bridge made her sigh and lean more heavily into the foundation of Chance's embrace.

7

Brown maverick vines twisted among the evergreens that scented the air along the bank of the creek where Anna and Chance set up camp. During their slow ride back to the Indian camp, Chance had talked about the country, which he seemed to know as well as Anna had known her tiny garden in Germany. The spot he'd chosen to spend the night was several yards upstream from the Indians, where the creek twisted, allowing them privacy. As Anna combed the twigs from her hair, Chance knelt and built a fire. The air was warm and an easy silence settled between them.

Aware that he was watching her out of the corner of his eye, Anna thought maybe his interest was as he had told her, nothing more than the fact that he hadn't been around many women. She wanted to believe they could be friends; otherwise, this would be a long year.

Chance stood, lifting his rifle from the grass. Slinging the barrel across his shoulder, he turned his face to the sun. "If you want to take a bath in the stream, I'll stand guard at that rock." He gestured toward the rock that marked the bend in the river.

Slowly, Anna lowered her hairbrush to the fabric-covered box that held her dresser set. Why, she wondered, couldn't life be as orderly as the dresser set, with its indentations for brush, comb, file, and hair receiver? Right now there seemed to be no order in the world. Maybe a bath would help. "You'll keep your back turned?"

"Of course."

She wished she could trust him without asking, but old habits weren't broken in a day. "I'd like to wash out these clothes, but my other dresses are in my trunk."

Without a word Chance moved to his saddlebag. He pulled a bar of soap and the white shirt he'd worn on their wedding night from his pack. "You could wear this until your clothes dry."

She hesitated a moment, then took his offerings. There seemed something very personal about wearing his shirt and yet it was the only practical thing to do. As Chance climbed atop the rock and sat with his back to her, Anna stripped down to her undergarments. She waded into the icy water and as she rubbed the muddy coat and skirt, the crude soap stung her hands. After several minutes, she tiptoed out of the stream and spread her clothes over the evergreen bushes that grew near the water. The sun was warm against her damp flesh, making the water seem even colder as she waded back into the stream and dunked her head.

The clean water washing through her hair felt like liquid heaven. All the days of muddy roads drained from her mind as she sank deeper into the sparkling water. She took great care to scrub her hair and body. Cleanliness had always been her passion, for somehow she felt if she kept herself clean then the dirt from her family would not touch her: her father's leaving, her mother's dishonor, the two times William had raped her.

Anna considered removing her undergarments but decided to wash the thin cotton on her body rather than risk being totally nude. All the months of basin baths in tiny cramped places made Anna doubly grateful for the open stream and the continuous flow of cool, clear water. Aboard ship she'd often been the second or third person to bathe in the water provided.

As she splashed from the stream and slipped into

Chance's shirt, the feeling of being clean and fresh enveloped her, calming her mind and relaxing her muscles.

She began to twirl around, letting her hair fly free; then Chance yelled, reminding her she was not alone. The sharp edge to his words brought her good feelings to a halt. "Are you finished?"

Slinging her hair over her head, Anna twisted it into the small towel she'd pulled from her bag and yelled, "Almost." When she raised her head he was only a few feet from her. His rifle was still slung over his shoulder, but the easy stance of before was gone. His narrowed eyes were focused along the line of trees.

"Someone's coming." He lifted his bedroll and wrapped the blanket around her shoulders just as someone stepped from the shadow of the trees.

Anna heard the air leave his lungs as Chance relaxed. Lowering his gun, he walked toward the visitor. A beautiful, young Indian woman—tall and slender, with tiny feathers tied to the ends of her braided, blue-black hair—greeted him with a formal nod. At her side she carried something wrapped in a hide.

Nodding in greeting, Chance said, "Anna, this is Walks Tall's woman." His next words made no sense to Anna, but the Indian woman looked from Chance to her, and Anna assumed she'd just been introduced. Anna nodded as she'd seen them do.

When the Indian woman spoke, she lifted the leather package in her hands and gave it to Anna. Glancing at Chance for a translation, Anna accepted the gift.

"She says her husband is going to heal. The medicine woman fixed his arm so it will mend straight."

When the Indian spoke again, Chance suddenly had trouble keeping from laughing. He translated for Anna. "She wishes to help you. She noticed the leather on your boots is hard and rises above the ground in the back like you are walking on sticks. She would like you to take this gift from her."

"But—" Anna opened the leather bundle to find a pair of soft Indian boots that looked as if they laced all the way to the knee. They were a warm brown, with a pattern stitched into the seams. They were unlike any boots she'd ever seen.

Chance interrupted. "Take the gift or you will shame her."

Anna smiled and accepted the gift. She ran her hand lightly over the leather, hoping to show how fine she thought the boots were.

Walks Tall's woman said a few more words and turned to retrace her steps. Then she disappeared into the shadows of the trees as quietly as she'd appeared. Anna wondered how Chance had heard her approach, for her steps were as light as a blossom's brush against the ground.

He grinned and winked at Anna. "We've been invited to dinner. You'll have somewhere to wear those new boots."

Anna looked at the leather leg wrappings and shook her head. "I'm not wearing these things."

"Oh yes you are. It must have taken her days to make those boots. Indian women soften the leather with their teeth."

Anna's eyes glowed with anger, but the tiny curve of her mouth betrayed her insincerity. "And if I refuse?"

Chance didn't smile. He was almost lost in the wonder of her eyes, but he remained stern as he spoke. "Then I will wear a redheaded scalp on my belt tonight when I go alone to dinner." With one finger he caught a damp curl that had escaped from Anna's towel. Your hair looks so much darker when it's wet."

Pulling her hair from his grip, Anna answered, "You don't frighten me."

His laughter was low and rich. "I guess not, but you will wear those boots tonight if I have to tie you down and put them on you myself."

Hiding her amusement, Anna turned her back. She almost said she'd like to see him try, but she feared he might accept the challenge. "If I wear the boots, you must shave."

Rubbing his two-week-old beard, he realized he hadn't thought much of shaving out here in open country, but if it would calm her, he'd dig out the razor. "Agreed."

"Good. You're beginning to look like a bear."

Chance laughed as he walked toward his saddlebags. "And you're beginning to sound like a wife."

Her only answer was the sound of a wet towel flying past his head.

The sun was turning the hills velvety shades of purple when Anna and Chance walked into the Indian camp. She'd combed her hair and tied it into a tight knot at the back of her neck, then pressed her skirt with hot rocks and brushed her coat. Her clothes were clean, with the fresh smell of evergreen dried into the fabric. At first glance she looked the same as the day she'd stepped off the boat in Galveston. But at closer range the soft brush of her leather boots against her skirts could be heard, and she now stood two inches shorter than before.

If she were being honest she would have to admit that the boots were warm and comfortable. The straps of leather held the hides tightly around her calf and ankle. Still, she couldn't help but wonder what the people in the society would think if they saw her tonight dining with savages.

"Now remember," Chance said as he leaned nearer, "stay close. These people are peaceful and only want to show us hospitality."

Nodding, Anna followed along the path a step behind him. He looked much like he had at their wedding: his hair was still damp from his bath in the stream, and his face was clean-shaven for the first time since the night they'd married. He was a fine-looking man with a masculine quality about him she'd never seen before. William had been the type of man to sit and ponder everything; Chance was always in motion. Even when he was standing still there was a restlessness about him, as though he were trying to break free from all civilization's constraints.

Anna smiled as she watched him greet the Indians, thinking she'd chosen wisely. He seemed to be a man of his word and yet he would never be the type to settle down. She would have her farm in the Fredericksburg settlement, and he would be gone in a year.

Pulling her against his side, Chance began the introductions. "Anna, I'd like you to meet Medicine Man's widow. She is the only medicine woman around." He laughed. "She's just told Walks Tall's woman that she is to be a mother."

Delighted, Anna smiled at Walks Tall's wife. The beautiful woman was patting her tummy and excitement radiated from her face. Anna immediately felt closer to the Indian woman. The life growing inside her own womb was her only ray of hope for the future, her one chance to love and to be loved—her one light in the lonely tunnel of her life.

The medicine woman came close to Anna. Her chest was covered with a thick necklace of odd trinkets and tiny bags, and she smelled like a spice peddler's wagon. She looked as though she'd been rolled in the dirt a few times before coming to dinner. Anna moved an inch closer to Chance as the old woman reached to touch Anna's stomach. Their eyes met and Anna knew the old woman knew of her pregnancy also, but the woman was silent and pulled her hand away as if it were being burned by Anna's nearness.

Suddenly Chance was pulling her away to the feast, joining the others in a huge circle around the campfire. There was much talking and laughing. The food was shared from a common bowl. Anna found that the meat stuck in her throat, refusing to move down to her stomach, but everyone was too busy to notice her lack of appetite.

Chance seemed to be a friend to many in the tribe. His words were slower, but he was able to talk with them in their language. Although he didn't talk to her, he planted his arm behind her and braced her back. After what he'd said about not being able to talk to her before the fight, she decided it might be part of these strange people's rules that he not address her. Anna was beginning to feel very much left out when someone sat down beside her, brushing her shoulder with his buckskin.

She turned to face the white man she'd seen in the camp before the fight. Unlike Chance and her, he'd made no effort to clean up for dinner. He reeked of months of perspiration and salty horse sweat, making Anna thankful she had nothing in her stomach.

The white man looked past her and addressed Chance. "I see you found your little runaway wife."

Passing a bowl of roasted vegetables and meat to the man, Chance said simply, "She was only frightened by the fight." He seemed in no hurry to introduce the stranger to Anna. Was it an oversight, or an obvious insult?

The stranger mumbled, "Hope you're all right now, ma'am." He bit into a large piece of meat and continued. "Name's Tobin Taylor. I tell you, I was powerful worried about a pretty young thing like you wandering off in this wilderness." The insincerity in his words had a scent worse than his body odor. "I wanted to help look for you myself, but someone had to ride over and talk the medicine woman into coming to help."

Anna leaned closer into Chance's side. "I'm fine now, Mr. Taylor." Her joy at having someone who spoke English was evaporating. He talked as he continued to eat. The sight of his food tumbling around in his mouth was nauseating.

"Yes, ma'am, we don't get many as pretty as you out here. Why, I can't even remember the last time I saw a white woman. You're powerful lucky to have that young man watchin' out for you or there ain't no telling what kind of trouble you'd be gettin' into."

Without looking as if he were listening, Chance slid his arm from behind her to her shoulder.

Tobin Taylor didn't seem to take the hint that Anna wanted to keep her distance. He spent the entire meal talking to her as if she were an old friend who was dying to hear all his stories. Anna found his yarns hard to believe and judging from the tightening of the muscle in Chance's arm each time Tobin spoke, Chance agreed with her.

As dinner ended and everyone stood to leave, Walks Tall emerged from his tent. His arm was strapped to a straight branch and tied from shoulder to hand. He walked directly toward Chance. A murmur spread among the others and Anna felt Chance's body tightening as if preparing to face a strong wind.

The hatred she'd seen in Walks Tall's eyes earlier was now replaced with pain. Tiny white lines were dug around his mouth where he had held back his cries of agony. "I come to tell you we fight no more." His words were in English.

Chance nodded. "We fight no more." He lifted his hand. "From this night on Walks Tall will think about teaching his son to hunt and no longer will we fight."

Walks Tall glanced at his wife. His pride in his future generation was reflected in his face. "My arm will heal by the full time of my woman. I will be ready to hold my child high to the Great Spirit."

Chance reached to place his hand on Walks Tall's undamaged shoulder, but his action was thwarted.

Medicine Man's widow pushed her way between them with a mighty twist, her long hair flying in their faces. She danced around the men, dust circling them as she let out frightening screeches. The trinkets around her neck rattled and she hissed like a snake before it strikes.

Her long, bony finger shot toward Anna like a gun being pointed at an intruder. Her voice rose louder and louder and Anna saw fear flash in the eyes of Walks Tall's woman.

"What is it?" Anna pulled at Chance's sleeve. "What is the old woman saying?"

"Nothing," Chance snapped at Anna; then he shouted something at the old woman, clearly trying to shut her up.

Tension mounted in the air. All the Indians were backing away from Anna. Hatred seemed to be overriding the pain in Walks Tall's eyes, and now he was looking at her with the same deadly stare Anna had seen in the eyes of his wife. Chance was yelling something in the Indian tongue and shaking his head, but no one seemed to be listening to him.

Anna glanced around the campfire in fear. This was a nightmare that made no sense. Her eyes met Tobin Taylor's. He was the only one not involved in this insane play with Anna at center stage.

"What is she saying?" Anna screamed at Tobin above the noise of the old woman's chant.

Tobin shrugged his shoulders and said calmly, "She says the child you carry will someday kill the Indian woman's child."

8

"No!" Anna looked toward Walks Tall's woman. How cruel the old woman must be to even suggest such a thing. She remembered how proud the Indian woman was of being pregnant. Then to be told that her child would die . . .

The terror in the Indian woman seemed to shake her entire body. When her eyes met Anna's there was a hatred in them unlike any Anna had ever seen. And she realized the Indian would gladly kill her to protect her own unborn child.

Tobin moved close to Chance. "I think it'd be wise, son, to get that little wife of yours as far away from here as you can. Walks Tall's woman is upset right now, and I wouldn't put it past her to see that the baby your wife carries never gets born."

The look in Chance's eyes spoke of agreement as he pulled Anna slowly away from the campfire and toward the trees and Cyoty. To their surprise Tobin stayed with them until they reached their camp. He helped them collect their supplies and saddle Cyoty. "Ride north. I'll join you in an hour. I know this country and can get you out of harm's way fast, even at night."

Chance put his hands around Anna's waist and lifted her into the saddle. "Thanks," he said, but the man was already darting away into the night.

Looking up at Anna, Chance molded her hands to the

saddle horn. "I'll walk and lead the horse. You hang on tightly to this. If you feel yourself falling asleep, let me know."

Anna nodded and they moved away from the Indian village without another word, but the fear in her heart continued to scream among the silent shadows of the night.

True to his word, Tobin met them within an hour. After sliding from his horse, he fell into step beside Chance without even bothering to address Anna. She could hear him whispering to Chance but was unsure whether or not she wanted to know what he was saying. Her eyes already ached from watching the shadows for movement other than the swaying of trees and the scurrying of animals. Something evil seemed to lurk just out of sight, waiting until Anna relaxed before attacking. The unknown fear was a torture greater than confrontation. Her fingers hurt from gripping the saddle horn so tightly and a scream would have to fight its way past her heart, which now throbbed in her throat.

For another hour they moved through the darkness; then Chance and Tobin stopped to water the horses. The moon was up and the land was flat, making it an easy ride. Finally, Chance swung up behind her in the saddle and whispered, "You all right?"

"Yes." Anna wouldn't have complained if she'd been about to die at this moment. All the danger they were in was somehow her fault. All her life, it seemed, anything that had ever happened to those around her had been her fault: her father's leaving, her mother's death, and now this.

Climbing atop his horse with a loud grunt, Tobin suggested, "If your little lady is up to it, we could make some time across this flat stretch." He paused only long enough to catch his breath, not allowing enough time for anyone to respond. "Course, I never seen a woman yet that wouldn't let a man know when she was uncomfortable. I know to civilize this part of the country we have to have women and children, but if you ask me, all they are is a heap of burden in this wild land. Way I see it, ain't the fightin', drinkin', and gamblin' that age a man. It's a woman walkin' along beside him remindin' him of how old he's gettin'."

Chance brushed the top of her head with his chin, and his words came low in her ear while Tobin rambled on in the background. "If you'll swing your leg over the saddle and turn sideways, I can hold you on; plus, you might be able to sleep."

Anna hesitated.

"Don't worry, I promise not to let you fall."

Slowly, she did as he'd instructed. Now his shoulder and arm braced her back and she could lay her head on his chest. Her legs lay across his thigh and for a moment Anna was embarrassed by his nearness. But the warmth of him and the comforting way he held her secure in his arms outweighed all else. How could lying in this man's arms have become so easy in such a short time? She'd already touched Chance more than she'd touched William in their five years of marriage. But then she and William hadn't shared a real marriage, only an arrangement made between him and her mother. She'd been used in a horrible game the two of them had played without any thought to how she would have to pay for their dishonor.

Memories of her mother chilled Anna. What kind of woman runs from her daughter's cries? What kind of mother kills herself when her child needs her? Anna wondered if she'd ever stop hating her mother for what she and William had done. Even in death they seemed to surround her like a mildewed memory threatening to contaminate any future happiness.

At least this time she'd planned her own fate. Her marriage to Chance might be a farce, but it was of her own making. Even in this wild land where fear fell like heavy rain, Anna felt safe in his arms. For a year she had someone she could depend on, someone who looked at her as a sister, someone who cared.

"Try to get some sleep." Chance spread his fingers out

along her waist and though she knew his gesture was only to secure her, Anna felt the caress in his gentle touch. "I'll hold you. It's all right," he whispered.

Wrapping her arms around him, Anna closed her eyes. She was in the middle of Indian territory and didn't know what lay ahead of her, but she suddenly felt more secure than she had in years.

By the time Chance lifted her from the saddle, dawn had already spread across the horizon. He held the reins and her fingers in one hand as he followed Tobin into a thick growth of trees.

Anna studied him in the morning grayness, wondering if he'd slept. His tanned face was lined around his smoky blue eyes and his shoulders were rounded slightly in fatigue, but his right hand rested firmly on the mahogany butt of his gun, ready as every to confront danger.

Several feet into the trees they found a small clearing already touched by the pale green colors of early spring. The brush and branches were so thick that the clearing seemed walled in by nature.

Tobin kicked at a few fallen branches. "This looks like a fair place to spread a bed."

"What about the Indians?" Anna spoke the words that had been on her mind for hours.

"Probably tired of followin' us, if they tagged along at all." Tobin stretched. "Besides, we're moving into Comanche country. They wouldn't wanna follow."

Pulling his saddle from his horse, Tobin plopped down in the grass. "Well, folks, I'd like to stay up for a while and visit with you, but I think I'd best take a little nap." Sliding his hat over his face, he began to snore loudly.

Chance winked at Anna. "Thank heaven."

Anna giggled. She'd listened to about all of Tobin's stories she could bear to hear, and she must have missed several while she slept. Still, she had to admit he was a good guide. They'd been able to move faster due to his knowledge of the terrain, and his constant talk made him easy to follow even in the dark.

Pulling the saddle off Cyoty, Chance walked several feet away from Tobin and planted their belongings between two trees. "I can hear a stream." He glanced over his shoulder at Anna. "I need to rub down Cyoty if you want to wash up."

Without a word, Anna grabbed her bag and hurried toward the sound of running water. The tiny stream was only ten feet from the clearing. Despite her fatigue, she took her usual care to wash.

When she returned, Chance was propped against a tree with his hat low, covering his face. His long legs were stretched out and crossed at the ankle and his rifle lay over his chest. He made no move to indicate he'd heard her return. She picked up her bedroll and spread it out beside him.

Chance used his thumb to shove his hat back. A slow smile spread across his lips as he raised one eyebrow in silent question.

Anna knelt on her blanket. "I don't want Mr. Taylor to know that we're not married in every sense of the word. I don't trust him."

Leaning closer to her with a devilish twinkle in his eyes, he whispered, "I was hoping you were getting used to lying next to me."

She wanted to laugh at his teasing, but every muscle ached. Hesitantly, she intertwined her fingers with his, enjoying the strong firmness of his warm flesh. "I want to say I'm sorry for all the mess I've gotten you into. You've been nothing but fair to me, and I've been nothing but trouble to you."

Turning his fingers over, Chance grasped her hand. "It's not your fault. I'm the one who got us mixed up with the Indians. I should've slipped past them and not confronted Walks Tall."

Anna pulled off her coat. "Maybe we'd better start fresh

now. In a few days we'll be back with the others and then we'll reach the settlement. We've been promised that all our supplies will be waiting for us. Our biggest problem will be which row of vegetables to plant first." She couldn't remember when she had last felt so comfortable with another person. It was nice to have someone to talk to about her plans. "Sleep well, Chance." On impulse, she leaned over and brushed his cheek with a kiss, then slipped beneath the wool of her blanket.

Chance straightened the covering over her shoulder and rested his fingers atop the blanket for a long moment before he answered, "Sleep well."

The sadness in his words told Anna he didn't believe all would be right. But he couldn't be expected to share her dream, she reasoned. He hadn't seen the contract all the families had signed in Germany; he hadn't heard the promises made by royal men, like Prince Carl, who led the German Immigration Society. She would explain it all to Chance when they had her new land in sight, but right now she needed to sleep.

Leaning back against the tree, Chance tried to sleep, but the memory of Anna's lips brushing his cheek reverberated through every nerve of his body. Finally, she'd started to trust him; she'd even lain next to him without fear. What would she do if she knew his thoughts? He'd enjoyed the feel of her legs resting across his thigh, her breasts pushing against his ribs, her warm breath brushing the sensitive hollow of his throat as she'd slept. She would probably hate him if she knew.

Very slowly, Chance unbuckled his gun belt and placed it on the other side of Anna. He smiled, remembering how her green eyes had turned fiery when she'd pointed his own gun at him and he'd shown no fear. She'd been surprised, which told him how little she knew about guns. The first chamber always had a dollar bill stuffed into it when a man was traveling. His Patterson Colt might be a fine weapon, but he wouldn't trust it if the first chamber were loaded. The unpredictable black powder might go off and shoot a fellow in the leg. But he would let her think he was brave for a while longer.

Sliding down beside Anna, his face only a few inches from hers, Chance brushed a strand of auburn hair from her cheek and marveled again at how beautiful she was. She looked like a china doll, her dark lashes brushing against creamy skin. Slowly, he pulled his blanket over them both and gently lifted her head so it rested on his shoulder.

She snuggled closer to his warmth.

Moving his hand across the distance between them, he touched her waist and, cursing himself inwardly, pulled her nearer. She complied with the urging of his fingers by rolling closer. Now he could feel her breasts pressed against his side and one of her legs lay over his. *Dear God,* he thought, *she feels like a small piece of heaven dropped to earth.* In all his life he had never dreamed a woman could feel so good. He let his fingers fan out along her waist; she was so fragile, so soft.

He couldn't stop himself from closing the inch between them and brushing his lips against her cheek. She smelled and tasted like spring dew. He knew she was stubborn and proud, but she was as soft as a miracle in his arms while she slept, and for the first time in his life Chance wished he was better than he was. She'd want a husband who knew the world, who could read better than a few words at a time. She deserved a man who knew the right things to say and who knew how to make love to her.

These thoughts sobered Chance and he leaned back to stare up at the trees. Even if Anna did ever treat him like something other than a brother, he wouldn't know what to do. She'd been married; she knew how to make love. The closest he'd ever gotten was once in Houston a few years ago. A barmaid had offered to spread her legs for him for free. Chance had followed her up to her little room and watched while she slipped off her underwear and pulled her skirt up to her waist. Then she'd laid there on the soiled sheets laughing at his hesitation.

Closing his eyes, Chance remembered how all he'd been able to do was stand there and stare at her blackened feet and dirty legs. He could still hear her laughter in his mind and smell the sour odors of whiskey and urine in her tiny room.

After that, he'd stayed out with the cattle when the other men went into town. It usually meant spending extra money, and the board due each year for his little sister was always in the back of his mind.

He sent Maggie every extra cent he could save, knowing that a little girl needs a few frills in her life. When he'd given his boss the hundred dollars to mail in Galveston, Chance had felt the security of being over a year ahead on her bill. Maggie was the only person in the world who had meant anything to him until now.

But Anna had touched him the moment he'd seen her, and her nearness was giving him thoughts that no man should have for a woman he'd said he thought of as his sister.

The morning wind rustled through the trees and Chance relaxed. He didn't want to think of Maggie, or of Storm's Edge, the Indian who'd led the raid on his parents' home. He only wanted to sleep next to Anna and let her dreams slip into him. In all the years he'd been alone, he'd never dreamed of finding happiness . . . and he knew that this moment might be as close as he ever got.

9

Chance rolled over Anna and grabbed his gun. In the time it took the sound of a twig's snap to reach his ears, he'd twisted the chamber and, was ready to fire, fully aware of the murmur of movement in the trees. Anna squirmed sleepily, trying to escape his sudden weight.

"Quiet!" he whispered an inch from her ear.

He felt the pounding of her heart beneath him, but she stopped shoving and turned to see what lay in the direction of his pointed gun. Their pulses seemed to beat as one as the moments passed, and both watched the movement in the brush as it grew nearer.

"Mornin', folks," Tobin yelled as he came through the tress in front of them. Two limp rabbits hung from his belt and his hands were full of roots. "Glad to see you two are finally awake."

Slowly Chance rolled out of Anna's way and holstered his gun. "You're up early, Taylor."

"Yup." Grinning like an old maid with her first offer, Tobin added, "Guess I don't have as much to keep me in bed as you do, son."

Chance sat up and blocked Tobin's view of Anna, resenting the other man looking at her with her hair falling all around her like a cloud and her eyes brushed with sleep. This new protectiveness made Chance uneasy. He could

77

think of no time in his life when he'd had more than a saddle and his horse to safeguard.

Tobin didn't seem to notice Chance's silence as he knelt in the clearing and continued to talk. "I think we're safe enough now to build a fire and roast a few rabbits. If the Indians are close enough to see the smoke, they probably can smell us whether we light a fire or not. Besides, it seems they dropped off our trail a long piece back."

After a glance at Anna, Chance stood and helped gather wood. As the fire warmed, he skinned one of the animals and staked it near the fire. Tobin did the same with his portion, then shoved the roots into the coals to bake.

When Anna joined them, Tobin grinned. "Your husband tells me you two are bound for the settlement at New Braunfels and then on north to set up another town. I've been near there and anything north would be smack in the middle of Comanche hunting grounds. Those Indians ain't like the Delawares; they'll skin you alive before you can get a cabin up. Why, I've seen whole towns wiped out faster than it takes a bull snake to swallow a field mouse. A few German settlers won't even be a full meal for those devils."

Chance was watching Anna, and he could see Tobin's words were upsetting her, so he kept his voice calm. "Maybe, maybe not. All we have to do is convince the Comanches that these people are another tribe of white men. They already hate the Texans and the Mexicans, but maybe they'd give another group a chance."

Laughter rumbled out of Tobin as easily as a coin from a fool's pocket. "You gonna ride up the Llano River and tell them bloodthirsty braves to hold off and give a bunch of farmers a chance?"

"I might," Chance answered as he turned the meat. "There doesn't seem to be anyone else applying for the job."

Tobin shook his head, and the boastful streak Chance had been counting on showed itself. "Why, son, I'm the only man who could pull somethin' like that off and I'm not crazy enough to try it."

Forcing his voice to sound matter-of-fact, Chance added, "And how would you do it?"

Taking the question as a formal invitation, Tobin began a long lecture, detailing all the things he might do if he were foolish enough to try such a thing. The advice continued all the way through the meal, and most of it was thrown out along with the bones and the root skins.

As the fire burned low, Tobin leaned up against a tree and began filling his pipe as though preparing for a long visit, but Chance slung his saddlebag over his shoulder and followed Anna to the stream to escape.

In the shadows, they washed up together. At first she seemed nervous at his presence, but he didn't want to leave her alone for long and she made no objection. They would have to get used to each other's closeness, for they could hardly spend a year avoiding one another. Without a word between them, Chance stripped off his shirt and started to shave.

The razor he'd sharpened in the pool only a month ago would never last the year at this rate. He'd bought the worn leather kit from an old-timer a few years back. The old man had sworn he'd never shave again and Chance used it only once a month as his beard was so heavy it seemed to grow back by the time he got the soap washed off. But the old razor was better than using a knife, and if Anna wanted him to shave, he figured he'd give it a try.

Watching her comb her hair made Chance long to reach over and touch the free strands before she braided them.

"Ow!" Chance yelled suddenly as the razor nicked his chin.

"Are you hurt?"

"Hell, yes," Chance yelled. He reddened at his use of such harsh language. "Guess I'm not used to shaving so often," he grumbled.

Laughing, Anna offered to help, but Chance backed

away. Watching her had gotten him this pain in the first place, and having her worry over him would only make him feel worse. He'd doctored a lot worse injuries than a tiny shaving cut.

' As he backed away, Anna cocked her head sideways and rested her fists upon her hips. "Well, it seems to me if you'd pay less attention to watching me and more to what you're doing, you would be less apt to cut yourself."

Smiling at her teasing, Chance answered honestly, "You're right, but my face will probably be a mass of scars before I get used to seeing you comb that hair of yours." He turned toward her, the towel held at his chin. "I've never seen hair that color."

Anna looked down at the stream. "Muddy, my mother used to call it. Muddy, muddy, ugly hair."

"No." How could anyone have insulted such a color? He remembered when he'd first seen her hair in the morning light. "Your hair reminds me of the rich river-bottom soil. It's warm and shiny at the same time. I wish you'd wear it down."

Blushing at his compliment, she met his serious eyes. "It would be scandalous for a married woman to wear her hair free."

"Still, I like to see it falling down your back." He checked to make sure his chin had stopped bleeding.

"Tell you what." Carefully, Anna inspected the damage the razor had done with her finger lightly on his chin. "You try not to get all sliced up, and I'll wear my hair down when we're alone in our house."

"Agreed." Chance wished he could lay the first logs today.

Tobin's whistle shattered the calm air. "Come on, folks. If we're going to reach the wagons by nightfall, we've got some riding to do."

Feeling suddenly lighthearted, Chance reached for Anna's hand and she gave it willingly as they walked back to the clearing, both smiling.

Tobin looked at them skeptically. "Too much washin' ain't healthy, you know, ma'am," he said. "I take a bath every spring and I've never been sick in my life."

Laughing, Anna rolled up the bedrolls as the men saddled up. A good feeling welled up inside her, as if her life had finally taken a turn for the better. She watched as Tobin took the horses down to the stream for water while Chance doused the fire and covered it with dirt until there were no signs in the clearing that they'd passed.

The quiet peace of the morning was shattered suddenly by Tobin's angry voice. He yelled like he'd been wounded, then took only enough time to suck in his breath before letting out a continuous string of curse words.

Chance lifted his rifle and ran toward the stream with Anna only a step behind. They reached the horses and found Tobin hopping around on one leg in a crazy dance of pain, his language keeping pace with each step.

"What is it?" Chance yelled.

With pain-filled eyes Tobin looked from Chance to Anna and closed his mouth, biting back pain-induced profanities. Plopping down on the ground, he waved his foot in the air like a signal flag. "Durned snakes bit me in the ankle. I can't believe I didn't see them. I must have stepped right on the sons of Satan's nest."

Using the butt of his rifle, Chance cleared the brush away and dropped to his knees beside Tobin. "Settle down. You're not doing yourself any good dancing around stirring up your blood."

"I know it, but I'm so mad at myself I could bite them little snakes' heads off. I deserve to die for being so stupid. Any toddlin' papoose would know better."

Chance handed his rifle to Anna and pulled Tobin to his feet. "I'll get Tobin back to the clearing; can you handle the horses?"

Anna nodded. "What else?" She admired how calm Chance seemed, since judging from the white lines around Tobin's mouth there was much to be concerned about.

"We'll need a fire. Boil water in every cup we have." Chance lifted Tobin and started back to camp. "And Anna, watch out for any more snakes. Tobin probably scared them all off with his yelling, but keep the gun butt ready just in case."

Sweat was already forming across Tobin's forehead. "You know, son, a baby rattler's just as poisonous as his great-granddaddy. I didn't even hear the rattles, so I must've startled them."

"I know. How many bites did you feel?"

"Three, maybe four." Both men knew each bite doubled his chance of death and halved the time until the poison moved from his leg to his heart.

Back at camp, Chance laid Tobin on the ground, slit his pant leg, and removed his moccasins. "If you'd wear boots you'd be better off."

With a whispered oath, Tobin clenched his teeth and lay back. "I always hated the hard leather around my foot." He pointed at his bedroll. "There's chewin' tobacco and whiskey in my bag. I'll start on softenin' a plug after I down some of the whiskey."

Chance handed him the whiskey; then, taking the wide strip of rawhide used as a strap around the bedroll, he tied it above Tobin's knee and twisted it as tightly as he could. "That should slow the blood some."

Glancing up, Chance saw that Tobin was too busy concentrating on his drinking to answer.

Moments later Anna appeared from the stream pulling the horses and carrying a load of wood. She helped Chance start a fire and brought water from the stream as Tobin drank and bit into a huge wad of tobacco.

After Tobin downed the last of the whiskey, Chance pulled his knife from his boot and poked it into the fire. "Anna, keep the water heating. He's lucky; looks like one bite hit the ankle bone and didn't do much besides break the skin, but the other two look deep. I'm going to cut them open then loosen the strap on his leg so the blood will run.

You pour hot water over the cuts so the poison will come out faster."

Following orders, Anna set to work. Chance's hand was steady as he crossed each bite with the hot blade of his knife. Tobin yelled like an Indian in battle all the while, but didn't move his leg. As Chance loosened the strap, blood flowed out of the cuts and Anna poured hot water over the wounds.

They repeated the bloodletting three times, and each time Tobin's face grew paler. Finally, Chance took the tobacco from Tobin and smeared it over the cuts. "This will draw more of the poison out," he told Anna as he wrapped his bandanna around the man's ankle. "Help me get him up on his horse. I think it's safer if we move on rather than stay here. We may not make it to the others by nightfall, but we can try. If there are Indians following us it wouldn't be wise to stay here too long."

While Chance talked Tobin had been silent, and when Anna looked at him she saw why. His face was gray-white. Although his eyes were open, he was beyond hearing. A chill passed over Anna. This land was a cruel place, pulling the life from people with no warning, as though one person was of little value. Everything here was sharper, more intense, than back in Germany, as if living and dying were painted with bright colors.

They lifted Tobin onto his saddle and tied a blanket around him. Chance walked beside his horse, guiding the animals while trying to hold Tobin in the saddle. "Can you handle Cyoty by yourself?" he asked Anna as he lifted her into the saddle of the huge bay and handed her the reins.

Anna answered, "I used to ride every day at boarding school. Then after I married, my favorite times were early-morning rides."

Chance patted Cyoty's neck. "He's not a boarding school mare; he's strong, with a mind of his own. I reckon you two are pretty fairly matched."

Anna pulled the reins taut. "You just have to let him know who's boss."

Chance winked. "I'll remember that."

Anna didn't know how to take his wink. She kicked Cyoty into action and was surprised at how good it felt to be back on a horse and in control.

They traveled northeast, hoping to cross the wagon tracks. The day was cloudy and gloomy, darkening the earth and their moods. Tobin sobered from the whiskey, but as the day continued his fever rose, and Anna silently watched the veins along his temple swell as sweat poured from his face. They covered him with another blanket when he complained of chills, but it seemed to give him little warmth.

Near dusk they reached a river with wide, sandy banks on either side, and Chance insisted on crossing in case it rained again during the night. On the far bank was a beach with overhanging cliffs. Anna, tired and irritable from both the ride and worrying about Tobin, didn't speak as they made camp. Chance built a huge fire under a cliff's edge, then hollowed out the earth and made Tobin a place close to the fire with a bank of sand behind him to block the wind.

Tobin was mumbling continuously now, making no sense. Anna wiped a cold cloth over his face as Chance checked the man's wounds. Dark purple veins climbed up his leg like weeds under the skin, and his foot was swollen to twice its normal size.

"What else can we do?" Anna whispered. She covered Tobin with their last blanket and still he shivered.

Chance shook his head. "Nothing left to do now but see if he can fight the poison that's gotten into his blood. The cold cloth on his head will help, and I'll keep the fire blazing." Chance lifted his rifle and handed it to Anna. "Will you be all right for a while? I'll catch us some supper."

Anna nodded, but she'd never felt less all right in her life. Wrapping her arms around her knees, she sat beside Tobin and watched black clouds gather along the horizon. Lightning flashed and thunder rumbled, but it was miles away.

By the time Chance returned, Tobin was resting peacefully. Chance laid three fish beside the fire. "I was lucky to catch these before dark." He cut the heads off the fish and covered them with the sandy mud by the river so they'd cook evenly in the campfire. Then he pushed them into the ashes of the fire. "You'll have time for a bath if you want."

"Thanks, I would like that. Every muscle in my body hurts." She glanced at Tobin. "He's finally sleeping quietly."

Chance threw another log on the fire, then stretched out beside his saddle and watched her walk to the water. As she rounded a corner, he tried to picture her slowly undressing in the moonlight. All day he'd walked beside Tobin and wished he was behind Anna in the saddle. His arms had ached to hold her and he'd counted the hours until nightfall. Tobin might have poison in his blood, but Chance could feel something equally dangerous running through his. The fever in him was frightening, and Chance wasn't sure he couldn't die of it just as easily as Tobin could die from the snakebites.

Restlessly, Chance stood up and walked toward the water. He relaxed among the shadows and watched Anna as the moonlight reflected off the river in shimmering pale light, making pearls of the drops of water on her skin. The thunder in the north was growing louder, adding a wild harmony to his pounding heart. Tonight she'd pinned her hair up like a crown atop her head. Her skin was almost as white as the cotton camisole that covered her. Feeling a hunger inside him suddenly eating away at his gut, Chance realized he wanted her and hated himself for having such thoughts. She was as far above his grasp as the queen of England. How could he even dream that such perfection would long for him as he now did for her?

Anna ran out of the water, shivering as she wiped the tiny towel over her bare arms and legs. Her chemise clung to her like a second skin. Chance could see the outline of her body, and couldn't help but study the way her hips curved above her long legs. Lightning flashed closer, breaking his trance as the thunder rumbled nearer, warning of the storm's approach.

Pulling his coat off, Chance walked slowly toward her. He placed the warm wool on her shoulders before she sensed his nearness. Instinctively, she jerked in fear, then relaxed into the warmth of his coat and arms, loving the way the heat left in his coat surrounded her cold body.

His voice was low in her ear. "A storm's coming. You'd better get away from the water."

Anna shivered and Chance pulled her tighter into his embrace, feeling the wet cotton of her camisole soaking his shirt. Her breasts pushed against the wall of his chest with a soft pressure that jolted through his body like a bolt to his heart. Lightning flashed again, and he saw the reflection of the flash in Anna's huge eyes. He raised one hand and pulled the comb from her hair, letting the shiny silk tumble around her shoulders like a cloud of dark fire.

"I love your hair," he whispered as he ran his hand over the mass. "It's as beautiful as you are."

Anna brushed her cheek against his shoulder. "No one's ever told me that before."

Chance wrinkled his forehead in confusion. Was it possible that her husband of five years had never told her of her beauty? He moved his fingers into her hair, filling his fist with the wonderful silk. "Don't lie to me, Anna. Any man would have to be insane not to see your beauty."

Resenting his suggestion that she'd lied, Anna pulled away. She'd always been honest with him, and he had no right to pry into her past. It was dead, buried at sea. His words were just words. She'd heard the truth every day of her life. "I'm not lying. My mother told me often enough how I looked. Muddy and ugly, she'd say. Poor, plain little Anna. Better marry at fifteen or you'll be an old maid. By the time you're twenty, any bloom in you will be long gone." Anna's voice broke.

Chance couldn't believe his ears. How could a mother tell her child she was ugly? And he could see that Anna, with her tight widow's bun and plain clothes, somehow tried to make it true. He wanted to hold her, to shout to the heavens that her mother had lied, but when he touched her shoulder, Anna pulled away, hugging his coat around her more tightly.

"Don't," she snapped. "I'm no longer cold."

He fought the urge to grab her and shake the truth into her. "The hell you're not," Chance swore. She was so lovely, but her scars were burned deep. He wasn't sure he could touch them with words. For the first time in his life Chance felt someone else's pain deeper than he'd ever felt his own.

Anna watched Chance stalk back to the fire. She knew he wouldn't understand. How could he know how beautiful her mother had been? How she had always been plain little Anna, the plain, sad child who had sacrificed a future to keep her mother's secret? How could Chance understand that her husband and mother had been lovers, and that she'd been married off to William so that they could live together without gossip. Telling such a thing would shame Anna to the core.

Braiding her hair into one long, thick rope, she dressed in the dark. No, she thought, no one will ever know. Let them think I destroyed William. Let them think my mother was insane. No one will ever know the truth of what happened the night my mother died. No one. Not even this stranger who is so full of kindness.

She picked up his coat and folded it carefully in her arms. The soft wool caressed her fingers as she touched its folds. Holding it to her face, she could smell the scent of Chance deep within the fabric.

* * *

When she returned, Chance had the fish cleaned and was ready to eat. Even as she approached, he didn't look up. He didn't speak. Anna thought maybe she'd hurt his feelings by pulling away, but better that than have him turn away from her, as he would if he knew the truth. He was only a stranger, a stranger she'd see for no more than a year.

After a silent meal, Anna pulled the loose strands of hair from her brush and placed them in the tiny hair receiver in her dresser set. Someday, when winter slowed her life and kept her inside, she would braid the hairs over a cord and make a comb to match her hair. Concentrating on her task as though nothing else mattered at the moment, Anna wanted to say she was sorry for the way she'd acted, but somehow the words wouldn't come.

Tobin's fever had broken and he was sleeping quietly. Chance laid one blanket down on the side of the fire opposite Tobin and stretched out, watching the clouds rumbling above. Finally, Anna moved to his side, silently lying down within an inch of him.

She turned her back to Chance and whispered, "Good night."

Chance stirred and a moment later she felt his coat go over her. Before she could speak, he pulled her against him, holding her tight as though challenging her to tell him again that she was not cold. The warmth of his body spread through her, and Anna relaxed, knowing that he meant only to share the warmth of his body and no more.

Long after both their breathing had slowed, Anna felt Chance's cheek against her hair. "Good night, my beautiful Anna," he whispered, half asleep.

Anna smiled, knowing his words were a lie, but a lie she could treasure and store against the coldness to come, when the only warmth she'd have would be her own.

10

The stormy heavens rumbled all night. Anna was aware of the wind and the thunder, but she kept her eyes closed tightly as she snuggled into the warmth of Chance's arms.

A nightmare of memories kept haunting her, flashing scenes across her thoughts, howling like rumors never spoken aloud but clearly heard by all. The brooding clouds above her became the murky lake behind their home in Germany. The pale half moon twisted into a vision of her mother's body, floating facedown in the choppy water. Crackles of thunder were Anna's frightened cries. Wind tore at her hair and clothing just as William had pulled at her gown that night months ago when he'd first invaded her bed.

Anna twisted in her sleep, feeling William's hands pawing her. His labored breathing reeked of whiskey. He pressed his fleshy cheek against her throat and called her mother's name as he sucked at her flesh. When she cried out, his fist silenced her. Terror rose in Anna as vivid in her dream as it had been that night. Suddenly, she was fighting with every ounce of her being—fighting the nightmare, fighting the fear, fighting her shame.

Strong hands crossed the nightmare. A powerful grip pulled her shoulders straight and stilled her thrashing.

"Anna! Anna!"

She opened her eyes to reality. A tall shadow sat above

her, pinning her to the ground with his hands. Anna froze. His voice was low and worry colored his words. "Are you all right?"

As her eyes adjusted, she could see his dark hair blowing in the wind. She knew the strength of this man she now called husband, and he was applying no more than needed to keep her still.

"I . . ." She focused on her surroundings as her nightmare dimmed: The firelight. The man sleeping across from them. The gentle stranger above her. "I had a nightmare," she whispered to the lean silhouette. "I hate storms."

Chance released his hold and lowered himself onto his side, resting his head on one elbow. His face was only a few inches from her own. "I've had a few of those myself. After my folks were killed, it was years before I stopped seeing them dead and the house burning. I thought I should have died with them. I'd dream over and over that I was running, trying to get there before the Indians killed them."

He rolled onto his back and stared at the clouds. She could see the hard lines of his strong jaw and knew without asking that he'd never told anyone of his nightmares.

When his gaze turned toward her, the firelight reflected in the caring blue depths of his eyes. A tear that the man would never allow to fall sparkled from a boy's nightmare. She could hardly hear his low voice. "Might help to talk about it."

She turned to her side. "I . . ." She glanced at Tobin. The man was resting.

Chance followed her stare. "Come on." He stood and tossed their blanket over his saddle a few feet away. "Let's take a walk." He offered his hand.

The energy left from the nightmare still pulsed through her veins as they strolled down to the water, picking their way through shadowy masses of brush. Wind rippled over the darkened water, making it slosh at the rocks near their feet as they walked along the bank in silence. She could feel his nearness, and it calmed her as did the shadows waving across the sand and the constant beating of the water against the land. Chance's hand was warm and strong as he guided and steadied her on the path.

Anna thought of how afraid of him she'd been. She'd shielded herself from him with her anger as though he were as evil as William. She'd been wrong. Chance had shown her nothing but kindness and tenderness. He'd cared for her when she had the fever and found her when she'd run away. He'd kept her warm with his body.

When they reached a cave that broke most of the wind, Anna stopped. Chance tugged her hand gently as he looked over his shoulder, a question in the shadowy tilt of his head.

Brushing a few strands of hair from her eyes, she began, "I want to say I'm sorry. I don't think I've been quite fair with you." He moved to face her but remained silent as she continued. "I seem to always be yelling at you and you don't deserve it. The sisters at the boarding school always said I had a mean temper."

Chance's voice was only a whisper in the wind. "I don't think anything about you could be mean." He cupped her cheek with his palm and Anna leaned into it, instinctively needing the touch of someone who cared about her. She could hear it in his words, feel it in his touch, see it in the dark blue warmth of his eyes.

"You're a good man." A tear spilled over her lashes and trickled down her cheek. How many times had she sworn there were no good men in the world? How many times had she promised never to allow herself to be near another?

His thumb caught the tear and for a moment he seemed lost in the wonder of its moisture. "I have to leave in a year." Pain echoed in his words.

"I know." Anna pulled away slightly. "I will hold you to our bargain."

"There is something I have to do, a promise I made years ago."

Anna remembered the night he'd called for Maggie in his sleep. What had he said? *Don't cry, Maggie?* Wrapping her arms around her waist, Anna wondered if his promise had anything to do with a girl he'd left behind. "You don't have to explain anything to me. I bought a husband for a year, nothing more." She turned back to retrace her steps. There was no need to hear him tell her he was only with her because of the money; she'd known that from the first meeting, when he'd asked for the hundred dollars even before he'd married her.

"Wait." Chance grabbed her arm and twirled her toward him. "I want to explain. I always seem to be starting conversations with you and not finishing them." Suddenly, her nearness slowed his words.

"There is no need." Her eyes studied the black outline of the trees. "You've been kind and I thank you. There is and can be no more."

"Anna . . ." He couldn't find the words. She looked so strong and lovely before him. Moonlight turned her hair to smoky fire and her eyes seemed to hold the pain of the world in their emerald depths.

Angry and stiff as an ice sculpture, Anna now stared at him. But he'd felt her warmth beside him. Her tear had touched his heart. Suddenly, he wanted her to know his thoughts. Her presence had added a softness to the world that he'd never known existed.

"If I tell you how beautiful you are, you'll only call me a liar again." He moved his hands around her waist and pulled her stiffly against him, needing her nearness more than air. "I don't know if I have the words to tell you how lovely your eyes are when they're filled with fire."

"No!" Anna's voice was whisked away on the wind.

"Dear God, Anna, do you know how you make me feel inside?"

"No," she whispered again, but her nearness was flooding his mind, intoxicating his reason. Chance spread his fingers across her waist and held her so close against him that their hearts seemed to pound as one. He lowered his lips to hers without thought, without logic.

The softness of her mouth sent a jolt through him and for a moment his pulse seemed to stop. There was no wind, no river, no night. There was only the wonder of Anna in his arms. Opening his mouth slightly, he circled her lips with his, loving the feel of her so near, loving the taste of her. He released her waist and slowly slid his hands up her sides as he tasted the essence of this beautiful woman.

She moved in his arms, twisting the fullness of her breast into his hand, and he slid his fingers across her blouse, loving the softness beneath his touch. When her mouth would have pulled away, Chance braced her head in his hand and pressed his lips harder into her sweetness. He'd never kissed a woman whose lips didn't taste of whiskey. Anna's mouth was as soft as butter and reminded him of fresh, wild honey.

A sudden pain slammed into his chest and for a moment Chance didn't react. He felt another hit, then her lips were gone, along with the warmth of her body against him. Watching in disbelief, he made no move to defend himself as her hand flew through the air and slapped the side of his face. His cheek stung from her blow, but he didn't move. Then reality began to register in his mind.

When her hand flew again, he ducked away from the blow. The angry blaze in her eyes was hot enough to set the horizon afire. "What?" he yelled as she kicked at him in rage. Her skirts hampered the severity of the blow.

"You said I could trust you. You said you wouldn't force yourself on me."

"Wait!" He stepped out of harm's way. "All I did was kiss you."

"I said there would be nothing between us." She forced her voice to harden. "Nothing, do you understand? Or are you too savage to know what I mean?" Anna's breath was coming in gulps now. "Don't ever touch me like that. It's wrong. It's bad."

Turning away from her, Chance dragged his fingers through his hair. He knew he wasn't worthy of her. She was so perfect. He called himself a hundred names for not thinking. How could he have kissed her when he'd worked so hard to gain her trust? He was her bought-and-paid-for husband. The job was to work her farm, not hold her in his arms. But, by God, she'd felt something when they'd kissed. She might scream and kick till hell froze, but she had responded for one moment.

"I'm sorry I upset you, but I'm not sorry I kissed you." He had to tell her the truth, or she'd never trust him again. He had the feeling she'd been lied to enough during her life. "I'm a man, Anna."

"You're an animal."

Chance took a step toward her, then hesitated. "No. Despite what you think of me, I'd never force myself on a woman." He lifted his hand to touch her shoulder, but she moved away.

Anna's voice was stone cold. "I've heard such lies before." The hurt in her eyes was too deep to have been caused by one kiss. "Give me your knife."

"What?"

"Give me that knife!"

Chance reached for the hunting knife at his belt.

"No." Anna pointed at his boot. "The one you keep hidden. The one that man named Bonham gave your father before he died at the Alamo. The one you said was so important to you."

Leaning over, Chance slid the blade from the lining of his boot. The pearl handle flashed ghostly white in the night as he handed it to her.

Anna shoved the weapon into her coat pocket. "I'll keep this with me for the rest of our year together. I know it means a great deal to you, and I promise I'll give it back the day you leave. Between now and then, however, I swear on the grave of my mother, I'll kill you with it if you touch me as a man touches a woman."

Chance's mood couldn't have been blacker if he'd just killed a dozen old people, eaten the last meal of some starving children, and hung his best friend. He'd always thought of himself as good and honorable, but her eyes told him he was beneath contempt. She'd said he was a savage. Was she right? Perhaps he'd lived as a savage too long, for even now his fingers longed to slide along her body, unhampered by her clothing. How could he have mistaken hostility for hesitation?

Watching her walk back to camp, her back straight and her head high, he still sensed she was frightened—just like that night back in camp when she'd walked among the men and asked for a husband. He'd admired her fire, her strength. That night he'd only wanted to help. He'd never dreamed her anger would be turned on him. Now he could see the hate in her eyes when she looked at him. How, in one moment of moonlight, could he destroy all the trust he'd worked for weeks to build?

He wanted to yell out, *Don't be afraid of me. I'd never hurt you.* But she wouldn't believe him. He'd have to prove to her that he wasn't an animal, and he planned to do just that even if it took every day of the next year.

Chance kicked a rock into the river. He wished he knew more about women. If he'd been around them a little more, maybe he'd be able to read her better. Maybe he'd have known that she'd cuddled next to him merely for warmth. He was unsure what he was supposed to have done, but what he did was obviously wrong. She was as mad at him as a pinned-up longhorn. He'd seen wild cows fight a fence until their heads were bloody. Chance walked slowly back to camp, thinking that the only one who might get bloody if he got near Anna again was him.

Anna watched as Chance stepped from the shadows. He slowly circled the camp, then slid down beside his saddle. He leaned against it and pulled his hat low without even looking at her. Snuggling into their only blanket, she waited for him to make a move toward her.

As the minutes ticked by, Anna released her grip on the

knife and let it fall to the sand. Maybe she wasn't as afraid of him as he assumed, but she wasn't going to let her guard down again. He'd stepped beyond the boundaries they'd drawn, and she had to stop him before anything happened, before she felt anything for him.

Finally, Anna closed her eyes and let her fingers touch her lips, remembering how gently his mouth had brushed hers. The feel of his hands moving over her body returned. He'd touched her so lightly, as though he'd been afraid she'd break. For a moment, she hadn't wanted to pull away. For one second she'd longed to throw her arms around his strong shoulders and melt into him just to see what it was like to touch a man without fear. Many other women her age had known the light touch of a man's hand, had felt the first gentle kiss. But not Anna. She was four months pregnant and twice married. And tonight was the first time she'd been kissed.

11

The light of dawn slithered between the low clouds, spreading across the earth like a prowler. Chance lifted his hat and watched the thick, humid air turn from black to gray. He stretched soundlessly, uncrossing his legs and straightening his shoulders, every muscle sore from his cramped sleep. The morning was as stormy as his mood, but it would take more than a rain to wash Chance clean of his troubles. The cold bothered him little, but the ache to have Anna cradled in his arms chilled him to the bone.

She lay sleeping, curled like a child in her blanket, only a few feet away. He stood and walked toward his wife, then knelt and studied her as though he'd just discovered a treasure. She was so beautiful when she was asleep, with her face relaxed, her hair slipping free from her thick, auburn braid.

Even in the half-light, he was hypnotized by her lips, now slightly open as she slept. How wonderful her mouth had tasted. She had a power over him whether her eyes were closed in sleep or blazing with fire. What had she said when he'd kissed her? It was wrong. Did she think him so far beneath her that even a kiss would be evil and dirty?

Standing, he looked away, studying the sky as a seaman studies his maps. He had to think of other things besides Anna's lips. Even the softness of the clouds reminded him of her. The low stormy rumbling to the north, the distant flash of light, the cool morning breeze that caressed his jaw . . . all whispered *Anna* in his mind.

He shivered as though with a sudden chill. "Stop it," he muttered to himself, shoving his fists deep into his pockets and trying to stop the urge to hold her. He'd given his word to leave in a year, and even if she didn't think so, he was a man of honor. He knew he'd have to leave her without a good-bye, even if it tore the heart from him to do so. No matter how it hurt, he'd leave her in one year and prove to her that he could be trusted. To hell with the heartache. To hell with caring about anyone. He didn't need a heart to find Storm's Edge. Chance would find the Indian who'd murdered his parents and kill or be killed. Once and for all, he'd put his own nightmares to rest.

"Chance," Anna whispered.

Whirling around, he found her sitting up and her beauty, as always, was like a blow. But he hid his feelings. "What is it, my wife?"

She stood and folded her blanket, her eyes looking to the north. "Will we ride today?"

Chance opened his mouth to answer, but Tobin's voice came first. "Hell of a dream I had last night."

They both turned to face the middle-aged man. His face was pale and his eyes were still colored with fever, but his voice was strong. "I reckon we can do some ridin' today. We should be able to catch the wagons within a day or two."

Shaking his head, Chance replied, "It looks like rain. Maybe we should stay here protected by the cliffs until the storm blows over."

Tobin huffed like he was planning a protest. But when he tried to stand, he sank back into his pallet. "Guess you're right, son." His breathing was labored. "I wouldn't want to get the little lady wet."

Anna smiled at his lie. "I need to change that bandage on your foot whether we ride or not."

For once there was no argument from Tobin as he looked

from Anna to Chance. "I've never been much for sayin' thanks, but I reckon you saved my life."

"Forget it," Chance answered. "You'd have done the same."

"Maybe, maybe not." Tobin leaned his head back. "But I'll find a way to pay you back someday. Might start by stayin' around till you get that wife of yours a proper cabin built."

The memory of Anna's promise to wear her hair down when they had a cabin flashed in Chance's mind and he said, "I might just hold you to that offer."

Tobin lay back on his blankets. "For quite a spell now, I've been feelin' like there's not much makes life worth livin', but after walkin' so near the edge of the world, I realized how much I'd like to stay around." He fell asleep still mumbling about climbing over a few more mountains.

Anna chuckled at the old man as she helped Chance change the bandage.

Chance looked up at her, but she looked away the moment their eyes met. Lord, how he wished he could say he was sorry for kissing her, but the truth was he wanted to do it again—probably would long to every day for the rest of their year together. But she'd said his touch was wrong and bad. Chance threw a log on the fire and wished he could believe it was because her first husband had just died and not because she found him so repulsive.

Grabbing his saddlebag, he headed off toward the water. "I'm going to clean up," he mumbled. She wouldn't have to tell him again to take a bath or shave. He might not be some fine gentleman like she'd probably had court her when she finished boarding school, but he wasn't the savage she thought he was either.

Almost a week passed before the threesome caught up with the wagons. The afternoon sun was hot and the earth steamed with spring heat as they cleared a ridge and saw the German caravans. Anna was shocked at the sight before her as they neared the band of immigrants. Her people looked like bony shadows following mud-covered coffins. Their clothes were as dirty and ragged as their faces. Chance picked his way between the wagons until he found Carl and Selma Jordan. Anna hardly recognized her only friends among the settlers.

Carl looked up as they neared, his face sunburned and vacant; then, after a long moment, he slowly raised his hand in greeting. "Welcome." His weak smile barely lifted the corners of his chapped lips.

Sliding from the saddle, Anna hugged Selma. Tears streamed from her eyes as she felt how thin the woman had become in only a few weeks.

With heartfelt tears of gladness, Selma greeted Anna, then Chance. "We thought you were dead. Many died the first few weeks when the rains were so bad." She couldn't seem to stop patting Anna's arm. "But my Carl, he kept telling them you'd be back. He wouldn't let them throw your chest out of the wagon."

"Thank you." Anna closed her eyes as she tried to imagine what she would've done if she'd lost her trunk with all she owned inside.

Chance shook Carl's hand, forming a bond of friendship between the two men that would not easily be broken. "We are in your debt."

Nodding as if he understood, Carl, as always, said nothing.

Selma had none of her husband's shyness. She continued mixing German words with English. "Almost all those from our village are gone. Walter Schmitz's wife died and all the Muller children, except the oldest." Her eyes were tearless as she spoke, as if no more tears could fall. "So many others. I can't think of them all."

Carl lifted his head as if about to dive into deep water. His words were slow and thick with accent. "Some died, some got tired, and stopped along the road. Reverend Muller says we'll be lucky if a third of those who sailed make New Braunfels." He placed his arm around his tiny wife. "But we are going to make it to our new home."

Selma's voice was weary from hoping. "Yes, but it's been a hard trip, plus I'm worried about Walter. Since his wife died, he's been acting like a man possessed. He even traded her clothes for some homemade liquor a few days back when we passed a settlement."

Carl looked at Chance, and his words were heavy with emotion. "Every man's got to deal with his grief in his own way. I don't know what I'd do without my Selma."

Chance was saved from having to answer by a cry from the front for the wagons to halt. Carl Jordan gave a heavy sigh and squeezed his wife, lifting her effortlessly off the ground. "One day closer to our home."

She smiled and looked at Anna. "We have sweet potatoes. You're welcome to share."

Anna knew from their hollow faces that they must have very few, and she wanted to hug them all over again for being so generous. She raised her eyes to Chance and he read her thoughts with a wink.

"That sounds mighty fine." Chance pulled Anna's bag and their bedrolls off his saddle. "But you have to allow us to share also. I saw some deer tracks back a ways and was hoping we'd have someone to share with."

The smile on Carl's face was genuine. "That sounds grand. The ammunition has been so low we haven't had venison for days. And to be honest, I never handled a gun. A hammer fits my grip much better."

Limping out from behind the horses, Tobin nodded at Carl and tipped his hat to Selma. "Reckon I should go with you, son. Ain't never took me more than one shot to down a deer." He bit into the last of his tobacco. "While we're huntin' I'll tell you about the time I downed two bucks with one shot."

Anna laughed and introduced the strange man to Carl and Selma. With each day of Tobin's recovery, he'd grown stronger and more outlandish with his stories. She knew he

persisted because the tales made her laugh and Chance
swear in disbelief. Tobin reminded her of a stray dog that
touches your heart with his need—you accept him, fleas and
all.

"We'll set up camp while you're gone," Anna said,
touching Chance's arm.

His dark, stormy blue eyes turned toward her. They'd
spent the week trying not to touch one another or look in
one another's eyes. The strain was tearing at both of them,
and now Anna wanted to start fresh. They were back among
her people. The music of the German tongue in the air made
her feel as if she'd come home. Surely he would act
civilized among the others.

Chance swung atop Cyoty and tipped his hat. With the
energy of a morning ride, he and Cyoty vanished into the
trees.

Anna knew he'd bring back enough meat to share, and
she felt a sudden pride in this wild Texan she'd married. He
might be half savage, like the Indians around them, but she
always felt somehow protected and provided for when he
was near. His silence toward her over the past week had left
her nerves on edge. He'd been polite, but never close.
They'd ridden double only a few times. His strong arm had
been like a brace, nothing more. At night he slept a few feet
away, no longer touching her. Anna missed his comforting
warmth beside her, but her pride wouldn't allow her to cross
the ground that seemed like a wall between them each night.

Darkness fell across the campsite. Family fires dotted the
land around the wagons. Anna and the Jordans chose a spot
near the stream, several yards away from the others. With
relief, Anna found her trunk and pulled out a fresh dress.
She scrubbed her traveling clothes and hung them to dry.
Pulling Chance's extra clothes from his bag, she washed
them also, mending them with skill and hoping her small
task might prove to be a peace offering. She searched
through William's clothes in the trunk, but all of them were

far too small to be altered for Chance. Night was upon them when Anna finally set up her tiny tent beside the Jordans'. She enjoyed the night sky, but it would be pure luxury to change into her nightgown and not have to sleep in her clothes. The privacy of her tent outweighed having the stars for a roof tonight.

Just after dark Chance returned with a deer. Tobin swiftly cleaned it and hung the carcass between two nearby trees, while Chance roasted two small pheasants they'd killed for dinner. They built small fires around the venison to slowly cook the tough meat.

Huddled beside the fire, Anna ate in silence while Tobin spread a horsehair rope around their campsite. Since he'd been bitten, he'd become obsessed with snakes. He'd told Anna that a snake wouldn't cross a rope, so they'd sleep safely at night inside the circle.

Everyone slowly found their places around the campfires. Anna could see Chance through the trees, brushing Cyoty down. His low voice drifted to her, but she could not make out his words. He talked to the horse as though there were no human company. Exhausted, Anna reluctantly crawled into the tent and slipped on her nightgown. It felt so wonderful to have the fresh cotton against her skin. Her skirt waistband was getting tight and she knew within a few weeks she'd have to let it out. The thought of a baby growing inside her made her smile. Someday she and her child would stand against the world. She'd have someone to love and who'd love her in return. She'd have land of her own and a child. What more could she ask of life?

It was well after midnight when Chance lifted the flap of Anna's tent. "I was just looking for . . ." His words died as his eyes fell upon his bedroll lying next to hers.

Anna raised her head slowly. "I spread it out for you," she whispered, her glance darting toward the Jordans' tent.

Nodding, he slid into the tent, leaving the flap open for

light. "For appearances," he whispered as he unstrapped his gun belt. He rolled the belt around the holster and placed it in the few inches between the two bedrolls.

The blade of the knife in Anna's hand reflected in the firelight.

Chance pulled his boots off and sat down on his blanket. "Do you really think that knife would stop me?" His whole body ached to feel her next to him. The memory of her lips brought a constant fever to his mind. But her bitter words and hate-filled look kept him away with a chill far more piercing than that of the knife, for her hate had singed his pride and his heart. "Can't we declare a truce to this war?"

She moved the knife slowly forward and placed it beside his gun belt. "I know this weapon would do little, but it's all I have to protect myself."

Chance could see the fear in her eyes, hear the trembling in her voice. The anger he'd felt toward her vanished. "You have me."

She turned her face away and he thought he heard a tiny sob. Chance slid down on his blanket and tossed the flap closed.

"One other thing," Anna whispered.

"What?"

After a moment, she answered, "In the morning I want all the people who need food to have part of our venison. Will you see that those who have children get extra meat?"

"I will," Chance answered. He was touched that she cared so deeply about a people who, except for Selma and Carl, didn't seem to even notice her.

"Good night, Anna." He forced the words out, wishing he could say more, wishing he could ask her if she cared for him.

"Good night." Her voice sounded weary.

Slowly, he slid his hand along the space between them until he touched her fingers. She jerked slightly, but he held her hand tight. After a moment she relaxed, his hand still over hers, and she didn't pull away.

"Trust me!" he wanted to shout, but the question *Do I trust myself?* whispered through his mind and echoed long into the troubled hours of sleep that followed.

12

"I've come to speak with Anna Meyer." Walter Schmitz's voice boomed, shattering the quiet of the morning.

Raising her head, Anna stared into Chance's questioning blue eyes. Neither moved for a moment as Walter continued to yell outside their tent. Chance touched his finger to his lips, indicating that she should remain silent, then he pulled on his boots and strapped his gun belt around his slender waist. When he left the tent, he was careful not to leave the flap open.

Anna scrambled into her clothes as she listened.

"May I help you with something, sir?" His words were simple, but his tone left no doubt that he considered Walter Schmitz a bother.

"I don't wish to talk with you, boy. I said I wanted to talk with Anna Meyer." Walter's voice sounded angry as though he were annoyed at Chance's interference.

"I know of no Anna Meyer in this camp. If you're referring to my wife, Anna Wyatt, I'm afraid she's dressing."

"You know damn well I'm referring to your wife, although there is not a person in the camp who doesn't see your marriage for the sham it is. She only married you so she could claim William's land. Why else would a lady of quality marry a Texan?" He said the word *Texan* as though it left a foul taste in his mouth.

Chance's words were frosty. "I think, sir, that our marriage, and my heritage, are none of your concern."

"The hell they are not. Anna is like family to me. Everyone knows you'll leave her as soon as the deed is signed. There she'll be with twice the land I'm going to get, her stomach ripe with child, and no man around to help her farm."

"Come to your point." Chance's words mirrored his tightly held temper.

Walter's voice slurred. "My point is that a single man only gets half the land a family man does."

"I don't see why that should concern Anna." Chance widened his stance and folded his arms across his chest in an effort to appear relaxed.

Anna stepped from the tent, her brown dress buttoned up tightly and her hair pulled into a neat bun at the back of her neck. "What do you want, Walter?" She couldn't command her voice to sound as indifferent as Chance's had. "And make no pretense of being like family." She hadn't missed the dull eyes and puffy features of the man who'd become too friendly with bad liquor. Sober, Walter Schmitz could be bothersome, but drunk he might be deadly.

"Maybe we haven't seen eye to eye on most things." The middle-aged man's chest puffed up with a prepared speech, but it still didn't outdistance his large stomach. "But I think I'm old enough to know what should be done. I don't want my best friend's child being raised by a woman who'd marry a man she doesn't even know. This Texan is a foreigner who doesn't know our ways." He took another heaving breath.

Anna almost burst out laughing. "I think, Walter, that if you look closer, you'll find we are the foreigners in this land, not my husband."

Walter shook his head, ignoring the point. "He's a lowborn vagabond. You and William came from good families. You were educated in fine schools. In our village you were welcomed in every home."

Anna fought to keep from laughing. With a father who'd

deserted the family after losing all their money at the gambling tables, and a mother who had committed suicide, her background could hardly be defined as "good" or "fine." And the schools she attended were only to keep her out of the way while her mother lived off of men like William Meyer. If families were valued for being weak and without morals, then she must come from one of the best. Sometimes she felt her mother and she were allowed to remain in polite society only because they gave the refined women someone to gossip about over tea.

She smiled at Chance and met his gaze evenly as she said, "My education will not keep me alive in this country. I'll depend on my husband's knowledge for that."

Chance winked as though her compliment had meant a great deal to him.

Walter raised his head in his best effort to look down on two people who were several inches taller than himself. He rubbed his runny nose and spoke in German. "I've given this some thought since my wife died. I come to you with an offer. You need a husband from your own people and I need a wife."

She couldn't believe his arrogance, and her anger made her words sharp as daggers thrown through the air. "I already have a husband." Her words were in English. She wouldn't insult Chance by using words he didn't understand. "And even if I were not married, I'd never consider becoming your wife."

"Why not? Your vow with this Texan must come cheap." Anger filled Walter's bloodshot eyes. He hadn't expected to be turned down, and her quick refusal insulted his pride. "You married him as soon as you met him. Were you so desperate to have a man in your bed that you took a boy?"

Walter's victorious laugh was little more than a hiccup. Chance shoved his arm into the man's throat with swift violence. Chance had moved so fast that the older man hadn't even seen him coming.

"I've heard enough. Anna is married and there's nothing

you can do." He held Walter firmly. "I know we're from different worlds, but I'm her husband." Chance tightened his grip until only a slight choking sound could be heard from Walter's throat. "I warned you once that I wouldn't tolerate your insults. You're new to this country, but you'd better learn fast that a man doesn't speak that way to a Texan and stay healthy."

Anna pulled on his sleeve and Chance slowly lowered his arm. "I suggest you leave, Walter." Only Anna's fingers stopped Chance from teaching Walter a lesson he wouldn't forget. His words froze the moisture in the cool morning air. "While you can still breathe."

"It's all right, Chance." She looked at Walter without fear for the first time. "The man is distraught over his wife's death. He doesn't know what he's saying. There's no need to fight with him."

Chance hesitantly uncurled his fists and placed an open palm over Anna's fingers, which still rested on his arm. His body was as still as stone beside her, but she could feel the animal just beneath the skin, waiting to pounce. Smiling, she realized the power she had over this young savage at her side. Her words had stopped his assault when no man in the camp could have.

Walter snorted and grabbed Anna's free hand, placing her fingers between his two hands as if he were praying. "Come with me. This frontiersman can never make you happy. You're accustomed to an older man's bed. This boy can know nothing of how to please a woman."

Anna could feel the muscles in Chance's arm tighten beneath her fingers. He was a fraction away from springing on Walter and beating the fat little man into the ground. She'd seen Chance fight. Walter would have about as much chance as a weasel would against a mountain lion. Jerking her hand free of Walter's, she slid her arm around Chance's back, relaxing the tight muscles with her gentle touch. "I've known nothing but kindness from this man. I thank you for your advice and offer of marriage, but I have a husband. I have no wish to take another."

Walter's watery eyes glazed over in anger. He moved half a step forward, then heard the snap of leather as Chance widened his stance and placed one hand on the mahogany butt of his weapon. "We'll see," the older man mumbled as he stormed back toward the other tents. "We'll see how happy this man makes you."

Trembling, Anna clung to Chance. Walter was an evil man and she would put little past him. She'd heard of his unfair dealings in Germany and had often wondered if someone had forced him to run to the States.

Chance tightened his arm around her shoulder and pulled her close. "Don't worry," he whispered. "The only way that lecherous old man is ever going to touch you is if I'm already planted six feet under."

"He frightens me. You don't know what he's capable of doing." Anna remembered all the evil looks he'd given her in the past, the times he'd tried to get her alone, the little hints he'd made that his wife and William hadn't heard.

"I'll be on my guard." Chance smiled down at her. The twinkle in his eye told her he considered Walter harmless; still, he enjoyed her sudden concern.

All day, Anna worried as she walked along beside the wagons. She knew Walter would do something. He was like a spoiled child accustomed to getting his way. He'd been shamed in front of the others. He wouldn't let it go unchallenged.

Well after dark, they made camp in a valley. As the sun melted in a pool of gold between the hills, Chance tipped his hat to her and turned his mount toward several men organizing a hunting party. She could tell by his smile that he'd had enough of the slow walking pace for one day and needed to stretch his muscles.

As Anna watched him go, she suddenly wished she were riding with him and not staying in the camp. With a start she realized it was not fear of Walter that made her want to be by Chance's side, but the feeling she had of being safe and protected when she was with Chance. But there was much work to do, and how could she be safer than in the middle of her own people? With a sigh, she turned and helped Selma do the laundry and mending.

Anna enjoyed talking with her friend, but Selma had only one topic of conversation: Carl. He was her life. She'd loaned him the money to secure passage, then eloped with him the night before the ship sailed. It mattered not what she'd given up; the only thing of importance in her life was Carl's nearness.

Selma seemed to need to tell someone all about how she and Carl met secretly for over a year before deciding to run away together. Anna laughed at her stories of almost being caught by her overprotective parents. She also had a habit of always telling everything three or four times, as though Anna needed the repetition to understand. By the time Chance returned, Anna was ready to snap like a dry twig from the other woman's constant chatter. As Chance moved to his saddlebags, she excused herself from Selma and joined him.

"Where's Tobin?" Anna smiled, knowing they both enjoyed the silence of his absence more than the noise of his presence.

Swinging around with a start, Chance relaxed as her nearness registered. "He rode ahead to scout. The people should have more to eat tonight. There was plenty of game." He pulled clean shirts from his bag.

Anna clasped her hands behind her. "I washed your clothes and mended a few. I hope you don't mind."

"I don't mind." Chance looked at the worn shirt as though it were new. "No one's ever done that for me."

"But I'm your wife. I'm supposed to do things like that for you."

Chance shook his head. "But you don't have to. I've been taking care of myself for a long time."

"I know." Anna felt her face turning red. Somehow, as Chance's fingers brushed over the stitches she'd made in the shirt, he was touching her. "I just wanted to," she whispered.

He laid the shirt carefully over one arm. "I'll clean up and put it on."

As he reached into the bag once more, a puzzled look crossed his face. He pulled a rich, brown, leather pouch from the saddlebag.

Nervousness tickled the hair at the back of Anna's neck as she watched him turn the case over in his hand. "I thought you could use that."

Chance opened the bag to find a fine, masculine dressing set, complete with a gold-handled shaver. He handed it back to her. "I can't take this."

"Of course you can."

"Was it your husband's?"

Anna nodded. To be honest, she'd never seen William shave. They'd lived quite separate lives in Germany, and on board ship she'd always avoided him as much as possible. She pushed the case back toward Chance. "You're my husband now. Take it. I want you to have it."

Chance held it carefully and headed down to the stream to clean up. He was halfway through shaving when he realized he hadn't even said thank you. Glancing over his shoulder, he watched Anna coming toward him.

She walked to the water's edge and filled a pan, then sat back to watch him shave.

"Much obliged." Chance smiled down at her.

"Much obliged?" she repeated.

Chance laughed. He'd finally found a word she hadn't been taught. "Thanks. I've never had anything so fine."

Anna brushed off his gratitude and allowed her practical mind to take over. "It was of no use to me. The only sensible thing to do was give it to you."

Desperately, Chance tried to think of something else to

say—anything—just to keep her near. "I heard you laughing back there with Selma."

Anna's soft laughter filled the air once more. "She was telling me of her romance with Carl."

As Chance shaved, Anna told him the story. He loved having her all to himself, and she loved watching him shirtless in the late sun. The shaver moved in his strong hand, and Anna couldn't imagine William ever holding it with such grace.

As an easy silence fell between them, they watched a cloud of dust appear on the other side of the stream. Leaning down, Chance lifted his rifle and wiped the remaining soap from his face. Anna could hear the faraway thunder of hooves coming inexorably closer as though danger were traveling at double speed.

"What?" She couldn't do anything but watch the dust cloud approach.

Chance stepped between her and the stream. "Get back with the others!"

"What is it?" She couldn't make her feet move.

Listening, he whispered, "Riders, moving fast. Three, maybe four." His words grew sharp. "Anna, go back to camp!"

Anna took a step backward, watching the dust cloud grow nearer. Her eyes focused on the front figure in buckskin. "Tobin!" she shouted. "It's Tobin!"

Chance raised his gun and took aim. He waited, ready to fire, as the riders grew closer. The other riders materialized from the dust, their dark hair flowing behind their heads and their bare chests flashing reddish brown in the sun.

They were almost within range when Tobin raised his arm and yelled, "Don't shoot, son!"

Lowering his gun an inch, Chance studied the Indians behind Tobin. "Comanche," he whispered as Tobin splashed across the stream at a wide shallow point several yards upstream from where they stood. The Indians held back, vanishing into the tress in the time it took the water to settle in behind Tobin.

"Lower that rifle, son. You're making me nervous." Tobin swung from the saddle as the horse reached the bank.

"What are you doing riding into camp like the devil's on your tail?" Chance lowered his rifle and picked up his shirt. "You just took a year off my life."

Stooping, Tobin drank a handful of water, ignoring the fact that he'd muddied it considerably with his ride. "Well, son, I reckon you got enough years to spare a few." He laughed and nodded at Anna. "I met up with them braves about a mile back. First I thought they aimed to have me for supper, but after a few minutes I knew all they wanted to do was play. They didn't pull a bow, and I've seen a Comanche string his bow, thread an arrow, and let fly in the time it takes a white man to pull a trigger."

Anna laughed and Chance swore under his breath as he carefully packed his shaving kit. To be honest, he enjoyed Tobin's stories because they always made Anna laugh, and for that he'd even pay the price of being called son. "You'd better watch out, Tobin, or they'll have what's left of your hair."

Tobin shrugged. "They was just boys tryin' their legs. They didn't mean nobody harm. I wish I'd had time to talk with them; maybe they'd solve our problem."

"What problem?" Chance asked, looking from Tobin to Anna, silently warning the older man not to share anything that might frighten her.

Brushing Chance's warning aside, Tobin continued rattling like a man running for office. "We're about a half day's walk from the Guadalupe River, son. New Braunfels is right across the river, but with all the rain, it'll be days before the river is low enough to cross. These folks are goin' to be real disappointed when we get to the river and can't cross to the settlement."

"Are you sure?" Anna moved between the two men.

Tobin took no offense at the question since it was asked

by a woman. "Course I'm sure. I rode up and down the river for miles. There ain't no way to cross that thing till some of the water goes down. That river would take half your people with it if you tried to cross now."

Chance had to agree. He'd been thinking they might have this problem after all the rain they'd had lately. "You'd better go tell the reverend."

Tobin nodded. "I did find an old fort nearby. Folks could camp there till the river goes down."

Disappointment shadowed Anna's face. "The people are sick in body and heart. Better to tell them now than to wait until they get to within sight of the settlement only to find they're unable to cross."

Pulling his horse along behind him, Tobin headed toward the others, mumbling, "Don't see how a few days will make all that much difference anyway. When they get to their new settlement, they'll be too busy fighting Comanches to plant any crops."

Before Anna could follow Tobin back to camp, Chance grabbed her arm. He held her back until the old man was out of sight. Looking up, she was startled by the anger in his face. His dark blue eyes were stormy and his face was twisted in rage.

His words were as cold as the north wind. "The next time I tell you to go, you'd better move. Both our lives could depend on it."

Anna twisted away. "The Indians were harmless."

Chance's angry stare didn't soften. "Yes, this time, but what about next time? I told you to get back to camp. If you ever decide not to listen again, I swear there'll be hell to pay."

"I'm not some empty-headed girl to be protected from the truth. You don't own me and I won't be bossed around by you or anyone else."

"You don't know what the Indians might do if they captured you." He spit the words at her as if she were a child. "I've seen what can happen to a woman."

"I doubt they could do anything to me that is worse than what I've already suffered." Anna lifted her chin. "You're not my lord and master and I'll not be threatened."

"That's right. I'm just your husband, bought and paid for. Nothing more. You've reminded me often enough." His eyes were the moody blue of an evening sky just before a thunderstorm.

The blood was pounding in her head. "It could be to your advantage. If I die, you can keep the hundred dollars and be on your way."

"Don't tempt me, woman, or I might become a widower tonight." A smile twisted the corner of his mouth.

"How dare you threaten me!"

"Threaten you! What do you think you've been doing to me since the night we married? You've threatened to kill me at least once a week since we've been together. I'm beginning to think living with you is far more dangerous than this country and every Indian within a thousand miles."

Anna shoved him hard, catching Chance off balance. He plunged into the stream, grabbing her shoulder as he fell and pulling her down with him.

They hit the cold water with a splash and a scream. Anna twisted to hold onto him as the current pulled her along. "Help!" she screamed, as water filled her mouth and nose. Terror flooded her mind, circled around her, and pulled her under the muddy water.

Grabbing her shoulders, Chance yanked her up. "Stand up!" he shouted as he gained his own footing.

Anna's feet touched rock. She stood, realizing the water didn't even come to her shoulders. Suddenly, laughter caught her in a current swifter than the water. She'd shoved Chance into the stream and almost drowned herself in less than four feet of water.

He slung wet hair from his face and lifted her silently into his arms. As he carried her from the stream, he smiled.

"Drowning me was not one of the ways you've said you might kill me."

Anna smiled, her anger cooled by the water. "I have to use whatever weapon is at hand." Then, in a more sober voice, she added, "It almost backfired. I can't swim."

Chance looked at her in disbelief. "Then I'll have to teach you. Looks like we'll have plenty of time and water while we wait for the river to go down. It could take weeks."

He lowered her feet to the ground but their wet bodies still touched. "I guess this was your first lesson. Don't go into water unless you know how deep it is."

Pushing her wet hair from her face, Anna looked directly into his eyes. "Is that an order?"

"Never," Chance answered. "Only a request—but I suggest you heed my requests in the future."

"I always heed requests." Pulling away, Anna gathered up her wet skirts and hurried toward their tent. "It's orders I never follow."

The evening breeze chilled Chance through his wet clothes, but he felt a warmth deep within him as he watched her go. "I'll remember that," he whispered to himself. The urge to hold her was an ever-growing need within him, a fire that might drive him mad before their year together was over.

13

The weary band of immigrants camped on the bank of the Guadalupe River for almost a month, waiting for the water to recede. Fish and meat were plentiful, but they hungered for fruits and vegetables. Several more of the troupe died of the fever, but most rested from the long walk and waited for the opportunity to claim their dream. Chance refused to sleep inside the old fort, for he feared the sickness more than Indians.

The days grew warmer and Anna found her waist thickening as spring approached. She spent her hours caring for those who were sick and helping out where she could. By the time the river was down enough to test the wagons, she'd made several friends among the people. Her gift for nursing surprised even her, for she'd spent most of her life alone and didn't think of herself as skilled at comforting the ill. Although she hated watching those who were sick grow weaker, Anna felt good that her body ached with exhaustion at the end of each day. She prayed with family members when someone died and rejoiced when death's hand slipped.

On warm evenings Chance dragged her down to the water and made her swim. The lessons were little more than play, but Anna began to relax around him. He'd strip down to his pants and she finally got over feeling exposed in her undergarments. The water soothed her exhausted body and

119

Chance's light banter made her forget her problems for a while. He showed more patience than she thought any man could. By the time the moon had completed a full cycle, she surprised herself and swam several feet.

Yet the day the water was low enough to cross, the muddy river still frightened her. She knew Chance was near, and all she had to do was keep a tight hold onto the wagon, but the water seemed to lick at the sides, trying to pull her to her death.

"Chance," she whispered as the wagon almost rolled on its side.

He was beside her before his name was past her lips. "Hold on, Anna. You'll be across in a few minutes." His gloved hand reached and molded her fingers to the wagon. She could feel the warmth of his solid grip inside the wet leather. "Even if the wagon rolls, you can swim to shore."

Looking into his undoubting eyes, she had to believe him. "Thanks," she murmured. He tightened his hand over hers for a moment before pulling away from her side.

Long minutes later Anna's wagon climbed the muddy north bank. She jumped into the mud and helped push the wagon. Glancing over her shoulder, she saw Chance riding beside another wagon, steadying it against the current. Without asking, she knew he'd be in the water helping until the last wagon was across.

It took all day for the Germans to cross the river. They were welcomed on the other side with music, food, and prayers of thanksgiving. The settlers of New Braunfels were happy to see more of their countrymen. They all talked and hugged as though they were one family. The women cried and told of their losses while the men smoked pipes stuffed with weeds and predicted the future. There was an old-world atmosphere that welcomed the newcomers like an open door and lifted everyone's spirits.

Well after midnight, Anna crawled into her tent. After she brushed her hair, she left it flowing over her shoulders in dark masses, too tired to braid it.

Chance opened the flap, balancing two steaming cups of dark liquid in his hands. He'd worked hard for hours, but there was a twinkle in his eyes as he looked down at her. She'd been aware of him watching her all day, checking every few minutes to see if she was safe and out of danger. Now he knelt beside her. "Want some coffee?"

Anna nodded and accepted the cup. When she smelled the smoke rising from the mug, a question formed on her lips.

"It's coffee." Chance laughed. "They make it here from parched barley and dried sweet potatoes."

Wrinkling her nose, Anna sipped the liquid. The warm fluid seeped through her, relaxing her limbs.

Chance settled cross-legged on his blanket. "There's some bad talk among the men." He hated to tell her now, but he didn't want her to hear it from someone else. "The German Immigration Society is in big trouble. The society, as you call it, is bankrupt. There is little or no money left and the debts are adding up fast."

"But we paid our money to come. They promised us land, a house, and food for a year until we got settled."

Although Chance hated seeing the disillusioned look in her eyes, he had to tell her all the news. "I know. But Prince Solms, who was the first to come over, made a few mistakes. He was swindled out of a great deal of money. Now there's not enough left to move the people to their land, much less set them up with food and equipment."

"But my land . . . ?" Anna was near tears. She'd traveled all these months—only to meet with despair. All her life the land she'd lived on, even the house where she'd slept, had belonged to someone else. Was she never to have a home to call her own?

With a gentle touch, Chance brushed her hair off her shoulder. "The land is yours. But Tobin was right; it's smack in the middle of Comanche hunting grounds. I talked to the new leader of your society, a John O. Meusebach. He's an honorable man trying to do the best he can in an impossible situation." Chance wasn't sure she was hearing him. "Meusebach has had the land north of here surveyed. We'll have land, but little else."

Anna's chin lifted. "If I have my land, I have enough. I will survive."

Admiring her determination, Chance added, "You'll have more than that. I've heard that the land along the Pedernales River is rich and well watered. There's ample timber to build your house, and I swear you'll have a door to bolt before the leaves fall."

Anna brushed a tear away with her fingertip. "We'll make it."

"We'll make it." Chance tried to sound as sure of himself as she was of her future. He took the cups and placed them outside the tent. "We'd better get some sleep. There will be much to do come morning."

With an exhausted sigh, Anna lay down on her back and watched Chance remove his gun belt and boots. The coffee had relaxed her insides and the hard work had tired her muscles. She stretched. "Do you always sleep in your clothes?"

He glanced at her. "No, but I thought it would be less embarrassing for you."

"I've seen you bare-chested when we go swimming," Anna replied. "I can't think a nightshirt would be any worse. I'll turn my head while you change."

Although she turned to face the wall of the tent, she heard no movement. When she glanced back he was still sitting there, fully clothed.

"Well?" she asked.

"I don't have a nightshirt." Chance looked nervous, unsure of his words. "I've never had a nightshirt. I don't sleep in anything if it's hot."

Trying not to look shocked, Anna whispered, "Nothing?"

Chance's rich laugh filled the tent and she realized she

hadn't heard it often in their weeks together. "Maybe I'd better just sleep in my clothes."

Anna nodded, feeling her cheeks grow warm. "Aren't you afraid of catching a chill without wool next to your skin in winter? It's not healthy to undress so."

"Near as I can see, the Indians run around with less, and I've never seen as many of them ill as there are in this group of your people."

Anna couldn't argue.

As Chance stretched out on his bedroll, he reached and touched her hand. "Good night, Anna."

"Good night." She laughed at the thought that anyone would sleep naked. "Keep warm."

The next few weeks flew by in a buzz of activity. The trunks were reloaded onto wagons, but no wagons rolled toward the new land because more people were coming down with the fever each day. There was only one doctor in the town, and he had been worked to exhaustion. Over a third of the new arrivals were suffering from scurvy or fever. The doctor set up huge hospital tents, but the fever spread to the townspeople as fast as a maverick grapevine climbs a tree. By the end of the first day, he was out of laudanum. The fever attacked quickly, sending people who were healthy only hours before into violent seizures of vomiting. The doctor was forced to stand by as his people were gripped with stomach cramps, and hours later their arms and legs tightened with pain.

Anna bathed the feverish, blanketed those with chills, and cleaned the beds again and again as more died and more came down with the illness. Chance spent his days burying the dead and chopping wood for wash fires. Every morning, all the sheets had to be boiled and scrubbed. He and Anna were too tired at night to speak more than a few words to one another.

On the first evening of their third week in New Braunfels, Anna straightened after scrubbing bile off a sickbed. She watched as Chance moved through the hospital tent entrance. He looked thinner, and dark circles framed his indigo eyes. She could tell by his uneasy stance that he disliked having to come into the hospital. The smell of vomit and human waste didn't seem to bother him as much as watching Anna work until her hands were raw from cleaning. He'd do the most hated task of all, that of burying the dead, but he resented Anna seeing the horror as her countrymen died.

Walking toward him, Anna prepared herself for another lecture about how she should get away from this place for a few hours. In truth she'd tried, but there always seemed to be one more task to do, one more bed to clean. Each day she worked more hours and Chance's anger grew. Anna hoped to start this conversation with him on neutral ground. "Have you seen Tobin?"

Chance frowned, resenting her asking about Tobin as though the man were their child. "I don't know where he is. I wasn't the one assigned to watch him today."

Anna didn't smile at his attempt at humor for she saw no laughter in his stare.

"You look tired," she said as she pressed her hands against the small of her back. She'd felt a pulling in her back for days, and twinges in her stomach, but she wasn't about to complain about such minor ailments.

"I'm fine," Chance snapped.

Anna finally took exception to his tone. "You don't look fine. Your clothes are filthy from digging and you haven't shaved in days." She knew she shouldn't find fault with him. He was working harder than most to fight the fever, but he had no right to snap at her.

Removing his hat, he ran his fingers through his dust-coated hair. "Tell me, Anna. Is there ever anything about me that's right? Since we've met you've managed to criticize just about everything from my manners to the way I dress."

Anna couldn't believe he was talking to her this way in

front of the others. Even knowing that many didn't understand English or were too sick to hear did little to stop the crimson spreading across her cheeks. "I don't wish to discuss this," she said, lifting her head.

Chance crammed his hat on. "I take it, then, that I've been dismissed."

"Take it any way you like."

He stormed out of the hospital without another word. Hours later, when Anna crawled into her tent, Chance's bedroll was gone. Wiping the sweat from her forehead, she tried to remember if her words had been bad enough to make him leave. But she was too tired to care tonight. Whatever their misunderstanding, it could be solved tomorrow when they'd had some sleep.

But the morning brought no answer. Chance wasn't at breakfast, and he didn't bring her wood for the wash fires as he had every morning. At noon he wasn't among the men returning from the cemetery, and when the evening fires were built she couldn't see him among the tents.

He seemed to have disappeared. She asked about him but no one had seen him, and as night fell on the second day he'd been gone, fear began to creep into Anna's heart. What if he'd had enough of her and the troubles in the camp? What if he could take no more of the illness and disillusionment? She'd heard the other men talk in angry voices filled with hate and heartbreak about the bankrupt settlement. What if Chance saw no way the settlement would survive? Could he have vanished as quickly as he'd appeared the night they'd met?

In the dark solitude of her tent, Anna gripped Chance's knife. "He wouldn't leave without this," she whispered. "He said he'd be here when I needed him." Turning her face toward the wall of the tent, Anna refused to allow tears to fall. "He'll come back," she said over and over, trying to convince herself, but the tent was smothered in loneliness. The ground felt harder and the night seemed colder than before—and all because Chance was missing.

By the third morning of his absence, Anna's worry had turned to anger. She stormed around the camp looking for him like a mother bear in search of her missing cub. She didn't care if people stared, or even laughed. She would find Chance if he were avoiding her even if she had to search every house and tent. If he had left her over a little argument, she'd give him another to send him on his way.

Finally, she trudged down the muddy road to the cemetery. She'd looked everywhere else; he had to be among the workers. But as Anna neared, her hopes fell. All the men digging graves were short or old. She could tell Chance wasn't among them even before she reached the cemetery gate.

One old man layered with dirt waved an arm in greeting. "Howdy, miss. Can I help you?"

Anna swallowed her pride. "I'm looking for my husband. He's tall and thin and has black hair." *And he's proud and as stubborn as a mule*, she added to herself.

The man shook his head. "I know the man you mean, but I haven't seen him for three days or more. He was a good worker, but last time I saw him he was riding a bay off toward those trees."

Thanking the man, Anna walked toward the trees he had indicated. She knew it was pointless, but she had nowhere else to turn. Chance had ridden off just as she'd feared, leaving her without a word, and she couldn't even remember what they'd fought about. He'd lied when he'd said she'd have a cabin by the fall, lied just like every man she'd ever known. Why was she surprised? Why had she depended on him?

She moved among the trees, not feeling the cool shade or the branches brushing her face. She'd made it to within a few days of getting her land and now had no one to help her get started. There was no doubt in her mind that she could run the farm once it was settled, but she couldn't build a cabin and a corral. She couldn't clear the land in her pregnant state. Now her choices were simple: marry Walter, or remain in New Braunfels and depend on charity.

A horse's snort startled Anna out of her self-pity. Quickly, she moved through the branches toward the noise. The sound came again, closer this time. Anna tried to understand the animal's cry. It could be a horse trapped in the brush, or a wild burro lost from the herd she'd seen roaming the river.

Lifting her skirts, Anna climbed over a fallen log to where the shadows grew as deep as those of the evening. The warm morning air was thick with humidity; it stuck to her flesh like a spider's web.

Anna pulled a thick oak branch away from her path. There before her stood Cyoty. The great bay shook his head in greeting, then stomped and jerked his neck on the rope that bound him to a tree.

Anna rushed forward, startling the animal with her sudden movement. "Cyoty." She held her hand, palm up, to allow him to recognize her. "Cyoty, what are you doing here?" She said the words as though the horse could understand her. "Who tied you up?" His line was long enough to reach both water and grass, but the half-wild animal had pulled at the rope until his neck was raw.

Unmindful of her clothes, Anna scooped a handful of cool mud from the creek and smeared it along his neck so insects wouldn't bite into the raw flesh. Cyoty seemed to understand her kindness and stopped stomping.

This made no sense. Who would tie Cyoty out here away from camp? Had someone stolen him? No one could have done that if Chance was alive. He wouldn't have allowed it. She remembered how he'd fought Walks Tall for the horse. A man would have had to hit him from behind to best Chance in a fight . . . or shoot him.

A knot formed in the pit of her stomach, spreading dread through her veins. Chance's body must be somewhere nearby. He must have been killed when he'd entered the woods. Fighting the urge to run, Anna forced herself to look around. She had to know if he was alive or dead.

The brush was thick and shadows seemed to form bodies beneath each tree. She walked in a circle, widening her area with each round. There was nothing: no saddle, no hat, no body.

Several minutes passed and fear crept up her spine. What if she found his body? What if she didn't? What if the murderer returned for Cyoty and found her?

Something brown flapped beneath the branches of a huge live oak. Anna moved forward, afraid of what she might find. The brown object moved again, flapping in the morning air.

Kneeling, Anna slid between the branches of the knotted old tree. The sight that greeted her stopped her breath in her throat.

Amid the dark shadows, Chance lay on his back beneath a blanket. His body was twisted with pain as he silently jerked in a violent cramp. Sweat blackened his hair to shiny ebony, yet his face was ghostly white. His eyes were as dark as his hair. His cheeks were sunken, making his face a bony, flesh-covered frame.

"Chance!" Anna closed the distance between them. "Oh, Chance."

Wild, unseeing eyes rolled toward her. He lifted his hand a few inches, then it fell against the blanket. Anna wanted to yell at him. How could he have been so foolish? What could have made him camp out here so far away from everyone? He had the fever and he needed help. His skin felt cold to her fingers as she reached for a pulse. She knew he was already more dead than alive.

Anna couldn't carry him to Cyoty, and she was afraid to leave him to go get help. Touching his face, she realized he was as near death as any of those she'd helped in the hospital. Relief at having found him and worry over his raging fever clouded her face. Anna set to work, her hands fumbling at her task.

She collected water from the stream and used his shirt to bathe his head and chest. Over and over she washed his face, cooling the fever only a fraction of a degree. She found his saddlebags and pulled out the small twigs from which she'd seen him shave chips to make tea. He'd told her the Indians called it feverbush. Anna now prayed the name bore some meaning.

The hours passed in a blur. She built a fire; then, undressing him, she bathed him in cold water. She had stopped blushing over a nude male long ago, during her weeks at the hospital. She sponged off his burning body until her arms ached, and still the fever raged.

When the water in Chance's cup finally boiled, Anna tried to make the tea as he'd made it for her in the cave. She had no idea if she were getting the proportions right, but it didn't matter—at least she was doing something.

As the afternoon sun turned the shadows long, Anna forced the hot liquid down his throat. He mumbled something about not wanting to leave Maggie alone, but his eyes never opened. Anna sat rocking his head in her arms, for once totally unafraid of him. If she took him to the hospital, he'd be put in a crowded tent with no air. Somehow, she knew her wild Texan didn't belong in such a place. He'd come here among the trees. He must have known the fever was overtaking him. But why hadn't he told her? Why would anyone choose to die alone?

She thought of what his life must have been like before they met, and of Maggie, whom he always called for in his dreams. Over the months she'd learned a great deal about him and found it hard to believe he'd abandon someone he loved. She stroked his hair and thought of all the nights he'd slept only inches from her. There was a wildness about him she didn't understand and a tenderness that frightened her even more.

Finally, Chance rested quietly, and Anna returned to her tent to gather her things. He deserved to die in the open where the stars were within his gaze, and she belonged with

him for as long as he had left to live. For with his fever so
high, she knew he would die within a day or two at the
most. Some folks lived through the fever, but none as sick
as Chance. She guessed his time left could be counted in
hours now.

As she hurried past the main street, Tobin appeared from
one of the doorways where only men ever entered. He fell
into step without a greeting, but the smell of whiskey told of
his adventures of late.

"Trouble's brewin'." He spit brown liquid out of the side
of his mouth. "These new folks ain't happy with the way the
society's treatin' them. I tell you, it reminds me of a mutiny
on board a ship. Men don't think straight when they're sick
with scurvy. Then you add the cholera to that; well, it ain't
a pretty sight."

"Cholera," Anna whispered. She'd known it was more
than just a fever, but she hadn't wanted to put a name to the
black death that had been killing her people since they'd
landed.

Tobin kept talking, pleased as always to have an audi-
ence. "Yeah, the doc says he may lose a third of the town,
maybe more. I figure it might be better for my health if I
leave in the mornin' with some men headin' toward
Galveston. There's still over a thousand folks waiting for
wagons and more arrivin' from Germany every day."

"When will you be back?" Tobin wasn't much, but any
friend is a good friend in a storm.

"A month, maybe more. But don't worry, Chance can
take care of you and I'll be back before the first log's laid on
that cabin of yours."

Biting her bottom lip, Anna forced the words out.
"Chance has the fever."

Tobin stopped walking. "Where is he?"

"He's camped in some trees past the cemetery." Tears
welled in her eyes. "He's in bad shape."

Nodding, Tobin lifted an arm as if to comfort her, then

dropped it in embarrassment. "He's better off out there than in one of those death tents."

Anna nodded. "I found him. He didn't even tell me he was ill. He could have died and I would never have known."

Tobin scratched his whiskers. "He's a Texan. Men like him don't take too well to being pampered and coddled."

"But he's just lying out there on the ground with sweat pouring from him."

"What does he need?"

Anna fought back the tears. "Nothing . . . everything."

Tobin turned around and began running in the direction he'd come. "Wait for me at the cemetery road. I'll be there in a few minutes."

Too tired to argue or ask questions, she moved along with her bundles, thankful that the sun was finally setting and the air cooling.

She was too exhausted to notice Walter Schmitz moving from shadow to shadow as he followed her.

14

The last rays of daylight streaked the sky as Anna climbed the road toward the cemetery. Long sunbeams gave a purple-violet cast to the evening and one lone crow glided like a black shadow above her, calling to a mate who gave no answer. The sunset turned the trees around her to a dark green; then they became only shadows resembling foothills on all sides. A dead oak tree beside the cemetery gate pointed toward heaven like a gun balanced on the earth. The barkless wood flashed a milky white against the moody sky. The tree looked strong in the waning light but Anna knew that brown rot lay at its core. For a moment she stared at the dead tree as though looking in a mirror, for in spite of her strong appearance, her fears and her past were eating away from inside her just as the rot was consuming the tree.

Tobin's voice startled her as he hurried up the hill. He carried several blankets, a lantern with a thick, white candle inside, a pouch of food, and a large bottle of liquor. "I picked up a few things I thought you might need. Fellow down at the store lost a few hands of cards to me last night."

"Liquor?" Anna raised her eyebrows.

"I reckon it couldn't hurt for those cramps. Doc says to give them milk, but I figure alcohol will kill off a fever faster. Never did find milk worth the time it took to pull it out. I ever tell you about the time I had these three milk cows . . . ?"

Smiling, Anna fell into step. "No, you never did." She could almost hear Chance swearing as Tobin related being able to get three buckets a day out of one cow by feeding her clover and milkweed. This wilderness man was full of yarns and always seemed to be missing when work had to be done or a bath was poured and waiting for him, but his chatter gave her comfort tonight.

As she crawled back beneath the oak tree, she found Chance much the same as when she'd left him. Anna began sponging him with cool water while Tobin helped set the camp in better order. He hauled enough wood to last through the night and stirred up a soup using vegetables Anna had never seen before. Then he treated Cyoty's neck and hobbled the horse so the rope would no longer cut into his hide. Well after dark he made a bed on the other side of the fire without waiting for an invitation, then began his nightly circling of the camp with his rope to protect against snakes.

Anna managed to get Chance to swallow two spoonfuls of soup and several gulps of whiskey. To her surprise, the whiskey did make his violent cramps slacken, and he rested easier. She used her lap for his pillow as she sat watching the fire, her hand gently stroking his hair. The thick, healthy mass curled over her fingers.

Tobin lay on his bedroll, watching the night sky. "You know, I wasn't too sure you favored our boy here much until tonight."

"What do you mean?" Anna looked up, but all she could see was Tobin's shadow.

"Oh, nothin', just talkin'." The smoke from his pipe curled slowly toward the stars. "Just that when I met him, I knew right away how much you meant to him, could see it in his eyes, but I didn't think the feelin' was returned until tonight." Anna was silent so he continued. "Not that it matters much. I figure in most marriages there's one who loves more and one less. Seems like it would take a powerful amount of luck to make such a thing come out even. I asked Chance the other day how long you two been married. He said the funniest thing."

"What?" Anna hoped Chance hadn't told Tobin about why they'd married. She could just see the man telling everyone of their strange arrangement.

"He said, 'Long enough to know what I'm doing wrong and not long enough to fix it.'" Tobin laughed. "I told him that's about what every man married less than twenty years would say. And them that's been married more than that either don't care anymore, or gave up tryin' to understand their women. I told him to give it a few years, but he didn't seem in too much of a mind to wanna wait."

Anna wrung out a rag and brushed Chance's chest lightly. Despite his illness, his muscles were firm beneath her touch. His chest was hairless except for a dark patch in the center. Dark, sunbaked skin covered cords of muscle. Suddenly embarrassed, she pulled the blanket tightly about his shoulders, noticing that his strong jawline was covered with short black hairs. Hesitantly, she brushed her fingers over them, expecting to find the stubble coarse and scratchy, but it was soft.

Without a word of warning, Tobin jumped up as though someone had thrown a hot coal into his blanket. "Someone's out there in the dark," he whispered. "I hear 'em circlin' the camp."

Afraid to move, Anna watched as Tobin lifted his gun and melted into the shadows. Her ears strained to hear movement, but there was nothing. The moments passed with only the sound of Cyoty's snort and the leaves rustling gently in the night air.

Her mind could see a hundred Indians surrounding them. Walks Tall's woman would be their leader. A chill ran down Anna's back as she pictured the beautiful Indian woman, her face transformed in rage, running toward Anna with a knife held high above her head. She would slash into

Anna's stomach and destroy the child the old medicine woman had said would someday kill her own.

Brushing Chance's hair back from his face, Anna whispered, "I'm so afraid."

He was too ill to answer, but she continued needing to tell her feelings, longing not to feel so alone. "This child is the one good thing that has come out of the ruins of my life. It's my hope for the future. If it died, I would surely die also, for there will be nothing left of me but rot and hate." Placing her forehead against his, Anna hoped the chill of her fear would melt in the fire of his fever. "Help me!" she whispered. "Don't die, please don't die."

Tobin climbed from the bushes as fast as he had disappeared. "Whatever or whoever it was is gone now." He stared into Anna's wide eyes. "Now don't you worry none. Before I leave in the mornin', I'll show you how to load Chance's pistol. You can hold off half an army with that Patterson gun. They don't call it a Texas pistol for nothin'."

Anna tried to swallow the lump of fear in her throat. "Thanks, you've been a great help."

"Hell." Tobin lay back on his blankets. "I ain't done nothin' but keep you company." He relit his pipe. "By the way, is there anythin' you need? Chance gave me twenty dollars in gold to buy seed and things he'll need for the farm, but there's gonna be a few coins left over unless this war with Mexico has driven the prices up."

Leaning against the oak, Anna tried to think. Chance had given Tobin twenty dollars of his own money for supplies. That simple fact told her two things: that he had no faith that the society would provide what was needed, and that he hadn't been as desperate for funds as she'd thought the night they'd married. But if he hadn't needed the money, why had he left her for several hours on their wedding night?

"Flour," she said to Tobin. "I could use some flour."

Tobin pulled his hat low and within minutes was snoring, but Anna stayed awake for a long time wondering why

Chance would give Tobin twenty dollars. She didn't understand it at all, but it somehow made her feel cared for.

The night passed in slow hours of backbreaking work. Chance tossed with the fever like a man fighting a grizzly. Anna sponged him when he was hot and held him in her arms when the chills came. When morning finally dawned, she was exhausted and he seemed no better than he had the day before. He was staying alive on pure stubbornness. His breathing was so shallow that Anna repeatedly felt his pulse to see if he was still alive.

Just after sunup, Tobin packed, promising to return, but Anna had a feeling he'd made such a speech many times. He piled up enough food and wood for another day with neither having to say what both knew: if Chance wasn't better by tomorrow, he'd be dead and there'd been no need for Anna to stay among the trees.

"Tell him"—Tobin nodded toward Chance's sleeping body—"that I'll check on that little lady he told me about when I get near Galveston."

Anna's cheeks burned as she realized Chance had told Tobin about the Maggie he'd whispered of in his dreams. "What lady?" Anna tried to sound calm, only slightly interested.

Tobin winked as if Chance having another woman was no great sin. "Reckon he'll tell you about her in his own time."

"What should I know about her?"

Tobin scratched his chin. "You got a full bucket of worry right now, missy." He turned and headed into the trees, still talking. "You just get that man of yours well first. He knows you ain't got time to handle any more problems than the Lord already gave you."

Anna opened her mouth to call out to Tobin, but knew he would just keep on walking. The man had the manners of a yard dog, but Chance had shared his story of Maggie with the old man and not with her.

When the sounds of Tobin talking to his horse had long left the air, Anna forced a few more swallows of whiskey down Chance's throat. As his body relaxed from the cramps, she curled beside him, planning to sleep for just an hour.

Afternoon shadows lay across the campsite when she next opened her eyes. Chance's arm was curled around her like a tight cocoon and the fire had died.

Rolling over, Anna ran her hands along his sides, familiar now with the muscular hardness of his frame. He was cooler. She continued touching him, making sure his face, his arms, and his chest were cooler. A sudden fear gripped her heart. Laying her ear against his chest, she listened to the steady thud of his heart pounding against her cheek. Relief flooded over Anna. He was alive and the fever had passed! Chance was alive. She hugged him to her and began to cry, her tears falling against his bare chest.

It took her several minutes to gain enough control to pull away from him. His violent cramps may have stopped, but there was still much to be done. She rebuilt the fire, washed his clothes, hung them on the nearby bushes to dry, and cut pieces of jerky from the hunk Tobin had left them. When the jerky was placed in boiling water, the meat swelled up and made a stew with a hearty broth.

Cradling Chance's head in her arms, she fed him a few spoonfuls, succeeding only in dripping it all over both of them. She washed him off, enjoying the feel of his flesh beneath her fingers now that it was no longer hot with fever. She knew she was spending far more time than necessary, but she'd never touched a man so, and the action sent a pleasant stir deep within her.

The shadows had melted into evening when Anna left his side and walked to the stream. With aching shoulders, she removed her blouse and washed in the cold water, longing to strip off all her clothes and swim, but an eerie feeling of being watched warned her against it.

Even when she returned to camp, Anna couldn't shake the feeling that someone was observing her every movement. Cyoty must have felt it also, for he stomped and snorted at the air, his ears up and alert to every sound.

Anna ignored the feeling, knowing she had enough to worry about without seeing ghosts behind every tree. She tried to feed Chance the rest of the stew, and this time he swallowed several bites before falling back against the blankets. Covering him gently, Anna stood and carried the empty pots down to the stream to wash them.

Just as she reached the water's edge, something moved from the brush. Before she could scream, a hand covered her mouth and the sudden jolt sent the pots in her fingers flying across the rocks by the stream. "Good evening, Anna," Walter said as he materialized from the shadows.

Anna jerked away from him, anger replacing her fear. "What are you doing? You nearly frightened me to death."

"I thought I'd come check on you. Now that your husband is dying, you may take my offer more seriously."

Shoving past him, she answered, "I'm not interested in you or anything you have to say."

"Now, Anna." Grabbing her arm, Walter stopped her progress. "You can hardly afford to play so highborn when you may be left a widow again very soon."

"I don't see that as your concern." Anna pulled away, but he grabbed her again before she could get past him. His fingers bit into her arms and Anna cried out in pain. "Let go of me!"

Walter's neck grew red with anger. "Now don't be in too much of a hurry. I know your problem better than anyone." He smiled a wicked grin that wrinkled his fat cheeks into a thousand ripples. "You see, I knew about William and your mother."

Anger and embarrassment blended in the fire of her cheeks. "What about my mother?"

Pulling her closer, he whispered, "It's not your mother I'm concerned with. What matters is that I know the whole story. William Meyer was a fool never to train you. You're like a fine horse that needs to be broken to the saddle." His laughter frightened her as much as his words. "You'll buck a few times, but then you'll gentle up and love it. Who knows? Maybe you'll take to bedding as ardently as your mother did."

As Anna opened her mouth to scream, Walter's lips covered hers. Pulling her tightly against him, he pressed his mouth upon hers with bruising force while his short fingers dug into the flesh of her arms, ignoring her struggle.

Wild, unbridled rage exploded inside Anna. *No!* her mind screamed. Not again. She kicked and fought with all her strength and pulled her mouth from Walter's.

He laughed and Anna saw the glimmer of insanity in his eyes. "Don't worry, Anna, I'm only giving you a free lesson today. After we're married, I'll have every night to ride you until your legs fall open with exhaustion. I'll have years to train you to be as good in bed as your dear dead mother was."

As he struggled to pull her closer, a shot rang in their ears. Anna heard the bullet fly past her, only inches from her ear. Walter froze, his grip still tight around her waist. The lust in his eyes was replaced with fear in the moment it took the shot's sound to die.

Chance's voice rang clear in the night air. "The only reason that wasn't through your skull, Schmitz, is that I didn't want to risk hurting my wife."

Anna felt Walter shake as though a great earthquake was rumbling inside him. "Chance," he whispered in her ear. She twisted to see her husband, but the darkness beneath the trees hid him.

"Turn her loose *now*!" The order was crystal clear. "Or this settlement will be minus one more member."

Recovering his voice, Walter answered, "Now don't get upset. I was just comforting Anna." He slowly released her. "We thought you were near death."

"If you ever touch her again I'll gun you down if I have to come back from the grave to do it." Chance's voice seethed with barely controlled hatred. "Get out of my sight, Schmitz."

Anna heard the click of Chance's gun as Walter dove into the brush. She listened as he ran, swearing and yelling in pain with every few steps. Laughter escaped her as she hurried toward Chance's voice. "I hope the brush scrapes the hide right off that pig," she said as Walter's German and English curses sounded from farther away.

When she reached the edge of their camp, Chance was leaning against a tree, his long form only a shadow. He'd slipped his pants on but nothing else. As she moved closer she saw the gun hanging at his side and his head drooping forward. When she touched him, his weight fell toward her as though he barely managed to hold on until she caught him. She almost collapsed under the load. Slowly, Anna put her arms around him and pulled him to the blankets.

Chance walked with great effort. "I didn't shoot him because I wasn't that sure of my aim." His words were short, uttered from between clenched teeth.

Anna laid him none too gently upon the covers. "I'm amazed you had the energy to move so far." He was like a huge rag doll in her arms as she tumbled down beside him.

"I would have been there sooner, but someone removed my gun, along with my clothes." She could see the hint of a smile on his lips as he rested against the blankets.

Anna wasn't about to talk of such things. "You were there when I needed you."

Gripping her hand when she slid the blanket over him, he asked as he recovered his breath, "Did he hurt you?"

She was silent for so long he wasn't sure she'd heard his question. Then a long sigh escaped her, making room for a calmness to settle in. Finally, she whispered, "No."

Chance pulled her against him. "Thank God," he mumbled into her hair as she rested atop his heart.

Anna lay beside Chance, wanting to feel the protection of his arms. "He only kissed me. I can still feel his mouth touching mine, and it makes me want to scrub my entire face with lye soap."

Chance's face was only an inch from her own. "The same way my kiss made you feel that night?"

"No!" How could he compare his kiss to Walter's? "Your kiss broke our agreement, but it didn't disgust me."

The firelight reflected in the twinkle of his eyes. "I'm glad." He moved closer until his lips touched her ear. "There's only one way to erase a distasteful kiss from your lips."

Anna felt an unfamiliar excitement within her. "How?"

Chance's beard stroked her cheek ever so gently. "You'll have to remain still for as long as the cure takes."

Anna knew it was mad to be this close to him, but for the first time in days she felt happy, and she didn't want the feeling to end. "I'll do anything. Give me the medicine."

Lightly, Chance's lips touched the corner of her mouth. "Then I'll do the best I can to help you." His full bottom lip slid across her mouth so lightly she wasn't sure he was actually touching her. "Although I've been promised death if I kiss you again, I figure I'm so near it I haven't got much to lose."

Anna lay back and enjoyed the feathery kisses he placed along her cheeks and across her lips. His hand moved up to pull the pins from her hair. As the thick mass tumbled free, he slowly moved his fingers through it as though touching silk.

"Tell me, Anna, would you take my life for this?" Chance brushed her nose with his cheek.

"No." Anna answered honestly. He'd been right about the cure; she no longer felt the bitterness of Walter's bruising attack.

As Chance's lips touched hers again, his hand spread wide along her waist. "Kiss me back, Anna. Let me feel your lips caress mine as your hands caressed my face and chest."

She tensed in the darkness. "You were awake? Why didn't you say something?"

He trailed kisses along her cheek to her ear before answering, "I was enjoying it too much." His voice grew low. "Touch me like that now when you know I can feel your hand sliding over me."

"No." Embarrassment darkened her cheeks. "I was only keeping the fever down."

"Don't lie to me." She felt his strong jaw tighten. "Lord, don't ever lie. Not when we both know the truth."

Tears welled up in her eyes, but she wouldn't let them fall. She ducked her head into the hollow of his throat and remained silent. She couldn't say the words, but she knew the truth. She'd enjoyed his gentle kisses. She'd loved the feel of him. Even now with his warm body pressed close to her and his hands at her waist, she loved the nearness of this man.

The strange pains came in her stomach again. She felt her insides turn and knew Chance had felt the movement with his hands.

"I felt it!" He leaned up on one elbow but didn't remove his hand from her stomach.

Anna hated to complain of such a small pain when only hours ago Chance had been ripped apart by fierce stomach cramps. "I've been having them for weeks. At first I thought I was getting the fever, but they seem to grow no worse or more painful."

Chance burst out laughing. "Don't you know what they are?"

She resented his tone but curiosity forced her to admit she didn't know.

Brushing her hair back with his hand, he whispered, "It's been a long time, but I remember feeling the same thing when my mother was pregnant. It's the baby moving inside you."

Anna pushed his hand aside and spread her fingers wide. "My baby?"

Chance's smile warmed her face with his concern. "Have you never been around a woman who was pregnant?"

Slowly, Anna shook her head. "I've seen a few, but my mother could have no more children after me. She told me nothing of such things, assuming I'd never need to know."

One dark eyebrow rose, but Chance didn't ask the obvious question. Instead he said, "I was pretty young, but I remember my mother saying she was over halfway there when she first felt the baby move. It'll grow stronger and bigger every day."

Feeling good to the very core for the first time in her life, she thought of her baby alive inside her. Her dream of having someone to love was growing within her. Now she let the tears fall. "I'm so happy . . . and so frightened."

Chance pulled her close. "Don't worry, I'll be there with you. Between the two of us we can figure out what to do. My mother delivered all alone because everyone else was out working."

He pushed her hand from her abdomen and spread his fingers wide. "Promise to tell me if there is more pain or if you bleed, and as your skin begins to stretch we can make an ointment that will make the skin softer."

Anna was too embarrassed to raise her head. She had never dreamed a man would talk of such things to a woman.

Chance stroked her hair and his words grew heavy. "We'll have to start feeding you better. You don't look like you're five months pregnant."

Anna looked up. His dark lashes rested against his cheeks. The firelight played across his sleeping face, throwing planes of light and shadow across it.

His knowledge had made her feel so happy and his caring

had lightened all her worries. On impulse she brushed his sleeping lips with a kiss.

"Good night," she whispered and cuddled into his open arms.

"Good night, Anna," he answered with a smile and a promise in his thoughts.

15

The next morning Chance was at the stream shaving when he heard Anna's footsteps behind him. Her soft moccasins brushed the earth with a whispery, swishing sound. He turned and watched as she walked toward him, an inner glow alight in her eyes. Without a doubt she was the most beautiful woman God had ever created. The only thing that could've made her perfection itself was if the child she carried had been his. But Chance knew that would never happen. He'd sworn to find Storm's Edge and kill him and Chance couldn't do that if he allowed love in his life. But the way Anna smiled up at him made his heart feel like it was turning faster than a windmill in a tornado.

"You look like you're feeling better." She sat down across from him.

"I feel like I've ridden a hundred miles in the past three days. A strong wind would blow me over, but at least I'm alive."

She had that funny way of looking at him with those forest green eyes that made him know he had to tell her the truth. Her words were light and conversational, but the wrinkling of her brow told him she needed an answer when she asked, "Why didn't you tell me you were ill?"

Chance wiped the razor dry on his pant leg. "I didn't want you slaving over me like you did all those folks in the hospital. I've been taking care of myself since I was twelve and I don't need any mothering now."

"Even though you could have died?"

Her questions were making him uneasy. "Could have. I figure I should have died eight years ago when my family did. The way I look at it I'm on borrowed time."

"Tell me about your family." She propped her chin on one open palm and watched him.

Chance hadn't talked about his family in years, but her eyes were so full and deep. She was open for the first time since they'd met. How could he pull back and lose the easy comfortable feeling between them?

"My folks bought a farm in the Austin Colony; it's probably not much over a hundred miles from here. Their land was beautiful. Dad planted apple, peach, and cherry trees all along the north side." He looked away from her as he spoke as if looking into the past. "They should be giving quite a crop by now."

"You still own the land?" She was shocked that someone who had his own farm would be roaming around the country.

"Sure, but I haven't lived there since the raid. It was spring, like now. The smell of blossoms filled the air for miles, and the days had turned warm and, for a kid like me, endless. My mom sent me off fishing while she and my sisters did the wash. Dad was in the fields. I followed along behind the plow long enough to collect worms, then ran off, yelling about how many fish I'd catch for supper."

Chance fell silent. He didn't speak for so long that Anna thought he might not continue. Then his words started again, low and painful. "I heard Mom scream first, even before I saw the fire from the barn. I ran as fast as I could from the pond, but she was dead by the time I reached her. Her bloody body had fallen on top of the cradle with my baby sister in it. I ran toward my dad in the field just in time to see a group of Indians cut him down. I yelled like the devil when he fell. They turned toward me."

Straddling the log she was sitting on, Chance looked into her eyes now filled with sympathy. How many years had he wanted to tell someone who cared, who looked at him as Anna did now? The day had haunted his dreams, stacking his peaceful moments with the promise of death. Now, as he poured the nightmare into the open, it somehow lessened his pain. The pictures of that day were as clear as if they'd happened yesterday and not eight years ago.

"There were twelve, maybe more, Comanches. A huge, young brave was the leader. I'll never forget how he looked, his face filled with blood lust and a white streak running through his hair like a lightning bolt through the midnight sky. They were all on horseback and I was just a kid standing there without a weapon."

He glanced at Anna; her eyes begged him to finish. "They rode past me at full speed. One swung his club. It slammed into my face. The next jabbed a spear into my back. I fell flat in the freshly plowed field and the world went black, like all the light just melted out of my sight. They must have thought I was dead, because when I woke up, they were gone."

"Will you ever go back to that farm?"

Chance shook his head slowly, as if he doubted his own words. "Someday I will, maybe after I've fulfilled a promise I made that day. I'm going to kill Storm's Edge, the Indian who murdered my parents, and until I do, nothing else can matter. That one goal kept me alive through my parents' funeral, through the years at the mission, through the hard nights on the trail."

"But how will you find him?"

"If he's somewhere in Texas, our paths will cross again. I ask about him. That streak in his hair is a brand most folks remember." Chance folded his shaving gear pouch and smiled at her frown. "Don't worry. I'll get you that cabin of yours built and the first crop in before I move on."

"I've been thinking about the cabin." She wanted to

change the subject, wanted to see the anger and sadness pass from his eyes. "I have a few ideas."

Returning to their camp, Chance downed morning coffee as she told him all about how she wanted the cabin built. They spent the day talking and resting. As evening settled in, Anna moved into Chance's arms. He held her against him, savoring the feel of her next to him and careful not to upset or frighten her.

By the time dawn touched them again, they were stronger. He woke her with a light kiss, and to his pleasure, she smiled up at him as she opened her eyes.

"Morning, beautiful."

Anna brushed the hair from his forehead. "Good morning. How do you feel?"

He wished he could tell her how he was truly feeling at that moment, but he knew he'd frighten her. "I'm starving."

"You're cured." Anna laughed. "Let's ride down to the settlement and eat a huge breakfast."

Chance pulled her to her feet and for a moment they stood facing one another with only a breath between them. A hunger grew inside him that had nothing to do with food.

She looked away first. "I'll pick up everything while you saddle Cyoty."

He stood there for a long moment before he moved, forcing his emotions under control.

A silence fell between them as they cleaned up camp and rode to town. Yesterday there had seemed a million things to say, but today both were lost in private worlds of thought.

An hour later they both noticed a strange quietness as they rode through the town. No men sat on the benches outside the stores, no children played. The streets were as deserted as though it were midnight, yet the sun boiled down upon them.

"What's happened?" Anna could feel the uneasiness in the air.

Chance shook his head. His first thought was that the

fever had struck everyone, but if that were true there would be some sign. The town doors stood wide open; the corral gate was swinging in the hot wind. No horses were tied up in front of the town café and it was almost lunchtime.

Urging Cyoty into a trot, Chance headed toward the immigrant camp. What if the townspeople had turned on the new arrivals for bringing the fever? He doubted if there were ten among the ragged tent group who could even defend themselves.

As they rode nearer, they suddenly heard shouts. Coming closer, he saw a group of angry men gathering in the center of the huddle of tents.

Chance circled the group, then slid from the saddle and pulled Anna down next to him. "Stay here. I'll see what the problem is." He could see the fear brightening her eyes and for a moment all he could think of was his need to hold her.

The shouts come again—angrier, louder.

Chance pulled her close and whispered, "Stay with Cyoty; I'll come back for you."

There was no time for discussion; Chance jerked his rifle from his saddle and hurried toward the voices. Their shouts were growing into a roar. He'd heard a mob voice before, and the language did little to change the hate that was airborne and far more contagious than any fever that mankind ever knew. He could almost smell the madness that all would participate in and for which none would claim responsibility.

Walking between the men toward the front of the gathering, he noticed many of them seemed to be arguing among themselves. Most were speaking German. Chance didn't understand their words, but their angry shouts hurled hate toward the heavens.

Moving forward, careful not to shove anyone lest they turn on him, Chance saw John Meusebach standing alone in the center of the group. He was a huge redheaded man who faced his problems straightforwardly and honestly, but as Chance neared, he saw only worry in the leader's eyes.

"Is there a problem, sir?" Chance slung his rifle over his shoulder in plain sight of everyone.

Slowly, John nodded. His voice was low. "Best back away. This isn't your fight."

A man several feet away yelled, "Ya, Texan, stay out of this. We aim to hang this man, and there isn't one thing you can do about it."

Looking at John, Chance saw no fear in the strong man's eyes, only sadness. "They blame me for the trouble the society's in."

"But . . ."

John shook his head and moved closer to Chance as he spoke. All eyes seemed to follow his every move. "I've tried to talk sense into them." He lowered his voice. "I'm about out of wind. If you've got any ideas, now would be a grand time to express them."

A voice from the crowd bellowed, "Get back, Texan. We've got a hanging to do."

"No!" Chance stepped in front of John. "You folks are half-sick and crazy from disappointment right now. John Meusebach is working night and day to try and keep this settlement going. If you kill him, you'd be cutting your own throats."

"Stand aside or get ready to hang with him!" someone shouted. Several others yelled their agreement.

With reflexes born of the need to survive, Chance raised his rifle. In the length of a gasp, he fired above their heads. Every man in the crowd leaned back as if struck by the shot himself, and a sudden silence fell over the group.

Before anyone could move, Chance lowered his rifle and pulled his pistol from his holster. "There's not going to be any hanging here today, but I won't make the same promise about a shooting." He pointed the gun at the crowd. "There must be some among you who see the injustice of what you're about to do. If so, come and stand beside John, now, before your countrymen make you a part of their crucifix-ion."

For a moment no one moved. All eyes seemed to be on Chance's gun, and no one wanted to be singled out of the crowd.

Finally, Chance caught movement out of the corner of his eye. Carl Jordan stepped from the others and stood beside Chance. "The Texan is right," he said, then repeated the words in German.

Chance had never liked Carl more than he did at this moment. The young carpenter, with his white-blond hair and rounded shoulders, stood tall.

Slowly, like reluctant sinners at a prayer meeting, men stepped forward to stand beside John. Chance let his grip on the pistol relax as he saw several turn away in anger. They would console one another in private, without the mob to enhance their bravery.

Breathing a deep sigh of relief, John patted Chance on the shoulder. "Thanks," he whispered and raised his hand to the others. "I wanted to tell all of you who are able that tomorrow we'll be loading wagons for the first group that wants to go claim Fredericksburg."

Chance didn't care anything about founding a town named after some prince in Prussia, but his hands ached to hold an ax. The first logs would be laid for the cabin by May. As his thoughts turned to Anna, he spotted her auburn head moving through the crowd toward him.

Anger melted in his face as he saw her excited smile. "Tomorrow," she said, laughing, as she stepped between John and him.

Chance heard the click of a rifle just as her hand touched his arm. Looking over her head, he saw sparks fly from a gun barrel sticking out between two tents.

"No!" he screamed as he lunged toward Anna. A puzzled look crossed her face an instant before the blast hit her.

Anna's body jerked, and she twirled as if someone were spinning her around in a dance with death.

Chance folded his arms around her a moment after the blast, but he was too late. He pulled her with him to the ground, but the bullet had already hit its mark. Her hands gripped the front of his shirt, and her head lay against his chest as it had so many times in sleep.

"Anna!" He holstered his gun and wiped her blood-splattered cheek. The dark red liquid seemed everywhere. He pulled her close. The smell of blood overpowered the light fragrance of spring that always surrounded her. The memory of blossoms and the burning cabin mixed from his past to multiply his pain. He pulled her close, refusing to see the blood, refusing to smell death's perfume.

John was above them shouting orders like a ship's captain in the middle of a storm. Men ran to do as he bid, but Chance couldn't make his brain understand the words. Part of him wanted to grab Anna and shake her for not staying where he'd told her, and part of him was bleeding with her from a wound long hidden but never healed.

Someone grabbed his shoulder. "Chance!"

He didn't want anyone else around. He could take care of himself, and he could take care of Anna. He jerked his shoulder away.

"Chance." The voice was softer but still persistent. "Can you carry her to the doc? We have to hurry; she's losing a lot of blood." There was a pause. "If not, give her to me and I'll carry her."

Shaking off John's hand, Chance answered defiantly, "I'll carry her." He stood, Anna in his arms, and walked, blind to everything but the pain in his heart.

16

The old doctor tried to shove Chance from the tiny examining room. "Now you wait outside while I take a look at your Anna. You can hear every word I say to her through the door."

Chance stood his ground. "I'm not leaving. You do the best you can with right here." He'd laid Anna on the table and stepped back a foot, but he would move no more.

The doctor threw his hands up in defeat and set to work, aware that Chance watched his every move. From the few doctors he'd seen in his life, Chance had about as much faith in them as he did in medicine men.

The old man cut Anna's dress away, revealing her shoulder and most of her left breast. He washed off the blood with great care, but every time Anna moaned, Chance touched his gun, making the doctor sweat and his hand shake slightly in fear.

Finally, the old man could stand the young Texan's gaze no longer. "Look, if you're going to watch, you might as well help."

After only a second's hesitation, Chance nodded and moved closer.

"The bullet's lodged in her shoulder. Do you think you could hold her while I cut it out?"

The blood drained from Chance's face. Could he hold

Anna while someone hurt her? He placed his large hands on her shoulder and arm.

The doctor took a thin knife from his bag. He wiped it on a clean cloth. With a determined hand, he dug into the wound. Anna screamed in pain as the blade slowly slipped into the bloody hole in her flesh.

"Talk to her," the doctor ordered as he worked. "Tell her to be still."

Forcing his gaze from her wound to her face, Chance noticed her lips were pulled tight in pain and her eyes were closed. "Anna," he whispered. "Don't move, Anna. It will be over soon." He didn't know if he was trying to convince her or himself. Every ounce of energy within him wanted to grab her and take her away. Each time she cried out, he felt the knife twisting into his heart. "Don't think of the pain. Think of your house we're going to build."

Anna tried to twist away, but he held her tightly, feeling her pain as though it were his own.

The doctor nodded for Chance to continue.

"In a few weeks we'll have a cabin. Then I'll start clearing the land." Chance remembered words she'd spoken to him once. "And our only worry will be what row of vegetables to plant first."

"Got it!" The doc yelled as he held the lead up between bloody fingers.

Chance relaxed his hold on Anna's shoulder and wiped the sweat from his forehead with his sleeve. He remembered the words his Irish mother used to say when one of her children was hurting. "We're going to get through this just fine, Anna me girl, just fine."

The doctor poured whiskey over the wound and placed a pad of bandages on it to contain the blood. Then he wrapped her shoulder. "If she didn't lose too much blood, she should be fine in a few weeks."

Chance tried to pull her dress back over her bandage, but too much damage had been done to the material. Pulling off his jacket, he draped it over her shoulders, then lifted her so that her undamaged shoulder rested against his chest. "Thanks, doc."

The old man waved his thanks aside as he opened the door. "Wish I had a place for her here, but there's not a private bed anywhere and she shouldn't be in with all the ones with fever."

"I can take care of her." Chance would never have left her here among the fever victims.

The doc shrugged. "And take care of that baby. It looks like you'll have a son or daughter by summer."

Chance had never thought of whether the baby would be a boy or girl. To be honest, he hadn't thought of the child much at all, although Anna was noticeably pregnant now.

John Meusebach was standing on the porch. When he saw them he stepped forward, his hat already massacred by his large nervous hands. "I'm sorry, Chance. I know that bullet was meant for me."

Chance shook his head. He could think of at least one person in this camp who wanted him dead. "It might have had my name on it."

John followed Chance off the porch. "Either way, I want to thank you for standing up with me the way you did. These people are good people; they've just had their share of bad times delivered in double doses lately."

"Haven't we all," Chance said as he brushed his chin against Anna's hair.

"I want to offer you something." John chose his words carefully, for he knew the Texan would take no charity. "My house will be empty while we go north to set up the new settlement. It's only two rooms, but it would be better than a tent. If you like, you could leave Anna there until we get back. There's a neighbor woman who would be happy to look in on her, and that way she could recover while you claim the land."

Chance looked down at Anna; she'd need days of rest before she'd be ready to travel. In the meantime, he could at least build a dugout. If he were alone he could concentrate on his work and not have to worry about her. Plus, this first group of people moving out would get first pick of the land.

As they walked, John continued, "I could sure use your help when we ride out tomorrow, and Anna would have plenty of company here at the settlement. The Basse family lives next to me and they have a houseful of children—so many I've never seen them still enough to get a count. The boys are not much better than wild Indians, but the girls are soft-spoken and kind."

Chance knew John's idea made perfect sense, but there was something in him that didn't want to let go of Anna even if she was safe. He wanted to hold her in his arms at night and wake up with her sleeping beside him. He was starting to care about her when he thought all caring had died and been buried with his family years ago.

John pointed toward a small house. "Here's my place. I can bunk in with some folks a few doors down. It'll be a few months or more before I get back, so she's welcome to stay as long as she needs to."

Chance carried Anna inside the two-room house. The main room was sparsely furnished and without the frills a wife might add to a cabin. A plump woman with a warm smile greeted him, fussing over Anna like a mother. She was like a huge hen with several chicks running unnoticed around her feet. She spoke only German, but Chance could see kindness etched into the wrinkles of her face.

John translated. "Mrs. Basse says to put Anna down on the cot by the fire. She thinks she will be warmer tonight if she stays close to the fire. Also, she's leaving her older girl here in case Anna needs anything."

Lowering Anna to the cot, Chance nodded to John. "Tell her thank you."

Within minutes Chance was gently pushed aside so that Anna could rest. Mrs. Basse showed none of the hesitation around this tall Texan that the doctor had shown. She was used to giving orders, and expected them to be carried out. Chance's size and his gun didn't frighten her. She'd already faced a house full of children and come out the victor.

Leaving Anna in the capable hands of Mrs. Basse, Chance went in search of the man who'd fired the shot. Maybe John was right; maybe the shot had been meant for him. But the name that kept crossing Chance's mind was Walter Schmitz.

It was after dark when Chance returned to John Meuse-bach's house. He'd searched the town, but no one had seen the shot fired except himself, and all he'd seen was the gun barrel. Also, no one knew where to find Walter Schmitz. Some thought he stayed away because he was afraid of catching the fever. Others said they hadn't seen him since the men left with the wagons to return to Galveston for more people. Chance couldn't tell if they were telling the truth or just protecting one of their own.

Quietly opening the door to the tiny house, Chance slipped in without a sound, hoping not to awaken Anna. It had been a long day, and her injury had taken its toll on his nerves.

Anna was sitting up in a chair with a quilt wrapped around her. She looked pale and very tired, but Chance still had to stop for a moment to fight the gut reaction that always hit him when he first saw her. He could not believe any woman could be so beautiful. Her hair was combed around her in a cloud of brownish red brilliance.

A shadow moved in the corner. "Mr. Wyatt," a girl of about twelve whispered. "My mom said I could go home when you got here."

Chance nodded and the girl slipped past him.

"Anna," he whispered as he closed the door softly behind him. "Are you awake?"

She looked up, her green eyes sparkling with reflected firelight. "I'm sorry," she answered.

Of all the things he thought she might say, this was not

among them. He crossed the distance between them and knelt at her side. She looked at him, a touch of fear in her eyes even though she held her head high, ready to face any storm.

Chance lifted her hand to his cheek. "You're going to be all right." The fear in her eyes when she looked at him was cracking his heart like a blacksmith's hammer against thin ice. The thought that he might cause her any worry or fright sickened him.

"You told me to wait, but I ran forward. I was so proud of the way you stood up to the mob that when I thought it was over, I just ran to you. I'm sorry."

Leaning forward, Chance brushed her cheek with his lips. "Don't ever be sorry for coming to me." He'd been so worried about her, he hadn't even thought about her not following his orders. He now remembered how he'd threatened her if she didn't listen to him. "Anna, you should have stayed with Cyoty, but don't ever be afraid to come to me. Don't you believe by now that I'd never hurt you?"

She smiled and brushed the hair back from his forehead. "I'm starting to." Her finger trailed along his jaw and paused at his collar. Slowly, with a feathery touch, her fingers combed through his hair.

His head felt like it was caught up in a whirlwind. Thoughts were flying past him so fast he couldn't distinguish one from the other. Her eyes had turned that soft dark green of a deep forest, the kind of color that made only truth exist in the world. "I want to hold you so desperately," he whispered, "but I don't want to hurt you."

Anna brought her fingers to rest on his shoulder in a gentle caress. "I'm very tired. I feel like all the energy has been drained out of me." Her fingers traced the seam of his shirt. "But you leave tomorrow and . . ."

Chance smiled, loving the softness in her voice and the feeling that they were all alone in the world. "And what?"

Their eyes met and held. He knew whatever she asked,

he'd give her. He loved the way she looked at him straight on to ask and didn't use some coy flirtation to get her way. If she asked him to leave he'd have to even though it was the last thing he wanted to do.

Anna's voice was filled with questions. "I would like you to kiss me as you did two nights ago." She looked into the fire for a moment. "That is, if you don't mind."

Mind! Chance felt like someone had just knocked the wind from him. This woman was a constant source of amazement, but he wasn't sure of her motivation. He straightened slightly, controlling his voice enough to answer.

Anna misread his hesitation. "I know we said there would be nothing between us. And I meant it. But I've never been kissed like that before and I found it very curious. I'll only ask this once; I promise not to repeat my request." Her words seemed to be tumbling into one another. "It's only that you're leaving tomorrow and some say that the Indians won't allow any white men to return." Her head dropped slightly. "I'm sorry, I'm being selfish. I understand if you don't want to kiss me."

Chance stopped her words, placing his finger lightly on her lips. He held it there even after she stopped talking, letting it run slowly across the fullness of her bottom lip. "No more talking." He let his fingertips brush her face. "Come here."

With great care he lifted her gently into his arms and carried her to the bed.

Anna lifted her head from his shoulder when she saw he was carrying her in the wrong direction. "Mrs. Basse said I was to sleep on the cot by the fire to stay warm." This room was cold and plainly furnished with a four-poster bed and a dresser. The bed was covered with colorful quilts.

Pulling the blanket from her shoulders he laid her between the quilts. Without taking his eyes from her he answered, "I'll keep you warm tonight." He unbuckled his gun belt and slung it across a nearby chair. "If this is to be our last night together, I want to spend it with you in my arms."

With sudden impatience, he pulled off his boots and shirt, then gently lay down on the other side of the bed, only inches from her.

She held back, curled into a ball under the quilts. The fire's light was enough for Chance to see the traces of fear still reflecting in her eyes, and he almost pulled away. Part of him wanted to move away and say he was sorry for his hasty action. Part wanted to pull her against him so tight she'd never be afraid of anything in her life. God, how he hated seeing fear in her eyes when she looked at him!

"Anna, I'm not going to hurt you." He touched her hair. "I'm afraid to even pull you near for fear of hurting your shoulder. Anna, don't be afraid of me. We've lain beside one another many nights before."

"But not in a bed."

Chance reached up and gently pulled the quilt she was wrapped in toward him. Without a word she raised her head as he placed his arm underneath for her pillow. "It doesn't matter if it's a bed or the ground. I'm the same person. I don't understand why you're so frightened. What kind of man do you think I am? I would never take advantage of a woman, much less a pregnant one with one arm wrapped against her shoulder."

Anna smiled. "I'm in pretty bad shape."

Chance held her cheek in his palm as he whispered, "You are so beautiful. The most beautiful woman I've ever known."

As Anna opened her mouth to argue, his lips covered her protest. He kissed her softly, gently, until she could no longer remember what she'd been about to say.

Finally, he trailed kisses to her ear and whispered, "Is that what you wanted?"

"Yes," Anna whispered, and turned her head until their lips touched again.

Chance fought the urge to touch her. He wanted to slide

his fingers over her as he kissed her. He needed to feel the flesh of her bare shoulder beneath his fingers. He wanted to pull her full-length against him, but he didn't dare. The slightest jolt might start her shoulder bleeding again, and he wouldn't risk Anna's life no matter how desperately he wanted to touch her.

Chance buried his hands into the silky mass of her hair. "I'm glad I was able to oblige you with a kiss, my love, but someday I want to show you another kind of kiss—a kind with passion."

Turning her face to the wall, Anna answered, "I want none of that."

Chance could hear the pain in her voice. He lightly kissed her neck until she turned to him. "Someday you'll ask for those kisses also," he whispered against the fullness of her lips.

"Never," she answered.

"Someday." He breathed in the honey-spring scent of her hair. "You'll touch me like you did when I had the fever."

He felt her laughter on his cheek. "I wouldn't bet on that."

Chance moved his lips to hers, kissing her so lightly they barely touched. "I would," he answered against her lips, thinking he'd probably already bet his heart.

He savored the way her lips felt against his own, wishing suddenly that he knew more of lovemaking. He could handle this kissing, but what if she did someday want more? What if she asked to be loved one night just as she'd asked to be kissed tonight? What would he do then? Just stand and stare as he had once before? Or would he love her the way such a woman should be loved?

Lowering his face beside hers, Chance kissed her cheek lightly. "Good night."

Anna moved her cheek against his bare shoulder. "Good night, and thank you for the way you make me feel."

"Anytime you want me, I'll be here," he whispered into her hair, wishing he understood her.

She fell asleep in his arms, but Chance lay awake for hours, not wanting to waste this last night with Anna so near. Tomorrow he would ride north with John into Indian hunting grounds. Tonight might be the last time he ever held her in his arms.

17

Dawn came, bringing with it a rumble of excitement that moved through the town like a runaway wagon wheel, gathering the speed of anticipation along with the wobbles of caution for the unknown.

Slipping from bed, Chance dressed without waking Anna. He could hear the rattle of harnesses and the squeak of springs as men began loading wagons. Since John Meusebach announced the morning before that the first families would be leaving at dawn for the new settlement, everyone in town had been hurrying about like squirrels on the last day before winter.

Chance silently strapped on his gun belt as he took one last, long look at Anna. She lay nestled among colorful quilts with her ravishing hair wild and free around her. An ache deep inside him spread through his very bones. How wonderful it would be to truly have such a woman as his wife, to wake up every morning for the rest of his life with her beside him. When she'd asked him to kiss her last night, he'd thought he might explode. The request still puzzled him as it had all night. How could a woman five years married and pregnant act as though she'd never been kissed? Well, he'd have a month to think about it before he saw her again, Chance thought resolutely as he lifted his hat and slipped from the tiny cabin.

He joined the other men outside as they loaded supplies

needed for the trip. The society was able to give each man only the bare necessities in terms of tools and supplies. Chance had dried enough meat to live on jerky for the next three weeks, but he was thankful for the ration of salt, coffee, and beans.

After saddling Cyoty, he helped with the wagons. There were twenty-nine heavy ox-carts and a number of Mexican two-wheeled vehicles ready for the trip. Even though over half of the people had died of the fever in the past month, today was a day of rejoicing. The sun was already growing warm by the time the long train started moving. Chance helped Carl lift the last trunk onto the wagon and turned to see folks lining the streets and waving good-bye to the families.

Tying Cyoty to one of John's porch posts, Chance went to say good-bye to Anna. The train of carts would move slowly, and he'd catch up without trouble. He had to see her one more time.

She was sitting up in the chair when he entered. The golden morning sun fell across her and for a moment he could see nothing in the room except her. Mrs. Basse must have combed Anna's hair into a bun and dressed her. Out of the corner of his eye, Chance noticed the plump old woman lifting a tray of dishes as she gave him orders he didn't understand.

Anna laughed. "Mrs. Basse told you to build me a fine house and keep me pregnant all the time. She is a great believer in having large families." When Chance raised an eyebrow she continued, "Mrs. Basse is moving her whole clan to Fredericksburg as soon as they block the town. She thinks this New Braunfels is too settled for her liking and she wants more room to watch her family grow."

Chance removed his hat and stood looking down at Anna. Her cheeks had more color today, but she still looked very weak. "Mrs. Basse should join and fight the Mexicans. With her organization and planning she'd have the troops in line in no time."

Anna laughed again, holding her shoulder as if she were restraining the pain. "She is a kind lady. I hope to be well enough in a few days to earn my keep. With eleven children, she has her hands full and she doesn't need me to worry over."

Chance lowered himself onto one knee. "You stay right here until that shoulder heals."

Anna's eyes sparkled with challenge. "Is that an order?"

He loved looking into her green depths and seeing no fear. "Yes, it's an order, and you'd better follow it."

For a moment he thought she might argue, but she only cradled her arm. Her shoulder was causing her a great deal of pain no matter how she tried to hide it from him. Somehow he wanted to help in her deception, even though it was meant for him. "If you don't," he made his voice gruff as he pulled the quilt snug over her shoulder, "I'll tell Mrs. Basse to send in her clan to sit on you."

Anna managed a laugh and a halfhearted look of horror. "Please, not all of them."

When Chance brushed her hair with his hand, her look turned serious. "When will you be back for me?"

"A month, maybe more. It will take quite a while to get to the land with all these carts, but when I ride back I can make it in only a few days." He saw the disappointment in her eyes, for she was anxious to see her land. "I'll be back as soon as I can."

Anna looked up into his warm, blue eyes and nodded, knowing she had to trust him. She had no one else to trust.

"You will be safe here." He leaned forward and kissed her cheek. "Take care," he whispered, then withdrew before he said more. All night he'd thought about the way he felt about her. He'd remembered how she'd cried in his arms, how she'd nursed him when he had the fever, how she'd kissed him. He needed time to get his feelings under control or he'd be telling her he loved her like some love-starved kid.

Chance walked to the door without looking back. He

knew she was watching him, but he wouldn't be able to leave if he looked at her even one more time. Hell, he thought, when his year was up and he left for good, he would still think of her every day of his life.

He swung woodenly onto Cyoty and kicked the horse into action. Anna was in his blood and no amount of running could change that. But he had a month to get himself under control before he saw her again, thank God.

Chance galloped to the front of the line, then slowed his horse beside John Meusebach. The man was a strong leader and the first sign Chance had seen that this settlement might work. He was the kind of man who never accepted defeat, and men tried that much harder around him because he believed in himself.

They rode north with John in the lead and Chance riding scout most of the time. The two men enjoyed the time they spent together and soon became friends. When they were approaching the banks of the Pedernales, they saw several Indians. Chance rode ahead with John only a few lengths behind. Trouble hadn't been expected so soon, but both men wanted to face it head-on. If there was to be a fight, now, while all the folks were together, was as good a time as any. In a month, when they were scattered throughout the valley, the Indians would have little trouble picking them off, but now, all together, the German people would make a good showing. There was not a fighter among them, but no cowards hid in their ranks.

As Chance neared the Indian camp, he saw that it held a tribe of Delawares. He lifted his arms high in the air and shouted his arrival. A moment later he heard John do the same. Chance was amazed at how fast John picked up words in the Indian tongue. Delawares were a peaceful and friendly tribe that Chance never minded running into. The only thing that bothered him was the knowledge that it wouldn't take long before the Indians ran into Walks Tall and told him where the German settlement was headed. If

Walks Tall was looking for Chance, he wouldn't have too much trouble finding him.

After a short rest, the wagon train moved on, going further into Waco and Comanche territory. Chance doubted the Wacos would cause any trouble. They weren't as warlike as the Comanches, but he'd seen too many burned out farmhouses to think the Comanches would let these people settle on what they thought of as their land without a fight.

After several days, they reached the place where the surveying party had erected a house. The weary immigrants rested and thanked God before plotting out their land on a town site. Chance quickly picked a lot in town away from the main street, then set out for the farmland. He knew Anna might someday be interested in a house in town, but right now the most important thing was the land. The land he chose was a spot north of town were the soil looked rich but rocky.

Working the first day from dawn until dusk, Chance cleared an area between the trees for a cabin. As the days passed, he dug down five feet and framed off a large room; then he built a fireplace in one corner, and cut logs for the cabin walls and the roof. Most of the cabins were built above ground, but Chance had decided this would be safer, plus it would be cooler for the summer. After the crops were in, he'd build a cabin on top of the dugout; then they could use the dugout as a cellar to store vegetables.

Twice a week he forced himself to leave the land and go back into town, where he helped others. Many of the men had little or no skill, but a few were fine carpenters and stonecutters. The Jordans settled on the farm lot next to Chance. During the first week, Chance made a deal with Carl. He agreed to supply Carl with meat and lumber for both houses if Carl would build furniture for his cabin. The lanky German with his rounded shoulders and strong hands set to work on the task with the vigor of youth. His long, thin fingers might be useless around a gun, but they worked magic with his carpentry tools.

Selma was about as much help as a butterfly, flitting around Carl, never getting enough of his presence. Her tiny body seemed to be always in motion, and her blond curls bounced around her face continually. Chance started teasing Carl about having to raise Selma before he could think about having a family. Selma squealed and argued and finally took the teasing good-naturedly.

At the beginning of his third week on the land, Chance managed to rope a wild calf. He pulled it into the corral he'd built and, as planned, the calf's mother followed. Chance spent an hour each day gentling the cow. He guessed the cow had been around humans before and probably had been separated from a herd somewhere or stranded on a farm after a family left or was killed. By the time he went to get Anna, the cow would allow him or Carl to milk her each morning. In a few months the calf would be fully weaned and they'd have plenty of milk for both families. Chance could get ten dollars for her, but she'd be worth more than that to them after the baby came.

As he rode back to New Braunfels, he felt good about what he'd accomplished. He ached to get to work on the fields. There were several tree stumps to clear and rocks half the size of a wagon that would have to be moved. But he'd chosen a good spot with a stream and a break of pecan and oak trees on two sides. Thinking of the land made Chance homesick for the first time. He remembered how his father had planned the farm, discussing every detail of the homestead as if Chance understood it all.

For the first time, Chance thought of what he would do after he killed Storm's Edge. He pictured working his farm. His father had paid sixty dollars for over four thousand acres of pastureland and almost two hundred acres of farmland in the Austin Colony. The colony's plan had been to use the rugged farmers as a buffer against Indian attacks. His land was so vast it made Anna's more than three hundred acres look small, but this would be enough for her and she'd be surrounded by her people.

Maybe that was the difference, he thought. Anna will be with her people. Except for Maggie, Chance had no people. His folks had hardly known their neighbors, and the only relatives he'd ever met were the second cousins near Galveston who'd taken in his baby sister. They'd been nice enough, but they'd made it plain they weren't interested in keeping Maggie unless Chance could come up with a hundred dollars a year. Desperate, he'd sold everything the Indians hadn't destroyed and managed to send them the first three years' board in advance. He'd tried making it on his own, but he ended up at a mission outside San Antonio for a while. After that he'd been able to make money by doing about every job that was legal and a few that he wasn't too sure about.

Maybe after Storm's Edge was dead he'd send for Maggie and return home. Austin had said the land would remain his until he and Maggie were grown. Chance found himself suddenly wishing he'd told Anna more about his farm and Maggie. All at once he thought of a hundred things he wanted to say to her. Urging Cyoty into a trot, he rode faster toward New Braunfels and Anna.

It was almost dusk when Chance rode into town. Wagons lined the street just as they had the day he'd left. A new group of immigrants was in from the coast. They looked less haggard than Anna's group, for they'd had more wagons and less rain to hamper their journey. Judging from the way everyone was shouting and hugging, he'd come in a short second to their arrival.

Picking his way among them, Chance realized he no longer felt like a stranger even though everyone was speaking German. He'd picked up enough words to feel comfortable.

As he pushed between two wagons, he spotted Anna on the porch of John's small house. She was talking with the new couples. Chance reined in his horse and watched her for a moment. How could it be possible that she was more beautiful than when he'd left? Her hair was in a bun, but now it was softer, not so tightly pulled against her scalp, and the brown dress he'd seen a hundred times had a new row of lace at the collar. The ivory lace broke the harsh stiffness of the brown dress and softened her face. Her arm hung in a thin sling that seemed no wider than a ribbon tied about her neck.

As she turned slightly, Chance noticed something else. Her abdomen looked as though it had doubled in size. There was no hiding the pregnancy now. And judging from the way she patted her stomach, her joy was great.

"Anna!" he shouted above the crowd, unable to wait any longer to see her eyes.

Raising her head, Anna shaded her gaze from the late afternoon sun as Chance jumped from Cyoty and ran toward her. He was unable to hide the pleasure he felt. All the tired muscles and long hours were forgotten as he watched her move toward him.

He reached her as she stepped from the porch, and lifting her in his arms, he swung her around as she laughed. Her arms were tight for a moment, as though proving to herself that he'd returned, then she pulled away slightly to look into his eyes. For Chance there was no one else on the street but Anna. Her face had been before him every day for over a month and yet the vision was pale compared to the reality.

Slowly the noise of the street invaded their paradise and Anna looked away. "Chance, put me down," she squealed as he rubbed his beard against her cheek. "You're covered with half the dust in Texas."

Chance set her back on the porch. "It's true. I've probably got ten pounds of trail dust on me, but you're more beautiful than ever." He patted her stomach. "And a little heavier."

Anna blushed but made no effort to hide her condition. "Must be Mrs. Basse's cooking or something."

"Or something," Chance echoed and placed his arm around her. Dear God, how he'd missed her! She grew more lovely with each stage of her pregnancy.

She smiled and introduced him to the people with whom she'd been talking. They greeted him warmly, asking questions about the settlement and commenting on the baby Anna would bear. After a few moments Chance realized that Anna hadn't told them that the baby she carried wasn't his. This knowledge confused him somewhat. She wanted the baby so badly, yet she never mentioned its father. And now she seemed content to let everyone think that it was Chance's child.

Chance was about to ask her why when a loud shout came from one of the wagons several yards back. They turned and saw Tobin coming toward them, a huge smile on his face. He was already talking to them before they could understand his words.

"Welcome back," Chance called as he took a few steps and shook hands with the buckskin-clad man. "We weren't sure you'd make the return run."

"Why, hell, son, to be honest I gave it some thought and talked it over with a little señorita I met. She really wanted me to stay, but her husband was bound and determined I leave."

Anna laughed. "We've missed your stories, Tobin."

Tobin studied her enlarged belly and smiled. "Looks like you got a little one on the way. Don't suppose you missed me enough to name the little fellow after me?"

"Not likely." Chance laughed. The man was starting to grow on him, but Chance wasn't sure whether he was more like moss or mold. "Did you bring the things I ordered?"

Tobin beamed. "Yes, sir. Plus, I brought you a big surprise." He glanced at Anna with a question in his eyes. "When I got to the coast, there was someone waitin' to come to see a Mister Chance Wyatt. She'd had her bags packed for weeks, waitin' to hear from him."

Chance looked doubtful; he was sure Tobin was about to embark on one of his stories.

"She's a mighty fine little lady, but I don't know what you plan to do with her. She'd already broke the hearts of half the men before I got her loaded up for here."

"What?" Chance didn't like this teasing. He could see the confusion in Anna's face. She was believing Tobin's tale: "That's enough." His tone was serious but Tobin paid no heed.

"That's right, son. Looks like you got yourself two sweethearts in one town." Tobin giggled like a toothless hyena. "A redheaded wife about to deliver and a tiny little pixie with black curls that sends every heart a-spinnin'."

"I said that's enough of your teasing. Anna will be believing your tale if you don't stop."

"Would if I could." Tobin winked. "But the wee little Maggie would be sorely disappointed if she didn't see her Chance. She hasn't stopped talking about seein' him since we left Galveston."

Chance's face paled as the name registered in his mind. Without a word he broke free of the crowd and started running toward the wagons yelling Maggie's name.

Anna turned away. Seeing the two lovers reunited was more than she could bear. Chance had never said a word about Maggie except in his sleep, but Anna, with Tobin's few comments, had put the pieces together. Maggie was the girl to whom he'd given the hundred dollars. Maggie was the one he loved and would go back to when the year was over. She'd seen the light in his eyes when Tobin had said her name. Chance would turn away as quickly in one year as he had when he heard her name. Without a backward glance, without a regret, he'd go back to Maggie's arms.

Tobin pulled at Anna. "Come on. You gotta see Chance's Maggie."

"No." Anna felt her face redden. "I've things to do inside."

"Don't be actin' as finicky as a pregnant cow in the

middle of a water crossin'. The girl won't bite, you know."

Anna flashed her anger at Tobin as he pulled her along. "I resent being compared to a pregnant cow!" she argued.

She pulled free of Tobin just as she heard someone scream Chance's name. Looking up, Anna saw a tiny bundle of arms and legs fly from one of the wagons and land in Chance's arms. The child looked like an angel as she squealed and hugged Chance's neck. She could have been no more than eight years old.

Lifting her high into the air, Chance twirled her around. "Maggie!" he cried. "My little Maggie!"

Tobin slapped Anna on the back. "I knew she was his sister the minute I saw that black hair and those bright blue eyes. She came runnin' up to me, dancin' around me and askin' questions the minute she knew I had seen her brother."

Chance propped Maggie on one arm and brought her over to them. "Anna, I'd like you to meet my little sister."

Relief and joy sparkled in Anna's eyes. Tobin was right; the tiny child had the same coloring as Chance. Even the dimple on her left cheek was a reflection of her brother. "I thought all your family was killed."

Chance rubbed Maggie's curls. "They were, except Mom's body saved my sister. She fell on Maggie and the Indians didn't take the time to notice such a tiny bundle. She's lived with my cousins since she was one." He looked at Maggie, expecting some explanation.

The little girl couldn't seem to stop hugging Chance and continued to do so even while she talked. "They sent me here when they got word of where you were. Tobin told them all about you getting married and since they were expecting their fourth, they sent me with him. He told them you were ill, but Cousin Bessie said I was to help take care of you or stay with your widow, she didn't care which."

One look at Maggie's smile and Anna's heart melted. "Are you Chance's wife?" She pushed at Chance and he set her on her feet.

Anna nodded as the little girl curtsied.

"Are you going to have a baby?" The child didn't come to but an inch above Anna's waist.

"Maggie," Chance scolded, but Anna held her hand up to stop his protest.

"Yes, I am." Anna loved the honesty of this child. Maybe some of it would rub off on Tobin.

Maggie twisted one finger inside her tiny fist. "I know I'm a lot of trouble—my cousins always said so—but I could help when the baby gets here. I'd try real hard and I don't eat much. If you have four kids, I'd even sleep under the bed so you wouldn't hardly notice me being in the way."

Anna brushed her fingers through the child's curls. "Maggie, you're welcome to stay with us for as long as you like. We'd love to have you."

"Really?" A look of surprise crossed the child's face, revealing much about the eight years of her little life with her cousins.

Kneeling, Anna folded the child tightly in her arms. She knew what it was like to grow up feeling unwanted and being told that you were always in the way. "Oh, Maggie, I'm so glad you're here." Tears sprang from her eyes. "You get your things and we'll start for our home tomorrow." She kissed the tiny girl's cheek. "We're very honored you'll be with us and there will always be room for you."

Maggie broke from Anna's arms with a smile that stretched from dimple to dimple. She glanced at Chance, who nodded, then she ran to get her bundle. They could hear her telling everyone among the wagons that she'd found her family.

Chance's hand went around Anna's arm and steadied her as she stood. "Much obliged," he whispered.

Anna looked at him, her eyebrows drawn together in puzzlement. "No, it is I who thank you." She meant her words so completely that she even surprised herself. "I can think of no greater joy than providing that child with a home."

Suddenly, she was in Chance's arms and he was holding her tightly against him. As she moved her hand up to stroke his black hair, she realized he needed to belong somewhere just as badly as his little sister did. Only he was a man so he'd never admit it.

18

"I'm not wearing the damn thing!" Chance stormed bare-chested from the bedroom and pitched the white nightshirt at Anna.

"But every man wears a nightshirt to bed." Anna looked up from braiding Maggie's hair. "What will Maggie think?"

Chance winked at his little sister. "I doubt Maggie cares what I wear. Right, sweetheart?"

Tittering, Maggie answered, "Right." Her love for her brother shone so strongly in her eyes it was obvious the child could love him no less if he were in bearskins.

Anna stood, one hand on her hip, the other pointing a comb at Chance as she frowned in her best imitation of the sisters at boarding school. "Well, you can't sleep naked with women in the house. Besides, it's not healthy. You'll catch a cold."

"I don't see what you're so upset about. You act like you've never seen me without clothing." He watched the blush rise in Anna's cheeks. "And besides, I haven't had a cold in ten years. I doubt this frilly shirt with the lace around the collar will save me from one."

Anna had heard Tobin bedding down earlier on the porch. He was probably snickering like a hyena right now. They would likely become part of his stories for the next folks he met. She took Maggie by the hand and crossed to the bedroom, trying to keep her voice low. "I don't care what

179

you sleep in, Chance Wyatt, because you're sleeping out here on the cot. Maggie and I will do just fine in the bed."

Chance's mouth fell open as she dropped the curtain over the doorway leading to the only other room in the house. Briefly, he thought of changing his mind or storming in and telling her she was mistaken about the sleeping arrangements, that he'd be damned if he was going to sleep in the kitchen on a cot while his wife slept in the bedroom. But he thought about how that would make Maggie feel if he kicked her out. He'd seen her love for Anna all evening. The child had never left his wife's side. He couldn't come between them. They were like two lost souls who had just found one another. No matter how much he wanted to hold Anna, he couldn't hurt his little sister.

Storming out of the house, Chance slammed the door loud enough to wake the neighbors. He almost tumbled over Tobin, who was sitting on the porch downing a bottle of whiskey. The evening was murky black, with only spots of tiny lights flickering in the distance. Chance fought the urge to run hard and fast into the night until he slammed into something and shocked the frustration from his mind. Pain, anger, even hardship, he could deal with, but not the feelings that churned inside him whenever he fought with Anna.

Chance plopped down beside Tobin and silently took a swallow. For once he hardly noticed the fiery liquid burning its way down his throat. Every night for the past month he'd thought about how it would feel to sleep next to Anna. Now all he had to look forward to was a cot in the kitchen. Even when he'd worked to the point that he'd been too tired to eat supper, he'd still lain awake thinking of Anna in his arms.

"Hell of a hole you dug for yourself, son." Tobin tipped the bottle and gulped down another swallow. "Way I see it, if you back down and wear that damn nightshirt you might as well be roped and tied for brandin'. If you don't, you ain't never gettin' in that woman's bed."

"I don't remember asking you what you think, Tobin."

Chance stared out at the black night. He could hear a lonely owl serenading the moon. Just now, Chance figured, he and that old hoot owl had a lot in common.

"That don't matter if you ask me, son. I'm happy to help out." Tobin passed the bottle back to Chance. "I can tell you, though, when you get to that cabin of yours, you best lay the law down or you'll be sleepin' in the barn most of your married life."

"Anna isn't the easiest person to lay the law down to," Chance said, more to himself than to Tobin.

"Ain't a woman alive that doesn't like her man strong. If you aren't stronger than her, she'll have no use for you at all. So you just stand your ground, son."

Chance turned to stare at the shadowy man beside him. "How did you get to be so smart when it comes to women?"

Tobin chuckled. "I've been married a few times. Never found a woman I wanted to warm my bed more 'n one winter. But then I never met a lady like your missus."

Leaning back against the wall of the house, Chance finished off Tobin's bottle. He wished he trusted the man enough to ask for advice. But he'd learned a long time ago not to bother asking for or giving any advice. A man could just as easily end up on the open end of a shotgun. He agreed with Tobin about one thing, though; he'd never met a lady like Anna. And he had no idea how to handle her. About the time he thought he was gentling her, she'd fly off the handle like a powder keg left in the middle of a brushfire.

Finally, Chance stood up and walked back into the house. He had no idea how long he'd been sitting outside staring at the moon, but the night had grown chilly. He could hear Tobin snoring, so there was no need to bid him good night. The man was like a barnyard cat: as soon as his belly was full he found a place to curl up and sleep.

The cabin was dark except for the dying fire. Chance stared into the coals, trying to think about where he'd gone wrong. Anna had been happy to see him. She'd moved into his arms as smooth as butter over hot biscuits. He remembered how she'd laughed at his jokes and wanted to know every detail of the cabin and the land. She'd even told him she'd been packed for a week and had walked the road to the edge of town waiting for him almost every day. Yet tonight she'd grown angry when he hadn't wanted to try on the nightshirt she'd made him.

Chance chuckled, remembering how foolish he'd looked in the thing. He'd felt like a turkey dressed for Thanksgiving with all that lace around his neck and wrists. He hadn't even bothered to let her see him looking so ridiculous. He'd pulled the thing off and slipped into his pants. Her first husband might have worn such a shirt, but Chance was no country gentleman. He'd be laughed out of camp if any of his friends saw him all duded up like that just to go to bed.

Anna watched him from the bedroom. His tan body glowed golden as he leaned against the mantel and stared into the fire. Somehow, he looked stronger, larger than when he'd left a month ago. There was a ruggedness about him that had been sharpened by living in the open. The muscles across his back were stronger, harder from the work. His face, even clean-shaven, bore the sun-darkened creases of a man who had faced the wind for many a day. His pants fit tightly across his hips as he leaned on one leg to stir the fire. Anna realized how much she'd missed him. Her eyes were hungry for the sight of him. Although she didn't understand why, Anna wanted to touch him, to reassure herself that he was back and that her dream of a home was going to come true.

She slipped from the covers and tucked Maggie in. The moon shone through the windows as she tiptoed across the floor and into the other room. Chance didn't look up, but she knew he sensed her presence because she saw his muscles tighten slightly. He lifted his head an inch as he listened to her footsteps approaching.

Touching the warm flesh of his shoulder, Anna whispered, "Chance, I'm sorry."

He looked at her then, his eyes the crystal blue of a clear summer day. The firelight danced within their depths. He didn't move, but stood with one hand gripping the mantel, the other stuffed deep in his pocket.

Drawing closer, Anna brushed his hair back from his forehead with her fingertips. "I've always been stubborn and quick-tempered, I'm afraid, but the pregnancy makes it worse. Mrs. Basse said she's two different people depending on whether she's pregnant or not." Anna continued to touch his hair, which was still damp from the swim he'd taken in the stream. He was so strong, so self-assured, but there was a little boy inside this powerful man—a little boy who touched her heart with his need.

"You don't have to wear the nightshirt. I'll make Maggie a Sunday dress out of it."

Chance's smile dimpled his left cheek. "I wasn't planning on wearing it. I'm not that kind of man." He saw the confusion in her eyes and continued, "I know you're used to a gentleman who can wear that kind of thing and treat you better than I ever could. I've spent most of my life sleeping on the ground and busting a bronco before breakfast. I think it'll take more than the months we have left together to make more of me than I am."

Anna slid her fingers along his shoulder. "No," she whispered. "I don't want to change you. I don't care if you wear the nightshirt or not. It's not important. And as for treating me like a gentleman would, I've never been treated more like a lady by anyone."

Anna's soft words, the whiskey he'd downed, the smell of her hair, all were like a drug to Chance's brain. He wanted to hold her, to kiss her as her lips begged to be kissed. As he leaned forward to touch her lips with his, Anna turned away.

"I want to tell you something before we leave tomorrow." She walked to the window and looked out as if the words were painted in the clouds. "I've been thinking about it, and I want to say this now so there is no confusion for Maggie."

Chance tried to concentrate on something besides kissing her. "What about Maggie?" he asked.

"When you leave, I want you to know that it would be all right if Maggie stayed with me while you're traveling. I'll try to give her a good home."

Chance's hopes snapped like dead wood in winter. That was why she'd come to him, then—not because she wanted him; not because she longed for his touch as much as he craved hers. It was Maggie. She was making it plain she wanted him to leave and stand by their agreement, but Maggie could stay. Maggie could be a part of her life, but he was to leave just as they'd bargained.

He shoved both hands into his pockets and his words were sharp in the sleepy air. "I'll send money every year for her keep."

Anna looked up at him and he thought he saw a hint of pain in her eyes. "Oh, no, that won't be necessary."

"Is a hundred dollars a year all right?" Chance's words were harder than he'd meant them to be. How could he have thought she'd come out here in the middle of the night to see him? She'd only wanted to remind him that he'd be leaving. Maggie could stay. Maggie was a child so starved for love she'd take it in huge gulps from Anna. But him, he'd stand by the agreement. He'd walk away although his arms ached to hold her. Even now, if he reached for her, he might crush her before he let go. But it would be his heart's secret, a secret never shared.

Suddenly he wanted her to feel an ounce of the weighty burden of pain he carried. Why had she touched him, brushed his hair back, and then stepped away as if playing a game? His words were angry. "Unless you want more money?"

His reward—the hurt in her eyes—was bittersweet. He knew she was proud and wanted to throw the offer in his face, but she was also practical and knew she might need some money. Her voice shook slightly. "One hundred dollars will be fine." Her heart flinched under the sting of his words. "If ever you can't pay, I'll still keep Maggie with me."

"Don't worry." Chance pushed his anger deep into his pockets with white knuckles. "I'll do *anything* to get the hundred dollars for her keep."

Anna had had enough of his baiting. She had no idea why he was angry, but she wanted to return fire for fire. Only the knowledge that Tobin was within hearing kept her from answering. "We'll talk about this later."

Chance bowed, acknowledging her dismissal with sarcasm.

"Well"—she hesitated—"that's all I came to say. Forgive me for my outburst, but Maggie has a home with me for as long as she wants."

She turned at the doorway. "Good night."

Chance held himself tightly under control. Even in his anger, he needed her so badly he could feel it in the very roots of his hair. If she had any idea how much he wanted her at this moment it would probably frighten her to death.

He forced his lips to move. "Good night, Anna."

19

Tobin loaded Anna's and Chance's supplies into the wagon he'd bought with the money he'd made hauling people from the coast. Even with Anna's trunk and all Chance had ordered, there was still plenty of room for Maggie to play in the back. They started out of town amidst the cheers of friends and the tears of Mrs. Basse.

Chance had learned the country well enough to pick the easiest way back to the Fredericksburg settlement. Anna rode in the wagon, too large with child to walk far or ride a horse. Tobin's rifle lay across her knees, ever ready in case of Indians. No one spoke of the danger, but everyone except Maggie could feel it in the air. They were being watched, observed like ants in a jar as they moved across the open country.

Each day they camped at sunset, keeping a watchful eye on the night's shadows. Tobin built a huge fire every evening and told Maggie stories. The old man was totally fascinated with the child and she loved his tales. Anna and Maggie slept in the wagon while Tobin bedded down underneath it.

Chance walked the campsite, constantly alert to possible dangers. He wanted to talk to Anna, but they never had any time alone. Tobin and Maggie were better chaperones than old maiden aunts with perfect hearing. The pain of seeing her was like a wound in his heart that wouldn't heal. He told himself that they had an agreement and nothing more. She was pregnant and within a few months of delivery. She'd made it plain that she wasn't interested in him. Yet still he longed to hold her. He admired her more and more each day for her strength and hated himself for his weakness, his wanting her. So by day he kept her in his sight, and by night he paced until he dropped, too tired even to dream.

They reached the farmland late one afternoon. The land rolled out like green velvet between two dark rocky hills. Chance pulled up alongside the wagon. "See that hill up there?"

Anna rubbed her back and nodded.

"That's the start of your land." Chance laughed as Anna stood up in the wagon in excitement. "Easy now!" he cried, not wanting her to tumble out.

Anna's face was filled with joy. "I can't wait any longer. Take me there now."

Shaking his head, Chance answered, "The wagon'll get you there soon enough."

"Oh, please?" Anna held her arms out to Chance, as impatient as a child.

"All right, if you'll hang on tight." He couldn't deny her request. He cradled her in his arms and nudged Cyoty into action.

As they rode, he pointed out where her land started and where Carl and Selma's place ended. There was a thick group of trees that separated the two properties. Chance had built Anna's house on one side of the trees, and Carl had built his place on the other. Only a short distance divided the two homes. Even now they could see chimney smoke coming from the other side of the trees.

Pulling out his pistol, Chance fired twice, quickly, to announce their arrival. A moment later, they heard a single shot in answer. "Neighbors are too close if they can hear a gunshot," Chance complained with a smile. He was thankful that the Jordans had elected to build so near; when he left, Anna wouldn't feel so alone. He'd heard that the

loneliness in this country was sometimes a woman's great-
est hardship.

Holding his precious cargo tightly, Chance guided Cyoty
toward the home. He drank in the feel of Anna in his arms,
loving the smell of her hair and its silkiness against his
cheek. She was maybe twenty pounds heavier than when
they'd ridden double before. Part was the baby, and part,
Chance thought, might be from Mrs. Basse's cooking.
Anna's thin figure had rounded out nicely in the months
he'd known her.

"There's where the barn will be." He pointed to the
north, where a hill of rock and trees made farming impossible, but where tiny ridges could be used for corrals and
pens. "Over there's where we'll plant your garden. It'll get
the morning sun and be shaded by the trees in the afternoon."

Anna shaded her eyes. "I can't see the house."

Chance reined Cyoty to a slow walk. "Now, don't expect
much. Remember we only agreed to build the dugout first.
When I have time I'll add a cabin."

"I know." Anna didn't care what it looked like. She just
wanted to see her home.

Rounding a group of live oaks, Anna held her breath as
the house came into view. It was almost hidden beneath the
evening shadows of the trees. The roof was made of logs
and at first glance the cabin looked as if it were only three
feet tall. The steps going down into the cellar-like home
were hidden by a mound of dirt covered with sunflowers.

Shouting with joy, Anna almost jumped off Cyoty.
Chance was hard-pressed to manage the horse and get Anna
down without injury to either.

She ran to the cabin and opened the door before he could
tie up the bay. "Oh, look!" he heard her squeal just as Carl
and Selma came through the trees on what was already
becoming a well-worn path.

For the next several minutes everyone talked and hugged
at once. Maggie was accepted as one of the family within a

heartbeat. Selma even hugged Tobin, which left the man speechless for a moment. While they unloaded, Carl filled Chance in on all he'd done since Chance had left.

When Chance walked into the cabin he could hardly believe the change. Selma had swept the floor until it was as smooth as hardwood. Carl had laid extra rocks in an oval around the fireplace, forming a ledge. He'd made a bed frame and a table as well as two chairs and a bench. Shelves lined one wall and pegs lined another.

Carl's sunburned face beamed. "I made you something special." He lifted a blanket, revealing a little bench with a high back made just for two.

Tears rolled down Anna's face. The little room with its primitive furnishings was the most beautiful home in the world to her. "Thank you," she said. "How will I ever be able to repay you?"

"Probably with a meal," Chance said with a laugh. "We've been stuck up here with Selma's cooking for a month. If you can't cook, Anna, you'd better tell us now so Carl and I can go live with the Indians. Selma's cooking will surely kill us by winter."

Selma slapped Chance on the arm. Her words were all mixed up in German and English, but everyone knew she didn't mind his teasing.

Anna watched, feeling a little envious of their light-hearted banter. She pulled her pots from the trunk. "I'll make supper tomorrow night. We have meat. Tobin brought me flour for bread and Mrs. Basse gave me dried peaches. We'll have a feast."

"And I'll bring wood to make Maggie a bed." Carl acted as though he were measuring the little girl. "I'll build it high so she can be up close to the windows at night and then hang all her clothes underneath."

Chance motioned Carl outside as the women talked. When they were several feet past the dugout door, he said, "There were Indians following us almost from the time we left the settlement."

Carl's freckled face creased with worry. "Are you sure? Did you see them?"

Looking toward the dugout door, Chance kept his voice low. "Didn't have to see them. I could sense them. We're being watched and I don't like it. Tobin's going to stay around for a few days in case there's trouble."

Carl stood up straight and tried to sound defiant, but his voice shook a little. "There will be no trouble. The society told us the Indians around here are peaceful."

Chance moved back toward the others. "Maybe you're right, but I'm sleeping with one eye open." He didn't want to think about what would happen if they were attacked, but he knew he had to be prepared.

Everyone was talking again, making plans for the morning. Chance watched Anna unpacking each of her things from the trunk. She'd smile at each treasure, then look around for exactly the right place for it. She was settling in, building her nest. She was home.

Chance left for the fields before Anna and Maggie were up. He'd slept outside, on guard, using the excuse of not wanting Maggie to be frightened her first night in the strange little house. In truth, he could feel the Indians nearby. It was too quiet to be more than a small band, but they were there.

By the time Anna had dressed and cooked breakfast he'd been working for two hours. She called him in from the fields just as he pulled a tree stump from the ground with Tobin's team. Chance was already shirtless and sweaty in the cool morning air. He allowed Tobin to go ahead as he washed up and put his shirt back on. The older man would never have allowed his attire to come between him and food, but Chance needed time alone before facing Anna. He couldn't allow his thoughts of her to show in his face, or he might frighten her.

Anna served pancakes with berries and thin venison steaks. Chance cleaned his plate, and she made a mental note to prepare larger meals. He was quiet, but Anna could think of no reason for his anger. Yet something was obviously bothering him.

As he walked toward the fields, Anna followed. "You forgot your hat."

Chance turned back and stared at her. "I don't need it."

Anna touched his shoulder. "You'll blister."

Chance pulled away from her touch. "I'll come in and work on the barn when it gets hot." His eyes looked tired. The sadness in them made Anna want to cry.

"What is it?" she whispered. "You've been angry about something since the night I gave you the nightshirt and now you look like you haven't slept for days."

Chance laughed, but there was no happiness in his eyes. "I'm not angry about that nightshirt. In fact, I'm not angry about anything. Maybe it's just your pregnancy."

"No." Anna resented him sloughing the problem between them off on her pregnancy. "There's something bothering you."

Chance looked toward the fields as if he were impatient to return. How could he tell Anna what was eating away at him? How could he say that every time she hugged Maggie, he felt a pain inside him. She seemed to have all the love and caring in the world for his sister, but none for him. Oh, she was fond of touching him. He could still feel the warmth of her fingers on his shoulder, but if he moved toward her, she'd step away. He was sick of being near her and not holding her. He was angry at himself for being jealous of Maggie when the child needed so much love and affection. And soon, Anna would have her baby and Chance would be pushed even further from her. But he couldn't tell her any of this. He didn't even want to admit it to himself.

Touching his arm again, Anna insisted, "Tell me what it is that's troubling you or I'll follow you to the fields and flutter around you like Selma does to Carl when he tries to work."

Chance smiled. He'd enjoy Anna flirting with him the

way Selma flirted with Carl, but she was hardly in a condition to tramp around the fields. "All right." He lifted his hands. "I give up."

Anna rubbed her back and waited.

"I didn't want to tell you about this because I didn't want you to worry." He had to tell her something that she'd believe. "Tobin and I think there might be a group of Indians camped not far from here. We've felt them watching us for several days."

Anna held her breath.

Chance chose his words carefully. He didn't want to frighten her. "They may be peaceful like most in these parts. Tobin left this morning, hoping to find out. I didn't want you to worry."

Anna relaxed. "I won't," she lied. "That explains why you've been walking the camp at night and why you didn't sleep in the house last night."

The corner of Chance's full lip raised slightly. "Would you like me to?"

Anna looked down and suddenly became very interested in straightening her apron. "I think for appearances . . ." Suddenly, Anna didn't want to lie anymore. There was no need to pretend out here in this land. She'd missed his arms around her. "I wouldn't mind." She ran her hand over her stomach. "I seem to be taking up more space every day. There may not be room for anyone to sleep next to me soon. But you need a good night's sleep, and the man of the house shouldn't sleep on the ground. Maggie will have her little bed tonight when Carl comes for dinner."

Chance knew she was rambling a little with nervousness, but she'd said what he wanted to hear. Tonight she'd sleep in his arms.

20

Lifting the iron pot from beside the fire, Anna rotated it slowly just as her cook in Germany had taught her. The fresh smell of bread blended with the aroma of roast turkey and filled the one-room home with the promise of a feast. Anna wanted to do something to please Chance. His dark mood of the past few days seemed to lighten only when he hugged Maggie. The child was a joy. Even if he'd only been out of the room a few minutes, each time he returned she flew toward him with her arms outstretched.

A touch of jealousy snuck into Anna's heart. She would like to have been encircled by those strong arms, but her pride wouldn't allow it. How could a man's embrace feel so secure when she knew it was as unsteady as the sandy cliffs around the stream beside their cabin? They too looked solid and steadfast, but when you put any weight on them, they shifted and crumbled. And this winter, on the anniversary of their marriage, Chance's strength would be gone from her life completely.

Sometimes she thought of asking him to stay, but he'd told her often enough that he planned to continue his search for his parents' killer, Storm's Edge. Also, if he stayed he might expect to become a real husband to her, and despite the fact that Anna liked having him around, she'd vowed never to allow a man to use her body in that way again.

Swiftly, she pushed her doubts aside as she swept the

extra pieces of dough from the table. Maggie was asleep in the high bed Carl had finished making for her only an hour ago. She'd worked beside Anna all morning, cleaning the little house, and was exhausted.

Anna rolled a piece of light brown dough flat against the table. All that was left to do was prepare dessert and cover the table with her finest linen cloth. Carl had gone home to fetch Selma and clean up. Tonight would be Anna's first dinner in her new home, and she wanted everything to be perfect.

A shadow moved over the doorway, blocking the late afternoon sun. For a moment Anna continued working and waited for Chance's voice.

The shadow over her work area remained.

She glanced up into the bright sunlight that shone in from behind the wide frame of a man.

For a moment she was unafraid. The shadowy man before her seemed made of stone, like a statue outside a store. His headdress brushed the top of the doorway, and his wide shoulders pushed at the door frame as if requesting more room to enter. His bare chest shone like polished oak.

Anna dropped the pie pan, sending a white puff of flour from the table. "Indians," she whispered, digging into her dress pocket for Chance's knife.

The knife! her mind screamed as if her hands were feebleminded and couldn't think of what to grasp.

The Indian moved a step closer. His skin glistened with a thin layer of sweat in the afternoon light. A huge knife at his belt clanged against a chair.

Anna stopped her search. What good would Chance's little knife be? If this savage pulled his blade, she would be slashed through before she could even draw blood.

"What do you want?" Anna moved back toward the corner trying not to look frightened. She remembered Chance telling her to show no fear. Yet her hands shook and the hair stood up along the back of her neck. Panic ricocheted off the walls of her mind.

The sun flashed across the Indian's face as he took another step toward her. His nose was wide and long and his high cheekbones made him look like a proud king. His parted lips revealed huge straight teeth.

Anna looked around for a weapon. She watched as he raised his hand slowly toward her. There was no doubt in her mind that his fingers could choke her before she could even get a scream past her lips.

Her body was shaking so badly that she could hardly think. She glanced down at the hot round bread she'd just pulled from the fire. In one mighty lunge she lifted the hot pan and flung it at the Indian.

The iron pan dropped to the floor, but the bread flew right into the Indian's hand. She heard the soft thud as it hit his wide palm. He could probably smash her skull with little more effort than he'd need to crumble the bread.

He looked down at the hot steaming thing as if he had no idea what to do with it. The bread filled his hand as he pulled it close to his nose.

In pure panic, Anna ran for the open door like a deer bolts after a shot is fired. Without looking behind her, she ran toward the fields where she knew Chance was working.

"Chance!" she screamed. "Chance!"

He lifted his head, then grabbed his rifle and ran toward her. "What is it?" he yelled as he crossed the distance between them in lightning speed.

Suddenly, Anna froze. She turned away from him and lifted her skirts. "Maggie!" she screamed. "I left Maggie in the cabin!"

Anna ran back toward the cabin. She'd left the tiny child alone with that savage. He could twist her body or smother her with one hand. *Dear God!* Anna thought. *How could I have left the child?*

As she turned the corner at the mound of dirt, the ground sifted slightly beneath her feet and she tumbled down the cabin steps.

A moment later Chance was at her side, pulling her up

almost as she hit the earth. His powerful arms lifted her off the ground, then set her down gently amid the sunflowers beside the door.

Shoving his arm aside, Anna pointed toward the cabin. "Indians," she whispered as the huge red man stepped out the door.

Chance raised his rifle, but the Indian just stood there staring at Anna. After a moment he raised one mighty hand and took another bite from the loaf of bread.

Instinctively, Chance pushed Anna behind him. He said something to the Indian and the man nodded, showing his huge teeth in what he must have thought was a smile. Chance spoke again and the Indian straightened with pride. Chance lowered his gun and brushed the air with an open palm. The Indian did the same and Chance spoke again in words Anna couldn't understand. Without a word the huge savage marched out toward the woods, holding his head high and chewing away on Anna's bread.

For a moment Anna clung to Chance's arm, too frightened to let go. His hand slowly moved along her side to her shoulder. His fingers touched her throat, then his thumb tilted her chin upward until he could see her eyes. "It's all right, Anna. He wasn't going to hurt you. He didn't realize the dugout was private property. He was only looking around."

Pulling Chance closer, Anna cradled her face into his shoulder. His warm flesh smelled of soap and leather and sweat. The scent of him was his alone, and Anna found the smell strangely comforting. She didn't want to let go of him. She wanted to stay in the protection of his arms forever.

Chance lowered his gun to the grass and sat down, pulling her into his lap. He pushed strands of hair away from her face and kissed her tears from her cheeks with a smile. "Don't worry, darling. He only wanted to sample your cooking." He moved his hands gently down from her shoulders to her waist. "Are you hurt?" The concern in his eyes surprised Anna.

Rubbing her hand over her swollen abdomen, she shook her head. "I'm shaken up. I thought he was going to kill me and then I just ran out, leaving Maggie asleep." Shame brought tears to her eyes. "I left Maggie. Oh, Chance, I'm sorry."

Chance held her tightly in his arms. "Don't be so upset. You were just frightened. You ran."

Anna shook her head. "What kind of mother will I be if I forget a child and think only of myself?"

Gently, he rubbed her back. "You ran to get help. That was the best thing you could have done. I don't think a woman in your condition could very well fight a stocky Tonkawa chief."

Anna agreed but couldn't stop crying. When Chance finally got her calmed down enough to explain, she said only, "I threw our bread at him."

Chance's laughter could be heard all the way to the Jordans' cabin. He could just picture the Indian's surprise when Anna tossed a hot loaf of bread at him.

An hour later they enjoyed the breadless dinner and another round of laughter. Anna remained silent, her body stiff from the bruises of her fall. Chance teased Selma about the Indian never stopping by to taste her cooking. All the men agreed that the Indian probably took Anna's bread as a gift, and if it were as good as everything else she cooked, he'd be back the next baking day.

Tobin helped himself to another slice of pie. "The Tonkawas are a friendly, honest tribe, but they see everythin' that's not nailed down as free. I've been in their camps before. They'd give you anythin' you wanted, all you have to do is show an interest, but they believe you should feel the same about them rummagin' through your poke." He refilled his mouth and continued, "I think Chance is right about our Indian comin' back. Think I'll call him Sourdough."

Anna frowned. "I hope I never see him again."

The men began talking about the advantages of having a friendly tribe nearby while Anna cleared the table. The pain in her back was increasing, and she was starting to think the fall might have injured her more than she'd first thought.

Excusing herself, Anna went to the stream to wash up before it got too dark. She needed a few minutes to be alone.

When she reached the stream, the sun was a huge ball sitting atop the low rolling hills. The land was brushed with gold and full of promise. Anna sat down on a large rock and relaxed for the first time since she'd seen the Indian. With the laughter of her friends in the background, the terror of the afternoon seemed far away.

As she enjoyed the sunset, Anna washed her face and hands, splashing water against her neck. Anna felt a wet trickle sliding down the inside of her legs and lifted her skirt so she could cool her sweaty limbs in the stream. What she saw turned her warm skin to ice: Blood! Dark, thick blood covered the inside of her legs like a coat of paint. Bright red circles stained her petticoats.

Anna bit her knuckle as she fought back a scream. For a moment she stared at her bloody legs without moving, as though they belonged to someone else. Then a pain tightened the muscles in her back, making her all too aware of her body.

She looked at the sky for a minute until the pain passed. Her hands trembled as she cleaned the blood from her legs. Another pain shot through her back. "No," she cried, "it's not time."

Mrs. Basse had told her what to look for: she'd said a spot of blood and pains and the waters. But this was no spot of blood. A crimson liquid was dripping from her, and there was no sign that it had been diluted with water.

Rinsing the cloth, Anna wiped her face. She pushed her skirt down and tried to think. It's not time. She knew the night she'd gotten pregnant. It had been when William raped her on board ship. That was less than eight months ago. It wasn't time. It wasn't time!

"Anna?"

She turned with a start and saw Chance crossing the rocky ground by the stream.

"Are you all right? You were gone so long I was starting to worry."

He squatted beside her, his rifle over his knee. "I thought I'd come . . ."

Their eyes met and Anna knew she couldn't hide her fear even if she tried. Worry crossed Chance's smiling face like a sudden spring storm darkens bright skies. "What is it?" he whispered.

He looked around, his hand moving to his gun. "Have you seen the Indian again? I'd never have let you come out here alone if I'd thought he was still around."

"No," Anna whispered, "it isn't the Indian."

Leaning closer, he ordered, "Anna, tell me."

Anna didn't want to tell him. She didn't want to tell anyone. She didn't want to believe it herself, but even in her moment of denial she could feel the blood seeping from her. "I'm . . . I'm bleeding," she whispered.

Chance knelt closer. "But you said it wasn't time for another month or more."

Anna didn't want to argue. She'd told herself the very same thing. "I'm afraid. You said to tell you if I was in pain and I'm in a great deal of pain right now. The blood . . . the blood won't stop."

"I'll get Selma." Chance started to stand but she reached out and grabbed his shirt.

"No!" Anna pulled him close. "I talked with Selma. She knows even less about babies than I do. I don't want her to see me bleeding. I don't want anyone to see me. I'm afraid I'll be a coward when the time comes." Anna knew she was rambling but she couldn't stop. "I don't want her to think I'm weak. You said your mother faced it alone. I can too. Please, I don't want anyone to see me."

Chance ran his fingers through his black hair as if he'd just been asked the impossible. "All right. I understand, but you can't stay alone. I'm staying with you. Maybe between us we can figure out what to do."

"No!" The thought that Chance would see such a thing made her cringe.

"Yes!" Chance insisted. "You're not going through this alone. Not when it's early and there may be problems. I've delivered animals. I watched my mother cut the cord from Maggie. I can help."

Anna had no choice. She wasn't sure she could do it by herself. The pain in her back was growing greater with each contraction. "All right," she agreed, and Chance lifted her into his arms and carried her back to the cabin. She held to him tightly as though he were her last hope.

In less time than she thought possible, Chance cleared the others out. He sent Maggie to stay with the Jordans and Tobin quickly decided he'd better be heading back to town. Chance's voice was calm and reassuring, explaining over and over to Selma that he knew what to do and she would be a great deal more help watching Maggie. Selma was like a child wanting to see the unknown and afraid to look at the same time. But when she saw Anna's face stiffen in pain, she quickly decided she could wait a while to see a baby being born.

After everyone left, Anna changed into her nightgown while Chance hauled water from the stream. He put a large pot on to boil and spread a deerskin over the bed, then laid all the extra towels and sheets on top of it.

"I saw Mother do this when she was in labor. She'd have to stop every few minutes for the contractions to pass. The hide will stop any blood or water from getting on the bed. When it's all over, we can lift this up and you'll have a dry bed to sleep in." His words were like soothing music to Anna as she followed his orders.

She gingerly lay down on the pile of towels. Chance

lifted a sheet over her, and she was thankful he respected her modesty.

"Pull your nightgown up to your waist," he ordered.

Fighting both fear and pain, Anna did as he instructed.

He wet a cloth in the bucket of cold water and squeezed it out, then handed it to her. "Here, lay this between your legs. It might help slow the bleeding."

Taking the wet towel, Anna did as she was told. Moments later another contraction came and she forgot everything except the pain. When it stopped Chance was holding her hand while his free hand moved slowly over her stomach.

"They'll get harder, I'm afraid. Before long they will be coming right on top of one another."

Anna nodded as he wiped the sweat from her forehead. "Mrs. Basse said they would." Anna tried to smile. "I don't want to cry out."

Chance nodded as if he understood. "You're quite a Texas woman, lady." He lifted the buckets of water she'd washed in and left without a word. In a few minutes he returned with clean water and a stick. He wrapped the stick in cloth and handed it to Anna. "When the pain gets bad, bite down on this."

Gripping the cloth in her hand, Anna raised it to her lips and drew strength from it. She would be brave, because everyone in her family had been a coward. Her father had run away rather than face debts. Her mother had killed herself rather than lose a lover. Even William, with his slobbering apologies when he'd forced himself on her, had been a coward. But not Anna. She would be brave. She hadn't cried when her father left or at her mother's funeral. There had been no scream when William had raped her, and there would be no cry when her child came into the world. She would show him from the moment of his birth that he must be brave.

Moving around her as the time passed, Chance measured time only from one pain to the next. He kept the fire going even though the evening was warm. He lifted the sheet at the foot of the bed and changed the cloth between her legs. She was past modesty now as each contraction twisted through her with choking force. He wiped her face with a cold rag and talked softly, and though his words didn't reach her, his comfort did.

Anna felt the baby move down inside her. Every inch was a knife thrust against her back. She would sleep between contractions only to be bolted awake by the sudden constricting pain.

Once between contractions her body relaxed and she looked up into the worried blue eyes of the man she hardly knew. He touched her cheek with his palm. "You're going to make it, Anna me girl. You're going to make it."

"Don't leave me," Anna whispered. "Don't ever leave me."

Chance wiped her damp hair away from her face. "I'll be right beside you for as long as you need me."

"If I die—" Anna began.

Chance cut her off. "You're not going to die. Remember when you had the fever and you begged me to bury you when you died? Well, I told you that you weren't going to die then, and you're not going to die now. We'll get through this. I swear it. I won't let you die."

His voice was so stubborn that Anna believed him. She pushed aside the knowledge that more women died in childbirth than any other way. She didn't think of the blood that kept dripping from her or of the pain. She clung only to Chance's words.

"Anna, listen to me." Chance wiped her arms and face with the towel. "Don't think about the pain. Think about the land. Think about the baby who'll need you."

Anna bit down hard on the stick and felt a sudden urge to push. She curled up in a ball and grabbed her knees. Chance pulled the sheet away and knelt beside her. With all the strength left inside her, she pushed. Sweat broke out over her entire body and still she pushed.

Through the sweat that dripped off her forehead, Anna saw Chance's hands cup a tiny head. Excitement colored his words. "It's coming. Oh, God, Anna, it's coming!"

With one great shudder, Anna felt her insides move as he lifted the baby out. She fell back against the pillows as Chance held the baby by its heels and patted it on the back.

With tears of relief and fear streaming down her cheeks, she waited for the first cry.

Chance slapped the tiny baby.

Anna waited, her body shaking with a sudden chill.

He laid the baby beside her and wiped out its mouth with his finger. The tiny blue body lay still against the white sheet. He cut the cord with a knife and twisted it into a knot.

"Breathe!" he screamed as he patted the baby's chest and back. "Breathe!"

Anna knew the child was stillborn even before she saw the truth in Chance's eyes. "No!" she cried grabbing the tiny body and holding it to her. "No!"

God wouldn't do this to her. He wouldn't take the one person in this world who would ever love her. She rubbed the slippery skin already growing cold with death. *"No!"* she screamed trying to make her child breathe. The pain of the birth was nothing compared to the explosion of grief in her heart as she hugged the lifeless body to her.

Chance pulled the baby from her arms. She fought him wildly, but he took her child from her.

"Stay here!" he yelled as he carried the lifeless form to the door.

"My baby," she cried. "Let me hold my baby."

Anna tried to follow but she was too weak to stand. She pulled herself to the edge of the bed and forced her weight onto wobbly legs. "Chance!" she screamed as he vanished into the night. "Chance, let me hold my baby." Anna collapsed beside the bed. She slammed her fist against the rug and cried, "Let me hold my baby." The room spun around and blackness edged its way into the corners of her mind.

She felt like her sanity might give way at any moment. All these months she'd thought of the child who was heir to all her love; the child that had never taken one breath of life; the child Chance had pulled violently from her and ran with as though her holding it a moment longer would matter. She wanted to die with her baby. She wanted to lie next to it in the ground and never again feel the pain she felt now as she stared into the black silence of the night beyond her door. Her bloodline had come full circle. She and all her kind were cowards. Her baby had not even fought to breathe.

She heard the sudden splash of water. Had Chance thrown her child into the stream so that not even a grave would mark its moment on earth?

"No!" Screaming, Anna buried her face in her hands. *"No!"* All she could think of was using the last of her energy to reach the stream and joining her child in death. But she was too weak and the blackness in her brain matched that of the night.

Far away, as if from another world, came a cry. For a moment Anna couldn't tell if she had imagined the cry or if it was the strangled sob that had been wrenched from her heart and echoed into the loneliness of all her future days. She took a deep breath and listened. Was she losing her mind? Or had a baby's cry filled the air as strong and crystal clear as the dawn on a summer's morning?

21

Chance stepped from the blackness into the long rectangle of light spreading from the cabin doorway. His bare wet chest glistened, and his hair fell across his forehead in dark locks. Anna stared at him, in too much pain even to allow her hatred to show. He looked so caring, so kind, as if totally unaware of the harm he'd done.

The haunting cry of a baby still whirled about her ears, pushing her closer to insanity. He'd ripped her child from her arms, and she would hear its cry to her death. He hadn't allowed her to kiss the only thing she would ever love good-bye. Now she wanted to run at him and pound her sorrow into his very heart, but her head swam with the loss of her own blood and she clung to the door frame, fighting the blackness that filtered through her mind like poisonous smoke.

Then she saw it: a small bundle in Chance's arms. As he neared she recognized the folds of his blue shirt around a tiny wiggling form. Reality and hope began to dance together until each blurred the other.

Reaching the door of the cabin, he shouted, "Anna, get back in bed!"

Anna stared at him as if the devil had just walked past her. "What?"

The black smoke filled her mind, and she felt her body go numb from her limbs inward until there was no strength, no light. As the darkness blanketed her brain, she felt Chance's strong arm go around her.

Anna awoke slowly, feeling as though she'd been sleeping for centuries. She felt the covers over her body and blinked at the firelight.

"Anna." Chance's voice seemed to come from all directions at once. "Anna, please wake up!"

Tears welled up in her eyes as she whispered, "I lost my baby." The pain of the words ripped at her heart for even now she could hear the cries of her child.

Lying down next to her, Chance pulled her under his arm. "No, darling," he whispered. "You fainted, but you didn't lose the baby. She's fine." He lifted the bundle on the other side of Anna. "I wanted to let you sleep, but to be honest I don't know how to make her stop crying."

With loving care he held the bundle close to him, but the cries continued. The child was still wrapped in his shirt. "She's been crying for an hour. I didn't figure it would hurt her much to yell a while. Might clear her lungs. But I think now she needs something I can't provide."

"But . . ." Anna couldn't believe her eyes as Chance laid the baby in her arms. The bundle couldn't measure up to a five-pound sack of flour. "How could she be alive?"

"I remembered hearing an Indian woman tell once about throwing her stillborn baby into the river to make the Great Spirit give it life. I didn't know what else to do when she wouldn't breathe."

"It worked?" She was almost afraid to touch the child, as if touching it might somehow make the dream shatter.

"The cold water must have shocked her tiny system enough to get her going." Leaning against Anna's arm, he pushed his shirt back enough to see the child's face. Her hair was almost white and formed curls around her head as she twisted and screamed. Chance stroked one red cheek with the side of his finger. "She's so tiny, like a picture I saw once of a little angel." He laughed. "But can she yell.

She screamed all the time I was cleaning you up. I finally tried rocking her, but it didn't seem to help. I made her a bed out of one of your bread pans and set it over by the fire, but she didn't like that either." Frustration crossed his strong features.

Small fingers reached up and Anna touched the hand of her daughter. "A girl," she whispered. The hand curled around Anna's finger and a bond formed that no power would ever break.

Leaning against the headboard, Chance relaxed. "There was blood all over your gown. I put you in one of my clean shirts. I figured I'd never be able to get one of those frilly, ribbony nightgowns on you."

Anna looked down and noticed for the first time what she was wearing. The long sleeves had been rolled to her elbows and the collar was buttoned to her neck. She blushed at the thought that Chance had changed her clothes, but the knowledge that he'd saved her and her child's lives registered more strongly.

Lifting her hand to his face, Anna cupped his strong jaw with her pale fingers. "Thank you. I am in your debt."

"No," Chance answered. "I should be thanking you. I got to watch a miracle tonight. I've never seen anything like it. Out of all the pain and mess came something so perfect. When I pulled her from the water and she was screaming at me, I thought I'd burst with joy."

The baby started to cry louder, as if on cue. Chance stood and crossed to the fire. "I'll put some coffee on." He seemed embarrassed as Anna started unbuttoning her shirt.

Anna laughed to herself. Here was a man who'd seen her in the worse possible shape. She didn't even want to think what it had been like to clean her up. And now he was embarrassed to think that she was about to breast-feed in the same room. She unbuttoned the nightshirt and put the baby next to her breast, surprised at her own immodesty.

Chance kept busy making coffee until the child fell asleep. When he returned with a mug of hot coffee, the baby was sleeping beside Anna. He stretched out on the other side of the tiny addition and leaned against the headboard. "What are you going to name her?"

Anna rested her head against Chance's arm. "I don't know. What do you think?"

Chance sipped his coffee. "Could name her after your mother or grandmother."

Anna shook her head slightly. "I never knew my grandmother and I want no memory of my mother."

He wanted to ask why, but didn't. He set his cup down and lightly stroked Anna's hair with his fingers. She closed her eyes and smiled contentedly as he continued to touch her. "My mother was a real fighter, just like this little girl. She wasn't very tall, but you wouldn't believe what she could do. I don't ever remember a day when she didn't thank God for the wonder of being alive."

Anna turned so that her cheek touched Chance's head as he continued to stroke her hair. "What was her name?"

"Her minister father named her Cherish Julia." Chance smiled, loving the feel of Anna's hair in his hand. "Dad always said he cherished Julia. I must have been five before I realized that Cherish was her name also."

"Cherish Julia Wyatt," Anna whispered. "I'd like to name my baby after her. If you don't mind?"

Chance leaned over and kissed Anna's forehead. "I'd be honored, and I think my mother would have been proud. With her hair almost white-blond and her eyes so blue, she's an angel."

There was no answer. Anna was sound asleep. Chance watched her for several minutes, then slowly lowered his hand between her breasts. Carefully, slowly, so that he wouldn't awaken her, Chance pulled the material over her breast and buttoned the shirt.

Just after dawn, activity hit the cabin with full force. Selma and Maggie came running through the trees and when they entered the cabin, they both squealed over the infant like old maids at a bridal shower. Carl showed up a moment later with a cradle in his arms. They passed tiny Cherish around until she began to cry. Then they all stood for a minute listening to her screams as though an orchestra were playing beautiful music right there in the cabin.

Carl and Selma quickly excused themselves with the helpless look of non-parents. After they left, Anna unbuttoned her shirt and fed Cherish without any embarrassment. Chance did his best to act as if nothing unusual was going on, but he couldn't help but watch her out of the corner of his eye. She knew a woman never breast-fed in the presence of men, but where was she to go in this one-room cabin?

When the baby was fed, Anna gently placed her in Maggie's anxious arms. The little girl laughed as if it were Christmas and her birthday all at once. She talked to Cherish about all the things they would do as soon as Cherish was bigger. Anna could even hear her whispering, "Call me Maggie, never Aunt Maggie, because after all, we're closer to sisters than anything." She rocked the tiny infant. "I'll never leave you, Cherish. You'll always have me to depend on. You'll never have to worry about being left alone with cousins who think you're a bother. I'll always be there to love you and give you a hug even sometimes when you don't really need one."

Closing her eyes, Anna fought back tears. Maggie's words made her love the child even more dearly. She wished someone in her life had said that to her just once. Anna would have given so much if just once in her youth she'd had a hug even when she didn't really need one.

Chance brought her out of her self-pity by sitting down on the side of the bed. He balanced a plate of food on his knee and spread a napkin under Anna's chin. "You need to eat something." He stuck a piece of meat with his fork and tried to feed her.

Anna shook her head, her lips tightly closed. When he lowered the fork, she said, "I'm perfectly able to feed myself."

Setting the plate aside, he lifted her shoulders up until she was sitting, and stuffed pillows behind her. "Then eat," he teased as he shoved the plate toward her.

Anna tasted the strange mixture of meat covered with a white greasy liquid. She couldn't suppress a snicker as she asked, "Did you make this, or did Selma?"

With a hand over his heart, Chance acted hurt. "How could you compare my cooking to Selma's?"

"What is all this white stuff?" Anna took another bite.

"It's gravy. I don't see how you people have a meal without it. I'm used to eating it with everything, including breakfast."

Anna ate another bite and raised her eyebrows.

Chance pointed a spoon at her. "Before long you'll be stirring it up for me every day. All you need is a little grease left from frying meat. And a palmful of flour and some salt. Then when the stuff gets hot, pour in half a skilletful of milk. As it boils it gets thicker. I've eaten at tables where gravy was the main course and the dessert."

Anna laughed, but continued to eat. She looked over at Maggie sitting cross-legged in a chair. The baby rested in her lap and both were sound asleep.

"Look."

Chance followed her gaze. "Selma said Maggie was up most of the night wanting to come over and see how you were."

"I love her dearly," Anna said between bites. "Thanks for agreeing to let her stay with me when you leave."

She didn't miss the hard twitch of the muscle along Chance's jaw, but he didn't say anything.

He tucked Cherish into her crib and carried Maggie to her bed.

Just as Anna thought he was about to speak, the silent morning was shattered by Tobin's yell from outside. He sounded like a man running from the devil. Grabbing his rifle, Chance opened the door.

"Come on out here, son!" Tobin shouted. "I got something you gotta see."

Chance disappeared for a moment, then returned. He leaned his gun against the headboard and asked Anna, "Are you up to being carried outside? There's something I think you should take a look at."

Anna lifted her arms to Chance in answer. She was amazed at how weak she felt. Mrs. Basse had told her to stay in bed at least a week, but surely that didn't include being carried out by Chance.

He lifted her up, blankets and all, and brought her outside. There, standing in front of the house, was a huge sorrel horse. The animal jerked at his rope and pawed the ground with wild, powerful muscles.

"Mornin', Miss Anna." Tobin nodded a greeting. "I hear from the racket that there's a new little Wyatt in the house."

Anna held tight to Chance. "Cherish Julia Wyatt," she said, and felt the muscles across his back tighten slightly. Had he thought she would use her first husband's last name? Or was he just shifting her weight?

"Well, that's real nice." Tobin scratched his dirty hair. "This family seems to be doublin' every time I turn my back. Before long you'll have kids runnin' around here by the dozen. You'll be worse than them Basses."

"Speaking of new arrivals, what about this horse?" Chance asked, changing the subject.

Patting the sorrel's mane, Tobin announced, "This here's a present from Anna's sourdough Indian. He loved your bread and decided to send you a gift."

Anna couldn't believe his words. This horse would have been a fine mount anywhere in Europe; he looked like a champion. He stood taller than any of the mustangs she'd seen and was far more muscular.

"It's a Chickasaw sorrel. I haven't seen a horse this grand since I was up north of the Red River."

Anna couldn't stop staring at the magnificent animal. He was dark red and had four short white socks.

As always, Tobin continued to chatter whether anyone was listening or not. "This is one horse you don't have to worry about some Indian comin' along and stealin'. There ain't an Indian with good sense who'd take a Chickasaw horse. They might buy them, or trade if they can find one, but they never steal them. I reckon they figure an animal like this would be easy to spot and so would the thief."

Chance moved closer so Anna could touch the horse. "I can't believe it," she murmured. "He gave me this for a loaf of bread."

Tobin laughed, making the horse jerk. "Well, I wouldn't say it was just for one loaf of bread. You see, if you take his gift he figures he's welcome in your wigwam anytime. He's liable to be back every baking day."

Anna touched the animal's nose, letting him have a long smell of her hand. "I don't care if it costs me a loaf every week. I have a horse and now I can ride. If there is trouble I can get to help. I can go visit other farms."

Chance pulled her closer. "Now, wait a minute. You've got some recovering to do before you even think about riding. Maybe by that time Tobin and I will have him settled down enough for gentle riding."

Anna would have argued that she could handle any horse she chose, but she was suddenly too tired. She leaned her head against Chance's shoulder and enjoyed being in his strong arms. The clean, masculine smell of him and the habit he had of rubbing her head with his chin made her feel sleepy and happy.

"I'd better get this lady back to bed," Chance said to Tobin. "I'll meet you in the fields in an hour. I've got planting to do, and I could use your help clearing a few stumps."

Nodding, Tobin led the horse off to the corral, still talking, although his only listener was the animal at his side.

Chance carried Anna inside and laid her back down. As he tucked her in, he whispered, "You sleep a while. Selma will check on you in a few hours and I'll be in before dark."

Anna didn't want to let him go. "You're going to work today after being up all night?"

"I've got to get the crop in as soon as possible. I'm not sure how long the season is, and a day or two might make a big difference. You sleep." He leaned over her and brushed her forehead with a kiss.

Closing her eyes, Anna slept, as did Maggie and Cherish—until gunfire rattled the air several hours later.

22

Chance barreled through the door as another pair of shots rang through the air. "Stay in here!" he yelled at Maggie and Anna as he grabbed his rifle. "Maggie, lock the door behind me and don't open it until I call!"

Maggie awoke from her nap, terror draining the color from her face. "Indians," she whispered and didn't need to be answered.

"And you"—Chance looked directly at Anna—"stay in bed."

Before she could speak he was back out the door. Maggie scurried across the floor and locked the door behind him as she'd been told. Then she crawled into bed with Anna and curled under her arm like a frightened animal.

Confused and angry, Anna resented being talked to as though she had no more sense than Maggie, yet she feared whatever could make Chance speak so sharply.

Anna and Maggie listened for another round of fire, but none came. The silence brought no comfort, but instead twisted their nerves tighter. Somewhere outside the safety of these walls, trouble walked on soft feet and the silent knowledge of its nearness was far more terrifying than if there had been constant cannon fire in their ears.

The minutes trickled by and Anna tried to calm Maggie. They played with the baby and talked of ways Maggie could be a help to Anna, like a second mother to tiny Cherish.

Although she made a sock doll for Maggie and told her stories, Anna's ears never stopped straining for the sound of another shot. She found herself watching the door, waiting for someone to try the latch. Once she thought she saw the wood move, but when she looked closer, the bolt was still resting in its slot. Somehow in her mind she believed the illogical: if she continued to stare, she thought, the latch would never move.

Finally, the sound of approaching horses broke the silence, followed by footsteps and low voices. Anna waited, but they didn't come any closer to the house. She couldn't tell who was talking, or even what language they were speaking.

Lifting her baby into her arms, Anna heard the horses retreating. She pulled Cherish tightly against her, preparing to protect the infant with her body. A shout shattered the quiet. Chance yelled for Maggie to unbolt the door and Anna breathed for the first time in several seconds.

Sunshine flooded the room as the door opened and Chance entered. He put his rifle up and collapsed on the bench. Exhaustion showed in the tilt of his head against the back wall of the cabin. "I guess I was a little jumpy. The shots were only to round up all the folks within hearing."

"There were no Indians?" Maggie asked.

"No, honey, there were no Indians." He looked over Maggie's dark curls to Anna and she saw the lie in his eyes.

He tugged at one of his sister's curls. "I'd love to have a cold drink from the stream. Do you think you could run down and fetch me one?"

Maggie was gone even before he could finish the request.

Anna looked directly at Chance. "Tell me!"

Chance rocked forward and rested his head in his hands for a moment. His whole body looked tired, bone tired. "They're warning all the people. The Comanches aren't too happy about us being here. A few of the men are planning to ride north and try to make some kind of peace. They're rounding up more to go, but with Walter Schmitz as the leader, I doubt many will follow."

Standing, Chance paced as if restlessness were being pumped into his body with each heartbeat.

Anna hated to say what she knew was on his mind. "You want to go."

"I should go with them, but with the crops and the baby, I'm needed here. Walter's liable to lead them right into a trap. They need a good gun with them and I'm more than a fair shot. Not one of them knows this country as well as I do."

Anna knew he was wavering, trying to decide what was right. Tobin had told her Chance had one of the fastest guns and surest aims he'd ever seen, and for Tobin to brag about someone other than himself was a rarity. Chance would be a great help to the men, but he was needed here more. She felt so weak she could only move in slow motion, and she wasn't sure she could lift a rifle, much less fire one.

Laying the baby in the crib beside her, Anna watched him. "I know I'll be alone in January when you leave, but I'll be stronger, better prepared then." She looked up into his bottomless blue eyes. "Don't leave me now."

Chance crossed to the bed and sat beside her, pulling her into his arms. He held her tightly, just as she needed to be held, and she felt secure.

"I'll get the crops planted, then I'll scout around for Indians. With any luck they won't be in any hurry to have us gone. Indians have a way of watching and learning an enemy's habits before they strike."

Anna felt safe and content in his arms. His strong hands rested against her back and his chin touched her hair. She knew he wanted to go with the men, but she couldn't bear to part with the one person she had ever leaned on in her life. She was too weak right now. "Stay with me," she whispered into his ear, then felt his body stiffen slightly as he pressed his heart against her own.

Maggie burst into the cabin, breaking the mood, and

was tickled to see them together. She considered Chance a knight in shining armor, and it was only fitting he hold Anna, who was no less than a princess in little Maggie's mind.

Chance downed the water and returned to the fields without another word about leaving. There was so many things Anna would have liked to have said to him, but there was no time, or privacy.

The days passed in a blur of work. Chance was gone from their bed each morning when she awoke, leaving only the memory of his arms holding her during the night. She would see him at meals, but there were always others around, and even after dinner, when the activity of the day settled, Chance continued to work. Well into the night she would finally feel his weight on the bed as an exhausted sigh escaped him. As if almost a reflex, he'd pull her near for warmth and within minutes his regular breathing would slow as it brushed her shoulder. Sometimes, in his sleep, he'd mumble her name, but he never tried to do more than hold her.

July passed and August's hot, steamy days lingered. Anna did all the cooking outside now to keep the cabin cooler. She put Maggie and Cherish on a blanket in the shade of the trees while she worked. She tried to keep busy and not think about Chance's touch, but more and more her mind drifted to the warm feel of his arm lying just below her breasts while they slept. Often she thought of the times she'd felt his heart pounding against her chest as if it were seeking entry into her very soul.

One morning Anna awoke just as dawn crept into the cabin, slicing the air into rows of day and night. She smiled, remembering the way Chance had held her so gently during the night. He seemed so careful, as if she were fragile china that he was only allowed to touch lightly.

Closing her eyes, Anna thought of how she'd miss having him near. The months were sliding by and soon he'd be gone. She wondered how many years it would be before she'd stop aching for his warmth next to her at night. Anna slid her hand out and stroked the sheets where he had lain, gently touching the pillow still indented from his head. She drifted back to sleep, thinking of the unexpected joy he brought her and how welcome it was to be able to lean on someone, if only for a short time.

Chance silently lowered his coffee cup to the table. He'd stepped back inside just before dawn to reload his gun belt. From his place in the shadows, he'd seen Anna stretch and reach for him in bed. He'd been hypnotized by her hand sliding along the sheets where he'd been and he could almost feel her touch on him even now. Her action had been a simple gesture he might never have seen, but it stirred his blood into hot lava.

To fight his need to touch her, he'd been working each day until he dropped. It had taken every ounce of his self-control not to press her body close to his own each night and enjoy the feel of every inch of her. He knew the only way he'd ever have Anna was to take her against her will, and he couldn't do that even if Maggie hadn't been sleeping in the same room. He didn't want to force Anna, he wanted to love her. She'd made it clear she wanted none of his advances. Even when she'd allowed him to hold her that morning she'd been afraid, she'd reminded him that in January he'd be gone and she would be strong enough to be alone.

But then she'd touched the place where he slept. God, how he wished she'd touched him. All day he saw her image before him, even when she wasn't there. Her waist was trim now and her breasts were full. The sight of her feeding Cherish almost blinded him with her beauty, yet she acted as if it were nothing but ordinary. Now as she lay sleeping he fought the urge to touch her.

Using all his willpower, Chance left the cabin and walked the fields. The morning was beautiful and the crops brushed his knee in soft whispers, but all he could see in his mind's

eye was Anna's hand touching the place where he'd slept.
He'd built and planted twice what any other farmer in the
area had. He'd chopped enough wood for winter even
though the air hadn't turned cool at night yet. He'd pushed
himself to the limit and still his need to touch Anna clung to
his every waking thought. She was a storm in his blood that
would tear him apart with its fury if he allowed it to surface.
Each night was a precious hell with her so near, and each
day an agonizing heaven of watching her.

An hour later, when he turned and walked back toward
the house for breakfast, he spotted Tobin's wagon and his
step quickened. The old friend always circled by when he
made a haul. Every few weeks he was bringing Anna
something, usually in exchange for her meals. As Chance
neared he could already hear Tobin's low voice spinning
another yarn. The man had more stories than the Bible and
more ways of telling them than a hundred traveling preach-
ers.

"Mornin', son," Tobin yelled from the door. "I thought
I'd drop by and taste some of your wife's cookin'. Damn if
she ain't the best cook in the country. No wonder that old
Indian, Sourdough, keeps showing up."

Chance hung his gun belt on a nail by the washstand and
splashed himself with water. "He's been around every week
about the time Anna takes the bread from the oven. Never
says a word, just walks in and waits for her to throw him a
loaf."

Anna's laughter sounded from the door. She appeared a
moment later with Maggie at her side. Chance stopped to
stare as he always did when he first saw her. Her hair had
been combed, but she hadn't braided it as she would before
the morning grew warm. Her white blouse was open at the
throat and her long, brown skirt hid the soft moccasins she
always wore. She announced breakfast and disappeared
again.

Staring after her, Chance remembered the way her fingers
had moved over the sheets still warm from his body and for

a moment there was no world outside of his dreams of her.

"Son." Tobin shattered Chance's daydream. "You beat anything I've ever seen in my life."

"What are you talking about?" Chance made his mind and eyes return to the present.

"The way you look at that woman you'd think you didn't sleep with her every night." Tobin's bushy eyebrows shot up almost even with his hairline. "You do sleep with Anna, don't you?"

Chance didn't want to talk about Anna to Tobin. "Of course," he said. "She's my wife."

"She's more than that to you, son. I've had a few wives in my time, but they didn't make me crazy like that woman makes you. She's got a hold on you that a blue norther couldn't loosen."

Chance strapped on his gun again and buttoned his shirt. "I just think she's nice to look at, that's all."

Tobin laughed. "Oh, you think a lot more than that. Just as she does."

"What do you mean?"

Tobin stared at the water in the washbowl as if considering cleaning up, then stepped back as he thought better of his momentary weakness. "I've seen the way she watches you. I saw the fear in her eyes back in the settlement when she thought you were going to die. She wouldn't even let me touch you."

Chance remembered the way she'd washed his skin and head. He could almost feel the way she'd kissed him on his lips now, but since Maggie came she'd shown no sign of wanting to repeat her action. Those sweet kisses had awakened an ache deep inside him, but they seemed to be only a passing fancy to her.

Tobin started toward the cabin. "Before we get around the women, I want to tell you somethin'. Those men who went down to check out the Comanches were found dead last night—all except Walter Schmitz. He sported a bump on the head, but the rest looked like they'd been used as target practice. No one knows if it were the Comanches, the Delawares, or who knows, maybe our friend who loves Anna's bread. Walter claims he can't remember a thing. Anyway, son, I'd keep my gun within twitchin' distance if I were you."

"The Delawares would never attack. They're not war-like." Chance had spent enough time around them to know that Walks Tall was the only one with more than a pinch of hatred for white men.

"That's what I figure too, but a fellow down near the Austin settlement told me a tall Delaware was asking about the folks up here. His description sounded a bit too much like your friend Walks Tall to me. Ya'll might have been buddies since you were kids, but the last time we parted I don't remember you being on too good terms with him."

Chance felt an uneasiness sprout from the tiny patch of worry he'd managed to keep pushed back in his mind. Walks Tall was asking questions. Chance and Anna wouldn't be hard to find in this country. The Indian was on his way—Chance could feel it. But Walks Tall hadn't been the one who'd killed the party of men who'd gone north. That wasn't Walks Tall's way. Someone else was responsible for that and Chance would bet anything that Walter knew who.

Resting his hand lightly on Tobin's shoulder, Chance whispered as they entered the cabin, "No need to worry Anna."

23

Tobin left after breakfast, but the uneasiness he'd brought clung to Chance all day. He worked hard cutting and hauling logs for the house, which he'd promised Anna he'd build before the first snowfall. Tobin had even agreed to haul a few loads of lumber if he had time so that she'd have a real floor and not just packed dirt to sweep.

At noon Chance didn't bother to stop to eat more than a few apples. He knew Anna and Selma were busy drying fruit and washing today. They were probably too busy talking to notice whether he came home for lunch. The dried apples and peaches would taste heavenly this winter, baked in one of Anna's pies. Anna was already getting a few vegetables from the garden and in another month the dugout would be full of stores of winter food. He'd even hauled sand in from the creak one evening last week and dug a deep hole in the cool earth to keep the potatoes fresh all winter. The crop would be good and there'd be enough to feed any neighbors who hadn't known what to plant.

When the afternoon sun finally drove Chance toward the shade, he noticed Anna riding toward him on her sorrel, which she'd named Cinnamon. He had to admire the way she handled the huge animal. She'd had a few laughs when he'd tried to give her riding lessons one evening last month. It made him proud that she was self-reliant and a little hurt that she didn't need him. She was just the kind of woman he'd want to raise his children; just the kind to stand by a man's side in this country; and just the kind who would never consider anything but a gentleman. He knew he could never be what she needed. He'd heard Walter say once that Anna's first husband had spoken five languages and had completed college. Chance sometimes had trouble getting English to come out right and he'd never even been inside a school of any kind.

Moving to help her down as she reached the shade, he couldn't help but notice how she slid into his arms and for a moment he didn't want to let her go. He wanted to press her body against his damp chest and make the hot day even hotter for them both.

Anna spun around and handed him the canteen. "I brought you water."

"Thanks," Chance answered. He downed several gulps, trying not to notice the way moisture sparkled on the warm skin at her throat.

"Maggie took Cherish over to Selma's. I thought you might ride over with me to the Mormons' camp. Tobin says they're very kind people and they have a way with bees. If we had a hive of bees, we wouldn't have to buy honey or wax."

Chance didn't want to quit work yet, but he wasn't about to let her go alone either. He had a feeling there was no use arguing with her about going. "I'll ride over with you."

The afternoon proved very informative. The small Mormon community had several hives and they were glad to show Chance and Anna how to build one. They twisted and bound a rope of long grass, then circled it into a cone much like a woman circles her hair atop her head. They told Chance all about how to get started and promised to drop by in a week to see if he was applying any of the lessons he'd learned. Chance found the people straightlaced and honest, but he didn't much hold with the practice of having more than one wife, though they seemed to have it working smoothly.

All afternoon Anna was near him, touching his arm to show him something, laughing when the Mormons teased him about having only one wife, and smiling the quiet smile that told Chance just how happy she felt. He couldn't help but wonder what her life must have been like in Germany if something as simple as beekeeping could excite her so.

Before sunset Chance and Anna returned home. There was a low bank of clouds to the north that promised rain and colored the evening sky a violet no artist could ever capture on canvas. Anna talked the entire way home about all the things she could do if she had honey and wax. She took great pleasure in planning her life and her future with Cherish and Maggie.

Chance was silent, his emotions as brooding as the clouds. He rubbed down the horses and took a long swim in the creek while Anna cooked supper. When he returned to the cabin, the food was on the table and Anna was sitting in a chair nursing Cherish. He sat down and ate, making no pretense at doing anything but watching Anna. He loved the way she looked with a child in her arms. Her soft song filled the cabin with peace. When she smiled and kissed the baby's curly blond hair it brought pleasure to him beyond any he'd ever known.

Maggie crawled into Chance's lap as he finished his coffee. "I hear thunder," she said. "It sounds like drums."

Chance cradled his little sister in his arms. "It's only thunder," he whispered as he kissed her cheek. But the uneasiness that had begun with Tobin's visit stayed with him. He wanted to tell Anna that the men had been found dead, but he didn't want Maggie to be more frightened than she was already. He'd have to tell Anna sometime or she'd be heading off alone as she almost had today, unaware of the danger.

Looking up from his thoughts, he noticed Anna staring at his hand as he patted Maggie's back. There was a look of longing in her lovely eyes. Did she wish to be a child in his protective arms? Or did she want his touch in a different way? Their eyes met and for a moment his heart outsounded the thunder. The need he saw in the green depths of her eyes had nothing to do with the longings of a child. She was thinking of him—just as she had thought of him at dawn when she'd touched the sheets where he'd lain.

Anna broke the spell. "She's asleep," Anna whispered.

Chance looked down at Maggie cuddled in his arms. He slowly lifted her and carried her to bed, kissing her forehead as he covered her up. When he returned he felt awkward, first shoving his fists into his pockets, then moving to the low fire. He felt like a boy at his first dance, not someone who'd lived next to Anna for eight months.

Trying to sound conversational, he began, "Tobin said the two men who went north last month were found dead. Somehow Walter walked away with only a bump on his head."

He heard Anna's sharp intake of breath. "You wanted to go with them," she whispered.

Chance shrugged. "Who knows, maybe if I'd been along they might be alive." He hated to think that he'd made the wrong decision. "After all, they didn't know the land or the Indians in these parts."

"Or you'd be dead." Anna's words were barely audible.

He took one look at her frightened face and knew he wouldn't tell her about Walks Tall. She had enough to worry about. This one warning would keep her near the house. He shouldn't have told her about the men, but she was bound to find out about them eventually.

"There's talk of sending others to try again."

"No!" Anna stood and laid the baby in her crib. "You won't go."

He resented her order and yet was curious about her reason. "I haven't decided yet." His voice deepened in warning for he was not a man to take orders. He'd lived too many years alone to allow someone else, even Anna, to dictate his actions.

She didn't take the hint, for all she could think of was that she didn't want him to leave. The picture of someone coming to her and telling her he was dead flashed in her mind with a sudden horror. "I don't want you to go."

"Why?" Chance could feel hope rise in his veins. Could she really, finally feel something for him? He took a step toward her. "Why shouldn't I go?"

Anna looked confused and suddenly unable to meet his stare. He could see a battle raging within her by the nervous way she pressed her hands together and her short intakes of breath. Then, slowly, her chin lifted and he knew pride had won. "You can't go because you haven't finished out your year. You gave your word."

His hopes crumbled.

"Then," Chance grabbed his rifle and was out the door before he finished his sentence, "I'd better get to work. I wouldn't want you to feel I cheated you."

He stormed across the yard until he reached the darkest part of the corral.

Leaning against the barn wall, he pushed his shoulders into the wood. What was the matter with him? Or was it her? He no longer knew where the trouble lay. The sky cracked apart with lightning and Chance felt like his heart was splitting also. Moving into the wooded area beside the stream, he leaned against an aging pecan tree and listened to the raindrops plopping into the stream. Dear God, how he wished the rain could wash her from his mind; but she was there, carved into his very heart, and she would be there until the day he died. Yet every time he tried to get closer, she pushed him away as easily as she swept dust from the steps.

Anna was within a few feet of him before he heard her soft steps. He whirled, his gun ready as she moved under the protection of the trees. In the flashing light she looked nervous and Chance knew the lightning bothered her as much as it did Maggie.

"I've come to talk with you alone." Anna's voice was shaking as the storm continued to frighten her.

"Now's a good time. There isn't a soul alive who'll hear

us over this storm." He wanted to hold her, to brush away
her fear, but her stance told him she'd come to talk, and she
planned to say what was on her mind, storm or no storm.
"So if you came out to here to say something, get it said."

"It's not your place to go settle things with the Indians.
Let the men of the colony fight this battle." Anna shot out
at Chance with an anger born of fear.

Resting one hand on the branch above her head, Chance
yelled over the thunder, "I know you consider me your
hired hand, but I care about this settlement. I don't have to
be German to hope these people aren't murdered. If I left
and made peace for them with the Indians, we'd all be safer
in the long run."

Anna could feel the blood climbing up her neck like fire
over dry brush. "You will not go!" she screamed, then bit
her lip as if to bite back the words.

"What is that? Another order?" Chance was so close she
could feel the heat of his words upon her face, but she stood
there, silent and proud, as he continued. "Are you ordering
me, or mothering me? You seem to do quite a lot of both.
I'm a man, not your slave or your child."

Anna's old fears stirred inside her. "I'm older than you."
She said the words as if they mattered, while hot tears stung
her eyes and the cool wind brushed her cheeks in bone-
chilling contrast.

With force born of desperation, Chance's arm went
around her waist, slamming her against the hard wall of his
chest before she could react. "I'm man enough to be a
husband to you." Chance's words were low in her ear as his
lips slid across her cheek and found her mouth. He'd
wanted to hold her like this for so long, wanted to feel her
body yielding to his. "I'm man enough to give you what
you want, Anna."

His kiss was hard and demanding, bearing all the desire
he'd bottled up inside him over the months. As the minutes
passed and she didn't fight, Chance's mouth softened. He
tasted the sweetness of Anna's lips as he'd longed to do

every day and night they'd been together. Her body felt so right in his arms. Her full breasts flattened against his chest, almost driving him insane with their softness. She smelled of soap and honey and home.

Covering her mouth with his own, he moved his hands along her back, molding her to him with each stroke. Her lips opened in a soft cry and he tasted the inside of her mouth. It was far sweeter than he'd imagined. Without letting her mouth free, he slid his finger to her shoulder and pulled the blouse open with one tug. Her breast stood exposed to the damp air only a moment before his hand covered it. The softness of her was maddening as he moved his fingers over the flesh he'd seen so often. The touch of her skin against his palm satisfied a need as deep inside him as the need to breathe. He circled her tender mound and felt the nipple tighten to the touch of his callused hand.

Breaking his kiss, he moved his mouth against her hair and whispered, "Dear God, you feel so wonderful. How I've dreamed of touching you like this—of holding you." She didn't move but remained still even as he kissed her neck and pulled her waist against the center of his need. "Anna, do you know how you've taught me desire these past months? I've never known such a fire. You are so lovely, my Anna, my wife."

He was drunk with her nearness. He'd sipped passion's awakening all day with the memory of the way she'd touched the sheets where he'd lain. He knew she wanted him, but he'd never dreamed he'd hold her in anything but a protective embrace. Now he'd opened the door to passion and it flooded his senses, overwhelming him with pleasure. He held her against him with one iron arm as his free hand roamed her body, loving the feel of her against him. As his fingers moved into her hair, he gently pulled, drawing her head back so he could once more taste her mouth. She was motionless in his arms as he bruised her lips in his eagerness and allowed his fingers to move from her neck down her open blouse to her breasts. Her flesh was softer than anything he'd ever touched and he spread his palm wide to feel every wonderful inch. Lightning flashed and she jerked as he pulled the material free to her waist, but he held her tighter, kissing her deeply to stop all her fears.

Chance pulled slightly away to look into her beautiful green eyes and see the dark fires burning in her as well—but there were none. He'd seen love when she'd looked at the baby and laughter when she talked with Maggie and determination when she'd argued; but never had he seen passion and there was none now.

The sight before him sobered Chance. He saw only stone coldness in her green depths. There was no fire, no desire. Her eyes were as lifeless as a china doll's in a store window. She stared straight ahead in terror, her hands at her sides, her breathing only a shallow whisper.

Fear touched Chance's heart. "Anna, what's wrong? What's the matter?" She was acting as if she'd never tasted passion on a man's lips, as if she'd never known love. He cupped her face in his hands. "Anna, what is the matter!" he screamed, not even knowing if she could hear him.

Her words froze the air between them. "You are my husband. Would you rape me and leave me with child as my first husband did?"

Chance's arm dropped. All the anger, all the bitterness passed from him and a sorrow as wide as a river filled him. He felt he might drown in the pain of her words.

"Anna, I wasn't raping you. I'd never rape you. I thought you wanted my touch, my kiss. If you didn't, why didn't you fight me or push me away?"

"I fought once. I fought with all my strength. He beat me unconscious and slowly raped me." Anger was tightening the strings of her emotions. She gulped air as if someone had been smothering her; then her words exploded from her. "Each time I came to enough to scream, he hit me again. He'd cover my mouth with his own as he pounded his fists into my body. When I'd stop screaming, he'd slap me over and over just to make sure I wouldn't make a sound, then he'd start raping me again, all the time saying he was sorry. All the time calling my mother's name."

Anna turned to run but Chance grabbed her arm. "Stay," he ordered. "I want to hear it all." Hearing her words was like looking at some horrible painting. He wanted to turn away, but he had to look closer.

"No!" Anna screamed and pulled away like a frightened animal caught in a trap.

"Yes!" Chance answered. "There is too much between us for you not to be honest now. Tell me, by God, or I swear we'll stand here all night."

Anna gulped back the tears and nodded. The whole world seemed to be crying for her. "The night I was raped, I found out my husband . . . and mother were lovers. He'd married me so that he could have my mother in his house without scandal since we had no proof that my father was dead. I was young and naive enough to believe he only wanted to protect me because he'd been a friend of the family all my life." She held her blouse closed with both hands. "He'd told me he was unable to do what men and women do when they are married. When he asked me to marry him, he promised never to come to my bed. I was to remain his wife to society and in exchange he'd provide for me and my mother. Only as I grew older I looked more and more like my mother had when they'd met, and William grew bored with her."

Chance pulled Anna into his arms and stroked her hair as she cried. "Don't be afraid of me, Anna," he whispered, but she was stiff in his arms. "I'm not William. I could never hurt you."

Looking up, Anna saw only the past as she added, "William planned to leave mother and take me with him to America. They'd had a horrible fight the night he raped me. It was stormy outside, and I thought their words were part of the thunder for a long time. Then, half drunk, he came to my room as if by doing so he would end the argument between them once and for all. At first I thought he only wanted to frighten me. I thought he was playing one of the games with me he sometimes played to show he had power. I cried for my mother's help. When she saw William in my bed she ran screaming, not caring about me. She didn't even try to stop him from raping me. William took great pleasure in telling me how many times he'd mounted my mother while we had been married. And each time I cried, he'd slap me over and over, yelling for me to stay quiet until he was through with me. Then he'd climb on top of me and call me by her name." Anna was silent for a long moment.

Thunder rattled more tears loose from the clouds as she continued. "We found her the next morning floating in the lake. It wasn't me she cared about, but the loss of her lover. If she'd cared for me at all, she never would have left me alone with him. I watched her body riding on the muddy water and I didn't care that she was dead, because part of me was dead also."

Anna pushed away from Chance. "William grieved for her and blamed me for her death. He promised never to touch me again if I'd come with him. When he was sober, he could be quite rational. The only thing we shared was a desire to keep the reason for my mother's death a secret. We let the town believe she'd gone mad."

Turning to face the dim light coming from the cabin, Anna continued. "I had no family, no home. I had to come with William. But one night on board the ship he took me again, the same as before. Only this time I knew better than to scream and take a beating with the rape."

"But wouldn't the folks on board help?" Chance saw the hatred of all men in her eyes.

"No man would interfere with a married couple. If anything, they would have hated me. They already saw how cold I was toward him and whispered about it. All I could do was lay there and pray for the pain to end. He was drunk and already a little sick from the bad food. It took a long time and afterward I went on deck to vomit. I thought of throwing myself into the ocean, but the memory of my mother's floating body kept me from taking my own life."

"I'm so sorry." Chance wanted to comfort her, but she stepped back each time he neared.

Anna lifted her chin. "I don't want your pity and I don't want your love. I don't want anything from you beyond our bargain and your word that come January you'll be gone. Every man I've ever known has lied to me. I'd like to know that once, just once, there was a man who would keep his word."

"Anna . . .," Chance whispered.

Raising her hand as though she could stop anything he was about to say, she shouted, "No. Don't say more. I'm not like my mother. I'm strong. I don't need anyone."

Showing no sign of even feeling the rain that pounded from above, she ran back to the house. For months he'd thought she couldn't bear his touch because she'd known another love, and now he knew all proud, silent Anna had ever known was rape.

Chance stared up at the sky, not knowing if the water on his face was rain or tears. One realization hit him like a bolt of white lightning. He loved Anna and would love her till the day he died . . . even if he never touched her again.

24

The rain continued through most of the night and soaked Chance to the bone as he sat beneath the trees watching the cabin. He wanted to follow Anna, but he knew she would only see him as part of the problem. His hatred for her first husband was so strong he knew he could easily have killed the man if William were still alive. How could any man have treated Anna so badly? How could he have frightened her so completely that she'd lost the instinct to fight?

Cursing himself, Chance remembered the rough way he'd pulled her into his arms and kissed her. He thought over all the times she'd stared at him and let him kiss her lightly, without passion. He thought of the way she'd touched the sheets and watched his hand when he'd stroked Maggie. She wanted him, he was sure of it, but not in the way he'd reasoned. She wanted to be held and protected, but not loved—not in the way a man loves a woman.

Chance swore in every language he knew. He wondered if he could live with Anna the rest of the year and never do more than hold her. Would she allow him even that after the way he'd acted? Could he leave and prove his honor when the year was over even though the cost would be his very soul? Her nearness had taught him the meaning of desire, and now her withdrawal would test his self-control.

As a golden dawn spread across the hills, Chance picked

up two buttons from the wet grass. He held them in his fist and set his will to iron.

A few moments later he walked into the cabin. Not a sound came from the shadows, but the smell of coffee welcomed him. Anna was sitting at the table. He knew she'd heard him come in, but she didn't look up. She was slowly picking the hairs from her brush and storing them in her hair receiver.

"Morning," Chance whispered as he poured himself a cup of coffee and straddled the bench beside her.

Anna looked up at him, her eyes red and puffy from crying. "You're dripping wet." She stood to get a towel.

"Wait." Chance stopped her with a hand on her arm. He could feel her stiffen at his touch. "It doesn't matter. I'll get some dry clothes in a minute."

Sitting back down, she pulled her arm from his grip, rubbing her hand over her sleeve as though his touch had scorched the material.

Chance took one long gulp of the hot coffee before he spoke. He sat his cup down and held out the buttons toward her. "I'm sorry about this."

Anna stared at the buttons. "I can sew them back on."

Covering her hand with his own, he wished he could patch the gap between them with a needle and thread. "We've got some things that need saying between us."

"But Maggie might . . ."

"Maggie's asleep." Chance lowered his voice. "I've thought about it all night and maybe we should be honest with each other."

"I have been honest." Anna lifted her chin. She tried to pull her hand away, but he held it fast.

Chance stroked her fingers. "In what you say, but not in what you do. Tell me, Anna, how you can snuggle up to me each night and not want my kiss? I'm not trying to hurt you, but I feel like a blind man in a maze. Every time I take a turn I end up hurting you." Chance let go of her hand and ran his fingers through his damp hair. "Maybe it's not you;

maybe it's me. I haven't been around that many women. You're so hard to read. I'm tired of guessing what you want from me."

"I don't want anything from you." Anna stood and moved to the fireplace. She leaned into the solid brick wall as if the stone could give her comfort.

Chance was only a step behind. "Like hell you don't," he whispered. "I've seen you watching me. I've seen the way you look at me when I hug Maggie. You want something, maybe more than I can give, but for the life of me I can't seem to figure out what it is."

Anna would have moved away, but Chance pinned her in the corner. His breath brushed the curls at the side of her face, while his powerful hands pushed her shoulders against the wall. "Tell me what you want, Anna, before I go mad."

Her eyes were filled with sadness. She no longer had the power to hide her pain from him. She'd told him too much of her past to ever turn back. "I want to feel safe," she whispered.

"What?" He relaxed his hold but didn't step away.

"I want to feel safe. I'm tired of being afraid. I'm tired of waiting for the evil side of every man to strike. I want to be held in your arms the way you hold Maggie." Tears filled her eyes. A single drop drifted down her cheek and drowned his heart with its pain. "I've never had anyone to hold me, and sometimes I think if you'd only hold me until you leave, I could make it last me a lifetime."

Chance's arms went around her, pulling her gently to him. "I'll hold you, Anna. I'll hold you."

The warmth of her body pressed into the cold dampness of his clothes. "Anna, I wasn't going to hurt you last night. I only wanted to love you. Making love isn't something horrible. I've dreamed of how it would be with you. I wouldn't hurt you; I'd love you. I thought you wanted it too. That was the reason I kissed you during the storm."

"No," Anna answered. "Never."

"Then I'll hold you each day until I leave." Chance

closed his eyes to the precious hell he was committing himself to. "Just don't ever be afraid of me again. I could show you that passion is not something ugly and evil, but I'll wait until you ask." How could she be this close to him and not feel a spark of the fire that raged within him?

"I'll never ask," Anna whispered as she relaxed against him.

He lifted her into his arms and carried her to the bed; then he laid her down gently and covered them both with blankets. She held tightly to him as he stroked her hair and whispered words of comfort in her ear. "Sleep, Anna. You're safe. I swear I'd never hurt you. Sleep, my love."

Anna lay her head against his shoulder and slept, but Chance lay awake for a long time. He'd almost lost her, but finally he understood her.

The rain continued all day. Chance stayed in the cabin most of the time, playing with Maggie and Cherish. Anna cooked meals and did mending, but the loss of a night's sleep made her actions a little slower. A peace settled between them, wrapping them in a blanket of small talk that warmed and healed them both.

The sun set, but they didn't bother to light candles. Maggie crawled into her high bed in the back corner and was asleep within seconds. Anna watched Chance rocking the baby in his arms. He was dozing off faster than the baby. Anna prepared the bed, then undressed in the darkest corner. She slipped into bed while Chance stood and placed Cherish in her crib.

As he stripped down to his undergarments, Anna watched him and realized he'd been right. She did enjoy watching him. His back was strong and tan and the muscles rippled as he stretched. He had a powerful grace about him.

Finally, Chance pulled the covers aside and rolled in, slamming his body against a hard piece of wood in the center of the bed.

"What's this!" He sat up and pulled up the long board that lay between them.

"It's called a bundling board. I've heard folks tell about using them in the colonies." Anna laughed at his confused expression. "In winter when a man comes to visit and there's no place for him to sleep, they place a board between the couple. Then all is proper. I put it in while you were feeding the animals."

Chance stood, pulling the board with him. "And you thought . . ."

Anna sat up. "I thought that would solve our problem of sleeping together."

The sharp snap of the board startled her. Chance threw the pieces into the fireplace and returned to bed. "The only wall that lies between us is your past. Do you really think one board would keep me from you?"

Anna hugged her side of the bed. "But I thought it would be easier." She clutched the sheet.

Laying beside her, Chance pulled her gently under his arm. "You have my word. I'll not take you against your will. It is a hell of my own making, and I'll be damned if a board will make any difference."

Anna fought back the old fears. He'd made no pretense of hiding his passion, but he had stopped when she'd asked. His arms felt so wonderful around her and she wanted to fall asleep on his shoulder.

"Anna, don't be afraid." Chance moved his hand along her back. "I'm not going to hurt you. I'll not even touch you if you like. If we can talk, we can understand each other."

"Tell me," she whispered, "how loving is different from rape. I see many women who don't look like they've been hurt each night, yet they sleep with husbands and have children every year, so they must be mating."

Chance tensed slightly, then forced his body to relax. How could he tell her all about love when he'd never made love to anyone? He remembered listening to his parents laughing and whispering long after they'd sent the children to bed. His mother would always get up and tiptoe in to tuck him in when the whispering stopped. Her hair would be tossed and her cheeks red, but she'd always be smiling as if a laugh were just an inch beneath the surface.

"Loving is a giving, not a taking," Chance finally answered.

Almost asleep, Anna nodded slightly. She'd gone without any sleep the night before and now the warmth of Chance next to her was intoxicating.

"When you let me love you," Chance whispered as he kissed her ear with his words, "I'll show you the difference. I've dreamed of holding you, of running my hand along your body with no clothes to mask the feel of your flesh. Someday you'll come to me and I'll show you my dream."

Anna's breathing was low and regular as she slept.

"Someday," Chance whispered, "I'll move inside you and you'll cry out with joy, not pain. I'll show you how much I love you. We'll taste passion together for the first time and drink our fill of one another."

Chance rolled closer to her, feeling her breasts flatten against his chest. Sliding his hand along her side to her shoulder, he slowly pulled the ribbon that bound her hair. "Let your hair free, Anna. Let you hair free when you come to me."

He lay awake for a long time, breathing in the wonder of her. He knew he could touch her anywhere and she'd probably not awaken, but he wasn't sure he could stop himself if he were any closer. Leaning his face into her hair, he whispered, "Dear God, how I love you, Anna. I love you enough not to touch you even though by the laws of man and nature I have every right."

With loving gentleness he combed her hair with his fingers. "I love you so much that I'll move slowly. I'll go one step at a time until you want my dream as much as I do." She moved slightly, adjusting her body to his side. He kissed the top of her head and fought the urge to roll over and cover her with his body.

Slowly, as evening passed, Chance fell asleep to the soft patter of rain that concealed the movement of moccasined feet outside the cabin.

25

Cyoty's whinny drew Chance from his place beside Anna. Like a mother knows her child's cries, he knew from the sound that something was wrong. He pulled on his pants, then walked to the edge of the bed, hating to wake Anna if it was a false alarm, but fearing what might happen if someone stumbled on her while she slept.

"Anna," Chance whispered as he buckled his gun belt, "something's going on out in the corral. I'm heading out to have a look."

Stretching, she pushed her hair from her face. The worry in his eyes drew her fully awake. She glanced at his gun, knowing if he thought it was a wild animal he'd have only taken his rifle. The gun he wore at his waist was for trouble that might take more than one shot. He stood before her with both guns. "Be careful," she whispered.

Chance leaned over and kissed her cheek. "Bolt the door when I leave."

Anna followed him, watching, as, shirtless and bare-footed, he moved silently out the door and up the steps. She closed the door as he disappeared into the gray light of dawn. A sudden chill covered her even though it was a warm fall morning. Anna slipped into her blue wrapper and moved to the window. She was thankful that Chance had built the windows high and too small for a person to slip through. If anyone wanted to get in the cabin he'd have to come through the front door and the bolt would hold anyone out.

The yard was silent, but Anna could feel danger. There were no birds welcoming the dawn. The cow in the corral was making no sound for someone to come milk her. Even the dust was motionless. Danger floated in the air like a thick, odorless vapor.

Glancing around the cabin, Anna realized she might need a weapon. There was only the knife of Chance's that she carried in her apron. It was small, but it might help protect her and the children. She poured water into the pot and shoved it over the low fire. If anyone came through the door, he'd have a scalding bath waiting. She searched the room, lining up everything that might be used as a weapon.

Maggie awoke. "Anna," she called as she pushed back her hair. "Is something wrong?"

Anna tried to smile. "No, dear. Get dressed as quietly as you can. I may need you to help me."

The sound of a gunshot rattled through the cabin. Anna raced to the window with Maggie close behind. The child couldn't see out at any window except where her bed was and it faced the back of the cabin.

"What is it?" She pulled at Anna's arm.

Searching the shadows for movement, Anna whispered, "Maybe just a mountain lion trying to get the calf. I don't see anything."

Relaxing, Maggie finished dressing, but Anna never removed her eyes from the empty space between the barn and the cabin.

A shadow moved by the corral. Another shifted among the trees. Anna felt her hand tighten around the knife in her pocket. She listened, straining to hear. Slowly, as if he had materialized on the spot, a tall Indian stepped from the shadows beside the barn.

"Chance!" he shouted at the barn door. "Come out. I mean you no harm. I've come for the child."

Anna's heart tightened. It was Walks Tall, and though he

was the only one she could see, she knew he was not alone.

Chance stepped from the barn. His stance was wide, his arms deceptively relaxed at his sides. "I've got five bullets that say you're not taking that baby."

The two men stared at one another, the hatred of a lifetime between them. Anna felt panic climb up her spine and explode in her brain. Chance probably could fight Walks Tall and win, but how many more were out there? How many would he have to fight before one finally knocked the door in and took her child?

She darted to the crib and lifted Cherish into her arms. "Maggie, can you run through the woods to Selma?"

Maggie tried not to look frightened. "Yes."

Anna pulled her toward the back of the cabin. "Take Cherish and run as fast as you can. Don't look back." Sending Maggie into the woods alone was dangerous, but it was better than all of them being trapped in the cabin. "Don't turn around no matter what you hear. Do you understand?"

Maggie nodded, her curls bouncing and her lips quivering with fear.

Anna climbed on Maggie's bed, then lifted her up. She helped Maggie slide through the back window. Then Anna passed her baby to the little girl. "Run!" she whispered. "*Run!*"

Maggie vanished without a sound into the trees behind the dugout. As she watched them go, Anna wanted to cry, but there was no time. Now that her child was safe she had to help Chance.

With no thought of her own safety, she ran to the front window. The two men were still facing one another. Walks Tall was pacing back and forth while Chance watched him, his fingers ready to lift his gun in a second.

Biting her bottom lip to keep from screaming, Anna watched what looked like stars twinkling just out of her line of vision. A man was in the trees, another by the stream, a third on the roof of the barn.

Just as she opened her mouth in warning, the one on the roof sprang like a huge bird falling on its prey. Chance twisted and pulled his gun just as the Indian's body hit him full force in the back. In a blink they were on him. Five, maybe six Indians.

"No!" she screamed as he fought them all. She couldn't allow them to kill Chance. He had to have help. Grabbing her knife, she unbolted the door and ran toward the men in a fury. The sound of fists hitting flesh filled the air in steady, painful beats, and the dust danced around the men as they twisted and turned in the battle.

As she reached the end of the steps, strong arms seemed to come from nowhere to grab her from behind. The knife was twisted from her hand with a mighty yank. The blade flew across the yard like a harmless toy. An Indian twice her weight slammed her against the mound of earth by the front door. His powerful forearm was shoved beneath her chin and his knee pressed against her chest.

Anna's struggles stopped as all air rushed from her lungs and her throat closed with the pressure of his arm. When she was still for a moment, he jerked at her shoulder and rolled her onto her stomach. He almost pulled her arms from their sockets as he grabbed her wrists and bound them tightly behind her. Anna could feel the thin cord cut into her skin as the sound of someone tearing up every inch of the cabin reached her. Cringing, she heard what must have been the crib being slammed against the stone of the fireplace.

Without a word, the Indian filled his fist with her hair and yanked her up with no more care than he would show to a wild animal. When her feet twisted in her skirts, he let her fall hard against the packed earth, then he jerked her upright again and shoved her toward the fight. Anna tasted her own blood. A bruise spread pain along her cheek. Sweat and blood blended with the dirt on her face, but she wouldn't allow herself to cry out. She would not show fear. She would not!

The Indian shoved her again as if testing her strength.

Anna fell once more to the ground, her shoulder breaking her fall. The Indian grabbed her robe and jerked her to her feet. He didn't herd her forward this time, but pulled out his hunting knife and pressed the blade against her throat.

"Stop!" Walks Tall's voice resounded in the yard. All the Indians backed away from Chance, who stood ready to fight. His eyes were wild with rage and the taste of death. Turning, he saw Anna for the first time. His intelligent, angry blue eyes darted from her to Walks Tall.

"Do not move or I will tell my brother to kill your woman." Walks Tall ventured closer to Chance as though testing the ground with each step.

Cocking his head slightly, Chance's words flowed like liquid iron across the still air. "You wouldn't kill a woman. You aren't a coward."

The Indian thought for a moment. "You are right. I would not. But I will hurt her if you do not allow them to tie you up. I will cut her hair away from her scalp so that none will ever grow there."

"I'll kill you and all your tribe if you touch her," Chance vowed.

Walks Tall laughed. "The way you always say you will kill Storm's Edge? You have made that oath since we were children, yet I see he roams north of here without any fear of you. I have killed ten soldiers for every one of my family who died. And you—you have done nothing."

Two Indians grabbed Chance's arms and bound them to a beam on the barn. Chance's eyes were filled with hatred, but he didn't move as he watched the Indian who held Anna.

Walks Tall moved closer to Chance. "I have no wish to kill you or your woman. You taught me much about the white people, as I taught you of Indian ways. I only want the baby. My wife grows more ill each day with fear that your child will kill mine. She has not eaten for over a moon's full journey. I will put an end to this. The two of you can live in peace. You can have more children. You people breed like wild mustangs on our land."

"Damn you!" Chance yelled, and kicked Walks Tall, almost knocking him down with the blow.

Walks Tall steadied himself and ran toward Chance, silencing the white man. Anger and hatred inflamed the Indian's face. He plowed into Chance with all his force, with the same anger he'd never been able to bridle since his youth.

Horrified, Anna watched as Chance took blow after blow without a sound or a cry. He twisted and pulled against his ropes, trying to free himself to fight back, but the ropes held and Walks Tall continued to vent his anger. Blood was dripping down Chance's arms from where he had twisted his wrists raw against the ropes. More blood sprayed from his mouth as Walks Tall doubled his fists together and swung a blow into his face.

Finally, Chance went limp, his head resting against his chest. Walks Tall jerked his head up by his hair. "Tell me where your child is or I swear I will end this game between us right now. I will let you watch while I make your woman scream for death's darkness, then I will kill you and burn all traces of you on this land. I can live no longer with the curse of Medicine Man's woman to haunt my family."

Chance's lip was swollen and blood dripped out of his mouth in a steady stream. "If you hurt Anna I'll cut your eyes out and you will walk the Forever Land blind."

As Walks Tall doubled back to strike him again, a scream sounded from the trees. In horror, Anna watched an Indian pull Maggie into the clearing. He yelled something to the others and dragged her forward. Maggie's arms were tight around the bundle she carried and tears were streaming down her face as she cried in fear.

The Indian pulled her before Walks Tall. He tried to lift the baby from her arms, but she fought him with all her might.

It took two of them to pull Cherish from her. Maggie screamed as Walks Tall lifted the tiny baby in the air.

Anna twisted and strained against the Indian who held her. She felt the knife's blade cut into her flesh as he pulled her tight.

"No!" Maggie screamed. "Don't hurt the baby. I tried to get to Selma, but they caught me."

The flat back of a brave's hand silenced the little girl's cry. Her tiny body rolled across the ground until she hit the wall of the cabin. One of Walks Tall's men went to stand next to her, grabbing her limp arm as if to ensure there would be no more interruptions from Maggie.

Anna suddenly remembered the shot she'd first heard when Chance went outside. If Carl heard it, he would be here in a few minutes. She glanced at Walks Tall as he pulled the blankets from Cherish. Carl would be of little help. He wasn't a good enough shot to fire from the trees, and if he ran into the fight, he would receive the same beating Chance had.

"Wait," Chance yelled as Walks Tall raised his hunting knife to pierce the child. "Undress the child."

Walks Tall hesitated. "Why?"

Chance spit blood and struggled to speak. "Because the baby is a girl. You said you have a son. Is the mighty Walks Tall's son so afraid of a woman that he would have his father kill the girl as a baby?"

Walks Tall was disturbed by Chance's words. "I swore to my woman that I would end the threat."

"What kind of a threat can a white baby girl be to the brave son of Walks Tall?" Chance watched the knife at Anna's throat lower slightly. "You will have to kill all of us and all the braves who are with you to keep the story from spreading. Your son will be disgraced for years when he must live with the shame that his father didn't think he could protect himself from a woman."

Walks Tall pulled the clothes from the baby to make sure what Chance said was true. He then dropped Cherish in the dirt as if she were below his level of interest. She continued to cry, angry but alive. The Indian holding Maggie let her go and she ran to the baby. She huddled over Cherish as if the little girl could protect the child with her body.

Walks Tall straightened in pride. "No son of my blood would fear a woman." He motioned for all the men to mount horses that had been hidden behind the trees. He was too proud to even think of being sorry for what he'd done, but he stopped as he passed Anna. "I will tell all to leave this place in peace."

Anna wanted to spit in his face. He'd almost killed Chance and her child, and now he was walking away as though all he'd done was pay them a casual visit. He saw the hatred in her eyes and the strong set of her jaw. He swung onto his pony and although his words were for Chance, his gaze never left Anna. "You have a strong woman. She will bear you sons someday."

In a cloud of dust he and all his braves were gone, leaving only the sound of Cherish's whimpering and Maggie's crying to fill the air.

Hurrying to Maggie, Anna shouted, "Get the knife and cut my hands free."

Maggie scrambled for the knife, then cut Anna's ropes. "I'm sorry, Anna. I tried to get to Selma's."

Anna hugged her. "You did the best you could. You were wonderful. I'm very proud of you. If you hadn't gotten her away for a while, they might have killed her."

Maggie smiled and cradled Cherish. "They didn't hurt her any, just scared her. She's just screaming now 'cause she's mad."

"Take her inside, darling." Anna lifted Cherish into Maggie's arms. "I know you can take good care of her while I cut Chance loose."

Anna kissed Maggie's curls and ran to the barn.

He was hanging by his arms with his head down, blood dripping from his mouth and a large gash at his hairline. For a moment Anna's heart stopped as she feared he might have died.

When she touched his shoulder he jerked toward her. His chest and face were covered with bruises and blood and his left eye was almost swollen shut. "Anna," he whispered as she leaned against him and cut the ropes binding his hands.

His arms fell around her shoulders and he pulled her against him, crushing her to him with a joy that outweighed all the pain. "Anna, you're alive."

Anna put her arms around him, helping to hold him up. "Yes, thanks to you, we're all alive."

Chance brushed one hand across her face, pushing her hair from her cheek. "You're hurt."

"It's nothing. First we've got to get you doctored."

With more noise than a buffalo in full run, Carl appeared from the trees, his gun in one hand and one of his carpentry tools in the other. "I heard the shot, got dressed, and came running."

Anna found it hard to believe that the entire confrontation had only taken minutes. It had seemed like hours, yet the sun was still not full on the horizon. "We had a visit from some Indians. Please help me get Chance into the house."

Dropping his weapons, Carl moved to Chance's side. "You both look like you fought a mountain lion."

"We're all fine," Chance said, coughing up blood.

Carl looked at Anna and shook his head. "Bleeding inside," he whispered as Chance coughed again.

Anna looked helpless. "What can I do?"

Carl lifted Chance and carried him the last few steps. "Get him flat on his back and don't let him move for a while."

Nodding, Anna hugged the children to her for a moment. "Can you take Maggie and Cherish home with you for a few hours? I'll walk over later."

Carl laid Chance on the bed and herded Maggie out the door. "I'll be back. You going to be all right?"

"Yes. Just look after them."

"That I'll do." Carl hurried out the door. Anna knew he wanted to get back and make sure his Selma was safe. He was so large; she sometimes forgot how young he was . . . how young they all were.

Anna washed her hands and face, then slowly began to clean the cuts on Chance's body. She taped the cut on his hairline, but the blood stained through the cloth in minutes. He was hurt in so many places she didn't know where to begin.

As she touched the cold cloth to Chance's swollen lip, he opened his eyes. His deep blue gaze seemed to cover her as he watched her work.

She tried to smile as she cleaned his face. "You are covered with blood and dirt."

"I can clean myself up. I've been doing it all my life." Chance started to rise.

Anna placed her hands on his shoulders. "No. You lay still. I'll clean you up. Carl says you may be bleeding inside and you shouldn't move."

"I'm only spitting blood from a cut inside my mouth," he mumbled as he drank deep from the dipper of water.

Anna touched his ribs and felt his pain in the tightness of his flesh beneath her fingers, even though he didn't utter a sound.

Raising his arm, Chance cupped the back of her head with his hand. Slowly he pulled her face near his own. "You've got a few bruises also." He kissed her cheek. "I was so worried that they'd hurt you."

"Would you really have killed them?"

"Without hesitation," he whispered as he pulled her lips to his. His kiss was light and she tasted the blood of his split lip, but she felt the promise in his grip and saw the longing in his eyes. "I'd kill any man who touched my woman."

He leaned back then and let her wash his face and chest. She wrapped his ribs where dark bruises marked his sides, and all the while she could feel his eyes on her. As she finished, she leaned back and stared at the white cloths crossing over his tan skin.

"I could use some more water," Chance said, startling her.

"Of course." She hurried to get him another dipper of water.

Chance covered her hands with his own as he drank. "Thanks," he said as he leaned back against the pillow and closed his eyes.

Anna studied him in the late morning shadows. He'd taken quite a beating and yet he hadn't complained. He'd seemed more worried about her bruised cheek than all of his cuts and bruises. She admired his strength. He'd been willing to fight to the death for a child that wasn't even his, and then he'd stopped and taken a beating rather than let them hurt her. She rubbed ointment into his wrists where the ropes had cut into his flesh, then she wrapped clean strips of cotton around each. His palm lay open, dark against the white sheets, and Anna slipped her fingers across his, noticing how much smaller her hand was. His hand was warm and the rough calluses he'd gotten from plowing tickled her palm.

Leaning closer, Anna kissed his hand in silent thanks for what he'd done for her. She slid from his side and moved to the table. Although she'd washed her hands and face, her whole body felt dirty after her falls.

Slowly, with pain in her shoulder, she pulled off her robe. She slid her gown to her waist and scrubbed her tender flesh with soap. The Indian's fingers had bruised her arms, and her shoulder felt feverish to her touch. She washed each inch of skin, then rinsed with cold water.

"Anna," Chance whispered.

She turned, pulling her gown over her breasts as she moved. "Yes. What is it?" Was he in pain and calling her name? Quickly, she moved to the bedside. "Do you need something?"

"Sit down," Chance ordered as he studied her. He showed no sign of being in pain or of having been asleep.

Carefully, Anna sat on the edge of the bed. She held her

gown up with one hand as she felt his forehead with the other. "What is it?"

"Your shoulder," he answered as his hand touched the dark bruises that now marred her cream-colored skin.

Anna smiled, relieved that he wasn't in pain. "I fell on it. It's nothing; only a bruise." She couldn't pull her eyes from his dark blue gaze. She saw the world in their depths, both the pain of his hard life and the pleasure he now felt as his hand brushed her shoulder.

Anna moved closer. "Don't worry about me."

"Does it hurt when I touch you?"

"No," Anna lied.

"What about here?" Chance slid his fingers over her shoulder until he brushed her throat. His touch was as light as a feather and he made no move to pull her close.

"No." Anna closed her eyes as his finger moved along her neck. She felt a warm stirring deep inside her that she'd never known before.

The air was thick with humidity and the clouds made it seem more like evening in the cabin than late morning. Anna's skin was damp from her bath and his fingers slid smoothly over her flesh.

His hand moved up to her lips and one finger brushed her swollen bottom lip. "Does my touch hurt you now?" His voice was as low as the wind in the hills.

"No," Anna answered, enjoying the feel of his fingers on her flesh.

He slid his hand down her throat to where the knife had scratched her neck. "And here?"

"No," Anna whispered. His touch was warming her skin now, making her feel alive all over.

His callused fingers moved slowly down until they reached the point where her hand held up her gown. He covered her trembling hand as he whispered, "Am I hurting you now?"

Anna felt the slight pull of his hand as he removed her fist from between her breasts. He lifted her fingers to his lips as she felt her gown slide dangerously low over her breasts. Her breathing was rapid as she felt his lips against her fingers.

"Anna," he whispered again, "am I hurting you now?"

"No."

He spread her palm open against his chest and she felt the strong beat of his heart as his fingers returned to her shoulder. "I would never hurt you, Anna. Your skin is silk to my touch."

Slowly, moving his hand over her shoulder, his fingers circled lower until he reached the softness of the swell of her breast. "Does my touch hurt you now?" he asked as his hand trailed across the line of her gown.

"No." Anna sucked in a sudden breath of air as her gown drifted down and Chance's touch crossed her nipple. She closed her eyes and floated on the wave of new sensations that overwhelmed her. His hands moved over her breasts and brushed the soft flesh just beneath each mound.

Leaning her head back, she was unable to do anything but enjoy the tender massage of his hand. She felt him slide the gown down to the flat of her stomach. There he spread his palm wide and circled her warm flesh. He returned again and again to brush her breasts as though he wanted to make sure every inch of her skin would feel fully alive.

His touch was something she had never wanted, never asked for, but its gentleness was impossible to turn away. He moved over her as silently as the sun covers the earth, spreading warmth and joy with each pass of his fingers.

"Anna," he whispered as his hand cupped one breast, "tell me you want more. Tell me my touch stirs a fire in you. Tell me you'll lay next to me tonight and let me touch you again." He pulled her gown over her bruised shoulder.

Opening her eyes, Anna stared into his smoky blue eyes and knew she didn't want his touch to end, but he was weak and this was not the time. "I'll . . ."

Chance moved the other side of the gown over her other shoulder and she wondered if the pain she saw in his eyes was because of his movement or because he, like her, didn't want the moment to end.

His voice was only a whisper. "Are you afraid? You've felt my touch, Anna. Would you back away even though I saw the pleasure it brought you?"

Anna stood, surprised at what had happened between them and a little embarrassed. But she wouldn't lie. "I was not afraid."

Closing his eyes, Chance drifted into sleep without another word.

All afternoon Anna thought of his touch as she worked. She could feel her whole being tense just at the memory of his caresses. Was this part of what he called loving? And if so, did she want any more of it, knowing that once he was gone there would always be a longing in her for more?

By the time the sun sank in the west, Anna had made up her mind. No matter how much she desired his touch, she would have to live without it. Yet she already knew her mind was lying to her heart, and her body would overrule them both.

26

Carl and Selma arrived at dusk with dinner in their arms, and Anna welcomed their questions and their company. Chance talked little, not even teasing Selma about her cooking. Watching his slow movements, Anna knew he was in pain even though he shrugged off her attempts to help.

Carl talked of all the things he planned to make in the fall and Selma played with the baby. The couple's everyday actions soothed Anna's nerves and gave her a warm feeling. She watched Carl's skillful hands put the crib back together by firelight. Later, over Chance's protests, they all checked his head wound and everyone, except Chance, agreed that he should stay in bed at least a few more days.

When Anna finally walked her neighbors to the path, she hugged them both and thanked them for all they'd done. She felt blanketed in family and friends for the first time in her life. There was no more fear for Cherish's life lurking in the back of her mind. Her daughter could grow up without watching over her shoulder to see if Walks Tall was following her, stalking her. All seemed as peaceful as the evening sky.

Anna walked slowly back to the cabin, enjoying the whisper of fall on the breeze and the smell of their dinner fire blending with the wilderness air. She studied the huge pile of logs Chance had cut and stacked, ready to become the walls to her new home. "My home," she whispered.

She could almost feel herself bonding with this country just
as the maverick grapevine wound around every pole and
stump. Each day this land became more a part of her, and
she of it. The morning's battle had only strengthened her
will to survive and build a life on this land.

Moving slowly into the cabin, she saw Chance asleep and
Maggie lying on the covers next to him, her small hand
resting on his bandaged ribs. Anna carried her to the high
bed at the window, then moved to the only dark corner of
the dugout to change into her nightgown. She sat by the fire
for over an hour feeding Cherish, relaxing and thinking
about how Chance had fought for her that morning. How
could he be such a wild man one moment and so tender the
next? How could the same man who'd threatened to kill
Walks Tall have touched her so gently, as though he'd never
touched a woman in his life?

Anna laid Cherish in her crib and slid into bed next to
Chance. She was a little disappointed that he wasn't awake.
Although she'd told herself she would say no if he wanted
to touch her again, she lay awake, waiting for him to pull
her near. The fresh, wild smell that always reminded her of
leather and horses and strength surrounded her, as his strong
arm rested beside her own. His muscles were relaxed, but
she knew they were always ready to tense if danger came
near. A part of her mind was frightened by him, yet a part
of her heart was fascinated. He was a good man, maybe the
best she'd ever known, but there was a wildness about him,
a part that would never be bridled or broken. She lay awake,
wondering what she would do with him . . . or without
him.

An hour before dawn, when the night moves on stock-
inged feet and even the wind rests, Anna heard Chance
whisper her name and she lay still as he touched her cheek.
"Anna, are you awake?"

Anna nodded, excited and afraid all at once. His mouth
was so near that she could feel the warmth of his words.
"Relax, my beautiful wife. Relax while I teach you about

touching." His words wove a magic all their own. "I'm not going to hurt you. I'm going to touch you just as I did yesterday." He buried his face into her loose hair. "I'm going to move slowly. If I do anything that doesn't make you feel good, tell me and I'll stop. Do you understand?"

Anna liked the smoky gray of the cabin, making everything that happened now seem not quite real, but more like a wonderful dream. She felt warm and protected. "I don't want you to . . ." She fought back the joy as his fingers slid lightly over her nightgown and she rolled toward him even as she whispered, "I'm not sure I want . . ." Her mind ordered her to stop him, but her heart begged for his touch.

"Anna," he whispered back as he softly kissed her cheek, "don't lie to me. When I came so close to death yesterday, I realized I'd have to have the heaven of touching you. Each time a blow struck I thought of you next to me like this and not of the pain of Walks Tall's fists. Over and over again, I thought of touching you."

Leisurely he pulled the ribbons open on the front of her gown. "You've never lied to me. Don't start now." He slid his finger down the opening of her gown, branding a line of fire along her flesh. "When I first saw this gown with all its ribbons, I wondered what it would be like to pull each free from its bow." He drew his finger back up to her chin and lifted it slighty. "Tell me to touch you." His voice was low and rich in her ears. "I have to know that you want this between us as much as I do."

"Touch me," she whispered and felt the joy of his fingers pulling her gown open. Her breasts slid free from the cotton and were brushed by the cool morning air before his warm fingers moved across them.

He touched her as he had before, with light, circling strokes over her body. His fingers brushed her breasts and spread over her stomach in a caress. She relaxed, enjoying the feelings he was awakening. As her pleasure grew stronger, his touch grew bolder, cupping her breasts and gently pulling at her nipples.

As she cried softly with pleasure, he pulled her against him, flattening her into the wall of his chest. His hands moved over her back, molding her along his length. She heard his breathing grow labored and stopped his hand. "Wait. Are you in pain?" Pressing lightly against his bandaged ribs, she whispered, "I don't want to hurt you."

Chance laughed. "I'm in pain, but not from my bruises." He pulled her hand to his lips and kissed each finger, wondering how she would react if she knew the full extent of his passion. He longed to roll atop her and push deep into the feather mattress with their bodies. But he would not frighten her. Gently, he molded her against him, feeling her warm flesh against his heart. Slowly, he pushed the gown to her waist. He moved his hands along her velvet skin. As his mouth lightly kissed her face, his fingers traveled over her hips and pressed her against him. She stiffened slightly in surprise, but his mouth covered her lips before she could protest.

His kiss was light, innocent, as his hands began stroking her back once more. This time when his fingers covered her hips and pulled her against him, his kiss deepened, pulling her with him into pleasure.

Her arms struggled at his sides and he released her. As he pulled away with a groan of dread and the knowledge that he'd gone too far once more, her arms slid over his shoulders and around his neck.

She pressed her body against him and whispered, "Teach me more of that kiss."

Chance laughed with relief and threaded his fingers through her hair. "What a demanding woman you've suddenly become." He moved his thumb to her chin and pulled her mouth open.

He'd meant to only show her one kiss, but the sweet taste of her mouth drove him mad. He kissed her full and hard as his hands gently explored her body. Her mouth was a sweet wine demanding to be drunk and Chance had waited a lifetime for a taste.

When he finally ended the lesson, Chance leaned back against the headboard. He closed his eyes, absorbed in the wonder of her. He needed her to be his wife, his woman, his love, but she was only playing a game of which a kiss was an end in itself and not a part of a journey to be traveled. He had to stop before she hated him as she had her first husband.

She stretched against him. "Is the lesson over?"

Chance opened an eye and saw her hair spilling across his chest as she rested her head. "Do you want it to be, my Anna? It will be dawn soon and Maggie will be awake. We must stop this pleasure." He moved his hand slowly from her throat to her side. "Tell me that you love my touch."

"And if I don't?" Anna laughed as he tickled her arm.

"Then I'll keep doing it every night until I get it right." His hand cupped one mound and pulled it slightly toward him. "I'd like to continue this in a few days without these bandages."

Anna cuddled under his arm. His fingers tilted her head up until he could lightly brush kisses over her face. His hand continued to move over her in gentle strokes.

She knew she could turn away and put a halt to his exploring fingers, but she didn't want him to stop. A need deep inside her began to rise to the surface. For the first time in her life she wanted to touch someone and be touched. "Thank you." Her breath was warm against his side.

"Anytime, ma'am." He held her a little too tightly for a moment before relaxing.

Slowly, he removed his hand and pulled her nightgown together. "Go back to sleep, Anna." His words were tight and low. "I can take no more of your pleasure and keep my word not to have you as my wife fully."

Smiling, she curled against him and let her breast push against his side. His whispered oath made her laugh.

* * *

At dawn Anna awoke alone. She ran outside, afraid of what might have happened to Chance. She'd known since the fight that he was in more pain than he'd allowed her to believe. What if their touching this morning had been his good-bye and he was lying outside somewhere, dying?

A noise drew her to the barn, where she found him feeding the stock. He looked up when she entered as if puzzled by the alarm in her eyes. "Morning, darling," was all he had time to say before she stormed toward him.

"You should be in bed." Her words rose with anger. "You're in no shape to be up. I can take care of the animals." She grabbed the bucket, angry with him and with herself for being so frightened at the thought of not knowing where he was.

"I'm fine, just a little sore." No matter how much he'd like to stay in bed with her forever, he had something he had to do. "I figure I'm not in any shape to work on the house today, but I could ride in and see how the settlement is doing."

She looked at his split lip and blackened eyes. The cut on his head had finally stopped turning every bandage crimson, but he didn't look fine to her. "We can all go in a few days. You're going back to bed."

"I'm riding out in an hour." He folded his arms gingerly over his chest and widened his stance. No one had told him what to do in years and Anna wasn't about to start now.

A sudden spark of stubbornness danced in his blue eyes before he turned away to lift a bucket of grain.

Anna watched him closely. "There's another reason you are going into the settlement?"

Chance didn't look up at her. "Maybe."

"I remember Walks Tall saying something about that Indian you'd sworn to kill. You're going to look for Storm's Edge, aren't you? You can't even wait until you heal from one fight before you go looking for another."

"Maybe." Chance pulled his saddle off the fence railing.

He knew there was no use lying to her; she knew him too well by now to believe a half-truth. How could she be so beautiful and soft one minute and so bossy the next?

"You're in no shape to fight him." Anna resented his obstinacy. "That was an oath you took when you were twelve years old. You can't fight him now."

"I know." Chance finally turned to face her. "I'm only going to check around and see if anyone else has seen him. I'll be back in a few days."

"I don't think you should go and I'm sure Carl and Selma would agree."

"I don't live my life by a neighborhood poll." Suddenly the number of people around him seemed suffocating.

Anger set her forest green eyes ablaze. "It's too soon. I need to check your ribs and rebandage that head wound."

Chance laughed. "Maybe I've had enough mothering. You know, I've been living for several years on my own without you to look after me. I've crawled off from fights worse than yesterday's and always managed to recover."

Each of his words kindled Anna's temper. "I am not mothering you."

"Then stop telling me not to go. You act like you have the majority vote on my actions."

"You're going no matter what I say, aren't you?"

"You guessed it, woman." Chance sighed, relieved that the discussion was over.

Anna lifted a bridle from the barn wall. "Then I'm going also."

Her words took a moment to register. "Oh, no." He held up his hand as if to stop her, but she continued.

"I'm not having you fall over dead along the road and have me learn of it days later. I'm riding into town with you." She passed him, throwing Cinnamon's bridle over the horse's neck before he could think of what to say. "We'll be ready in an hour."

Chance twisted the bridle in his hands. He marveled at the way she had of making him almost insane with love one moment and crazy with anger the next. She had no business going with him. She'd only slow him down. He needed to find out what he could about Storm's Edge before the Indian moved on. The last thing he needed was a wife, a baby, and his little sister with him.

But by the time Chance got the horses saddled and the cow milked and fed, Anna was dressed and ready. She'd tied her shawl around her neck with a wide sling in front. Cherish was nestled in its folds. Maggie danced around wearing her new dress made of Chance's rejected nightshirt. Her black hair was tied into a ponytail and ribbons curled around the ebony mass.

Chance had to smile. They might be a nuisance, but they surely were a fine-looking group of females.

Anna climbed carefully onto Cinnamon, who always seemed as gentle as a hand-fed old nag around Anna's touch. The huge sorrel knew his mistress and never failed to read her every command.

Anna smiled down at Chance's scowling face as he lifted Maggie up behind her. "We could stop by and see if Carl and Selma want to go with us," she teased.

"No!" Chance snapped. He'd felt fine when he'd gotten out of bed, but his bruises were already starting to ache, and his head was pounding to the point where he was sure anyone could see the throbbing from ten feet away. Although he wasn't about to admit that Anna might have been right about him waiting a few days, he was already dreading the hours of riding.

He swung onto Cyoty's back. "I already feel like an Indian with my tribe following me. All I need is Carl and his lovesick midget of a wife along."

"Selma's not lovesick," Anna protested, somehow enjoying getting under Chance's skin.

"She's always flitting around him like a butterfly. Won't let him get any work done." The corner of Chance's swollen lip rose. "She follows him everywhere."

Lifting her chin as if she hadn't heard his innuendo, she added, "Some men need more help than others."

"Some men feel a little smothered with too much mothering." He rode close to her. "Indian women don't ever question their men, and they always ride behind."

Anna laughed. "Maybe if they'd question, they'd be living in more than skins."

Chance leaned and ran his hand along her leg to her knee. The soft leather of her high-strapped moccasin was cool compared to the warmth of her flesh at the knee. "You don't appear to complain about wearing skins."

Kicking her horse, Anna rushed ahead. "We'd better ride or we'll be all day getting to Fredericksburg."

Chance laughed and followed, suddenly very glad she'd come along.

They rode slower than he would have, but he enjoyed her company. When they stopped to rest the horses, Chance watched Maggie collecting flowers as Anna nursed Cherish and he wondered how he'd ever thought he'd enjoy a little time to himself.

It was midday when they arrived at the settlement. Anna couldn't believe how it had changed in only a few months. A small town had grown overnight, with shops and homes and even the beginnings of a church. The roads were wide enough for a team of oxen to turn around and people were everywhere. There were farmers selling early crops and fruit as well as wagons bearing newly arriving immigrants, and everywhere Anna heard the music of her native tongue. German was spoken in trading, yelled in chants from the children playing, and whispered among friends and lovers. She hadn't thought about how much she missed hearing her own language.

Chance stopped at John Meusebach's office to check on how the leader of the settlement was faring. As usual, times were hard. More people were coming every week and there was little money to get them inland from the coast. John was a true leader, a genius at figuring out ways to make a few dollars stretch into enough, but he was the leader of a small group trying to fight a landslide of problems.

Chance left him, promising to call later that evening. He wanted to talk to John and several others alone, and the easiest way to do that was take Anna to Mrs. Basse, who'd moved her family from New Braunfels. The Basses' friendship with John had led them once more to settle as neighbors. With the sound of their many children filling the air for a block, Chance had no trouble finding the family.

Just as he'd suspected, Mrs. Basse almost swallowed Anna in welcome. Cherish was enveloped by her daughters, who made funny sounds as if they had never seen a baby, and Mrs. Basse couldn't have looked prouder if she'd been the grandmother herself. She ushered Anna and Maggie onto the porch and pushed Chance aside, telling him to go on about his business while they had a visit.

He heard her shouting over the noise of her sons wrestling in the yard. "A daughter's a fine thing. Gentle, like a flower to raise. Now sons, all you need to do is feed and water them. They grow up wild like weeds. But a daughter is a mother's song and the answer to a father's prayer as he ages."

Chance raised an eyebrow at the tough group of boys playing around him, compared to the fine dainty group of girls on the porch. Weeds and flowers were an accurate way of describing her brood.

A few hours later he thought of a few other names for her sons when they tricked him into letting them tie his arms behind him against the horse's stall. They all laughed and ran in to dinner, leaving their catch of the day hanging.

Chance twisted against the knots, praying he'd get free before Anna decided to come looking for him.

His prayers weren't answered.

27

Anna walked into the barn looking for Chance. She'd seen him ride in thirty minutes before, yet he hadn't come in when everyone was called to dinner.

The barn was cloaked in evening shadows. Huge piles of hay blocked the sun's dying light coming through the high windows running along the west wall. Anna paused, letting her eyes adjust while she enjoyed the solitude after spending the afternoon surrounded by all the talkative Basses. Before, she'd wondered why Mr. Basse never seemed to be around. But after only a few hours of their full-volumed household she understood his absence.

As her eyes grew accustomed to the shadows, Anna strolled to Cinnamon's stall. The huge sorrel greeted her with a snort and she patted his long, wide head. He was a fine animal and well worth the loaf of bread he cost her each week.

Wood creaked in the darkness as though someone were straining against a thick stock of lumber. She turned, suddenly aware of a man standing across from her. A tall form materialized from the dusty interior.

"Chance," she whispered in relief. He was leaning against Cyoty's stall, his arms behind him. "Why didn't you come in to dinner?"

Anna moved closer, puzzled by his stillness and the vexation in his eyes. Anger was reflected in the twitch of his jaw and the cocky way he always leaned his head to one side when he was controlling his rage. She was within a foot of him before he spoke.

"You should ask those demons Mrs. Basse calls her sons."

"Ask them what?"

"It seems I'll be late to dinner because I'm tied up at the moment."

Anna noticed the ropes as he spoke. Laughter erupted from her even as he jerked in anger.

"Oh, no." She was laughing almost too hard to even talk. "They wouldn't."

"The hell they wouldn't! This place is a breeding ground for savages."

Leaning beside him, Anna continued to laugh until tears streamed from her eyes. She placed her hand on his shoulder in a comforting touch.

Chance jerked away from her sympathy. "Stop acting like your brain's in the clouds and untie me." Although her laughter warmed his soul the way her touch set fire to his flesh, he didn't want to be the object of her mirth.

Suppressing her amusement, Anna faced him. "I think not." She raised one eyebrow. "The little darlings may have done me a favor. I've been trying all day to get you to hold still long enough for me to check your bandages. This may be the perfect time."

Anna retrieved her carpetbag from beside her saddle and plopped it down in front of him.

"Untie me, Anna, or I swear I'll . . ." Chance was in no mood to be teased, but his anger only made Anna laugh more.

"You do far too much swearing if you ask me. I'm no longer frightened by your growl." She slowly unbuttoned his shirt with feather-light touches. "Don't threaten some-one who's mothering you. She might just leave you and go back into the house. It could be hours before the boys return. And then there's no telling what they might do to someone as mean-tempered as you."

Hesitantly, she pulled his shirt free from his pants and slipped the cotton garment off his shoulders. With the nervous caution of an explorer determined to cross unknown territory, she unwrapped the bandage around his ribs. Chance stopped twisting and allowed her hands to glide over his chest. Each time she circled the wrappings behind him, she pressed against him with her shoulder and the softness of her breasts. He closed his eyes, savoring the feel of her nearness and cursing the ropes that kept him from holding her. The memory of their closeness before dawn now flooded him at full gale.

Her voice was the whisper of slow-moving silk against his ear. "That's better. Just hold still and I'll be finished in a minute."

"I love the way your hair smells," Chance whispered, hypnotized by the feel of her warm breath on his shoulder as she worked. "Untie me and let me bury my face in it like I did this morning. Let me teach you more of touching."

She lay the bandage aside and examined his bruised ribs. "The light isn't very good. I'll have to touch you and you tell me when it hurts."

Her fingers moved over his chest from his waist to his shoulder, and though he'd felt her touch before, this was different. And that ounce of difference weighed upon his flesh as heavily as the desire pounding in his ears. This time her fingers were a caress upon his skin. This time her touch burned his flesh with passion.

"Does that hurt?" she whispered, his nearness suddenly flooding her senses. What had started as only concern was becoming more . . . far more.

"No," he answered as he leaned down to brush his lips against the tiny curls at the base of her neck.

Moving her fingers over his body, she delighted in the rippling of his muscles and in the warm feel of his smooth skin that seemed layered over an oak-hard frame. So many times she'd watched him work, glistening with sweat in the fields, and she'd wondered what it would be like to touch such a man. He seemed so wild and free—part savage, part civilized. He was a breed apart from all the people she'd ever known, this man who called himself a Texan.

As she spread her palm wide over his chest, she heard his sudden intake of breath. "Am I hurting you?" She withdrew in alarm.

"No," he answered, slinging his hair from his eyes. Their blue depths were dark with need. Chance looked up at the loft, not wanting her to be frightened by the hunger simmering in his eyes.

Anna brushed the thick blackness off his forehead as he straightened, closing the gap between them. She let her fingers comb through his hair, loving the way it felt. So many mornings she'd watched him stand at the washstand beside the cabin. He'd dunk his head in the water, then comb the dark mass back with long fingers. She'd longed to touch his hair just as she was doing now. The feel of him against her brought a pleasure unlike any she'd ever known.

He lowered his lips to hers with a kiss as soft as spring leaves. Anna knew she had only to step away and he couldn't follow. If she moved an inch or more she would be free of his kiss. But she didn't want to move. She didn't want to pull away. The knowledge that she had the choice was the courage that created boldness.

Breaking the kiss, Anna let her lips drift along his skin to his throat. She kissed the short growth of beard under his chin until she reached the soft, pulsing hollow at the base of his neck. Her hands moved over him, loving the feel of him. Amazed at the way her touch changed his breathing, she pressed her body against him and felt his heart through her clothes. Slowly, she moved against him, feeling the pounding of his heart between her breasts.

Chance stared at the roof above him. "God, woman, untie me!" he whispered.

Leaning against him, Anna listened to the racing of his heart. "Not yet. Not until I've bandaged you again."

"I don't need a bandage. I need to pull you against me. You're driving me mad with your touch." His voice was low and seemed to ripple over her senses like the first warm breeze of spring. "I need to feel your heart against mine, Anna."

Looking up at him, curiously unafraid, she knew she'd caught the wild animal and he wanted to be free. She saw the passion in his eyes. She saw the hunger, but it didn't frighten her the way it had the night of the storm, for she knew him better and feared him less. When he'd grabbed her during the storm, all her bad memories had flooded over her. Now he was the one tied and trapped and it was she who held his freedom.

Anna lifted a fresh bandage. "We must get back to the others." She wrapped the cloth around him. "They'll miss us and come looking."

"Not before you touch me once more." Chance brushed her ear with his lips. "Not before I taste your mouth."

Anna dropped the bandage as her lips found his.

At first she teased him by pulling away, but his kiss drew her to him. As it deepened she opened her mouth to his and loved the way his tongue explored. As his kiss brought her pleasure she moved her hands over him as he had touched her before. When her fingers closed about his hips and pulled him against her, he moaned softly and his kiss deepened to a passion neither had ever known.

Finally, Chance raised his head. "Dear God, Anna, untie me."

The rope snapped free with her sudden tug and Chance pulled her against him. His embrace was wild and free with hunger. She clung to him, holding fast as a tidal wave of need overpowered them both.

He wound his fist into her soft hair and was almost lost to any world but her arms when he heard Maggie's voice.

"Chance," she called from what seemed like miles away. "Chance, Anna, supper."

Anna pulled away from his arms, but the pain of her leaving was overshadowed by the promise that smoldered in her eyes. "It will be good to get back to our place," she said as if they'd been gone for days and not hours.

Chance smiled. "Yes," he whispered, as he fought the need to pull her against him once more. "It will be good; in fact, it may be heaven."

At dinner Chance didn't scold the boys for tying him up, and they lost interest in their pranks because of his lack of concern. He and Anna were so wrapped up in watching one another that the dozen other people in the room might as well have been furniture. She watched his movements, and his eyes never seemed to leave her. Sitting beside her on the bench, his leg accidentally touched hers beneath the table and Anna had trouble concentrating on what Mrs. Basse was saying.

Turning suddenly toward Chance, Anna let her breast brush his arm slightly. He stumbled over his words, silently revealing how greatly her small action had affected him.

Wordlessly, he took her touch as a challenge, and began a silent game of affection that paralleled their everyday actions on the surface but stoked an inner fire within them both.

He lowered his hand beneath the table and ran it lightly over her leg as he talked about next year's crops.

She lay her fingers over his while she refilled his coffee cup.

An hour later, as she rocked the baby, Chance knelt beside her. He stroked her arm with the back of his hand as he pretended to touch Cherish's sleeping face.

While the children dressed for bed, Anna leaned close to Chance once more as she helped clear the table, apologizing with soft insincerity as she brushed his shoulder.

The game continued until bedtime without anyone except

Anna and Chance aware of it. Yet each slight touch was responsible for the glow in her cheeks and the twinkle in his eyes.

As the candles burned low, Anna was assigned to sleep with the girls in the loft and Chance had his choice of the boys' room or the barn. He took the barn without hesitation. As he stepped to the door, he pulled Anna close and touched her cheek with a kiss. The endearment was more of a promise than a farewell.

Mrs. Basse gave the order for sleep and to Anna's amazement the house quieted and settled in for the night. Within minutes, it seemed that everyone except Anna was sound asleep. She nursed Cherish for a while, thinking of the way she'd felt when she'd touched Chance. It had been exciting and frightening at the same time.

Closing her eyes, she remembered all the months they'd been together. She thought of how often he'd helped her, touched her tenderly, cherished her. He'd never hurt her. He'd never taken; he'd always given. In less than four months, their time together would be over and she would never know his touch again.

A need deep inside her grew. Could passion be such an ugly thing if it were a part of loving someone? Would she go her whole life without knowing the feel of a loving man?

Anna pulled her wrapper tightly around her waist. She had to ask Chance how he felt, she told herself. She had to check on his wounds. But inside she knew the reason for her journey to the barn and it had nothing to do with Chance's injured ribs.

She would taste his love before her fear overwhelmed her and forever quieted her need. She would go to him and ask him to hold her, to touch her, to make her his, if only for one night.

Crossing the moonlit yard to the barn, Anna heard the low sounds of the horses and smelled the damp, sweet aroma of hay. The night was heavy with heat and the air so still it was almost tangible, as though you could sweep it up in your hand.

She slipped between the doors and whispered Chance's name in the darkness.

There was no answer.

Moving into the center of the barn where she'd seen the lantern, she gripped the flint and struck. The candle inside the iron lantern flickered to life. "Chance," she called as she moved to where he'd spread his bedroll.

The straw poked at her bare feet as she walked, and the candle multiplied her shadow on the walls like sentries following her every move.

At the sight of Chance's bedroll lying tied beside his saddle, Anna's spirits plunged. He wasn't in the barn. Finally she'd been brave enough to give love an opportunity, and he was gone.

She walked slowly back to the house, disappointment making each step heavy. In the morning, she'd be glad, she told herself, but tonight all she felt was a hollow need inside her.

Flickers of light from the house next door drew her attention. She looked up and saw Chance through the window of John Meusebach's house. The two men were talking with a third man whose back was to the window.

Curiosity drew Anna closer. She couldn't hear what they were saying, but she could see Chance's face and knew he was arguing with the unknown man.

Suddenly, Chance threw up his arms and stormed out of the house. He was off the porch and around the corner before Anna thought to step into the shadows.

"Anna?" Chance snapped. "What are you doing out here? Were you listening?"

"No!" Anna felt her face redden and was thankful for the darkness.

"Then what are you doing up at this hour? We have to leave early in the morning to get back to the farm." He was moving closer as he spoke. She could hear the anger in his voice but couldn't tell if its fire had been from the argument he'd just had or if he was mad at the thought that she might have been listening.

"I . . ." The reason for her coming suddenly disappeared. "I . . ."

His fingers closed tightly over her arm. "I'm sorry for snapping at you. What we were saying shouldn't be heard by women. I don't want you getting worried about something that John and I are never going to let happen."

Anna tried to pull her arm away. "I couldn't hear you. I only just came from the barn." She didn't like the idea that he wanted to protect her as though she were a child. Suddenly, she realized her journey outside had been a mistake. "Let go of me."

Chance released her but didn't step out of her way. After a long moment he gently put his arm around her waist. Now his touch was not protective, but loving. His hands moved along the folds of her wrapper as he pressed her against him. "So you weren't spying. You were looking for me." His lips touched her cheek. "Could it be, my beautiful wife, that you wanted my touch? My kiss? Or did you come to torture me as you have all evening?"

Anna answered by lifting her arms and running her hands through his hair. She pulled his mouth closer and felt him stiffen in shock at her boldness. His kiss was hesitant, as if he were testing, checking, but hers was not. She opened her mouth willingly to his kiss. His hands slid over her hips and pressed her against him as their kiss deepened. All the longing of the evening climaxed in a sudden need to be closer.

Anna didn't understand what he'd been angry about or what the meeting had been about. She would worry about that tomorrow. For now she only knew she wanted this man to hold her. The longing he'd started with his touch had built until there was no denying her need. She held him tightly and leaned against him as he drew her into the magic of his kiss.

For the first time there was no hesitation in their relationship . . . no holding back . . . no fear.

"Well, well." A voice shattered the silence of the night. "What have we here?"

Groaning, Chance pulled his mouth from hers. His arms didn't loosen as his fingers pressed against her waist. For a moment she saw the passion in his blue eyes, a fire that would have consumed them both in a few more minutes.

He pulled her close and faced the intruder. "What we have here, Walter, is a man kissing his wife."

Walter's laughter fouled the evening air. "I saw that, and quite a show it was. I tell you, Anna, I didn't think that brittle stiff body of yours was capable of molding so closely against a man. You certainly showed no such passion to my dear departed friend William. I was beginning to think you had inherited none of your mother's hunger for men."

"That's enough, Walter." Chance's voice was low and deadly. "I've had quite enough of you tonight. If you want to be alive at sunrise, you'll say good night."

Walter bent in a mocking bow. "Certainly. I must leave you to your breeding."

He started to say more, but the sound of metal sliding against leather silenced him. Walter disappeared even as the click of Chance's gun snapped like a twig in the night.

They stood for a moment, listening to Walter's footsteps moving away. Chance returned his gun to its holster and pulled Anna closer.

"Forget him," he whispered, brushing his chin against her hair.

Anna was as stiff as a corpse. "I must go." She hated being compared to her mother. All she could think about was how many men might have seen passion in her mother's eyes, how many men had tasted her lips in the shadows.

Chance tried to kiss her but she turned her head away.

"Anna?"

"No!" Anna pushed at him. "I'm not like my mother. I need no man."

"But Anna . . ."

"No!"

He released her with his hands spread wide as if in surrender. "Then go, but don't come to me again at night unless you want me. I can't take more of this game you play with loving. I want *you*, not your mother. I want to hold you and make love to you, but I can't turn it off and on as fast as you can. How can you kiss me like you just did and still be so afraid of me?" His voice resounded with the frustration of all the long months of needing her—of all the months of loving her and always having her pull away.

Anna ran onto the porch. "I'm not afraid of you. I just don't want to feel dirty."

Chance thought of the one time in his life when he'd almost been with a woman and how dirty it had seemed to him. The vision of the barmaid lying on filthy sheets as she spread her dirty legs before him suddenly turned his stomach, just as it had before. Could Anna have that same feeling when she looked at him? Couldn't she see that what he was offering was more, far more?

"It wouldn't be dirty between us," he snapped as the door closed. He'd dreamed a thousand times of how it would be with Anna, but in reality he could make no promises. He turned and walked toward the barn, forcing himself to whisper, "Good night, Anna."

Anna leaned against the closed door, wrapping her arms around her and fighting back the tears. It had been so right before Walter had interrupted them. She'd felt like she belonged in Chance's arms and she hadn't been afraid. But then Walter had compared her to her mother, making her feel cheap.

Tears welled in her eyes, and she wanted to run away and never see another man again. She felt so alone, just as she had all the years she'd been growing up. There was never anyone to hold her when she woke from a nightmare. Her mother was always out with a man, or "entertaining," as she called it, in her private chambers. There was never anyone to kiss away Anna's fears.

Anna pushed the tears away roughly with her palm. There was someone who would hold her tonight and all she'd done was hurt him. He would kiss away the fears and he was an honest man. Nothing Chance had ever done had been dirty or cheap. She opened the door in time to see him vanish into the barn. He would make the nightmares go away. She would have one night of having someone care about her, one night that would have to last for a lifetime. All she had to do was cross the yard to him.

Chance closed his eyes and pushed his shoulders against the barn wall as though he could push his frustration into the wood. How he wanted her, needed her. The hunger for her even now was eating away at his gut like a pack of starved coyotes. When she'd pulled away, he'd wanted to crush her beneath him and smother her with his love. But he couldn't. When she turned to ice in his arms, he couldn't seem to warm her, and he couldn't hold her knowing he was hurting her, no matter how great his own need.

For months now he had admired, respected, and loved Anna, yet he couldn't touch her without bringing her pain. He pushed deeper into the shadows, hiding himself as he hid his need for her. He didn't want her to know how great his hunger was, for that fact would surely frighten her away forever.

He rubbed his hands as though they were suddenly covered with mud. The knowledge that Anna thought his touch was something dirty twisted at his insides like a pair of newly sharpened bowie knives. Yet all he could think of every waking hour was holding her against him. Even now he must be going mad, for he could hear Anna's soft steps coming toward him.

28

Slipping between the open doors of the barn, Anna walked softly across the hay. She knew Chance could hear her coming, yet he said nothing as she moved hesitantly until she stood in the center of the floor. The first long rays of a full moon poured in from the barn door, spreading a silver beam along the hay.

Something rustled behind her, yet she remained still. She'd come this far; now he would have to cross the final few feet. Anna would not ask or beg. She was neither the predator nor the prey. His words had been simple: *Don't come to me again at night unless you want me*. He would know why she was here, and she would make no pretense.

In the damp stillness Anna felt the warmth of his body inches from her own as he circled her. She wanted to cry out, to explain her actions, the fear she felt even now, but his nearness was flooding her senses. The feel of his warm breath against her hair and the scent that was his alone circled about her.

Touching her shoulder lightly, Chance slid his flat palm down her arm without allowing his fingers to curve. When his hand reached her fingers he intertwined their hands, bonding them in the darkness. Without allowing his body to touch hers, he leaned forward and brushed her lips with a kiss. The lightness of his kiss was counteracted by the tight grip he had on her hand.

His lips left hers with a low moan as his shadowy form knelt and shouldered his blanket.

When he stood he was so close that she could feel the moisture of his breath against her hair. "Anna, are you sure? Don't play games with me. We're heading into deep water. If we go much further, we'll have to swim to the other side."

"Yes, I'm sure," she whispered, wanting to add, *Yes, just this once. I want to fill this need I have for you and store this one memory forever.* But her heart was pounding too hard in her throat to allow her to say more.

"Then come with me." He pulled her close. "I'll not love you in a barn. We should be under the stars, just like when we were married."

Leading her into the yard and behind the row of houses, Chance walked in silence along the path that ran to the stream. Anna followed, feeling as if she were shedding layers of her past with each step. Soon she would be clean and free from all her memories. His hand was warm and firm around hers as they left the village behind and moved uphill.

The land was lush and green with late summer, yet fall crackled even now among the oak leaves already littering the soft grass. After several minutes they came to the end of the path. The town was behind them, a wilderness yet untamed before them. She felt like her civilized world lay behind and his wild world lay ahead. Anna hesitated as Chance stepped into the brush.

He stopped as her hand pulled back and his voice came low, blended with anger and sadness. "Have you changed your mind? Would you back away again?"

"No." Anna swallowed her fears. "I want you to touch me." She suddenly wanted to stop all the pain that had passed between them over the months. She'd always thought of herself and her needs and fears. With the impact of a thousand shattering stars, Anna saw his longing, his years of starvation for another's touch. She felt honored that it was her touch alone that would satisfy his hunger.

Brushing his arm with a soft caress, Anna remembered how often he'd spoken of being alone. "I want to follow, but I have no shoes."

Chance swung her up into his arms without a moment's hesitation. She wrapped her arms around his neck and laid her head on his shoulder, memorizing the feeling of being surrounded with tenderness. He moved through the brush that grew thick next to the stream. Tall, waist-high grass swished in the warm breeze as he moved further away from the town.

Anna's heart pounded as he carried her. The warmth of his chest excited her and she delighted in feeling the power of him so near.

The moon danced along behind them, peeping in and out from between the trees. "Where are we going?" Anna whispered as she played with the hair at his neck.

Chance smiled down at her. "Does it matter? You called me a savage once; well, now I'm taking you into my wilderness. Are you frightened of being lost in the wild with me?"

She felt his arm tighten just below her breasts. "No."

His laughter started low in his chest and rumbled past his lips. "I want to be alone with you. Truly alone, without children, or friends, or neighbors." He brushed a kiss past her ear. "God, how I want you all to myself. I want to crush you to me and hear you cry for joy. I want to be drunk on your nearness and drown in the smell of your hair before the sun rises."

As he spoke he stepped into a tiny clearing, well hidden from town by a growth of century-old oak. The stream bubbled wide as it bent around a huge rock and pooled for a moment before continuing its journey. Just beneath the rock a small space of ground drifted flat and grassy into the water for several feet before another rock sent the stream on its way once more. The spot was perfect, blanketed in green and bathed in silver moonlight: a private paradise. A moon as bright as daylight shone above them, while thick trees and brush guarded the grassy earth like a fortress behind them.

Lowering her until her feet touched the soft grass, he kissed her forehead, then cupped her face in his hands as though he held a great treasure. Slowly, he kissed her eyelids and cheeks.

Anna closed her eyes and enjoyed the wonder of being touched so tenderly by such powerful hands. She felt the late summer breeze brush her hair as he released it from its pins. The quiet sounds of the night blended with the pounding of her heart.

"I've wanted your hair to be free like this so many times," he whispered as he circled his hand in the long tresses. "Just as the only way I wanted you was if you came willingly. Many mornings I've cursed the sunrise knowing that you'd bind your hair with the light." He tugged at her curls until she leaned back, her face turned up to him. He studied her pale skin in the light. As her eyes danced with anticipation and excitement, her lips parted, ready to be made his.

His kiss was light at first, like a stream dancing over rocks high in the mountains, but his passion grew and deepened until it was a mighty river pulling them both into a current of white-water desire.

Anna clung to him. He'd kissed her before but never as he did now. A lifetime of loneliness pulled her completely into his passion as her years of need answered his longing.

Tugging at the belt on her robe, he pulled it free from her waist. His powerful yet gentle insistence forced her arms from around his neck so that he could slide the garment free. Moments later, the blue wrapper fell silently to the grass as her arms returned to encircle him.

She watched him in the moonlight, his eyes dark with approval and a smile lifting his full lip. He pulled her hands to him and moved them down his shirt until every button was freed by her own fingers.

"What about your bruised ribs?" Anna parted his shirt with her fingertips and touched the sides of his chest.

"The pain is nothing compared to the ache I have to hold you." His breath was against her ear. "Dear God, I've needed you for a lifetime."

She touched his eye where the shadows hid the deep purple circle.

Turning his face into the palm of her hand, Chance kissed her fingers lightly. "Forget the bruises; they'll heal. But this need I have for you may kill me."

He covered her hands and guided them to his waist, then his strong fingers covered hers as he helped her unbuckle his gun belt. She realized how few times she'd seen him without the weapon strapped to his side. The simple act her fingers performed made her feel that she was opening up his very soul. For him to stand unarmed before her made Anna somehow closer to this strong, wild man.

The holster and gun joined her wrapper on the grass. Anna slid her fingers along his thigh where the gun had rested. His leg muscle seemed no less hard than the gun, but she could feel the warmth beneath the rough material of his pants. Suddenly, she wanted to be close, very close, to him.

"What is it you want, my love?" Laughter filled his voice, already low with passion.

Anna pulled at his shirt. "I want to feel you next to me."

He smiled down at her without moving closer. "In all these months there have been many times when I would have given my very life to hear you say those words."

He raised his hands to her shoulders and gently turned her around to face the stream. She stood with her back to him as she heard his boots fall and his pants slip from his legs. Anna smiled, touched by his modesty. She'd seen him naked before, but she knew this time would be different.

Chance's hands touched her shoulders and he pulled her back against him. She felt the warmth of his body from her

knee to her shoulder. His fingers moved slowly down the
front of her gown, unbuttoning each button as though
unwrapping a precious gift. When he reached her waist he
pushed his hand inside and spread his fingers low across her
stomach. Anna leaned her head back against his shoulder
and sighed as his touch spread a hot glow over her skin and
a need began to grow deep inside her.

His lips trailed fire down her neck as he pulled the gown
from her shoulders and let it fall; then, at last, his hands
owned her flesh, and he moved his fingers from her hips to
her breasts. The feel of his body pressed against her back
and his hands moving across the front of her drove Anna
mad with pleasure. When she would have turned to return
his touch, he held her fast and chuckled at the need he'd
kindled inside of her.

Spreading his hands wide, his touch moved over her.
"You feel so wonderful," he whispered as his hands molded
her against him. "I've never held anything so soft." He
cupped her breasts in his hands and felt her melt against him
with a sigh.

Anna curled her face against his shoulder and treasured
the pleasure his fingers brought her as they moved over her
skin. His mouth descended to her throat and his touch grew
bolder with each caress until there was not a place on her
body he hadn't touched and explored. He shifted her head to
his other shoulder and pushed her hair away from her neck.
As he brushed warm kisses over her throat, his hand cupped
her breast, now half covered with her cascading hair.

"Anna, be mine." He stroked her hair away from her
breast and gently circled its fullness. "Be mine tonight and
forever."

Anna arched her body against him as his hand slid below
her waist. She wasn't sure if she whispered his name aloud
of if only her heart was singing it. All she knew was that
what he offered was far more than something physical and
for this moment she wanted everything. She wanted this

man and all he offered; she wanted there to be no past, no future, but only the now of his embrace.

Turning to face him, she felt their flesh touch full-length and marveled at the way his chest pushed against the softness of her breasts. "Love me," she whispered against his lips. "Teach me."

His kiss was gentle as he lifted her into his arms. Walking to the stream, he waded in until the water was past his waist. He lowered her into the cool water with a laugh and he silenced her squeal with a kiss.

Anna felt the water circling around her hips and waist as his kiss deepened. The moist fire of his mouth and the cold water circling about her legs sent a thrill through her. His arms held her tightly as the stream parted and rushed around them. He lowered them both into the water until her breasts floated like polished ivory in the silvery liquid. Then he reached and lifted her legs to his waist. Anna wrapped her legs around him as his face sank to her breasts. He buried his face in their fullness. The night was liquid velvet around her. She'd never felt so free, so wild, so cherished.

When she lowered her legs, she felt his manhood. He gripped her hips and pushed himself between her legs with a powerful force that could no longer be restrained or tamed. She opened her mouth in surprise, and he answered her with loving kisses as the center of his need pressed deep into her.

She tensed, then slowly relaxed as the water whirled around them and he moved inside her. There was no pressure smothering her, no drunken slobbering, no apologies. There was only Chance with his tender ways and gentle loving. All about her was fresh and clean and wild. All was new and tender, whispering to Anna that she'd only now come alive.

Leaning back, she floated on the water as he pulled her hips again and again against him. She'd never felt so free, so fulfilled. The water circled and splashed around them as if nature were pleased with their coupling. She tasted the clean water and smelled the freshness of the world around her. The pressure of him inside her seemed a part of it all as she floated, her arms above her, trusting him to hold her above the water.

Finally, she felt his hands tighten on her hips, then relax. He cried aloud as though the pain of a lifetime of loneliness were passing from him in one mighty, shuddering jolt.

Drawing her up close against him, he warmed her with his body, embracing her so tightly that she could barely breathe. Without a word, he lifted her into his arms and carried her to the moonlit grass. He laid her gently on the blanket, then spread his damp body beside hers. He seemed as though he couldn't get enough of her touch, and she was amazed that she felt the same way. The closer he was to her, the closer she wanted him to be.

"Anna," his voice was low with passion. "You are so wonderful." He slid his hand over her wet flesh. "You are so beautiful. Anyone who ever called you plain was lying. I can't imagine anything more perfect in the world than that which is in my arms now. Tell me, my love, how to make you happy."

"Hold me," she whispered, and he pulled her into his arms. "I want you to hold me." He silenced her whispers with sweet kisses.

They lay watching the moon pass over them as though its journey were for their amusement alone. Anna thought about how wonderful this time had been. He hadn't hurt her as William had. Chance's loving was a gift, not a price to be paid. All her life she'd remember the sweet feeling of floating on the water while he moved inside of her.

Anna was almost asleep on his arm when she moaned with pleasure as his thumb circled her breast. She hadn't been aware of when he'd stopped just holding her and begun to touch her, yet with sudden pleasure, she lay back on the wool blanket and stretched her arms above her head, allowing him full access to her body.

His fingers played along her flesh like a magical tune,

circling, pressing, loving. He seemed to be experimenting, exploring ways to bring passion to the surface. Each time she sighed, he repeated the action that had brought her pleasure.

"I want to make you happy, my love." His words warmed her heart as his touch warmed her body. "There will be nothing in the world for you tonight but my touch, my lips. I want you to cry for joy and only be able to measure time by the pounding of your heart against mine."

She felt her pulse speed up and her blood begin to follow his hands. Her body twisted and moved to his touch, craving his every caress. He kissed her until her head felt as though it were floating again; then he moved his mouth over her, tasting each inch of her flesh until every part of her body begged for more.

Kneeling above her, he covered her with long, wide strokes of his hands, and he laughed as she moaned when he stopped. The fire inside her was building with each touch. Her blood felt like it had turned to lava, spreading warmth all over her. She couldn't get enough of his igniting touch; her body told her there was more pleasure just beyond. There had to be more or she felt like she would explode with need for him.

He leaned over her, pressing his chest against her full breasts. His tongue circled her ear as he whispered, "Tell me how to love you." His voice was low, whispering an excitement that rumbled through her blood like the promising first wind before a mighty storm. "Tell me how to give you pleasure." He moved slightly, his chest molding her soft mounds against him.

Crying aloud with delight, Anna closed her eyes and relaxed as his body continued to brush over her.

"Tell me!" he demanded as he lowered his weight.

She opened her mouth, but he silenced her with his kiss, deep and seeking.

When finally he freed her lips and began kissing her face, Anna stretched against him. "You are pleasure."

He brushed her wet hair away from her throat. "I want to climb to a mountaintop with you." He moved his hand over her. "We're going together this time, my love. Don't be afraid; just let go and climb with me."

"I'm not afraid," Anna whispered as she drowned in the pleasure he stirred to life inside her. "I'm not sure what to do."

Chance laughed. "I'm not either, but if dreams count as experience, I should be an expert guide."

Brushing her hands over his shoulders she savored the warmth of him. "Tell me how."

"Touch me the way you did in the barn tonight."

Anna followed his order but knew the action brought her even more joy than it did him. She knelt beside him as he placed his arms behind his head and watched her. She loved the way his eyes turned to blue fire as her hands moved over him. His gaze boldly raked over her nude body and she felt the warmth of a blush travel over her. For the first time in her life, Anna knew she was beautiful.

"Tell me more," she urged as she lay back down beside him.

His mouth covered hers with more passion than she thought was possible. He kissed her while his warm hands lay claim to her body. After several minutes he pulled away and whispered, "Ask me to love you."

Her heart told her to linger, but the words raced to her tongue. "Love me," she answered as his heart pounded against her own.

He moved until his body covered hers. He pressed his knee down, nudging her legs apart. "Ask me again, my love."

Excitement had risen inside her until she felt she might go mad with pleasure at any moment. As she moved her legs slowly against his body, tears rose in her eyes. "Love me, Chance. Please, love me."

She felt him gently ease himself inside her. As his body pressed her against the earth, his mouth covered her lips and his tongue pushed into her mouth, making their oneness complete. There was no more time for words or instructions. Anna knew she had found her own happiness for the first time in her life. She'd made him happy, but she'd never expected to be caught up so completely in the avalanche of emotion. He'd predicted correctly: there was no measure of time except in the beating of his heart against her own.

She joined him in his dance of desire, and with each move wanted more and more of him. She wanted him closer, his hands everywhere on her body, his kiss to last forever. Now, his measured strokes released the eternity of her love.

The volcano of sensation exploded suddenly inside her as he pushed deep into her being. A flood of joy washed over her unlike she'd ever known existed in the world. She clung to him as her body took the shock of happiness she felt. She was floating, floating on a cloud of joy and belonging.

His body tensed above her, then he relaxed into her waiting arms. She slid her hand over his back and felt the thin layer of sweat. Had this wondrous joy they'd shared affected him as completely as it had her? She felt as though she'd exhausted every muscle in her body all at once; there was no energy left.

Rolling to his side, Chance pulled Anna with him in his arms. "God, I love you." He held her tightly.

Tears of joy spilled onto her cheeks. She lifted her hand to brush them away but Chance touched them first.

He pulled away slightly. "What is it? Did I hurt you? Oh, no, Anna, don't tell me I hurt you."

Anna tried to laugh as more tears rolled down her cheeks. "No, you didn't hurt me. It was wonderful. I've never felt anything like that before."

"I know."

"But I never thought I would. When I came out to the barn I was curious, but I never dreamed it would be anything like this. I was just hoping it wouldn't be painful. I never thought about the pleasure."

He kissed the top of her head. "I'm glad I made you happy."

"More than just happy. You made me feel whole for the first time in my life." She couldn't believe she was telling him her feelings, but somehow, lying there in the moonlight, it was impossible to lie. "Hold me," she whispered.

Chance kissed away the tears. "All night, my love. All this glorious night."

29

They made love again in the enchanted light of early dawn, then Chance carried her all the way back to the settlement. When Mrs. Basse stepped out of the house to greet them, Anna explained that they'd been bathing, but the smile on the older woman's face left no doubt that she knew exactly what they'd been doing.

She waved their excuses away and told Anna in German, "Now don't you worry. Little Cherish woke up a few minutes ago. I quieted her down, but she'll be wanting her breakfast soon." Mrs. Basse continued to chatter, knowing that the two lovers before her probably weren't hearing a word she said. "You should think of taking her completely off the breast as long as you have a cow. I'm just keeping my youngest nursing till the lady three houses down has her baby. Last year she gave birth and didn't have enough milk. I aim to help her out when she delivers this time."

Mrs. Basse finally wandered back into the house, talking more to herself than to Anna. She closed the door behind her as if she sensed they wanted to be alone.

Pulling Anna under his arm, Chance kissed the top of Anna's head. "It'll be full light soon. I'd like to get an early start."

Anna leaned against his chest. "I'll be ready in an hour."

As she turned to follow Mrs. Basse, he pulled her back

against him. "I don't want to let you go. I wish this night would never end."

"I know." She stretched and kissed his cheek. "It's been the best night of my life."

Hugging her against him, Chance thought of all the things he wanted to say to her. He wanted to tell her how much he loved her, but when he'd said the words before she hadn't answered. What if she didn't feel as he did? He knew not all people who enjoyed loving were in love with one another. The thought that Anna might not return his feelings kept him silent.

Anna slid her fingers over his shirt. "It was wonderful. I'll treasure it always in my memory."

"You sound as if we won't be together again." Chance didn't want to talk. He only wanted to hold her. Yet even now, he could feel Anna stiffening in his arms, pulling away from him even while her eyes were still warm with the glow of his loving.

Her fingers pushed lightly on his chest. "We must talk about what happened."

Tightly, he cradled her against him. "We talked last night. Your body told me everything my heart wants to know."

"But . . ."

He ended the discussion with a kiss almost brutal with the loss he already felt.

As he kissed her, Anna felt the warmth of his love as strong as the arms that bound her to him. Her fingers moved up his chest and encircled his neck as her last rational thought faded. There would be time to tell him later that last night must never happen again.

Finally, Chance broke the kiss and whispered, "I'd like to continue this conversation, but there are riders coming."

Anna pulled her wrapper tight just as riders turned the corner at full speed. Frantically, she tried to push her hair back into some semblance of respectability, but she knew it was hopeless. A dozen men or more rode up to John's house next door and dismounted as though they were in a race.

By now, Mrs. Basse and half her clan had joined Anna and Chance on the porch. The men destroyed the stillness of the morning with their shouts for John, and their horses stomped and snorted until a brown dust cloud rose from the ground like smoke from an evil witch's brew. The excitement infected the children immediately. Other neighbors poured outside in their nightclothes to see what was happening. Everyone was talking and shouting at once, and Anna couldn't understand a word being said.

Maggie clung to her waist in fright. "What is it, Anna? Why is everyone yelling?"

Anna patted her black curls so like her brother's and answered truthfully. "I don't know."

Chance walked over to the men and Anna watched as he calmly talked with them. She spotted Walter's plump frame pushing through the crowd. Then he climbed onto John's porch and shouted, "I say we ride out and kill every Indian we find!"

Towering above Walter, John shouted to the men around him. "That's not the answer. We have to reason with them and somehow make peace. I thought I made it plain last night, Walter: there will be no killing unless all else fails."

Walter puffed like a biscuit full of soda. "If you ask me, all else has failed."

John's normally kind face hardened slightly. "I don't remember asking you."

The two men stared at one another a moment, then Walter looked away.

Someone in the crowd yelled, "What about the men we sent out last time? They were murdered."

John shook his head. "We have to try. From what Walter says, they made some mistakes. If we act hostile, the Indians are as likely to kill as any people."

Walter stormed off the porch, having lost his following. He pushed his way through the crowd like a fat pig rooting

through knee-deep mud. When he reached the Basses'
porch he was heaving and wiping sweat from his face.
Looking up, he saw Anna and his anger seemed to flare
anew.

"You look as wild as this land." His eyes roamed from
her wild hair to her bare feet. "Tell me, how is the Texan's
wife?" His greeting was meant as an insult. This year hadn't
been good for him, and the past months had etched years of
bitterness into his deeply wrinkled frown. It had been a
mistake for him to pull up roots, but he hadn't been strong
enough to hold fast, and William had swept him along with
his dream. Now he seemed unable to grow on alien soil, so
he festered, unable to turn back.

"I'm fine." Anna looked down at him and for the first
time pitied him. He'd been a big man in their little town,
with a large circle of lifelong friends and an old family
name. Now he was someone who was pushed aside without
a second thought. Mrs. Basse had even said that many
didn't put any faith in his story of how the other men had
been killed by Indians. Rumors spread about their deaths
because all the men had been single, and Walter, because he
held the notes for their land, was the only one who benefited
from their deaths.

He snorted in an attempt to laugh. "You seem to be faring
well with your half-civilized husband. Back home you
would not be welcome in a single home with such a man,
and yet out here he'll probably fight those Indian butchers
on equal ground."

Anna knew there was just a grain of truth in his mountain
of lies. Chance wasn't the kind of man she could have taken
to dinners given by gentlefolk like those her husband and
mother hosted, and she couldn't imagine him sitting in the
drawing room discussing politics or poetry. But Chance had
never hurt her as they had. He would never live a lie; and
he'd loved her with a tenderness she'd never known existed.
Anna stared at Walter. "I'm fully confident that my husband
can protect me from any enemies—of any color."

Hatred flickered in Walter's eyes and centered suddenly on Anna. "You stand pretty high and mighty with your savage to protect you. It sickens me to think that this dream of a new life took my wife and my best friend and left you. But then, weeds thrive on any soil."

Anna tried to remain calm, for she knew Walter had never liked her, and grief for his wife had left him a penniless and bitter drunkard. "I'm sorry your wife died," she answered.

"Don't go giving me any of your pity. I'm pulling out of this. I might even come up on top with more land than anyone. Who knows? I might even have that little farm of yours before next spring."

"You'll never own my land."

"We'll see." Walter laughed and melted back into the crowd of men.

A chill passed over her and she knew he was up to something. He wasn't an honest man, and she knew he'd had schemes in Germany too, but there had never been any evidence to prove it.

A wagon clamored into the clearing at almost full speed. Anna recognized Tobin and Selma bobbing on the seat. Chance stepped from the others to help slow the horses. The tiny woman jumped from the seat as soon as she saw Anna. She lifted her skirts and ran toward them with tears streaming down her cheeks.

"Anna! Maggie!" she cried as she hugged them both wildly. "I'm so glad you're here. We didn't know where you were. When the report came of the Indian raids, we were so worried about you."

"Indian raids? Near our land?" Chance spoke from behind them.

Selma nodded vigorously. "There've been some farms raided nearby. None of the Germans yet, but we could be next."

Chance caught Anna's gaze over Selma's head. "Maybe we'd better talk about this without the children around."

Anna agreed and noticed Mrs. Basse had already taken the hint and was sweeping all the children into the house with reassuring words and healthy pats on their behinds.

Chance sat Selma down on the porch's only chair and instructed her to start at the beginning.

Gulping several deep breaths, she said, "We got word yesterday, and when Tobin came by with a load of lumber for your house, Carl ordered me to town where I'd be safe. He says he has to stay with the farm or the crops will rot in the fields and we'll starve this winter." Her round eyes filled with tears. "I've never been away from him. Not one day since we were married. He's not a fighter." She grabbed Chance's arm. "You know that. You've shot every piece of meat we've eaten this summer. You've got to go to him now."

Chance straightened. "I'll saddle up." He looked at Anna. "I'll check with John and Tobin and be on my way within an hour."

He patted Selma's hand. "Don't worry, I won't let anything happen to any man who's lucky enough to have a woman like you crying over him."

As he stepped from the porch, he glanced at Anna and she saw a touch of sadness in his eyes before his gaze turned to blue stone. Was he only sorry for Selma, or did he wonder if anyone would cry for him? Did he think she cared so little for him? A flood of tears welled behind her eyes, but she held them at bay and choked back the fear that wanted to beg him not to go.

An hour later, Chance walked into the barn to saddle Cyoty, knowing he'd have to travel fast to be of any help to Carl. If the Indians were raiding farms, they wouldn't take many days off. He'd taken the time to talk to several men, and so far all he'd heard were rumors, but rumors had a way of hatching from a kernel of truth.

As he lifted the saddle onto Cyoty's back, Chance saw someone enter the barn. For a moment he thought it was a man, but there was no mistaking the soft curve of Anna's hips even in a pair of pants. Her hair was tied back at the base of her neck and her moccasins were laced to her knees.

"What the hell do you think you're doing?" Chance knew, but didn't want to admit it even to himself.

"I'm going with you."

"I don't suppose it would do me any good to order you to stay in town." If Chance hadn't been so angry he would have admired her stubborn spirit.

"No." Anna led Cinnamon from the stall. Someone had already saddled the huge sorrel and Anna's carpetbag was tied onto the back of the saddle.

"I need to ride fast."

"I won't slow you down. That's why I borrowed some clothes from one of the Basse boys." She swung into the saddle with a grace that proved her point.

"But the baby?" Chance wasn't giving up. He wanted her safe in town.

"Mrs. Basse can feed her and see after Maggie. Cherish is almost four months old now; she'll be fine. I had Mrs. Basse wrap my chest so that my milk will dry up."

Chance placed his hand over hers as they gripped the reins. "Much as I want you with me, you can't go. It's too dangerous. I'll check things out and in a week or so I'll send for you."

"It's my land and no one is going to take it from me. If the Indians try, they'll have to kill me. I'm going and there is nothing you can say to stop me."

"Dammit, if you're not the most headstrong person God ever dropped from heaven. I've a good mind to pull you from that saddle and teach you a thing or two."

Anna kicked Cinnamon and was out of the barn before Chance could react. "You'll have to catch me first."

Chance mounted Cyoty and followed in a cloud of dust. They were over a mile outside of town before Anna slowed and he caught up to her.

"All right." Chance shoved his hat back. "You made

your point. You can ride better than most men I've seen. But that doesn't change the fact that you have no business going back with me."

"I have every right to go back with you. I can shoot as well as I ride and I'll be more help than Carl in a fight."

Chance couldn't argue that point with her. He'd rather have her at his back than Carl any day. "If you go, you agree here and now to follow orders. I don't want you questioning me in the middle of trouble."

"Agreed." Anna smiled, knowing she'd won.

"And we ride hard. I have no time for complaints." He knew there was no need to say it, for Anna was not a woman to complain. "I'm not sure what we're going to find."

"You think it's Storm's Edge, don't you?" Anna's words startled him.

Frowning for a moment, he didn't know whether to lie to her or tell her the truth. "It could be, from what some of the men were saying. John's been getting reports from the west about a small band of Indians. That's why I'd feel better if you were in town. He kills women and children without any thought." Chance's jaw tightened at the memory of his mother lying facedown, slaughtered like a farm animal.

"I'm not going back," Anna answered. "If you go to fight, I fight with you."

Chance kicked his bay into action and was proud to see Anna stay only a half a length behind him as they crossed the open country and rode north. He had one hell of a strong woman with him, and the knowledge that she'd come willingly to him during the night filled him with pride. If her strength equaled her stubbornness and passion, any Indian who crossed her was in for a fight.

Determined, he pushed hard all morning, not allowing Anna or his bruised ribs to slow the pace. As the sun grew warm, they stopped beside a stream to rest the horses.

Anna slipped to the ground before he could help her. She

walked beside him to the water's edge. "You're still angry about my coming."

Chance knelt and trailed his canteen through the water. "I just wish you'd put something ahead of your land."

"Like what?"

"Like your life, or Cherish, or my peace of mind."

Accepting the drink he offered, she answered, "I have no life without my land and neither does Cherish. As for your peace of mind, that is something I can't control."

Chance started to say something, then stood suddenly, listening to the breeze.

"What is it?" Anna stood beside him.

"Nothing," he whispered. "Just a feeling I have. We'd best ride."

They crossed the land in half the time it had taken them to travel to town. Anna wasn't sure what she'd expected, but there was nothing amiss at the farm. They circled by Carl's farm and found him hard at work on his cabin.

Chance and Anna agreed to stay the night with Carl, using the excuse that Chance could help Carl put up the frame of the second room of the cabin. Carl might not be a fighter, but he would be offended to think they were there to protect him.

The men worked until dark, with Anna helping. It amazed her how fast the room was going up. Over a supper of dried meat and baked sweet potatoes, Chance and Carl agreed to take shifts sleeping.

Anna slept in the only finished room and both men bedded down outside. She knew that Chance was probably more alert sleeping than Carl would be awake. Anna curled fully dressed atop the bed and tried to sleep. The silent alertness of Chance all day was finally getting to her. He'd worked, as always, with power and force, but she'd caught him glancing at the hills often. And once when he thought no one was watching, she'd seen him touch the ground, as if he could feel the pounding hooves of approaching horses.

30

Three days passed without a break in the pattern. Anna worked alongside the men, not wanting to be alone should Indians appear. They talked of little except the chores, but she knew the fear of an attack was in all of their minds. The fear was slowly destroying the foundation of confidence they'd first felt when they'd settled so near the hunting grounds.

Midmorning on the fourth day, Tobin appeared, bringing news that all had been quiet in town, but that Selma had about driven him mad with requests to come and check on Carl. He offered to help Carl with his crops so Chance and Anna could farm their own land. In exchange, Carl declared that a place would always be made at his table for Tobin.

Tobin rolled his eyes at Anna, telling her he'd already tasted Selma's cooking and would gladly favor hardtack and beans. Anna hid her laughter in her excitement over going home. She and Chance were saddled and racing toward their farm before Tobin had time to think of some excuse to return to town.

They found the farm as they'd left it except that the cow had gotten out. It took Chance an hour to find her. When he returned, Anna had a lunch of scrambled eggs and ham waiting on the table.

Chance ate in silence now that they were finally alone for the first time since their night together. It seemed as though they were both acting out roles, unsure of what to say. She knew he'd been angry about her coming with him, and she'd pulled away when he'd tried to touch her. Every time she'd tried to talk with him, they'd only had a moment before Carl was within hearing distance. Chance had resented her coldness and she'd resented his silence.

Anna tried to think of some way to explain to him that the night by the stream was a one-time occurrence. Even now she knew his departure would leave a wide hole in her heart. If they grew closer it would be even worse. He wasn't the kind of man to settle down. The fact that he had a farm he hadn't seen in years was proof of that. She couldn't ask him to be penned up after he'd always been free, and she wouldn't break the agreement they'd made.

Working through late morning in silence, they stored the vegetables in the cool hole Chance had dug in the sand of the cellar. The grain wasn't ready, so Chance turned his energy to the real house that would replace the dugout they'd been living in. When they stopped for supper, Anna was amazed at how much work had been done. She'd noticed Chance stacking logs and Tobin hauling lumber for weeks but she hadn't really seen a house amid the stacks. The stone fireplace had sat alone for several days as a silent promise of her home. She'd watched Tobin and Chance mark off the ground and lay the floor, but now, suddenly, it had all come together. Within hours, there was a roof and walls up to her waist in the room that was to be the bedroom.

As darkness crept in around them, Anna decided that dinner wouldn't be as wordless as lunch. "I can't believe how fast the house is going up." Trying to keep her voice calm, she reminded herself that they were having a meal together just as they had done for months. She tried to push the thought that they were alone aside.

"Rounding up all the lumber is the hard part." Chance seemed to jump at the opportunity to bridge the silence. "I wanted enough for two big rooms with a dog run in the middle. That way in summer you can move the table between the open space of the two rooms and enjoy the breeze."

"It's a fine cabin." Anna lifted his empty plate from the table.

Slowly, Chance stood up, and he would have touched her, but she moved away as she had for four days. He looked outside, not wanting her to see how much her withdrawal hurt. "I'd best check the fence. I don't want to lose that cow again."

Anna forced herself to speak her idea before she grew any more nervous. "I think I'll sleep down here on Maggie's bed since you moved the other bed up to the new bedroom."

Chance didn't move, but she saw his knuckles turn white as he gripped the dugout's door frame.

"I've been giving it some thought. It's better this way." She could almost feel his anger vibrating in the air. For a moment she wished he could see her pain. How could he understand that she'd miss him every day for the rest of her life? Every time they touched would be one more memory to carry when he was gone. He must see that a clean cut now would be the only way the wound of his leaving might heal. "I tried to tell you before. What happened that night by the stream was only one night. It does not change our agreement." She would not let her need for him bind him to her when all he'd ever been was free.

Slowly, as if forcing every step, he left the dugout. She heard him working on the cabin until dark. Each slam of the hammer rattled the countryside with his anger and was an intangible blow to her heart.

It had to be said, she told herself over and over. She had to stop what was growing between them before it went further. Only a fool would nurture a love that would only be uprooted before it bloomed. He would be gone in three months, and she could not bear it if she allowed his impending absence to become any more painful than it was already.

Anna bathed and dressed for bed without lighting a candle. The night grew dark, low clouds hiding the moonlight. She crawled into Maggie's high little bed and hugged herself, wishing the children were there to ease her loneliness.

Sleep wouldn't come. The rumbling sky twisted her nerves and faraway lightning made her restless. The sound of Chance working above her by lantern drifted to Anna and she knew he would work until he dropped.

When finally she dozed, she dreamed of being back in Germany the night William had raped her, the night her mother had died. The thunder of the night blended with her nightmare and the lightning flashed terror through her mind. She could see William's drunken face above her as his fists silenced her screams. The nightmare rolled on in angry waves. She was alone again, crying for a mother who would never come, screaming for help when she knew there would be none.

She could feel William's hands pawing at her, ripping her gown as she screamed. The storm outside the dugout outmatched her cries and the rain drowned her tears. In her dream the storm was the same as before and terror ripped reality from her mind.

The door slammed against the dugout wall with a sudden, violent explosion. Anna jerked upright in Maggie's tiny bed, almost hitting her head on the ceiling. Fear danced across her flesh as she strained to identify the shadow blocking the door. His chest was heaving for air and his fist was wrapped around the handle of a hammer. She was lost in a hell between the nightmare and reality.

"Anna!" Chance's voice echoed in the dark room.

She didn't speak, but instead clutched the covers to her. *This was it,* she thought as haunting fears and reality collided. The dark side of him that she knew would someday surface no matter how kind he'd been was now at hand. Tears welled in her eyes as she slid her fingers along the windowsill in search of the knife he'd given her. She would face the animal that lived in all men with a weapon this time. He wouldn't beat her senseless as William had without suffering also. A clap of thunder strained her every nerve and tightened her grip on the knife.

In the flash of lightning that followed, Chance saw Anna huddled in the bed, her face pale with fear, her hand gripping the knife as if the devil himself stood before her. Her eyes were wild with hate and terror.

"Come closer and I swear I'll kill you!" Her voice was high and unnatural with the nightmare that still overshadowed her reasoning.

"Anna!" he shouted, not knowing if his words would reach her. "Are you all right?"

Anna stared at him with hate-filled eyes. "What do you want?"

Moving a step closer, he answered, "I heard you cry out. I thought you were hurt or afraid of the storm."

Anna lowered the knife as she tried to sort dream from reality. Had she cried out in her sleep? The nightmare slid into blackness and the truth registered.

"I had a bad dream. When the door slammed open, I thought . . ."

Something heavy flew across the room and slammed into the fireplace as Chance swore. "You thought I'd come to rape you!" he yelled above the storm.

"You were angry at me. You've been angry since we left Fredericksburg."

"Hell, Anna, I'm still angry. I want you safe." He slammed his fist into the table as his words cracked the air between them. "But my anger has nothing to do with the look you just gave me. I am sick to death of seeing hate and fear in your eyes. What do I have to do to convince you I'm not William? No matter how mad I might get, I'll never take you against your will."

He stormed up the steps as Anna realized how much she'd hurt him. He was a strong man trying to do what was right, and she'd let the cruel injustice of her nightmare judge him.

Pulling the blanket around her, Anna followed him into the rain. She had to convince him that it was her past and not a fear of him that brought on her doubts.

He was standing in the center of the yard letting the cold downpour wash away his anger. His stance was wide, with his fists raised to the sky as though he challenged the storm.

She touched his shoulder, but he remained like a statue before her. "I'm sorry!" she shouted above the rain.

He didn't move.

"You've never hurt me. I had no right to say what I did." She saw the raw pain in his strong, blue eyes.

His words were as cold as the wind from the north. "Sometimes I hate you." Running his fingers through his wet hair, he added, "And I hate myself for wanting you."

"I want you, also."

"Then why did you sleep in Maggie's bed?"

"I didn't want to make it any harder for us to say good-bye."

"Could the pain be any greater than sleeping only a few feet apart for the next three months?"

Anna couldn't answer, for his hand moved over her wet nightgown, warming her with his touch. She closed her eyes, remembering the gentle way he'd made love to her.

Without a word he lifted her into his arms and carried her to the newly built bedroom. He pulled off her gown and wrapped a dry blanket around her, then he sat her atop the high workbench.

She watched as he stirred up the fire until it blazed in the half-finished room. The lye he'd used to make the mortar was overwhelmed by the smell of fresh-cut wood and the cedar fire.

Finally he stood, the fire alive behind him, the sounds of the storm echoing between them. "I've thought about our arrangement. I've gone along with every rule you've set, but not this time."

He moved to stand before her, their eyes level. "Tell me you hate my touch and I'll stop, but don't lie to yourself or to me, Anna." There was no end to the depth of love in his eyes. "Don't push me away when we both want to be together for the little time we have left."

Cupping her face gently in his hand, he whispered, "I'm going to love you tonight and every night until the year and our agreement is up."

"But . . ."

His lips brushed hers lightly. "You're going to sleep next to me for as long as we have left and I'll let no nightmares haunt your dreams. I'll see no more fear in your beautiful eyes."

"It will only make the pain greater." She touched his wet shirt with her fingers, delighting in the way the thin material covered his warm flesh.

Pushing her blanket from her shoulders, Chance pulled her against him. "Then let me die in three months, for I would have this time of heaven."

He lifted her onto the bed and rolled beside her.

Anna heard the thunder and saw the lightning, but she was no longer afraid, for she felt warm and protected in Chance's arms. He loved her with a tenderness and a passion that was even greater than their night by the stream.

Later, when the storm had quieted to a slow drizzle and their passion had been spent, Anna heard Chance whisper her name in his sleep. She cuddled close to him and memorized his young face, now relaxed in sleep. A single tear drifted from his eye, burning its way into her heart with its slow journey down his tanned face, and Anna tried to imagine how she would ever survive without him.

31

"**Mornin'**, folks," Tobin shouted on the other side of the four-foot barrier that would soon be a bedroom wall. "I would have knocked, but I couldn't find the door."

Jumping from the bed, Chance grabbed his pants while Anna pulled the covers over her head in embarrassment. Tobin only chuckled and strolled down to water his horses. When Chance joined him a moment later, Tobin was smiling from floor to ceiling.

"I know it ain't good light yet son, but it ain't like you to sleep so soundly. If I'd been a liquored Indian lookin' for a scalp to hang on my belt, you'd be a dead man."

Chance splashed water on his face and steadied himself for more teasing.

"Course, when I was young, I could go all night with a good woman and still be up before the sun."

"Of course." Chance tried not to swear. He patted the team hitched to Tobin's wagon, wanting desperately to change the subject. "Where're you headed?"

Tobin laughed. "I just thought bein' in town with Selma was bad. It took her three days to talk me into coming out to check on Carl, but it only took that slow-talking German a day to convince me to go get her. I also visited with Anna's Indian. He kind of likes being called Sourdough, by the way, and said there weren't no trouble around these parts that he knew about."

309

"He should know," Chance answered. "I've talked with him several times. His tribe's not the kind to brag, but I gathered that he's much respected by his people in these parts. If he says there will be no trouble, he's probably right."

Tobin nodded, agreeing with Chance's assessment of Sourdough. "I stopped by to see if you think it's safe enough for me to bring the kids back. I kind of miss that little monkey, Maggie, around the place. Till I ran into you last winter I can't say as I cared much about anythin'. Now I feel like I got a family. I figure in a few years when I get too old to run around the country, you and Anna will kind of take care of me in my old age."

"Don't plan on it," Chance said, laughing.

Tobin shrugged as if he'd give his planned retirement another shot some other time.

Chance looked toward the dugout as Anna stepped to the door. She was dressed, but her hair was still wild and free down her back and as always the sight of her made his heart catch in his throat. Even in her brown work dress and muslin apron, she looked like the finest lady he'd ever seen. She smiled at Chance, then asked Tobin to stay for breakfast.

Tobin jumped at the offer of food with much thanks, knowing full well that Anna had already set him a place. He winked at Chance as if to tell the younger man that his hope for a place in retirement was not lost.

Chance watched Anna disappear into the cabin as he asked, "When do you think you'll be back?"

"Two, maybe three days. I have to wait on some supplies Carl needs." Tobin chuckled as he studied Chance. "Damned if you ain't the most bit man I ever seen."

"Shut up, old man," Chance answered as he walked to the house. But he couldn't resist touching Anna as he passed her, and even Tobin's laughter couldn't slow the fire that was already building. Watching Anna move, Chance knew he'd spend the day wishing for nightfall and thinking of

Anna in his arms. He saw no shame in loving his wife. Even if she never came to feel the same, he knew he'd never stop loving her. Tobin's teasing was rooted in envy, but no one would envy Chance come January when he had to say good-bye or else break his word to Anna.

Anna playfully pushed Chance away as he patted her and tried to hide her enjoyment of his mock disappointment. "Do you think we could have the house finished by the time the girls return?"

Chance nodded and Anna turned back to the stove, missing Tobin's wink at Chance as he said, "Depends on how much else you've got to do, son."

The girls returned to their new home a few days later. Maggie loved her loft. It was the first time she'd had a place of her own. She climbed up and down the ladder in excitement. Cherish's crib was placed close to the fire in the bedroom, but Anna promised Maggie that as soon as Cherish was able to walk she could sleep in the loft also.

The dugout had been warm and cozy as their first home, but the cabin was well lit and smelled of freshly cut wood. There was a sense of digging in roots as each peg was hammered home.

Anna had never known the happiness of a true home where the rooms were filled with love. She'd wake early just to listen to the sounds of the house: the timber creaking in the roof and the slight tap of shutters in the wind. And inside she treasured the crackle of a low fire and the steady sound of Chance breathing at her side. When she heard these sounds she'd smile to herself with the pure joy of being home at last.

Fall brought a peace that none in the cabin had ever experienced. Chance finished harvesting the crops, then turned his labors to building a shed beside the barn and a wide porch for the house. Anna braided rugs from rags and gathered their first honey crop. The honey and wax brought a good price in town, thanks to Tobin's bartering skills.

As winter closed in around them, Anna bought material and yarn. She enjoyed the quiet afternoons watching Maggie and Cherish while she sewed. But the best time of all was when the girls were asleep and she was alone with Chance. Each night he'd go out to check the stock while she bathed and dressed for bed. When he returned there was always a fire in his eyes and his hair would be damp from his swim in the creek. They'd sit and share a last cup of coffee together by the fire, then he'd pull her into his arms with a hunger that surprised and thrilled her.

"The nights," Anna whispered to herself as she rocked a fussy Cherish one cold morning, "the nights are heaven."

Cherish coughed, shaking her tiny body and startling Anna out of her daydream.

"Hush, darling, and sleep," Anna whispered.

But Cherish didn't sleep. Each time she closed her eyes the cough came again, rattling her body.

By the time Chance came in for lunch, tiny lines of worry marred Anna's face.

Chance's sharp eye took in the cold stove and the breakfast dishes still on the table. He dropped his ax at the door and knelt beside Anna. "What is it?"

Cherish coughed and Anna tried to keep from crying as she answered, "She keeps coughing and she's hot, real hot. I've tried to give her milk but she won't take any. She won't even play with Maggie."

Putting his arm around Anna's shoulder, Chance tried to reassure her. "Don't worry; babies get colds. We've been lucky so far: six months and she hasn't had a sniffle." He couldn't bring himself to say how many folks lost their children before the tiny ones had even had time enough to have a birthday. Almost every homestead in this country had a tiny grave behind it.

Chance stood and warmed his hands by the fire, then took Cherish from Anna. "You relax a minute. Maybe I can walk her to sleep." He began to pace with the baby in his arms.

Leaning her head against the wall, Anna forced herself to

relax. When she'd been alone she'd been terrified, but now Chance was with her. Now there was someone to help, someone to share the worry. She watched her tall man with the tiny girl in his arms. He was patting Cherish on the back as he walked, and keeping up a rhythm of nonsense talk that only Cherish seemed to understand.

Anna fixed a cold lunch, but Maggie was the only one who ate it and Chance didn't return to his work, but stayed to help Anna instead. The look he shot her over Maggie's head told Anna that he, too, knew it wasn't just a sniffle. With each hour her cough grew worse, shaking her small frame with each spell.

They took turns walking Cherish and playing with Maggie, but by nightfall even little Maggie knew something was very wrong.

"I'll build the fire up real high and then get some water from the stream." Chance lifted the bucket. "We've got to get that fever down, but we don't want her catching a chill."

Anna stared at her child, who'd been so healthy only hours ago. Now she looked pale and thin. Her tiny body was hot to the touch and she hadn't eaten in hours. She was so tired from coughing that she whimpered no matter what Anna did. Cherish's breathing sounded raspy, and Anna knew that fluid was already starting to fill her lungs.

Chance and Anna paced beside the crib all night. When Cherish got too hot, they'd bathe her and then wrap her to keep her from a chill. Chance tried a mixture of the fever tea he'd used with Anna, but they couldn't get Cherish to swallow any.

Finally, Anna sat in the center of the bed and held her close. "I feel so helpless. We have no medicine." The realization of just how alone they were hit full force. Back in Germany there had always been a doctor in town and old women whose families had weathered every illness. Now there was no one to turn to for advice.

Chance wrapped a blanket around Anna's shoulders. "I

could ride to Fredericksburg, but I doubt I'd find much help."

Anna gripped his arm. "No! It's too cold. You'd never make it back in time." Tears spilled from her eyes as she realized what the words *in time* meant.

The morning brought only exhaustion and a baby now too weak to cry out when the coughing spells hit. They could hear the rattle in her chest each time she breathed. Maggie came down to breakfast, her eyes puffy from crying. "I could hear you talking and walking down here last night. I've seen babies cough like that. Cherish is real sick, isn't she?"

Chance lifted Maggie into his arms. "Yes, darling, she's real sick."

"Can you make it better?" She said the words as if she truly believed her big brother could do anything.

He smiled at his little sister. "We'll try."

But by afternoon, Cherish's skin was pale and she looked wasted and thin. Chance looked up at Anna, worry aging his face far more than work ever would. "We've got to get some liquid down her fast." He pushed his thumb against Cherish's tiny arm and stared as the imprint of his soft touch did not disappear.

Anna was to the point of complete panic. "I've tried milk. She can't keep it down, and she won't take the tea or even water." She saw what she feared reflected in Chance's face. Cherish was dying.

Pulling her baby close to her, Anna prayed, "Don't let her die. Please, God, don't let her die."

Chance turned away without a word. He couldn't stand to see Anna fall apart. He knew how important Cherish was to her, and that Anna saw the child as her only chance at loving or being loved. Why couldn't she see that he loved her too? Why couldn't she turn to him instead of pulling more and more into herself as each hour passed?

An idea hit him with such a force that he ran from the room, optimism touching his heart for the first time all day.

Within seconds he was back with a jug of honey. Anna watched him, one last ray of hope in her eyes.

He dipped a clean rag into the tea he'd made from brewing a branch of the spicebush, then layered the damp rag with thick honey. He knelt beside Anna. Cherish rested quietly in her lap, too weak even to cry.

Chance lay the rag against the baby's tiny pale lips. Slowly, almost hesitantly, Cherish began to suck on the rag. The honey coated her throat, quieting the cough, and the warm tea eased her fever.

The next few hours tiptoed slowly through the cabin, bringing the soft patter of hope. Maggie fell asleep at the foot of the bed, and hour after hour they bathed and rocked the baby. When she awoke they gave her more of the honey-laced tea, and each time she seemed to take a few more swallows. Now the rattle in her chest lessened.

Anna curled beside Maggie and closed her eyes for a moment to rest as Chance sat by the fire with Cherish. When Anna looked up, she realized she'd been asleep for some time. Cherish's coughing had stopped, and the silence was shattering.

Panic deep inside her brought her to her feet. Hurrying to the fire, she knelt beside Chance. Cherish was sleeping quietly on his chest as he leaned back against the wall. Anna touched her daughter's forehead and felt no fever for the first time in two days. Then she touched the black hair falling across Chance's forehead. He was sound asleep, but the worry lines were still etched in his face. He was in bad need of a shave and his clothes were wrinkled and stained, but the steady rhythm of his breathing had lulled Cherish to sleep, her arms outstretched, her face tucked under his chin.

Leaning against him, Anna kissed him lightly. At this moment, in spite of all the wrinkles, whiskers, and stains, this man before her was the most handsome man in the world.

Chance opened his eyes and smiled at her. "The fever broke," he whispered as he lifted Cherish.

Anna carefully carried her baby to the crib. She felt a blessing had been handed to her, a blessing she already possessed but never cherished until now. "We'd better get you to bed also."

He stood and stretched his long, tired muscles. "Let's make a pallet for Maggie. I don't want her sleeping in the loft and waking up afraid."

Anna threw a heavy quilt beside their bed. "She'll be warm here. That north wind is really starting to howl." Anna wondered how she could talk calmly about the weather when she wanted to shout for joy.

Chance lowered Maggie to her bed, threw a few more logs on the fire, then sank into bed with a low sigh of exhaustion. Anna lay beside him, resting her head on his chest. He pulled her tightly against him and kissed the top of her head. They were both too tired even to undress.

Anna curled in his arms and cried, releasing all the fear she'd held inside. Even now she couldn't stop listening for Cherish's next cough. But Chance held her tightly and whispered in her ear until she fell asleep on much the same spot her daughter had.

Morning dawned with Cherish's cry. She was weak, but the cough had not returned. Anna greeted the morning with a smile as she looked outside to find winter's first snow thick upon the ground.

Chance took the day off to play with Cherish and tease Maggie. It was as though he felt he had to make up for the hard day of worry with a day of leisure. Cherish was fussy and nowhere suited her but Chance's arms. He'd lean her against his chest and hold her with one hand as he moved about the cabin.

Anna made hot apple cider and oven cakes for lunch. The cakes weren't cakes at all, but potatoes split open, roasted, and spread thick with bacon drippings. Just as they sat down to eat, Carl and Selma hurried in without knocking.

Selma danced across the room like a tiny snow fairy. She was one of those women who would never stop being a little girl. "We had to come, even in the snow, to tell you." She smiled with delight at the oven cakes. "Those look just like what we had in Germany."

Anna handed her a hot potato. "I had to cook them on a skillet, but they should taste the same. Now let it cool and tell us your news."

Selma looked up as if she'd suddenly remembered. "Oh, yes." She held Carl's hand with both her own. "We're going to have a baby," she said in her most grown-up voice.

Everyone started talking at once. There was laughter and dancing and shouting.

Anna hugged Selma hard. "When?"

"I thought I might be with child when I was in town. Mrs. Basse told me not to tell anyone until I felt it move, and then I'd only have four months to go. I felt it move last night. We'll have a child before spring."

Maggie was pulling at Selma's skirt. "What are you going to name it?"

Carl answered. "Herschel if it's a boy, and Texas if it's a girl?"

Everyone laughed, but only Maggie was brave enough to say, "*Herschel*, who'd ever call a baby that? And what kind of name is Texas for a girl?"

Selma patted her on the head. "Don't worry, I've got four months to work on him. Maybe you can help me think of another name."

Suggestions flooded the room for several minutes, with each name getting wilder and more outrageous. Finally, Carl ended the discussion by saying he'd give the names some more thought. He pulled on his coat. "I'm going out to the barn to look at something with Chance," he said, winking at the other man. "We have to leave the women alone to talk about those things that no man in his right mind wants to hear."

Nodding, Chance followed him and left the women to make pies and talk.

The shadows outside had grown long by the time Carl

and Selma left. They'd had a great visit, but Chance had remained silent during most of the discussions about the future. He smiled at Carl's kidding about catching up with him on children and laughed when they talked of their children someday marrying one another. But Chance seemed relieved when they finally left. For him there was no future with Anna, and listening to the others only made him more aware of how little time they had left.

He carried Maggie up to bed while Anna tucked Cherish into her cradle. When he returned, Anna was staring out at the moon reflecting off the snow. He stood behind her, encircling her with his warmth. "What are you thinking, my love?"

Anna leaned her head against his neck. "I was thinking what if I were pregnant."

Chance chuckled. "You've been loving me for months now and the thought just crossed your mind?"

"No, I've thought of it before, but it always seemed far away."

He slid his hands over her abdomen. "I can think of nothing more beautiful than your body swelling with my seed."

Anna pulled away. "I'm not the earth—something to be planted."

Chance realized he hadn't said it right. "No, you're not. I just remember how lovely you were when you were pregnant and I would be proud if we had another child. I think sometimes of what a son of ours would be like. Does the thought of another pregnancy frighten you?"

"No." Anna turned away from him. "With Maggie here to help I could handle another baby." She loved the idea that a part of him would always remain with her.

Turning her to face him, he asked, "Do you honestly think I could leave you if you were pregnant?"

Anna didn't want to think about it at all. She didn't want to tie him down or try to cage him, but her plan for having her own farm without a man around was as ragged and warped as a novice's quilt. What had seemed like such a good pattern had somehow gone off center, and now that it was about to be complete, Anna felt a growing hatred for the end she'd made for herself.

She looked up at this man who'd become so much a part of her life. "I'm not pregnant, but if I were I'd be proud to bear your child."

Chance pulled her to him. God, how he wished she'd begged him to stay. He wanted nothing more than to live with Anna and have a dozen kids, but his pride kept him silent. For he was a man of his word, and he'd keep his part of the bargain even if it ripped his heart out to do it. If she wanted him gone, he'd leave on the third day of January, just as promised.

But tonight, and every night for the weeks he had left, he'd love her. He'd build up a lifetime of memories in that time.

32

Christmas came wrapped with joy and tied with silent sadness. Chance had almost forgotten how families celebrated the holiday. For the past several years he hadn't even noticed the day's passing. But not this year. Anna made a feast and invited Tobin, Carl, and Selma, then insisted on decorating a tree and having presents for everyone. The strain that was growing daily between him and Anna seemed to ease for this one day. Yet an ocean of unspoken words that neither knew how to cross floated between them.

Carl and Selma arrived early in the afternoon with their arms loaded with gifts. Pregnancy weighed heavily on Selma's tiny frame, making her look like a buoy floating in her long skirts. Even though she was only in her sixth month, she was already waddling.

Tobin soon followed, his wagon loaded with gifts. He'd always practiced the philosophy of never carrying more than he could pack in his saddlebags, so he'd spent the money he had left after restocking his supplies on gifts for everyone.

Laughter filled the house to capacity as everyone opened their gifts. Chance touched the shirt Anna had made him as though he were holding something priceless. She'd used all her saved strands of loose hair to braid him a chain for his watch. He looked at it questioningly until Selma explained that many German women made things like watch chains and combs out of their hair. Some even made wreaths with finely embroidered flowers made all of hair, she told him.

Maggie squealed, drawing everyone's attention. Selma had made her a doll and Carl had carved tiny furniture to match. Chance gave her a miniature dresser set like Anna's, and Tobin had bought the matching mirror. Anna had made her two new dresses and a long knitted shawl. The child moved from one gift to the other thinking she was surely the richest little girl alive.

Chance watched as Anna opened all her gifts of hair ribbons and things for Cherish. When her lap was empty, he stood and pulled her silently with him across the open space to their bedroom. All the others followed with excitement.

Opening the door, he smiled as Anna gasped. There, where only a bed and crib had been, was a roomful of furniture. Chance beamed. "Carl helped me." He moved beside the dresser. "I thought you needed a real dresser for that fine dresser set of yours and Carl suggested the desk and wardrobe. We had one heck of a time getting it through the door this morning while you were cooking without you noticing."

Running her hands over the soft cedar, she whispered, "It's beautiful."

"That's not all," Carl yelled form the porch. "Selma and I thought you'd need this for all those babies coming in the future." He uncovered a finely crafted rocker with a cushion made from the same material Selma had used for her curtains.

Anna couldn't tell if she was laughing or crying. She felt very much like Maggie with too many presents all at once. She'd worked for weeks to give everyone gifts without thinking about what they might give her, and now she was overwhelmed.

She hugged everyone. When she moved into Chance's arms, he held her a little too tightly, as though with each touch he realized they were one step closer to the end. She pulled away, trying to laugh at Tobin's teasing, but she could see the pain that seemed to grow daily in Chance's eyes.

Anna hurried everyone into the kitchen, not wanting to think about Chance's leaving in only a few days. They all crowded around the table, which was loaded down with food.

The laughter and hubbub of food being passed blocked out the sound of gunfire for a moment. Then, all at once, everyone heard it. Anna grabbed Maggie and Cherish and ran to the dugout with Selma at her side. The men raced for their guns as another round of fire sounded from the direction of the road.

Chance was on the porch with Tobin and Carl at his side when a rider rounded the bend from town and headed toward the house. Silently, Tobin raised his rifle, ready to fire.

"Wait!" the rider shouted. "Don't shoot!"

Chance swore under his breath as he recognized the rider. "Walter," he whispered as Tobin lowered his gun only an inch, still debating whether or not to fire.

Walter rode close, almost falling from his horse as he reined to a stop. "I was beginning to think there was no one around. I was over at Carl and Selma's place and—"

Chance cut him off. "What do you want, Walter?"

The fat man dusted himself off, offended by Chance's directness. Walter could see by the Texan's wide stance that any hopes of being invited in were only dreams. "I came to tell you that the society officials will be around tomorrow or the next day to check on how all the homesteads are coming. If there's no one home, the land will be reassigned."

"It's pretty obvious we're living here." Chance didn't like Walter and made no attempt to be anything but blunt.

"Yes, but some of the farms have been abandoned this winter. Not all farmers planted crops like you folks did. Some thought it was too late in the season, and some just didn't know how. Anyway, I was just sent to tell all you folks that there best be someone around the place when the society comes."

"Anna or I will be here." Chance wished he could say that he would be on the land, but he knew in a week he would be leaving.

Walter nodded as if Chance's news were bad. As he turned to remount, he raised an eyebrow at Chance. "I heard tell you were looking for an Indian who goes by the name Storm's Edge."

Chance stepped from the porch, interested in Walter for the first time. "What have you heard?"

"Not much, only that he's camped up by the north river. An Indian from another tribe spotted him and told John. He said they looked like they were resting and would be moving on in a few days. May already be gone."

Chance studied the fat man. He had made no secret of looking for Storm's Edge, but did Walter really know something or was he just hoping Chance would leave and he could somehow frighten Anna off long enough to claim that the farm was abandoned? "What makes you think it's Storm's Edge?"

"Just hearsay. Don't know for sure. The Indian said he's got a white streak in his hair."

Chance's blood turned cold. If Walter was right, this might be as close as he'd ever get to the Indian who'd killed his family. This might be his only chance.

As Walter rode off, Carl went to tell the women it was safe while Tobin followed Chance into the barn. He watched as Chance drew a bridle and saddlebag from their hooks.

"I don't see that this can't wait until tomorrow, son. We haven't even finished Christmas dinner yet."

Throwing supplies into his saddlebag, Chance answered, "I'm not asking you to go. In fact, I want you to stay here until I get back and make sure Walter doesn't try anything. This place is all that matters to Anna, and I want you to keep a watch until I get back. Don't worry about me. I'll be careful. If I can't get a clean shot at Storm's Edge without starting an Indian war, I'll come back in a day or two."

Tobin nodded. "I guess sometimes a man's got to do what he thinks is right no matter what folks think. But if you ask me, son, you may be buying yourself a ticket to eternity."

"I swore on my parents' graves I'd avenge their murders," Chance answered.

Tobin sighed. "I'll stay, if you want it. But be careful, son. You may not know it but you matter a hell of a lot to those little ladies in there."

Watching him leave, Chance for once thanked the old-timer for his brevity. They'd both learned a long time ago that in this country it was best to keep good-byes short.

Tobin bumped into Anna as she stormed through the barn door. He hurried away, wanting no part of the scene that was about to take place.

When Anna turned to face Chance, fire as hot as an August sun shot from her eyes. She stormed toward him with her hands balled into fists.

Chance smiled, suddenly realizing there was no escaping her wrath.

"Carl said you're leaving." Her words were full of anger.

"That's right. Storm's Edge is camped up the river to the north, and I aim to catch up with him this time."

"You can't leave; it's Christmas."

"I've got to go." He concentrated on his work so he wouldn't have to look at her.

"But we haven't finished our dinner."

"Anna, I have to go." He strapped the saddle on Cyoty.

"No!" Anna was fighting back the anger that threatened to well over into tears. "You said you'd stay a year. I need you here. I'm not ready to say good-bye. I thought we'd have another week."

Chance tried to touch her, but she pulled away. "I'm not leaving for good. I'll be back tomorrow or the next day at the latest. Tobin will stay around and make sure there's no trouble."

Shaking her head as if she knew his words were a lie, Anna shouted, "The man you want is no lost Indian. He's a killer." She bit her lip until she tasted blood. "If you leave me now, don't come back."

Chance pulled her to him abruptly, his words brushing the soft curls by her ear. "You don't mean that."

"Yes I do. You'll be leaving in a week anyway. This way I'll never know if you got killed or just rode away. If you go, go forever." All the pain she knew would hit her when he finally left slammed into her heart now. She could not say good-bye to him more than once or her heart would surely explode from the effort.

Chance felt her body grow rigid in his arms as her words chilled his heart. He kissed her roughly, but she was stone-cold and he pushed her away. "Dear God, you had me thinking you cared for me, but if I stayed around here another hundred years I'd never be gentleman enough for you. You'd break us both trying to make me into something I'll never be."

"I only want to break this insane promise you made when you were a child."

"I'm a man of honor. Can't you understand? I have to go."

Tears flooded Anna's eyes. Somehow she had to stop him. "You've broken your word before. You said you'd lay no claim to me."

"And that bothers you," he observed. "Not because I claimed you as my wife in every way, but because you loved it."

Anna shook her head, but she couldn't make her mouth call his words a lie. She knew this argument was about far more than his riding out today. It was about all the hopes and dreams she'd foolishly allowed to form in the back of her mind, all the tomorrows she wanted to share with him. But if he left there might not even be a tomorrow. "I thought you were different. My father promised he'd be back but he left forever. I never want to see you again if you think killing this Indian is more important than keeping your promise to me."

"It's not that, Anna." Chance wanted to shake her until she understood, but when he touched her, he felt only ice beneath his fingers. "I have to go. I'll come back and we can talk."

Anna jerked free. "No!" she screamed. "If you leave, don't come back. I can make it without you. I have no use for a man who considers one Indian more important than . . ."

"Than what? Than you? Than love? Or than this farm?"

"This farm," Anna snapped.

"That's the bottom line with you, Anna, isn't it? Not me, not love, not even you, but always this damn farm. You're not worried about my leaving and being killed at all. You're only worried about losing the farm."

Tears rolled down Anna's hot cheeks. "That's all I have."

"You're wrong, Anna. You had my love, but you never valued it. Whether I die tomorrow or ten years from now I'll always love you, but all you ever wanted was this farm. Well, now it's yours. I'll lay no claim to it, just as I promised." He swung into the saddle. "Only remember this one thing, Anna Wyatt: this farm can't hold you at night."

"Just as you never will again."

Chance crumpled his hat as he tried to gain control of his turbulent emotions. "Anna, I'm sorry. I settle my own debts. If you wanted a country gentleman or an old man for a husband, maybe you got shortchanged."

"You're no gentleman. You're a savage boy who leaves his family and rides off to kill another man."

"I am who I am. I've never tried to be anything else with you. I'm a Texan and out here men take care of their own debts."

"If you leave me now, I swear I'll hate you for the rest of my life." Anna no longer had any control over her temper.

Shoving his hat low, he answered, "At least you'll feel some emotion. If you'd just once said you loved me, I'd have held you forever, but I guess you're not capable of feelings for anything that isn't measured in acres." He kicked Cyoty into action. "Good-bye, my love!" he yelled as the horse sped away.

Anna collapsed on the hay, too angry and upset even to cry. She wanted to scream for him to come back, but it was too late. He'd been right about everything he'd said, but her pride had kept her from admitting it. She was hurt that he would leave her when she needed him and she'd only wanted to strike back.

It was almost dark when Tobin came into the barn, strolling over to her as if nothing were amiss. "Mighty fine pie." He patted his stomach. "I told the others to give you some time alone, but they were a little worried and wanted me to come out and check on you."

Anna brushed the tears away from her cheeks. "He's gone."

Tobin sat down beside her on the hay. "He'll be back."

"No. I told him I never wanted to see him again if he left now."

"He's a man. He has to do some things no matter how much it might hurt others or himself."

"But he might be killed. And for what? To pay a debt that is years old."

"Would you love him as much if he weren't bound by his word?"

"I don't love him at all," Anna said quickly, knowing it wasn't true.

Tobin chuckled. "Sure you don't, honey, and the sky ain't blue."

"Even if I do love him, it doesn't matter anymore. He's gone off to get himself killed."

"I wouldn't worry too much about that. Chance is no babe in the wilderness. He can take care of himself."

They stood and walked to the barn door. The sun had disappeared over the hills, and Anna pulled her shawl tightly around her, feeling the cold wind chill her bones.

A shadow moved at the corner of the corral. Tobin touched Anna's arm in warning, but she'd seen it too.

The old man slowly drew his gun as he studied the darkness.

The shadow moved again.

"Who's out there?" Tobin shouted.

The solid wall of muscle that could only be Sourdough stepped into the light. His shoulders were covered with a bear-hide cape and his legs were wrapped in warm skins. He said something in words Anna didn't understand. Tobin answered, then pulled Anna back into the barn.

"The Indian wants to tell you something. He doesn't want anyone to hear except you and me."

Anna nodded. "I was hoping he'd come. I have a gift for him."

Tobin frowned. "Now's not the time. This is no social call."

Sourdough spoke again. His words were hard and his face grave. Tobin listened, nodding slowly in respect.

When the Indian finished, Tobin turned to Anna. The lines around his mouth were white with tension as he spoke. "He says Chance goes to a trap. The man who came here earlier has met with Storm's Edge, and they will be waiting for him."

"But . . ." Anna felt a chill far greater than the wind.

"Sourdough says all the Indians around know about it. He only tells you because he doesn't want you to lose your man. Storm's Edge has twenty men waiting to kill Chance, and Walter help set up the plan."

"But why?"

Tobin shrugged. "Maybe Storm's Edge is tired of Chance trailing him. Maybe Walter's paying him. Storm's Edge is hated by his own people, so you can bet he's not a man of honor."

"I've got to warn Chance!" All the questions about her life slid aside and one thing became crystal clear.

"Now hold on a minute, Anna. You don't even know

where he is, and even if you could track him, you've got the
girls to think about. You can't leave them and the farm."

"The girls can stay with Selma. She loves keeping them.
You can help me track Chance."

"Sure, but then no one would be at the farm. Don't you
see? You're playing right into Walter's hands. If you leave,
he'll have the society out and have this place claimed for
himself. Better you stay here and I go."

"That would be two against twenty. No, I ride with you."
Anna pulled Cinnamon from his stall. "You saddle up while
I get changed."

"But the farm . . . ?"

"I don't care about the farm. I have to find Chance in
time." Anna started for the house, but Tobin held her back.

He started to argue, but when he looked into her face he
knew no amount of reasoning would help. "All right, but
we'd never find him tonight. We'll leave at dawn."

Anna didn't want to wait, but she realized they might
pass Chance at night and not see him. Tobin was a good
tracker if his stories were to be believed, but no one could
track in the dark.

"I'll be ready before dawn," Anna answered, and turned
to thank the Indian for his help.

But Sourdough had disappeared back into the shadows,
along with the two meat pies and loaf of bread she'd left on
the porch for him. In their place lay a bearskin and two
freshly killed rattlesnakes.

Anna packed the girls off with Selma for the night and tried
to sleep. Her new bedroom looked wonderful with all the
furniture and rugs, but Anna barely noticed them. Her longing
for Chance was a hunger that consumed her dreams. Each time
she dozed, she reached for him in her sleep, then awoke with
a start, feeling again the pain of his absence.

Sometime deep in the night she came to realize the truth: no
matter what else she had, without Chance's arms to keep her
warm the world was a cold and lonely place. He had been
wrong. It was not the farm she wanted, it was only him.

33

Anna was dressed and pacing the floor by the time she saw Tobin walk from the barn.

Running to the porch, she handed him a saddlebag filled with leftover meat and bread. When he mentioned breakfast, she dropped a biscuit into his hand and without a word, mounted her horse.

Tobin laughed, took a huge bite of the biscuit, and mumbled, "Don't look like you got much sleep last night. You're about as cagey as a polecat who's had his tail braided. Well, don't you worry none. We'll find this man you don't love and bring him back to the farm he doesn't care anything about."

For the first time Anna wanted to swear instead of laugh at Tobin's constant chatter. She was in no mood for conversation, and after a few tries, Tobin gave up and just rode.

They headed north along the river. Tobin had little trouble finding Chance's tracks, for he'd made no attempt to hide them. They rode hard all day but couldn't seem to catch Chance.

By the time the sun set, Anna was exhausted and disappointed. All day the vision of Chance surrounded by Indians had kept flashing through her mind. When Tobin suggested they stop, she shook her head. "We have to find him."

Tobin studied the terrain like a fortune-teller examines a rich man's palm. "If I was him, I'd be beddin' down in them hills up ahead a few miles. I reckon he'll figure he's too close to the Indians to light a fire, but if you give Cinnamon his head, that Indian pony might just lead us right to Cyoty. Horses have a way of finding their own in the dark." Tobin reined in his mount.

Anna did as Tobin had suggested and Cinnamon headed into the woods. She was too tired to do more than dodge the branches that hampered her way. Leaning low, she tried to stay awake. The night was black and the moonlight was blocked out by thick pine trees. The constant winter wind had frozen her cheeks, and her fingers were sculptured in a grip around a knot she'd tied in the reins.

Tobin slung one leg over the saddle horn and dusted his pants as though just noticing the mud that had been caked there for days. "I'll ride uphill and come down along the riverbed. If you reach the water without finding Chance, wait for me there."

Anna pulled her coat tightly around her and agreed. A sudden violent gust of wind threatened to tear her from the saddle, and she pulled her hat low as Tobin vanished into the frosty night.

The tree branches swished passed her as Cinnamon continued moving, his steamy breath rising in white puffs as he picked his way between trees and dried brush. She had no idea if the huge sorrel knew where he was going or if he was simply searching for a warmer place to spend the night, but she was too tired and numb to question him.

A branch snapped beside her and Anna leaned into Cinnamon's neck, bracing herself for a blow.

Without warning, a long arm grabbed her, pulling her from the saddle with such force that Anna felt the air leave her lungs. She rolled like a rag doll onto the hard ground, unable to suck in enough air even to scream. Powerful hands slid along her arms and pinned her on her back as the assailant straddled her. Anna struggled with her attacker, angry at herself for having stumbled into death's arms without a weapon ready. Her knife was out of reach and his hands cut like bands of iron into her wrists.

As she clawed to free herself, she twisted her leg, slamming her knee into the attacker's side. The movement caught him off guard, and he released one of her hands. In an instant, Anna grabbed her knife and slashed it toward him blindly, praying she'd hit her mark.

His arm blocked the blow and he twisted the knife from her fingers. "Hold on, I'm not going to hurt you."

Anna relaxed suddenly. "Chance?"

Chance froze for a moment above her. He slowly released his grip and slid his hand along her side. "Anna?"

She rose into his arms, holding him with all her strength. "I found you," she whispered as her cheek brushed his. "I was so afraid you'd be dead before I could catch up to you."

Chance pulled her a few inches away, twisting her hat off, but the night was too black to see her face. His words sounded angry, but his touch was gentle. "Anna, what are you doing here?"

She didn't want to talk for a moment. All that mattered was holding Chance close. Moving her hands up his chest, she cupped his rough, stubbled face. Before he could ask more questions, she kissed him with such boldness she felt the shock run through his system.

For a moment she thought he'd pull away and demand an answer, but slowly his mouth warmed to her kiss and his arms pulled her against him. He lowered her in the dried leaves and covered her with his warmth. Anna pushed her hands into his coat and slid her fingers over the cotton of his shirt. He moaned with her touch and his kiss deepened to a passion that made them forget the cold.

When finally he broke away, Anna continued to play with his hair and brush tiny kisses along his throat.

"God, woman, how I missed you! All day you were on my mind."

Anna laughed softly as she tugged at his hair until he

kissed her again. The cold, the night, even the Indians didn't matter as long as she was in his arms.

When his lips left hers again, he whispered into her ear and his hand pushed the material aside at her waist. "Before you say anything and I get madder than hell for you being out here, I have to tell you something. Anna, I am who I am, only half as civilized as you'll want me to be, but one thing's a fact, Anna Wyatt." He pushed his hand beneath her clothes until he felt her bare skin. "You're my wife and nothing under God's heaven can change that."

He kissed her soundly, and Anna laughed with sheer joy for the first time in her life. She didn't care that they were exhausted and rolling in the dirt, for she was with him and that was all that mattered. Her Texan was alive and warm in her arms.

A whistle sounded from the trees and Chance pulled her beneath him as he slid his gun from its holster. A moment passed in silence, then Chance answered with the same low tone.

His arm relaxed and he pulled her up beside him. "Show no fear," he whispered as something moved in the brush.

Anna's heart jumped into her throat and the pounding was deafening as she tried to see beyond the curtain of black before her. The night was a velvet ocean of life swimming around her in the scurry of four-legged creatures and the whine of a dying wind. Chance pulled her into a clearing where an anemic moon washed winter's black to a murky gray.

The shadows parted with a snap of brush. Walks Tall appeared in all his war-painted glory. He stood regal and defiant in the moonlight.

"You bring your woman?" He pointed at Anna as if to even mention her was below him.

"I bring my woman," Chance answered, raising an eyebrow to her. He switched to Walks Tall's tongue, leaving Anna out of the conversation.

After a few minutes, the two men gripped arms as if

sealing an agreement, and the Indian disappeared back into the night.

"What—"

Chance's words interrupted her. "No. First, what are you doing out here alone?"

"I'm not alone; Tobin is with me. He's riding downstream and should be here soon. We came to warn you. Storm's Edge has set a trap for you."

Chance showed no surprise. "I know," he whispered. "Walks Tall warned me this morning. All these years, ever since we were kids together, I thought Walks Tall hated me. Now he comes to fight by my side against Storm's Edge."

"Are you sure it's not a trick?" Anna knew little of Indians, but Walks Tall's behavior to date didn't exactly resound with brotherly love.

"Walks Tall is many things, but a liar isn't one of them. He hates Storm's Edge and knows that it's men like him that keep this war between the Indians and the settlers going. He won't help me kill him, but he'll stand on the side and make sure we have a fair fight."

Pulling Anna's horse with him, he led Anna toward the stream. "He'd been watching the farm for days, waiting for me to take the bait. He did not want to come down and warn me because Storm's Edge might have seen that as his helping me, but once I left, Walks Tall caught up with me." Chance held her hand in his. "But how did you know about the trap?"

Anna had just started telling about Sourdough when Tobin came splashing down the stream. He picked up the story with far more flair.

Chance talked with Tobin, but his arm never left Anna. He pulled her against him every few minutes as if her touch were his breath of life.

"If we stay with the stream for another few miles we can be camped above Storm's Edge by sunup." He turned to Anna. "Can you stay in the saddle for a few more hours?"

She smiled and nodded, thankful that he hadn't suggested

she turn back. As he lifted her up onto Cinnamon, he asked, "What made you come?"

"Ich liebe dich," she whispered.

"I've never heard those words. What do they mean?" Chance looked toward Tobin, knowing the old man was listening to everything they were saying even though he pretended to check the leg of his horse.

"I'll tell you later," Anna answered. She'd never said the words before and, somehow, the first time had to come in her native tongue, even though she'd promised to speak English.

"Tell me now." Chance closed his hand over hers. His words were determined.

"I'm not a slave or a hired hand. I don't take orders."

Chance laughed softly. "Tell me something I don't know. What do those words mean?"

Anna leaned low so Tobin couldn't hear. "I'm not afraid of you, Chance Wyatt."

He moved his hand slowly along her leg. "It may be me who'll have to be reminded to show no fear when we are alone again. And we will be alone again."

Tobin's voice broke the mood. "You folks ready to ride, or are you planning on talking all evening?"

Chance swung into his saddle, swearing under his breath, while Anna's laughter hung like crystal joy in the heavy air.

They rode in silence for hours, each lost in their own thoughts and dreams. When finally they tied the horses and continued on foot, Anna was too tired to do more than follow blindly. After half a mile of walking, they rested among a stand of trees.

Pulling her into his arms, Chance kissed Anna's forehead as he lay his rifle an inch from her spine. If trouble came, he could reach for his rifle and her at the same time. "Good night, Anna," he whispered as calmly as he had every night for almost a year.

She curled beneath his shoulder and let his heartbeat lull

her to sleep. "Ich liebe dich," she whispered, loving the way the words tumbled off her tongue.

Chance groaned in frustration, too tired to pry an explanation from her. In the cold blackness before dawn, Anna was warmed by his fingers as they traveled over her clothes, promising a pleasure that would come when they were alone. He turned her back against him so his hand had full freedom as his body molded behind her.

Carefully, he slid his fingers beneath her coat and pressed his palm against her breast. As his fingers tightened slightly he whispered, "You are, as Walks Tall says, my woman, Anna."

When she would have turned to kiss him, he held her tightly in his arms. His lips brushed her ear and moved into her hair. "No matter what happens tomorrow I want you to know one thing. There has never been or ever will be any woman but you in this world."

He kissed the back of her neck, driving her wild with need. When she tried to turn to him his arms tightened. "No," he whispered from behind her. "This fire will build."

He moved his fingers over her body, making her skin ache for his touch. "Tonight you'll have an ounce of the longing I've felt all year for you. Tonight you'll dream of me." His hands were bold, pulling at her clothes. The material moving over her flesh warmed her and excited her. Anna pushed her back against him and moaned softly, wanting him to love her more than she'd ever wanted anything in her life.

"Tomorrow night," he whispered as he tasted her neck. "Tomorrow night there will be no world outside my arms and no need for words between us."

Morning whispered through the trees and brushed Anna's cheek with sunlight. She rolled to move closer to Chance's warmth, but he was gone. Fear gripped her with icy hands and she came fully awake. Chance was gone!

Rolling onto her stomach, Anna looked down into the valley below. They'd camped on the edge of a twenty-foot cliff overhanging a small bank. One lone Indian dwelling sat beside the stream. At first she saw no signs of life, but slowly Chance's outline materialized only a few yards from the tent. He was sitting with his back to her. She couldn't see his face, but his head was tilted slightly in alertness. His right leg stretched straight before him. It took her a moment to see what was wrong. Then the knowledge iced her heart. Nothing before her could have frightened her more than the absence of his holster strapped to his leg. He was waiting, alone and unarmed!

For a moment she thought he must be mad, then realized that he planned to fight Storm's Edge in the Indian way. If he'd just shot the Indian, Storm's Edge would have died with honor, but this way he would die a beaten man.

Slowly, he stood as an Indian stepped from the tent. The red man was not tall, but his barrel chest was wide and strong. His hair was long and black except for one streak that began just to the left of his forehead. One white line flowed down his hair like a stream of milk through sable. "Storm's Edge," Anna whispered, and gripped Chance's rifle at her side.

The Indian looked at Chance and showed no surprise. With a turn of his head, he made a shrill sound like a hawk who's spotted prey. The forest came alive with a dozen of his followers. They stepped into the clearing, circling Chance, fencing him away from freedom.

As the men closed in around Chance like a pack of wolves on the day's first kill, horses sprang into the water from across the river and splashed into the clearing. Walks Tall halted his men and shouted something Anna couldn't understand. He pointed to a cliff over their heads where Tobin appeared, his gun already anchored on his shoulder. She didn't need to understand Walks Tall's words to know that the Indian had just declared a fair fight; and Tobin added the insurance.

The men circling Chance backed away and allowed Storm's Edge to face his enemy without assistance. Anna crept closer to the cliff's edge so she could see, yet still be hidden by the overhanging branches. The two men stripped to the waist and both pulled long hunting knives from their belts. Storm's Edge smiled and she saw the blood lust in his eyes.

Anna pulled the rifle close. This would be a fight to the death, but should Storm's Edge's knife pierce Chance's heart, Anna would see that a bullet struck the Indian before he had time to taste his victory. It might not be the honorable thing to do, shooting from the brush, but she would do it all the same. Every Indian below would probably turn on her, but she would lie with Chance tonight, be it in life or in death.

The two men circled one another, slashing and dodging. Storm's Edge was twenty years Chance's senior, but his skills were honed and refined from many battles. His stocky build gave him the advantage of power but Chance's reach was swifter and longer.

Anna watched in horror as the silver blade of the Indian's knife flashed again and again. She could see the love of killing in the man's eyes. He began to heave like an animal, sucking in the quiet air, then blowing it out in smoky white hatred. Sweat glistened off his hairless chest as he lunged at Chance in an attempt to end their dance of death.

Like the silent creeping of dawn on a foggy morning, Anna slowly realized that Chance was playing a game with Storm's Edge. Chance was younger, stronger, more agile. He was wearing the Indian down, humiliating him in front of his men. A swift death of honor would not be allowed the savage who had spent his life murdering families. He would fall to his knees in exhaustion before the mercy of the blade would pierce his heart.

Anna turned her gaze from Storm's Edge to Chance. His face was drawn in concentration. He moved with a warrior's grace and stamina, but there was no emotion in his eyes. He was doing what had to be done, as a man kills an animal mad with disease.

She glanced at the Indians of Storm's Edge's tribe. They were watching their leader carefully. If he had been killed quickly, there might have been one who would lift up the banner and continue the cause. But not this way. The fight was draining the loyalty from them with each lunge of the knife. By the time their leader fell to his knees, they too would be defeated.

Chance's blade struck Storm's Edge's arm, drawing only enough blood to be a mark of insult. Another strike landed on the Indian's shoulder. He bellowed like an angry bull and lunged without caution.

Stepping aside, Chance again drew his opponent's blood. Anna turned her head, not wanting to watch this killer of women and children die.

A flicker in the trees beside her caught her eye. She glanced across the brown forest and saw a flash of silver between the trees, the long finger of a gun. Glancing at Tobin on the cliff above the fight, Anna noticed he was too busy watching the fight to see the rifle in the trees. She saw a rifle lifted shoulder high with the barrel pointed toward the fighters . . . pointed toward Chance.

34

Chance wielded his knife through the crisp morning air and struck Storm's Edge in his side, ripping the skin. He pulled the blade back, careful not to slice too deep. The smell of human blood was sickening, but he had to continue. He not only had to kill this warrior, he had to best him. The men who traveled with Storm's Edge would only respect Chance if he took their leader in a fight. They considered white men little better than dogs, and Chance would have to earn the right to walk away after he'd killed.

Storm's Edge fell to the ground, heaving for breath and bleeding now from a dozen wounds. He hadn't the stamina nor the reserve for many more lunges. His years of fighting had left him heartless and cold; however, as he faced his own death, a touch of fear blinked in his eyes. But his proud blood would allow him no shame. He ran suddenly toward Chance with all the energy he had left.

With one mighty cry he fell on Chance's blade, allowing his leap into death to be clean and complete, not slow and painful. The long hunting knife pushed through his chest, cutting a wide gaping hole.

Chance fell backward from the thrust of the Indian's body against his knife. In the instant he flew between air and ground, he heard a round of gunfire from the trees.

Rolling in the dirt, he looked toward where he'd left Anna as another round sounded. He watched in horror as

341

she tumbled from the cliff's edge and fell twenty feet onto
the sand below. His rifle tumbled with her, slamming into
her head with a sharp crack of wood against bone.

Storm's Edge's body was forgotten. All the years of
craving the sight of the Indian lying in his own blood were
nothing as Chance ran toward Anna. She lay lifeless on the
sand, his gun beside her.

Pulling her to him, Chance was unmindful of the others
as his hands moved over her body. Thank God there were
no wounds. "Anna!" he yelled as his hands touched her
skull. A huge welt the size of his hand was swelling on her
head.

Chance was aware of others around him, but he couldn't
understand what they were saying. All that mattered in his
world lay in his arms. She'd come to stand by his side and
somehow she'd been the one to get hurt. Time had no
meaning as he held her, not feeling the cold wind against his
bare chest, nor the sun growing brighter.

"Son," Tobin said as he knelt beside Chance, "she's still
breathing, but that was one ugly fall. Appears she saw
Walter in the woods and fired your rifle to protect you.
Walter's gun had been fired; we found it beside his body so
the first round we heard must have been aimed at you.
Guess it's your good fortune Anna was a better shot. The
recoil from your gun must have knocked her off the cliff."

Lifting her in his arms as he stood, Chance said, "We've
got to get her home."

Tobin nodded. "I'll ride in and fetch the doctor. Maybe
he'll come. You take her home, son."

Anna remembered little of the ride home. Her head felt as
if it were on fire, and when she opened her eyes the world
began to spin around her in waves of pain. She was only
vaguely aware of Chance carrying her into the cabin and
putting her into bed.

In what seemed like only minutes, she felt someone
poking around on her head and opened her eyes to a blurry

vision of the old doctor. He was saying something about bed rest for at least a week. Then she heard him talking to Tobin, saying the society leaders wouldn't be coming out to check farms until after the New Year's celebration.

Anna closed her eyes and didn't open them again until dawn touched the sky once more. Chance was beside her, sitting on the bed with a cool towel in his hand.

He laid it over her forehead. "How are you feeling, my love?"

Anna tried to answer, but even a whisper brought pain as violent as a church bell ringing between her ears. Her brain felt like it was off center in her skull.

"Rest now," Chance whispered. "Carl and Selma are here. With the snow, they've decided to just stay with us until you're better."

Closing her eyes once more, Anna slept and the day moved slowly past as if in a dream. She was dimly aware of Selma moving around her and of Maggie sitting on the corner of her bed holding her hand for a long while. By the end of the third day Anna awoke with a clear head. She felt weak but enjoyed all the attention everyone paid her as they took turns sitting by her bed. In this country, friends quickly became as close as family. Slowly, she was able to move about the cabin on her own.

When Chance finally got a moment beside her without someone else present, he grumbled about building a bigger house.

As hard as Chance tried the next few days, he couldn't find a moment alone with Anna. He finally gave up hanging around the house and tramped through the snow to the barn with Carl or Tobin at his side.

January blew in with windy, cold days and Anna recovered. She loved having a house full of friends, but she missed the passion she'd shared with Chance when they'd had a room to themselves and no people within whispering distance. Tobin was just across the way, sleeping in the kitchen, Selma and Carl were in the loft, and both girls were on pallets beside Anna's bed.

On the third day of the month, she was busy cooking breakfast when Tobin wandered in from the barn, shaking more snow on her floor than he'd left out on the steps.

Anna smiled, for she'd grown to love the old loner. "Is Chance coming in soon?"

Tobin shook his head. "He just did the craziest thing. He saddled Cyoty and packed his saddlebag. Told me he had a promise to keep that he'd made a year ago today." Tobin didn't seem to notice the blood drain from Anna's face. "Then he looked at me real sad and said good-bye like he meant it to be forever."

Anna dropped the skillet, spilling eggs across the floor. "No!" she shouted. "No!"

They hadn't had time to talk, but she thought he'd known how much he meant to her. When she'd left her farm to warn him, she thought he'd understand that he was more important to her than anything. Didn't he know that she'd just been waiting for the snow to melt and everyone to go home before telling him how there was no life in her without him?

"No!" she whispered again as she opened the door. She thought back over all the things he'd said to her. He was a man of his word. She'd made him promise to leave and now he'd gone. He'd left her without even saying good-bye.

Anna looked at Tobin as she felt pain climb her spine. "Do you know where he went?"

Tobin shrugged. "I don't know; toward town, I guess. I heard him talking about joining up with Ben McCulloch to organize another ranger company to fight the Mexicans. Chance served with him once and said that even with Ben's crippled arm he was the best fighter he'd ever known. Course, now that McCulloch is in the legislature, he might not be so interested in fighting Mexicans but Chance seemed to think it might be worth the time to head down . . ."

"Tobin!" Anna couldn't stand by and calmly listen to him ramble when her entire life was falling apart. "Saddle my horse—fast! I've got to find Chance."

Tobin started to argue, but her strong stubborn jaw made him decide to just shake his head instead. He slapped his hands against his legs and headed for the barn mumbling, "Hell of a mornin'. Everyone in the place must have eaten loco weed in their dreams."

Grabbing her wool shawl, Anna ran through the patchy snow toward the barn. A moment later she was on Cinnamon's back and headed down the path to town. The road took a bend after half a mile, then lay straight for a good distance more. If she could make the bend while Chance was on the road, she'd be able to stop him.

She took the bend at breakneck speed, her shawl forgotten as she rode with the wind blowing her hair and her dress. There, just past the bend, she saw Cyoty grazing by a cluster of live oak trees.

Panicking, Anna reined her mount and jumped down. She ran to Cyoty. What if Chance had fallen or been shot? Why hadn't she told him how she felt? Why hadn't she begged him to stay?

As she reached the oaks, Chance stepped from behind a wide, old trunk. "What kept you?" he asked with a wink.

Anna was gulping for breath. "I thought you'd left. I thought I'd never see you again."

"We agreed one year ago today that I'd leave without a word of good-bye. I promised and I'm a man of my word." He moved slowly to shorten the distance between them until they stood in the clearing only an inch apart.

"You can leave if you like. I don't want to tie you down, but I'd have no objection if you stay." Anna wanted to hold him forever, but she wanted it to be his choice.

Chance played with one strand of her hair. "You mean we could extend the agreement for another year or so. And during that year I'd lay no claim to you, just as before."

"Whether you go or stay must be your choice. I'll not beg

you to stay when you want to go. But I'll not tell you I want you to go when you know it would be a lie."

"My precious Anna. Proud enough to risk all and fight for me, but too proud to beg. I told you once I'd never leave you if you said you loved me. So tell me, and not in German this time, that you love me."

A smile touched Anna's lips. "You knew what the words meant?"

"I had to ask Carl." Chance circled her throat with his fingers. "Some ribbing I took about it too, thanks to my cruel wife."

Anna laughed. "I love you and I love being your wife."

Chance pulled her to him, brushing her face with light kisses. "If you only knew how long I've waited to hear you say that. I think I've loved you from the moment I saw you, but I only dreamed that you would ever love me." His lips found her, and he made her feel light-headed with the passion in his kiss. As he molded her closer, he whispered, "We'll extend this contract between us, but I insist on a lifetime agreement." His kiss made it plain there would be no forfeiture of his love.

After several minutes, Anna pulled away. "If you knew what the words meant, why did you leave this morning?"

He lifted her into his arms. "You're a headstrong, stubborn woman. I knew you'd follow just like you did before and I've been dying to get you alone all week. I want to love my wife out of sight and sound of others. I have a promise to keep that I made the night before the fight with Storm's Edge."

Anna laughed as he carried her into the center of the grove of live oaks. There he built a fire and spread his bedroll. And there, amid the wilderness that was so much a part of him, her wild, tender Texan staked an eternal claim to her heart.